Pol
Poling-Kempes, Lesley.
Canyon of remembering
                    $ 24.95

CANYON
of
REMEMBERING

CANYON
of
REMEMBERING

Lesley Poling-Kempes

Texas Tech University Press

This book was set in Galliard and printed on acid-free paper that meets the guidelines for permanence and durability of the Committee on Production Guidelines for Book Longevity of the Council on Library Resources. ∞

Printed in the United States of America

Book and jacket design by Lisa Camp

Cover art by Judith Roderick

Library of Congress Cataloging-in-Publication Data

Poling-Kempes, Lesley.
   Canyon of remembering / Lesley Poling-Kempes.
     p. cm.
    ISBN 0-89672-363-1 (cloth : alk. paper)
    I. Title.
   PS3566.0464C3   1996
 813'.54—dc20   96-12980
                                   CIP

96 97 98 99 00 01 02 03 04 05 / 9 8 7 6 5 4 3 2

Texas Tech University Press
Box 41037
Lubbock, Texas 79409-1037 USA
1-800-832-4042

This book is for Jim Harrill, Jim Kempes, and John Poling; and the land, cats, and stories we loved and shared.

Acknowledgments

I am indebted to a circle of friends who have, for years, fanned the fires of creativity and hope with me and for me: to Jim, Terry, Sam, Jan, Jeannette, Christine, Carolyn, Stede, my brothers John and Andrew, and my parents, Dave and Ann, a thousand thanks. I am grateful to my brother Charles, who gave personal and professional insights to early drafts of this novel. And to my children, Christopher and Marianne, who kept me smiling with their hugs and sweet words of encouragement, a million kisses. I am so blessed.

I am also indebted to my wonderful editor, Judith Keeling, who took this book under her remarkable and enthusiastic arm and guided it to completion.

Contents

All our knowledge is partial and approximate; if we are to know electrons and chimpanzees less than perfectly, and call it good enough, we may as well understand phenomena like love and death, or art and freedom, imperfectly also.

Annie Dillard

Although Santa Fe is the name of a real city occupying a real place in New Mexico, the people and places in this story exist in a mythical portion of Santa Fe and northern New Mexico. There should be no attempt to place the fictional story within the context of the actual place.

Atencio de Jesús

Atencio de Jesús wavered on two skinny legs in the afternoon wind coming up from the bosque. From under the lone elm tree in the parking lot of the post office, Atencio could view the comings and goings at the Mi Ojo General Mercantile and Grocery, his mother's trailer home that sat to one side of the adobe mercantile, and the pock-marked adobe wall of his own house beyond them both. In his left hand, he clutched the top of a paper bag surrounding a vodka bottle that everyone including the Mi Ojo state trooper knew he was holding. But Atencio lifted the bottle's open top to his lips and drank only when he was certain no children were watching.

There had been enough children contaminated.

When the Mi Ojo county school bus returned mid-afternoon, Atencio held the bag against his pant leg as if it were a sack of peanuts. Or candy. Or a loaf of bread he had just bought for his mother at the mercantile. But everyone in the valley knew Atencio did not live in his mother's trailer anymore, and that the bag was for him if it was for anyone.

"My man! Atencio!" old friends still called from their trucks and cars while pumping gas across the highway at the mercantile. *"¿Cómo está?"*

No one actually crossed the two-laner to shake Atencio de Jesús' hand anymore. *"Bien, bien,"* Atencio mumbled in a voice no one farther than four feet could possibly hear. *"Bien . . ."*

Atencio smiled foolishly through glazed eyes. His black hair had not been cut since he'd returned. It was tied with a piece of his mother's yarn and hung down his back like a long, thin snake.

"I'll be having a good day, maybe tomorrow; come for supper," he wanted to say. "I'm still here." Instead, Atencio raised one arm in farewell to some Mi Ojo buddy, and with the other arm tilted the bottle and gulped the vodka. Surely his old friends could see he was having some trouble coming home?

He meant to cut his hair. Every day he meant to decide to cut it. But Atencio never did decide anything about his hair or anything else, even when he had a job with the highway crew up at Tomita; or when he went to Utah with his brothers to pick potatoes for a few months. He had worked hard back then; he was okay then.

"It's not the hair," Atencio heard his mother, Dominga, tell her friends. "His great grandfather had beautiful long hair like that. Atencio's pain is not his Apache blood."

The nameless problem living under Atencio's hair, deep in his head, came from over there. Everyone knew. Everyone saw Atencio walking the highway, and everyone drove on by. Even Dominga, who loved him most, who still touched his unshaven cheeks like they were fine baby skin, drove past him, left him behind in the rearview mirror, her first, her last, her only blood child looking for not quite empty beer cans in the roadside brush.

Dominga de Jesús gave Atencio the old adobe house in spring: the old Garcia house, with packed mud floors that were the pride of his grandmother's hands; the house with the cool, adobe plastered walls, with ponderosa beams the size of a man's chest holding ceilings ten feet above the ground.

"It holds your history, Atencio," Dominga told him the day she reopened the old house, "your memory may be clouded in your head, but it lives clear and strong in these walls."

Atencio stood with his beautiful mother at the open door looking into rooms that had been closed to light for ten years. "Maybe the past life in this house will touch you, and you will remember that you are home," Dominga had told him. "You will stop looking backwards to the pain that belongs to another place."

Atencio watched Dominga's hand rub the unpainted wood of the door frame. "We should never have moved into the trailer," she said, gripping the wood like an old friend, "it is a house without a foundation. But we didn't know, then, about the war."

Dominga crossed herself and left Atencio standing at the doorway peering into the dark, dusty interior of the house. This was her gift, she told him, for staying alive.

"Your gift to me will be living into old age in the house where you were born."

One month had passed since Atencio moved into the adobe house on the edge of Mi Ojo. One side of the house faced the highway and the village that sat up the mesa beyond. The opposite side faced north, toward the open mesa land and the uncultivated fields that began as sage and chamisa, but soon turned to prickly pear and cholla. Wild country. Not even cattle were adventuresome enough to stray out there.

Every day for a month, Dominga brought her son tortillas and green chile stew and whatever else she made in her trailer home kitchen. Sometimes Dominga stayed and watched Atencio while he ate. Atencio knew Dominga watched over him from inside her trailer, too, and from her clothesline out back. He knew Dominga watched the old adobe house like she once watched his cradle for signs of movement and change.

After the first week, when Atencio tore the boards from the windows and fixed the hinges on the doors, there was nothing for Dominga to watch, except Atencio leaving in the afternoons, and returning sometime between dusk and dawn.

Atencio spent the morning on the back stoop with a bottle, if he could find one, and with his old boyhood pocket knife. He passed time carving cedar sticks, left in the yard from a half century of wood splitting, into slim slivers. He stood the cedar needles, smooth and fragrant, side by side in the sand surrounding his feet. Over there he had seen traps, man traps, made of spears stuck upright in deep holes; he had even seen a person, not yet a man, speared.

A long time ago, Atencio de Jesús carved cedar *santos* for the good padre Leo and the village *capilla*—*santos* so perfect the padre publicly proclaimed Atencio's hands a gift from God, a physical manifestation of God's grace. From the back step facing the mesa land, Atencio de Jesús counted exactly forty-one cholla cactus trees climbing the sand hills sloping north to Colorado, sixty-eight carved cedar sticks aimed towards heaven near his feet, and two hands with ten fingers from which the grace of God had been removed.

When Atencio was tired of sitting on the back stoop, he stood under the fragile elm at the post office trying to keep abreast of life in Mi Ojo. Trying to get a hold on what it was that was holding him here. Ernie's Bar next to the Mi Ojo community center on the dirt plaza held him all evening. Old buddies bought Atencio drinks, for awhile, and then forgot about him, left him in a lonely stupor on his chair by the open window where Atencio stared out into nothing in particular. Atencio knew his friends left him for a ride with their girlfriends, or an evening at home with their children.

Atencio could not get a hold on their children. Boys, men now, sitting near him in the bar, childhood buddies he had fished the river with a lifetime ago, had children.

Some had even been in Nam.

◎

"At least I'm not on the heavy stuff," Atencio told his mother and his brothers.

He was the baby de Jesús, the youngest son of Feodoro, only son of Feodoro and his second wife, Dominga Garcia. He was perfect, the de Jesús family story went: Atencio was gifted. Eight years ago, the very last year of the draft, Atencio de Jesús was found to be so perfect that he was signed into service without a hitch. The other three de Jesús sons escaped the journey into war overseas because of age or physical peculiarities; two even wanted to go, wanted to get out of Mi Ojo, wanted to travel and catch communists.

Atencio explained to his family that he had escaped the hard stuff because of his fear of needles.

"You ain't escaped nothing, Atencio, unless you quit the booze and get a job," his brother, Tomas, said when the liquor started showing up after breakfast.

Tomas de Jesús had a permanent job with the highway department, and two children and a wife. They lived in a trailer house ten miles west of Mi Ojo, near Tomita.

"You're recycling bad dreams. Around and around they circle your head," Tomas liked to tell Atencio. "Shake 'em off, Atencio! Get your head out of the bag. Do it for mama if not for yourself."

But Atencio could not do something for mama he could not do for himself. Not just yet.

"Any day, though, I'll be back," he told someone at least once each night at the bar on the plaza. "I'm coming back."

After the highway department job ended in early winter, Atencio returned to wearing the baggy cotton trousers and flat, jute soled shoes he'd found in some import store in Santa Fe. Atencio wanted to melt into the landscape. Atencio did not want to be noticed, to stand out. Atencio de Jesús did not want anyone to mistake him for a soldier anymore.

During the winter, Atencio had managed to find few odd jobs—with the highway crew holding traffic signs, as a trash collector pushing Mi Ojo's garbage up to the dump above the village in his wheelbarrow, and later as a ditch digger, cleaning out the valley irrigation ditches before the spring flow began. But Atencio had not worked in six weeks now, and he had nothing left but pennies. There was something demeaning about never being able to buy himself a drink. Atencio did not want charity. He just wanted alcohol.

Atencio was watching his mother's trailer. It was Wednesday afternoon and she would be leaving to help the good padre Leo with his laundry. Atencio was planning to go into the trailer while Dominga was gone to see if there was any cash around.

Atencio did not want to steal money from his widowed mother. He just wanted to drink without her knowing it.

Across the highway behind and to the side of the mercantile, in her fresh cotton dress, Dominga de Jesús walked out of her narrow trailer home to her car. She had the quick stride of a young woman. Atencio wondered just how young his mother was? Forty-something now? Was it possible that Dominga was getting younger and that he would soon be older than his own mother? Surely he would die first. Dominga's young hands would toss dirt onto his grave.

Dominga drove her old, white station wagon slowly away from the trailer and through the mercantile parking lot. She paused, the engine idling, at the edge of the blacktop. Atencio smiled through the haze of late afternoon at his beautiful, young mother. His lips quivered, but he did not care. He wanted to smile. Dominga smiled, too, and waved to him. And then she drove slowly across the two-laner, still smiling at her baby son, and headed up the hill to the old plaza of Mi Ojo. Atencio kept his eyes on the mercantile's tin roof after she passed. When his mother's car crested the hill and disappeared into a cloud of dust on the village plaza, Atencio relaxed his shoulders. The smile for his mother slid off his face and joined the other lost expressions in the bottle of vodka inside the paper bag.

Atencio had no sense of time. so he measured his wait with gulps. When the bottle was empty, he tucked the bag under his arm and shuffled across the highway, past the mercantile and down to his mother's trailer home. The trailer was not locked; no one ever locked in Mi Ojo.

Rummaging through the desk built into the kitchen wall, Atencio looked out the square window over the dinette at the old adobe house that had been his grandmother's. Atencio forgot, running his hands over the checkbooks and receipts and gum kept in the drawer, that someone now lived down there in that ancient mud dwelling. The mud building was just another disintegrating adobe house perched on the edge of mortal life, waiting for rain and sun and waves of sand to reclaim it. Bury it.

Atencio was startled by this idea and paused in his stealing to consider the house that was disappearing. The trailer door opened behind him. Dominga walked across the narrow kitchen and placed her hand on his hand in the desk drawer where it had just found two ten dollar bills.

"This will have to stop, Atencio," Dominga said, putting the money back into the drawer and closing it. Atencio was now kneeling on the trailer's linoleum floor. The pattern was beginning to come to life, to slide away from his knees in water-like ripples speckled with yellow and green flowers. "This stealing and everything that goes with it. *¡Dios mío!* I'm your mother. " He knew she was crossing herself behind him. "I can't imagine what you do to people who aren't family."

"I do not . . . not one, mom. *Sí, no. Es . . . verdad.*" Atencio's knees slid apart and sank into the foaming sea of floral linoleum. He fell onto the paper bag, which muffled the sound of splintering glass as the empty bottle shattered inside. Before he fainted, Atencio covered his face with his hands and wondered if this bomb would take the gift of his eyes? Or would God retrieve another piece of his brain, take it on ahead to heaven where Atencio could pick it up, put it all back together again, when he finally arrived?

Dominga told Atencio, his three brothers, their families, told all their friends and neighbors, that things were going to have to change. If Atencio would not look for work, she would. Dominga asked everyone in the valley to help find work for Atencio.

Atencio sat on the back stoop and waited for work to come. He whittled sticks into spears and stuck them side by side like a sea wall in the earth surrounding his back door. Dominga would have to be very fast finding Atencio work, finding things that were going to bring change, because Atencio himself was seeing nothing that was going to stop that army of sand coming to bury him in the old house.

Whitney Slope

The sky over the mountains was blue black with the storm sliding north and east out of Santa Fe. When the sun dropped below the dark ceiling of the western clouds, brilliant streaks of light shot through the streets. Whitney Slope pushed open the screen of the double window and leaned his bare torso into the pristine fresh air. The city glistened after the drenching, and the adobe walls across from Whitney's second-story apartment were a deep, mud red.

This was one of Whitney's favorite city sights, the wet sheen of the uneven walks, the dripping wood of the hundred-year-old portals, the sun warming the canvas awning of the drugstore on the corner. Santa Fe was again the primitive New Mexican beauty who in the spring of 1976, eight years ago now, had seduced him to set down his paints, put up his boots, and stay awhile.

Nowadays, it was difficult to get away from the little city. Even Santa Fe had become possessive. Whitney had allowed it to happen, was a full participant in his entanglement with the city, but even a beautiful place like Santa Fe exacted a price from its inhabitants.

Whitney's price this year would be missing his niece's high school graduation in Ohio this coming Friday. Whitney generally avoided trips to Ohio, but he would do almost anything for Caroline. Caroline's mother, Connie, Whitney's only sister, had died of cancer less than a year ago. Whitney had always adored his niece, but since Connie's death there had sprung a new camaraderie—born partially out of their shared grief, partially out of a renewed sense of connection—between them. Caroline's father, Alan Westbrook, believed Whitney ought to stop playing with paints and get a real job in a real place like Ohio. But her father's opinion seemed to have little effect on Caroline's adoration of Whitney, especially now that he was "my famous uncle!"

"My girlfriends saw that story in *Time* magazine," Caroline had told Whitney on the phone last night. "They ask me if you're married! Not Uncle

Whitney, I tell them! So now they want to come out to New Mexico with me and follow you around—carry your paints and canvasses around the desert!"

Whitney reminded Caroline that he was forty-something and really quite a boring fellow to follow around.

Whitney stood in his apartment smelling the rain wet street beyond the window. He would have a can of soup for supper. Or maybe wander up to the plaza and into the High Noon Cafe for tacos and a beer. No, he might be depicted as the glamorous loner, the painter of the desert sky, but he certainly did not live it. Whitney was rarely alone, and his aloneness was never glamorous.

Caroline had cried on the phone last night. So had Whitney. Not just because he could not fly to Ohio and watch Connie's daughter leave childhood; but because life was so unfair—his summer show opening in Santa Fe the same night as graduation; unfair, Connie dying and missing out on the rest of Caroline's life. And her own.

Whitney offered to fly to Cleveland the day after, but Caroline would be off to the Cape. They agreed, instead, that Caroline would, over her father's objections, come to New Mexico for a visit before college began in the fall. They would see the sights around Santa Fe together. Whitney would show his niece his world, boring as it was, and Caroline would tell her uncle what she hoped her world would become. And together they would look through Connie's sketchbooks.

Last winter Connie had told Whitney about her drawings, about the work she began after the tests showed that her cancer had moved out of her breasts and into her bone marrow. Connie told Whitney she could not verbalize what she felt, but that she might be able to draw it: the insides of her body. The interior of her mind.

"Not gorgeous landscapes and skies, or weathered adobe buildings that have survived generations of people," Connie told Whitney over the phone. "Not like your work, Whit. You get to paint the immortal of the earth. Me? Why I get to ponder the tangible form of my mortality."

Connie had been the Slope who won the art contests in high school. Connie's school drawing of a leopard was made into a National Audubon poster when she was twelve. Both Connie and Whitney won college scholarships. Connie graduated summa cum laude and then married Alan Westbrook.

After working in the post office and putting Alan through law school, Connie had birthed Caroline. Whitney received his bachelors degree and went on to graduate art programs, but he had never finished graduate school. Instead, Whitney had opted for several years of footloose wandering and painting through Europe and the Mediterranean.

Whitney looked at the calendar hanging on the wall with the photograph of the old High Noon Cafe. Friday was crowded with pencil scribblings: there was to be a cocktail party before the show of his paintings opened to the public at the Mud Street Gallery at six-thirty; afterwards, there would be a dinner for art patrons and wealthy Santa Feans at the Upper Canyon Road home of Anna Farina, Mud Street Gallery owner and manager. In between, there was a birthday party for Juan, the High Noon cook, that Whitney hoped very much to attend. But like Caroline's graduation, Juan's birthday was probably going to take a back seat to everything and everyone having to do with The Show.

The Show was the capstone of Mud Street's annual art events, orchestrated and emceed by Anna Farina, starring Santa Fe artist Whitney Slope. Or rather, as Whitney kept reminding Anna, starring Slope's paintings. Anna continually confused the two, Whitney the publicly known—or was it owned—painter, and Whitney the privately unknown, unowned person.

Anna Farina had trouble separating the public domain from the private: the painter from the painting. She assumed that because Whitney's canvasses enjoyed such a huge reception in the art world, flesh-and-blood Whitney enjoyed the same attention. But he did not. It was as if his paintings were extroverted children who dragged Whitney along on their adoration-seeking adventures. Whitney preferred his adventures to unfold in the privacy of his own home; within the confines of his own life. But unadorned moments were becoming fewer and fewer, except like now, when a rain storm found Whitney alone for a few hours in his apartment, staring down at the wet streets.

Whitney hadn't made his life any easier last winter when he crossed the line between friends and lovers with Anna Farina. Whitney was fully cognizant of his mistake, of his own role in sabotaging the last remnants of his sedate, private life. When he became Anna's lover, he had erased the thin line he had drawn and hoped to maintain between business and pleasure. He had also crossed the more dangerous line into another man's wife's bedroom.

The affair had lasted only a few months. Even so, Caroline's father Alan would have every right to be skeptical of Whitney's judgment.

Whitney sighed and penciled *call Caroline* on Saturday, the ninth of June, above a scribbled note to himself about some New York collector who insisted on coming by the apartment to view Whitney's work. Studio visitors were surprised at the frugality of Whitney's material surroundings, but even his lack of outward pretensions was interpreted to be part of his charismatic aura. Whitney's sparsely furnished rooms solicited comments about artistic ambiance and native charm from out-of-town collectors and writers. One art magazine spent half a page describing Whitney's furniture: the white cotton sofa and long oak table made by monks in North Africa; his three ladder-back chairs from someone's garage sale, and two faded oriental rugs brought by freighter from Morocco. "Slope Style" the writer called it. When the magazine's editors chose to run a full-page glossy photograph of Whitney's paint tubes and coffee cans crammed with brushes, of stretched and gessoed canvasses leaning against the kitchen cabinets, Whitney's landladies were outraged: why hadn't he cleaned up his apartment before the photographer came?

Although his material possessions belied the fact, the last few years had brought Whitney substantial success in the art world. His accountant told him to buy a house, an expensive one, because a single man with a large bank account, living and working in a rental apartment, was an unmoving target for the IRS. Whitney could afford to live wherever he wanted, but he had never wanted more than these two-hundred-year-old rooms above a narrow Santa Fe street.

The clouds over the mountains pushed north. It would be a clear evening in Santa Fe; a warm, sweet, early summer night. Whitney would walk up to the old plaza and have supper with Jon and Samantha Gateworthy, the High Noon Cafe's owners. Tomorrow or the next day, he would figure out why he had not sketched or painted a single line in almost three weeks. After The Show on Friday night, Whitney would figure out why his heart felt like it was sliding north with those storm clouds, unanchored to his body, or to any person or living thing in his forty-four-year-old life.

Whitney pulled on a tee shirt and boots. He grabbed his denim jacket and sprinted two at a time down the steep, creaky steps to the door to the street. His apartment was above the Martinez sisters' A and M Tortilla Factory. Whitney glanced in the windows. The tortilla sisters, as he had called his elderly landladies all these years, were sweeping the floor and washing the counter tops. Whitney knocked on the glass pane of the door. Aguelita pattered over and opened it for him.

"Come in, come in, Señor Slope," she said, waving her broom at his feet as if he were a cat who needed direction. "We have some tortillas and a few sopaipillas still warm in the back. Marguerite! Bring those tortillas in the basket by my purse for Señor Slope!"

"No, no, Aguelita, I'm just saying hello." Whitney squeezed her fat, soft arm. The tortilla sisters wore crocheted shawls, even later in midsummer when the ceiling fans could not spin fast enough to give the shop even a hot breeze. "Just a hello! Aguelita, will you come to my show Friday?"

"Oh, *sí*, I saw your picture in the paper," Marguerite said as she untied her apron and hung it behind the counter. Both Aguelita and Marguerite were widows. They lived together in a new house in a subdivision south of Santa Fe. They had been born and reared in the upstairs rooms Whitney now rented. "I told my daughters you were a very famous man. They said I should charge you more rent."

"And you should, Marguerite," Whitney said, laughing.

"I don't like the plaza on Friday night," Marguerite continued, frowning. "The people and the cars, *ihijola!* The noise makes me feel like a stranger in my own town. We'll watch some television, won't we, Aguelita?"

"Oh, Marguerite, you are becoming an old, lazy woman." Aguelita stood by the door smiling at Whitney. Like her sister, she was gray haired and stoop shouldered, but Aguelita's eyes still had the glimmer of a teenage trickster.

"Well, ladies, just so you know I would love your company."

"We're too old for you, Señor Slope," Marguerite said. "I keep telling you, find a nice woman to give you muchachos and good food. You are always a little thin. And you are too old to live alone. You need another love besides the paints that stain your fingers. Do nice women come to those art parties? What did you paint this time? More of those skies over old mud houses?"

"Ah, Marguerite is a pest," Aguelita said from behind the counter where she was putting pans back into cupboards. "She likes your work, Whitney. That calendar you gave us? It is over the crucifix in the kitchen. I like the painting of the apartment window the very best: I used to sit there as a child on evenings like this."

"Watching the rain clouds leave the city and move into the mountains?" Whitney asked.

"*Sí.*" Aguelita stood up and smiled at Whitney over the counter that was as high as her shoulder. "I don't want to climb stairs anymore. I like my yard and my washer and dryer. But I like to look through that window the way you have painted it. It is not so long ago. Now I can always remember, even when I am a loco-crazy *vieja* like Marguerite."

Whitney waved a hand in farewell and turned to the street. The sisters chattered on in Spanish as he closed the door.

The streets of Santa Fe were beginning to fill with the folks who had run for cover when the rain swept in. Whitney left the main avenue and headed down the alley beside his apartment. He was in no hurry to leave the freshness of the open streets and walked past the avenue that led up to the plaza. It had not really occurred to Whitney that he had a second destination until he reached the rough, hand-hewn sign for Burro Alley. He glanced at his watch: six-thirty. Alejandro's would be closed, but his friend might still be in his shop.

The five burros—Moreno, Porqué, Little Bit, Wonder and Worry—stood in an obedient line, ear to oversized ear, on the far side of the adobe wall that edged this end of the alley. Whitney stopped and scratched the white, baby burro, Wonder, while the other four watched, placid and unblinking. The burros had only a small dirt field wedged between an abandoned adobe house and the rear wall of the Barcelona appliance shop, but Alejandro and the other shop owners along Burro Alley kept them fat with oats and hay, and with sweets and treats brought daily by their surrounding community of admirers. No one actually claimed the burros: they came with the alley. The local *historia* said there had always been a field of burros here, that Santa Fe had built itself up around the old street, not around the plaza, as the tourist brochures claimed. The burros, just like the ancient village, had become landlocked from the mountains and the old days, a shadowy sliver of living history clinging to time in this forgotten alley.

Across the alley from the burro field, the double doors of the Burro Alley Boot Repair Shop were wide open. The long flagstone step, once the entrance to a stable, had been washed clean today by the rain. Whitney rapped his knuckles on the wooden door frame and then stepped into the cool, musty shop. Alejandro was in the back bent over a pair of shoes held under the yellow light of a single lamp.

"¿*Alejandro, cómo está?*" Whitney walked back through the long shop. Alejandro glanced at Whitney over his bifocals, waved a hand, and then returned to his work. He was lacing the tip of the toe of a styleless, orthopedic type leather shoe. Probably, Whitney thought, they belonged to some old woman whose ablity to walk on her own depended on Alejandro's ability to keep those shoes intact.

"You're working late," Whitney said, taking a seat on a high stool beside a box of leather scraps.

"Oh, *sí*, old Mrs. Tibber needs these back tonight. I feel sorry for her. She doesn't walk, really. She just stands. Stands beside her lilac bushes with that deaf dog she's had since Mr. Tibber died. But she stands best in these. What can I do for you, Whitney?" Alejandro looked down at Whitney's booted feet. "I fixed those boots, what, a year ago?"

"Yes. And they're fine. I was just out walking."

"Out walking?" Alejandro pulled the lace tight and then looped it back under the leather before trimming it with a knife. He set the shoe down on the table and turned off the single light. The sun streamed in the wide doorway. "I didn't think you had much time anymore to be out walking. I hardly see you, Whitney Slope. Except in the newspaper."

"Yeah, I know, I don't get out visiting friends like I'd like, anymore." Whitney shrugged and smiled at Alejandro. "You coming to the show?"

"Me? With all those fancy people? Where do they all come from?" Alejandro waved his hand at the shelves of cowboy boots and women's flats, and sturdy-toed work shoes. "I never see their shoes in here."

"No. I don't suppose you do." Whitney took a toothpick from a glass jar kept on Alejandro's counter. Alejandro had given up smoking the first year Whitney was in Santa Fe owing to an emphysema scare. He had a jar of toothpicks in every corner of the shop.

"The *Duster* article said that some countess from Austria bought five of your paintings. Five." Alejandro laughed and raised his black eyebrows. "Big ones, they said. Now tell me, Whitney, what do Austrians do with paintings of the old adobe and blue skies of New Mexico?"

"I don't know," Whitney answered, laughing. "Dream of the Old West, I guess. Just like the rest of us."

Alejandro put Mrs. Tibber's shoes in a paper grocery bag on the counter and stood up.

"My niece graduates tomorrow night," Whitney said suddenly. "Connie's daughter."

Alejandro rubbed grease into the side of someone's cowboy boot and then set the boot down and wiped his hands with a cloth. "*Sí,* I remember. Caroline. How is she doing?"

"I guess about like most people when they lose a parent young."

Alejandro walked to the doorway of his shop and stood under the carved wooden boot swinging on hinges that served as the shop sign.

"Nice rain, wasn't it," Alejandro said quietly. "The June rain always comes in from the desert country, due west. When I first came to the city from my parents' village, the wind that brought the spring rain made me homesick. I wanted to return to the places that made the rain, that smelled like that. To my childhood. But my family needed me to work. In time, I came to enjoy the desert wind that brought the sand and bits of sweet sage into the city, reminders of home, of people gone but not forgotten."

Whitney joined Alejandro on the stone step. Ravens strutted along the top of the adobe wall. The burros had wandered to the far side of their little field. Miles behind them, beyond the low buildings that made up the west side of Santa Fe, the sun neared the top of the faraway mountains that rose in dark blue hues from the desert floor sixty miles away.

"Me and the burros won't be here much longer, you know," Alejandro said matter-of-factly. "The whole block, the alley, has been bought up by some *rico* gringo from Texas. My lease is up in September. We'll move out then."

"No, Alejandro! This is your place!" Whitney looked at the burros, suddenly an endangered species. "Their place! They can't move you out! It's been, what, three decades?"

"Mr. Robertson, the new owner, is going to build here. Right here. A restaurant. Maybe a fancy hotel. Dress shops. New shoes of Italian leather. I suppose they will put a high rise over there in the burro field. We wouldn't see the horizon anymore, anyway. Better to leave before some changes come about."

"Oh, God, that's terrible." Whitney turned and looked at the dusty shop behind him: leather and wood and dust. Soon just dust. "Jesus! What will you do?"

"People will still find me with their boots." Alejandro laughed and looked at Whitney. "Oh, I won't sit at home. Eliza would make me crazy. She cleans all the time. I'll fish, maybe, in the mountains like when I was a boy." Alejandro looked up at Whitney with a sad smile. "Of course, Eliza won't cook the fish. I'll throw them back. But going fishing isn't really about food, is it?"

"No . . . I just don't understand why someone would want to raze this old street."

"It's those big buyers, the ones you meet in your gallery. You're to blame, Whitney Slope."

"Me?"

"*Sí*. Your paintings make this city, those mountains, even the clouds and rain, something everyone has forgotten and suddenly has need to remember again. But when they come to this place, they can't forget what they've become. What they can't live without. Maybe they just need to put in indoor plumbing. Or fix the street so that it drains away from their front door. But I don't think so. They will make this old place into something new, something familiar. Something of theirs that was never ours. *¡Dios mío!* It's an old story in this old land."

Whitney stepped out onto the cobbled street of Burro Alley. His stomach tightened as he imagined some developer's crew tearing down the old adobe and *jacal* walls, scattering the burros and uprooting the catalpa tree growing too close to the street. But what made Whitney even sicker was knowing that at this very moment Anna Farina and her assistant were hanging his paintings of this very alley, this very shop, on the Mud Street Gallery's spotlit walls.

"I remember when you first came to Santa Fe. I thought you were just another spoiled gringo," Alejandro said. "Another drifter. But you were good. You worked hard. I was glad to know you, Whitney, glad to mend your boots every year. Your soles have the wear of a man who walks with a strong stride. I like you, you know that. But now I think you are too good. You paint too clearly what is of value in this place. Everyone who sees your pictures wants to come here and have a piece of it."

Alejandro saw the concern in Whitney's face and jabbed Whitney's arm playfully with his elbow. "I will come and see what you have painted. But you'll understand if I do not come to the party with the Austrian princess."

Whitney smiled and nodded that he would and then turned to watch the ravens ruffle their wings and prepare for the air. Alejandro mumbled something about Eliza and Mrs. Tibber, about the luck of fish hooked but thrown back into the water, before walking back into his shop.

Whitney remained alone on the doomed curb of Burro Alley with one of Alejandro's toothpicks still in his mouth. He watched as the black birds effortlessly opened their ragged wings and then soared west over the nearly transparent ears of the baby Wonder into the radiant glow of the setting sun. The ravens could fly away from the hands of developers, could leave behind the money of *rico* Texas gringos. Take to the clouds. But for his old friend Alejandro, and maybe for Whitney, too, it was too late to learn to fly like that—untethered and bold, the horizon the only destination.

Dominga de Jesús

Dominga de Jesús stood alone and wide awake on the edge of the mountain canyon. The faraway below bottom of the cool canyon was still held in predawn darkness. Dominga's brothers, Porfirio and Virgil, and her youngest nephew, Tim, were asleep in their down bags fifty yards behind her in the clearing. Only the four hobbled horses watched Dominga in the half light. Dominga peered through the ponderosa tree trunks at the horses: she knew they were wondering if she were about to saddle one of them up, and head him nose first into that cold canyon.

From the other side of the canyon, high in the walls across the open grey space from Dominga, birds began to chirp and nudge the world around them towards dawn. Dominga listened and tried to identify each call as she took in and let out long, vaporous breaths. She wondered if her forty-seven-year-old lungs could still handle the chilled air, and the descent and then ascent of such a steep slope as this one beginning near her boots? In the old days, Dominga de Jesús—Garcia back then—would be halfway down by now, easily reaching the sandy arroyo at the bottom where she would explore the dry river bottom, and then scramble back up to camp before any of the boys knew she had left. Dominga wanted to do just that, right now—down and up in time to make the breakfast fire, and a pot of cowboy coffee, before her brothers and nephew stirred.

Dominga pulled her wool hat down over her ears and zipped up her parka. It was early June, time to push the cattle to high mountain pastures, but in New Mexico in the thick of a ponderosa pine forest at first light, the air felt like late November.

Dominga looked back at the men rolled in their bags, and at the horses now feigning sleep and disinterest in the far clearing. She had not climbed down such a rock slope since childhood. Since marriage to Feodoro, which was really childhood, or the end of it, at eighteen years of age. She had not used her feet to scramble over sandstone or shale, through piñon or juniper, or around the cactus growing in-between, since before children, before grandchildren, before the confronting and acquiring of adult pain about which young Hispanic girls are not forewarned.

Here on the edge of this canyon, she was feeling she could climb like Dominga Garcia again. Not to leave the children and the life of the last thirty years behind, but to find some piece of herself that felt this morning as if it lay somewhere down in that canyon. Like a flung shoe; a mistaken toss made years ago, and now she wanted the pair together again.

"Nonsense," Dominga whispered to the sky, "I just want to climb!"

Dominga descended the rock ledges like a slow but experienced deer. She sang bits of an old Spanish holy song into the collar of her parka because a tide of fear rose into her belly as the true distance between her feet and the canyon floor came to light with the ebbing dawn.

Thirty minutes later, Dominga de Jesús touched the sandy bottom. She had removed the wool cap halfway down and now thought about removing her parka; she was drenched with perspiration. Dominga walked to a large rock, one that had tumbled a lifetime ago from the maze of boulders she had just climbed down through, and sat on its cold shoulder. It had been a laborious but exhilarating descent.

Dominga sat in the thick of a cottonwood grove where the canyon's upper rim was not visible. The morning sky of soft blue and pink clouds lit the ceiling above the old trees. What were they? Cirrus? Grandmother would know, but she would say their name in her Apache tongue. Dominga used to know all the clouds, each name, English, Spanish, some Apache. Cirrus. Grandmother's Apache people would have their own name, but Dominga was certain everyone else would call those thin bands of dawn fleece cirrus clouds.

Dominga waited for the panting of her lungs to subside. She closed her eyes and leaned her head against her arms, which rested heavily on her knees. Cumulus nimbus were her favorite. Cumulus. Clouds of fleece—*borregos*. Sheep clouds. Sheep tumbled like clouds in the wind.

It had been too long: too long since Dominga had exerted herself in the dawn air, too long since she had remembered how grandmother would watch the sky and mumble the old words of her mother and father; too long since Dominga had searched her mind for the names of clouds, or stumbled across the memory of sheep hurled across the desert, *el milagro de Mi Ojo*.

Dominga sighed. People around the village still spoke of the miracle of the flying sheep, even if they did not believe it to be true. They still spoke of the young Garcia girl and how she saw five sheep tumbled in the wind ahead of a thunderstorm, wool balls at the infinite mercy of God's hand. Dominga's parents and brothers, and most everyone else around Mi Ojo, believed that seven-year-old Dominga had been struck on the head by lightning that day. Even when the sheep were found dead five miles out in Recuerdos Canyon, their wool tinged with hues of purple and pink, like the tips of the clouds at sundown, people around Mi Ojo believed Dominga's story to be nonsense. The miracle, they said, was that Dominga Garcia was alive at all, loco or not. But Dominga knew *el milagro de Mi Ojo* was the five flying sheep, even if her neighbors were too stubborn to acknowledge it.

Grandmother would have believed Dominga's story about the sheep. Grandmother died in her sleep two years before that late spring storm, but Dominga always knew in her heart that grandmother would have understood about the sheep. Just as grandmother would have understood why Dominga cried yesterday morning when she found her cowboy boots chewed by mice.

Grandmother would have understood about Atencio and why Dominga needed to climb down into this canyon at dawn.

When Feodoro de Jesús went to war, Dominga Garcia was ten years old. Dominga remembered how everyone in Mi Ojo feared it would be Feodoro's wife, Leona, who would be left alone to rear their three sons. Who in 1945 could have foreseen how it would be? Feodoro returned from overseas, a war hero, "skinny but alive," Dominga's mother used to say when he passed them in the shiny De Soto willed to him by a GI buddy. Feodoro survived two years of hell somewhere in the Pacific, and four months in a prisoner of war camp; but his plump wife, Leona, died of influenza the winter of 1953 when the illness settled into Mi Ojo with a vengeance.

In the clean, bare seclusion of the dawn canyon, Dominga de Jesús got to thinking about her narrow trailer home—how she wanted to take down the rows of faded pictures hung on its metal walls. Dust-collecting clutter, she said to herself. There was clutter she liked—bread baking clutter, books for her reading class clutter, the grandchildren's blocks scattered across her carpeted floor; and then there was the clutter of time gone by that held no meaning anymore. Her family held meaning, but not necessarily their possessions—not her dead husband's clothes still hanging in the closet, not his guns and war medals in the locked shed; not her mother's faded afghan on the weary, overstuffed sofa that came with the trailer house twelve years ago; not the knickknacks her daughters-in-law felt obliged to give her each birthday, as if the crowding of her trailer with trinkets might ease her descent into older age.

Dominga sighed loudly into the lightening canyon. Why, she was just remembering the feeling of ascension again! That feeling young girls, teenagers, or almost, hide inside when they first get an idea of themselves growing away from the bodies of their parents. Dominga had grown away from her parents, but she had grown into the widower, Feodoro, and his three sons. Dominga's body became their body one afternoon during a wedding mass. The body and spirit of Dominga Garcia was needed by someone else. Needed for the next thirty years. A good thirty years, but sometimes years that seemed more like Feodoro's, and his sons', than Dominga's.

Except for the years with Atencio underfoot—her first, her last, her only blood-and-flesh child. Atencio's birth was the gift of a second self, a cherished twin, with grandmother's etheric green eyes and melodic laughter. Atencio's years near Dominga's body flew past too quickly, a fragrant wind she could not contain, but that lingered always, a ghost scent around her head.

Now the ghosts of a thousand bodies veiled the beauty of Atencio's eyes, and the sound of his laughter was something even God must have forgotten by now.

Dominga could not change what she saw, nor what had happened to Atencio. She could not even give it a name. The good padre Leo told Dominga to be thankful Atencio was alive. At least Atencio was alive. Some village boys never returned home from Asia. At least Atencio was alive.

Dominga opened her eyes and leaned her head back to view the canyon rising to touch the brightening sky. The clouds, whatever their names, were gone, dissipated by daylight.

Dominga de Jesús thought how she could change the interior of her trailer. Clean it out. Tomorrow when she was home again, saddle sore and lonely for these mountains, she would begin cleaning. Feodoro had been dead seven years now. It was time to remove his material past from the trailer. She needed the space. Not to fill, but to leave empty; vacant, for awhile, until the filling of space with life was easy again.

The Garcia brothers were nearly outraged by Dominga's dawn jaunt alone from camp.

"As if you weren't someone's mother," Virgil said when Dominga reached the rim. Dominga had taken longer than she planned climbing back up the canyon. Virgil had watched her climb the last twenty yards, his forehead furrowed with disapproval and worry. Her brothers had already begun the fire and the coffee.

"You could have fallen. You could be lying hurt or worse down at the bottom."

Dominga stood on top of the rocks and looked back down into the canyon. She tried to subdue the heaving movement of her lungs beneath her flannel shirt. "I didn't fall. I'm not hurt."

"What did you expect to find down in that canyon?" Virgil asked, still frowning and glancing down the steep rocks.

"Mother used to say," Porfirio called from the firepit, "if you can't find Dominga, look for the highest tree or the farthest ledge."

Tim was looking at his aunt as if he had never before imagined her to be a child. Dominga smiled at him.

"That's exactly the sort of thing you used to do as a girl," Virgil added.

"*Es verdad,*" Dominga said, touching Tim on the top of his head. "And do you know what I went looking for? Sheep." Dominga chuckled as Virgil shook his head and snorted. "Lost sheep."

"*¡Dios mío!* Not the sheep." Virgil looked down at his son, who was smiling quizzically at his *tía* Dominga.

"*Sí,* sheep. Have I told you about the flying sheep, *¿mi sobrino?*"

By the time the eggs were fried and the bacon crisped, even Virgil was more amused than annoyed with Dominga's friskiness. Dominga took her breakfast to the canyon rim. With Tim sitting on the earth beside her, Dominga surveyed the mountains that rose up and away into the Rockies and beyond. It would be very warm, like summer, by noon. Dominga looked forward to the day's work, another day on horseback, rounding up the last of her brothers' stray cattle. There would be no sheep found out here today. But as the clouds piled into brilliant white mountains in the blue above them, Dominga would be thinking of the dawn alone in the canyon and remember sheep and days past that were suddenly alive again.

Leaving Santa Fe

For three years, or more, Whitney Slope had wanted to face at least one spectacular sundown alone on the Mud Street balcony. But until tonight he had never found the way out at just the precisely right moment, when the sun was exactly there, and the clouds hovering above the far mesa line were exactly there, like that, like this moment now.

Tonight Whitney had not so much found the way out as stumbled onto it. All he was wanting was a square foot of space to call his own and the only one he could locate was this corner beside the upstairs balcony wall. Someone had left a plastic punch glass full and untouched on the top of the wall that held what had to be one of the finest views of the western desert in all of Santa Fe. Whitney had already had one too many. Whitney did not need nor want this drink. He held the glass up to his bloodshot but still discerning eye and was struck by the gorgeous light of the sun sinking into the wavering horizon. There it was, precisely in place, everything right. Maybe it was the sheen cast onto the evening by the tequila polished punch, or maybe it was just the inevitability of too many issues not finding answers, but it was suddenly very clear to Whitney why he had come up here. He wanted to remember out there.

Whitney placed the glass, full and unlipped, back on the adobe ledge and leaned his elbows next to it. The sun finished its slide down the far side of the desert in a flaming red hush that Whitney strained to hear over the escalating din of fine art talk in the gallery behind him. What he wanted was some of that—that sky, the desert it courted, and the magic, harmonious silence he imagined existed between them. Whitney Slope wanted out into that and he wanted out now.

As they promised, the tortilla sisters and Alejandro had not attended the The Show opening. Moments ago, his friends Jon and Samantha Gateworthy had left the gallery for the High Noon and the birthday party for Juan Lopez. Most of the familiar faces still in the crowd downstairs would soon depart for that beer and salsa fiesta, which promised to be the real party of the evening.

"We'll hold a plate for you," Sam had told Whitney before leaving the Mud Street Gallery. "Rose baked a birthday cake shaped like a chile and decorated it the most vile green. Please come if you can."

"He can't come," Anna had said, placing her perfumed and meticulously pressed and fashionably dressed body between Whitney and Samantha. "Whitney has a previous engagement."

Sam had rolled her eyes as Anna walked away. Jon had whistled under his breath and shook his head. Whitney's eyes had continued to follow Anna's promenade through the crowded main room of the gallery. A sleeveless red silk chemise clung to every hill and valley of her toned Texas form. Anna stopped and gregariously greeted people she knew, even people she did not know. One-to-one exchanges were a challenge to Anna, but she was in her element at large, impossibly impersonal social events, especially if they were on her turf.

"We will keep a plate warm, Whitney, all night, if you want." Sam gave Whitney a friendly peck on the cheek and squeezed his hand. "Come late if you have to."

"By the way, nice show," Jon added. Sam nodded in agreement. "We'll tell you which ones we want later."

Whitney had smiled and then watched from the doorway as Sam and Jon walked out of the gallery and up Mud Street towards the plaza. He had suppressed the sensation to sprint like a quarter horse after them.

Below in the alley, a black cat scampered alongside the adobe wall and disappeared under Anna's red Mercedes. Whitney's eyes struggled to hold onto the last scraps of the sunset. As openings went, this one tonight at Mud Street was nothing out of the ordinary. Whitney had even enjoyed himself until the last ten minutes. He had met at least one person—a mother, a receptionist of some sort—he wanted to meet again in less surreal circumstances.

"I like your simple adobe doorways," a slight woman about Whitney's age said when she caught his eye. "I own all of your posters, and your calendars. But I don't think I'll ever own an original. You know, just framing those large posters costs a small fortune. I mean, to me."

"What do you do?" Whitney asked the woman. She had the sweetest voice, lyrical, almost shy. Whitney did not think anyone left around Santa Fe was shy. Where did this woman keep herself?

"I'm a clerk for the Santa Fe phone company," she said. "I used to do pottery and some watercolors in college. Now I only do those things with my children. I want them to have some sense of the artistic in life, no matter what they do. It can seem very dry without it. Of course, what I do is nothing like what you do. You're, well, you're gifted."

"Everyone is gifted," Whitney said quickly.

"I suppose."

The woman blushed and laughed. Whitney smiled. For some reason he wanted to tell her about Connie, how she did watercolors when Caroline was a baby; how his sister filled sketchbooks with drawings of her dogs and cats and her baby daughter that she would not share with Whitney. "The mundane," Connie used to say over the phone. "I'm not going to expose my middle-class, suburban mundanity to you, Whitney Slope."

Whitney wanted to tell the phone clerk about Connie and her unused gifts, and how she died with enough unfinished dreams to cover canvasses from Ohio to heaven. But the phone clerk was looking self-consciously around the room. People were watching.

"I better let you go . . . nice to meet you . . ."

"Well, you and the children keep painting . . ." Whitney reached out a hand, but she was already out of reach.

Whitney felt someone's eyes on him, and then another hand took him by his still outstretched wrist and turned him around.

"Hello, Whitney Slope. I'm Adele Morgan."

Adele Morgan held Whitney's hand between her two moist and warm palms. She turned Whitney's hand over as if she were reading the bones and lines for clues.

"Of course. I've seen your films, Ms. Morgan." Whitney extricated his hand.

"Whitney, call me Adele, please. I feel like we're old friends. I adore your work." Adele Morgan wasn't much more than fifty. She had recently retired from motion pictures. Santa Fe was her new home. "I own two grand paintings of yours, both of Greece. I plan to put them in the house I am building here in Santa Fe. I'd like to talk to you about a commission. Ms. Farina said you will not do commissions, but I would pay you very well. Your colors are my colors exactly: I had the factory in Mexico match my tile to blend with the steps up that painting of a steep Greek street in . . . ee or ii something."

"Ios."

"The one. How often do you get to Greece? I love the islands, especially Santorini. I want you to paint the little villa I stay in. I'll even send you there, on me."

"Oh, I don't have the time I used to to travel," Whitney said. And he absolutely boycotted the accessible villages, and all beaches that provided lounge chairs and hotels with room service.

"Will you come and see me? We'll have a dinner party with some Hollywood friends. They would all love to meet you."

Whitney sipped the drink he did not remember taking from the bar. What else was he not remembering? Whitney gave Adele Morgan his best noncommittal yet still reasonably polite smile and then stepped back into a large man who was standing, really lurking, behind him. Adele Morgan watched his clumsy exit, chuckling. Obviously, she was the better actor.

Whitney looked at his watch. Eight-thirty. He could still make the party at the High Noon. It suddenly occurred to him that he had forgotten to find Juan a present. Whitney stared into the air above the crowd and wondered what stores besides galleries and overpriced dress shops were still open around the plaza. The tortilla sisters would know. He could call them. Meet them at Woolworth's for a chili dog and a coke and a consultation in regards to what middle-aged Hispanic men liked to receive for their birthday.

Across the crowd Whitney spotted a bar buddy. Tom was a part-time painter and long-term Santa Fe resident with whom Whitney could share serious evaluation. And a few needed laughs. Whitney gestured for Tom to meet him at the end of the punch table.

"What I can see of the work," Tom darted his head around the bodies bumping like cattle rear to rear, thigh to thigh in the Mud Street Gallery, "is very good. Really, Whitney. Some allude to something quite different. Like you've altered your perception, or changed your focal point . . . attitude, or is it altitude? You've been thinking a lot about the sky, untouched space, this year, haven't you?"

"I suppose we long for what we can't have," Whitney said, leaning towards Tom's ear. Tom laughed and agreed. Whitney wanted to expound upon Tom's insight about space and unflinching light when Anna's hands pulled him by the elbow away from the food table.

"Whitney, there are some people I want you to meet. Come over here." Anna dismissed Tom with a nod of her head and then steered Whitney through the crowd to a couple watching his approach from her office door.

"Mr. and Mrs. Eric Robertson, this is Whitney Slope."

Anna was smiling as if she were reuniting Whitney with his dead parents. Whitney looked blankly at the middle-aged couple, trying to remember why he knew their name. "Eric is one of Jack's business partners from Dallas. They are very interested in hearing about the Chaco painting, which, I might add, they now own. Tell them how you went out there in your truck, in the snow, how you decided to paint this walkway."

Anna's eyes instructed Whitney to continue with the presentation, and then she sashayed back into the crowd.

Whitney looked across the large room. The Chaco painting was a five-by-seven vertical canvas. It was placed by itself on the far wall. Whitney liked that piece. He had liked it when he did it, and he had come to like it even more over the two months it hung in his studio. And he finally remembered where he had heard the Robertson's name.

"Oh, well, that painting is really a work in progress. I can see from here how the shadows down the left side are much too strong for the light, for the time of year."

"Oh, no, it's a done deal, Mr. Slope." Mr. Robertson winked at Whitney over his plastic glass. "We'll take it just as it is. You can change the shadow on the next one."

"Tell me, Mr. Slope, when you paint, do you know exactly what it's going to look like, or do you explore as you go along?" Mrs. Eric Robertson had the most petite voice carrying the softest southern drawl. Anna had that drawl sometimes, but it was never soft.

"Well, it depends a good deal on the subject," Whitney said looking at Mrs. Robertson, "but most of the time, I have no idea where I am at all. It's an adventure, if I'm lucky."

"Well, your work is just so romantic, don't you think?" Mrs. Robertson asked.

"Romantic, hell," Mr. Robertson said, laughing loudly. "There's nothing remotely romantic about the size of profit this man turns in an evening. My dear, the Xerox Corporation, and its ability to do something right again and again, has nothing on this man. He knows exactly where he is: in the middle of a gold mine. Your work is a major investment, isn't it Mr. Slope? Maybe a spot on the stock exchange in a few years?"

"You overestimate my robotic abilities, Mr. Robertson." Whitney's voice had an edge to it. His opening night cordiality was beginning to wear thin. If he went to the High Noon now there was a good chance he would not insult anyone.

"Perhaps you can tell me, Mr. Slope, I'm not an artist, of course, I'm a manufacturer of tractor parts. Big parts. Hundreds a week sent out all over the world. But tell me, in terms I can understand, a painting like this, large, not a lot of paint, seems to me, but large, still, tell me, when you ask $25,000 dollars, exactly what does that work out to an hour? For your time?"

Whitney studied Mr. Robertson's face.

"I really haven't the slightest idea," Whitney said. "I'd rather not put my time, my work, into those terms. As a friend of mine says, going fishing is not really about catching food, is it?"

"What?" Mr. Robertson leaned closer to Whitney, who stepped back into the shoulder of someone behind him. "I'm talking about money? Would you do all this work without it?"

"Probably you'll never have to find out," Anna said from Whitney's left elbow, adding a light laugh that helped Mrs. Robertson regain her smile.

"Speaking of investment, are you the Texas Robertson who bought Burro Alley?" Whitney felt Anna's fingernails digging into the skin of his forearm, clear through his shirt. She was trying to relocate him, steer him to a less potent part of the room.

"Burro Alley?" Mr. Robertson frowned. "Here in Santa Fe? I have bought some real estate. I don't know the names."

"Burro Alley," Whitney repeated, pointing to his boots. Mrs. Robertson stared stupidly at Whitney's toes.

"Whitney, there are folks waiting to talk with you," Anna said. "Will you excuse us, Eric, Ladelle? You can talk with Whitney later, at dinner."

Anna hooked an arm through Whitney's and walked him into the crowd. Whitney stopped and faced her, still holding the drink he did not remember taking.

"Anna, do you know about Burro Alley?"

"What? No. But Jack will. You can ask him at the dinner party tonight. There's some talk about moving the gallery. Maybe that's the place."

"Jack Farina is going to be at the dinner party tonight?" Whitney made a point of untangling his arm from Anna's.

Jack Farina was not someone Whitney ever wanted to know, socially or otherwise. Unfortunately, Whitney had not learned the extent of Jack's reputation as the best of the worst sort of Texas businessman until after he had taken off his boots in Anna's Upper Canyon Road bedroom.

"Whitney, don't be so self-absorbed! Jack doesn't know about you." Anna was drawling, amused. "And he wouldn't care. Besides, there's nothing to hide anymore, is there?"

"Oh God, Anna, that's the problem exactly. There's way too much to hide."

Anna was pulled away by her devoted assistant, a recent art history graduate named Candy. Whitney headed for the balcony stairs and a piece of ground to call his own. Halfway up, he looked back down at the crowd and saw Tom at the door. The phone clerk was gone, gobbled up by the Robertsons and Ms. Morgan and the size of their pocketbooks and self-importance. Tom caught Whitney's eye, raised a thumb and was gone, too.

Whitney reached the clear, fresh air of the balcony and wondered why it was that the people he liked were always out of reach and the nameless, pushy people he probably could come to detest seemed to hold carte blanche to be directly underfoot? Was there no escaping them? Against the sunset, an abandoned glass of punch atop the balcony wall caught his eye, winking the obvious answer.

It was a good thing that Alejandro had not come tonight. Or the tortilla sisters.

"Slope, there you are!" Burt Rapp, the *Santa Fe Daily Duster's* editor, pulled himself up the last stair, then paused to catch his breath. Twenty pounds overweight and a smoker, Burt Rapp could always be counted on to share balconies and patios and other designated smoking areas, beautiful or not.

"I need a few quotes for the paper." Burt tugged a small pad, a badly chewed pencil, and a cigarette from his white cotton shirt pocket. A regular at local art openings, book signings, and other real or feigned highbrow events, Burt always looked and acted like the old-time Santa Fean he was.

"Nice show and all that. I'll let my art editor do the dissections and philosophizing. But I've been thinking—this is the third show I've seen of yours in three years. Always jammed, most of those expensive canvasses have red dots beside them, sold. I'm thinking, how can you go on like this?"

Whitney picked up the abandoned glass and took a robust sip before rousting up an answer for Burt.

"Is this on the record, or are we shooting the friendly breeze, Burt?"

Burt blew a long, deeply appreciated exhalation of smoke into the clean, crisp, evening air.

"Both. No, actually, I'm thinking, see, about how from where I sit behind my desk on Francisco Street, there are a lot of things still out there I want to do. We're about the same age. I figure I keep pushing the pen because I haven't done my best yet. Haven't really tested the water. But you, what do you do now? I mean, for an encore? How do you keep your own attention?"

Whitney took another sip of the punch. It had enough tequila in its fruity bouquet to preserve that ghost cat skulking around Anna's car in the darkening alley.

"Maybe I'll take up fly fishing; or homesteading. There are a whole lot of things I haven't tried my hand at yet."

"Yeah, yeah, I know. But you wouldn't. See, that's what I mean. No one walks away from this kind of success. You are what you do."

Whitney drank half of the punch and then set the glass down on the wall again, promising himself he would not touch its plastic side again with his hand or his lips.

"I'm just razzing you, Slope. I love your work. I just wondered if you ever take risks? I mean, *¡Jesuchristo!* You would have to risk failing in front of thousands."

"Burt, I never show anyone my failures."

"Oh, right. I'll quote you on that one." Burt laughed and put away his pencil and pad.

"I've got to go to the High Noon," Burt said, stubbing out his cigarette on the adobe wall and flicking the butt into the alley, just missing Anna's convertible. "You coming?"

"I'm hoping. But I might be a little late."

"See ya, Slope." Burt walked down the stairs and into the crowd.

Forgetting his promise, Whitney took a last sip from the plastic glass and wiped the punch from his mustache. There was something else he was forgetting. He turned and faced the western line of mountains, but only a flicker of purple remained of the sunset. Whatever he had seen out there was now swept away into dusk. Soon it would all be black. Just black. Whitney could not see what he wanted anymore, but he could feel it drumming like a hammer against his temples.

Whitney turned and walked quickly down the stairs. He was thinking about the party at the High Noon, how everyone he knew and liked would be there. And how everyone at Mud Street would know how Whitney had left The Show and gone to The Bar.

Whitney skipped the bottom two stairs and, with one last long stride that would make Alejandro proud, stepped out. Just like that, Whitney was on Mud Street, so named because of its historic and stubborn habit of regression to a major Santa Fe arroyo during the late summer monsoons. Whitney walked in a quick, semi-intoxicated march towards the corner where he turned onto unlit Chamisa Street and the longer but less traveled route to his apartment. In the three or four minutes since he had left the balcony, the high desert air had turned cool. Or maybe, Whitney thought, it was simply the return of his five senses to his body.

Without the aid of light, Whitney pulled clothes from the bedroom, paints, rolled canvas, papers and pencils from the studio, and various pots and pans from the kitchen of his apartment. His semi-inebriated but highly stimulated brain settled into a smooth, functional rhythm, dictating each step in the plan as he needed it: pack essentials and camping gear; gather credit cards and cash; turn off the water heater; put perishables from the fridge into his cooler; locate extra truck keys; depart.

Depart for where? Expecting to be found, and then cornered and cuffed by the art, adultery, and alcohol-abuse police, Whitney loaded in three trips, stuffing and heaving his belongings with unceremonious alacrity into the truck's covered bed. After locking the apartment, Whitney returned to the truck and sat with his hand on the ignition, his eyes squinting into the black of the alley around him.

Thirty-five minutes had passed since his leave-taking of the Mud Street Gallery. Whitney figured that was about all the time he was going to get. Anna would begin to get agitated and curious; then she would become miffed. He started the truck and drove without lights up the alley to the street. After mentally driving various routes into and out of Santa Fe, he remembered in which direction those unfettered ravens had flown. Whitney pulled on the truck's headlights and drove purposefully, and probably too quickly, out of Santa Fe and into the west.

The little pueblo capital twinkled against the mountains outlined by the early June moon in Whitney's rearview mirror. Whitney had no tangible idea where he was going except that it was west, and west of Santa Fe meant into the high desert, into the deep mesa country. Out there. To that.

Sixty miles later, having passed nothing more identifiable than the white and yellow lines of the rough two-laner, various cactus growing within the territory defined by his headlights, and countless kamikaze jackrabbits hell-bent on making his life and their own an intimate brush with death, Whitney read a sign announcing the village of Mi Ojo.

"My Eye," Whitney said aloud, slowing the truck to the legal limit for the first time in an hour, "My *ojo*. 'Where did ya say ya went to, Whitney?' My eye, God dammit, into the country of my eye!"

Whitney pulled the truck off the two-laner into a gas station. Actually it was the decrepit remains of what had been a gas station maybe ten or fifteen years ago. He parked the truck near the rusted gasoline islands and pulled his sleeping bag over him on the front seat. Whitney was asleep before the engine began to cool, but not before he heard a posse of coyotes courting the luminous moon.

Snakes and Stones

Atencio left Ernie's Bar on the plaza early that evening because he had been asked to leave by Ernie himself. No one was going to buy him anymore drinks, Ernie said, and he was tired of Atencio pestering the paying customers.

Atencio entered the deep dark of his house. He went directly to his room, feeling his way through the black by running his hands along the cool, smooth walls plastered with grandmother's mud. He stumbled onto his cot and after stripping himself, waited for sleep.

Atencio did not sleep, but drifted in and out of his body. From the edge of his dimming consciousness, Atencio heard soft swishing sounds somewhere in the black. Atencio sat up on shaking elbows. The sand was coming to begin the burial of the old house. With great physical effort he lit the kerosene lamp on the floor near the bed. When Atencio held the light up in the dark room, he saw it was not the desert sand invading the house. It was the desert snakes.

Suddenly sober, Atencio stood on his cot with the lamp held high near the ceiling. It was difficult to see if the snakes had flat, triangular heads, but Atencio had to assume the two slithering along the far wall were prairie rattlers.

Atencio moved slowly off the bed towards the door to the kitchen. If he could close the snakes in his room he could look for a suitable snake stick. His father used to keep a long handled hoe by the back door, but that was years ago, back when rattlesnakes came only into the garden. Atencio's heart tried to break through his chest with each beat, but he moved like a cat across the packed earth floor to the doorway. As he pulled the wood door closed behind him, he looked back at the far wall just as the snakes disappeared in silent single file into the floor.

Atencio held the lamp high and scanned the mud floor beneath his bare feet, and then around behind him in the kitchen. Nothing moved. But he had known good men—alert men—to be fooled before, ambushed, killed in the blink of an eye, the flash of a fang.

An empty, rusted bucket sat in the kitchen. Atencio set the lamp down near the doorway, and slowly lifted the bucket after checking its underside for movement. He walked noiselessly back across the floor of his bedroom to the corner where the snakes had disappeared and placed the bucket over the round, black hole he discovered there. Atencio then went outside and found a large stone on the back stoop behind the house. He carried the stone inside. After weighting down the bucket, Atencio returned to the step by the back door with a blanket, where he dozed fitfully under the silver moon the remainder of the night.

Atencio watched sunrise thread through the forty-one thorny skins of the cholla cactus sleeping on the mesas far across the sand. As the warmth slid up the side of his blanket and onto his cold face, he forgot just then why he was sitting alone on the back stoop. Atencio stood and saw he was a naked stick under the blanket. He wrapped himself in the old wool and opened the door into his mother's kitchen. Instead of his mother's coffee steaming from her kettle on the wood fired stove, Atencio saw the kerosene lamp on the floor of the barren, unlit kitchen. Atencio remembered he was grown. He remembered how he lived alone in a house full of snakes, and how he had to stay alert, keep thinking, if he was to stay alive.

It was a kind of thinking—of figuring and ordering—that Atencio had not done in years. It was going to be difficult, keeping his thoughts on the problem at hand in the house, and off the drifting urge to get a bottle from somewhere and watch the world instead of participating in it.

After retrieving his clothes, Atencio again closed up his bedroom. Before eating his breakfast of day-old tortillas, he inspected the remaining four rooms for holes in the packed mud floors. He found two more holes in two other rooms and carried heavy stones from grandfather's garden wall inside and placed them over the holes. The stones were only temporary solutions. Atencio knew snakes could find a way into anything.

Dominga came down to the old house in the middle of the afternoon. Atencio knew she often came down to his house when he stood at the post office, or wandered the highway. He liked thinking of his mother here. But he was never home when she visited, until today. Dominga was so surprised to find Atencio on the back step empty handed and nearly clear-eyed, she sat down silently on the earth beside him.

"*Hola,* mom."

Dominga smiled and then lifted her hand to push hair away from Atencio's light green eyes.

"*Hola, Atencio. ¿Cómo está, mi hijito con los ojos verdes?*"

Dominga shaded her own green eyes, and looked across at Atencio. Atencio could not hold her gaze and did not try.

"Snakes, mama, live in my house."

Dominga looked quickly at the kitchen door, which was closed.

"No, snakes have never lived in the house! Not your grandmother's house. No! *¡No es verdad, Atencio!* It is the liquor in your veins. You have seen demons before."

Dominga stood and brushed the sand from her jeans.

"Mama, I saw snakes in my room last night. Go and look for yourself. Holes in the mud floor. Snake holes. In the front rooms, too."

Dominga entered the old house. Atencio heard her opening the doors of each room, and then heard each door closing again.

"Maybe only racers, or bull snakes," Dominga said when she returned and stood behind Atencio. "Not rattlers. Not in my family's house."

"Maybe, mama, maybe."

"I'll call Tomas; he will come and do something. Tomas will have an idea."

Dominga began to walk around the side of the adobe house towards her trailer. Atencio stood and went after her and took her wrist in his hand. He was thinner than she was; he was thinner and maybe even older, now. But his hands were strong.

"No, mama, not Tomas. This is my house. I will stop the snakes in my house."

Dominga looked down at Atencio's hand holding her arm.

"All right. I won't call Tomas."

Atencio released his mother's arm and returned to the back step, which was now in the shade of late afternoon. He sat down on his haunches, his ankles folded beneath him, his arms resting on his bony knees.

"I will sleep outside tonight," Atencio told his mother. "Until I can make my house secure from snakes, I will sleep outside."

Dominga stood near the side of the house, looking out at the desert, her hands on her hips.

"Like when you were boys," she said after a long silence. "I brought you matches and candles after the moon set and the owls began to call." Dominga laughed. "You were so brave, Atencio, you and your brothers, sleeping under the stars near that cottonwood, huddled together like spoons; waiting for your father. He said he would not sleep outside on the hard ground when his own soft bed was a stone's throw away. But he always came to join you, anyway. He always came for you."

"He slept sitting up, his back against the tree," Atencio said, pointing at the cottonwood to the left of the garden wall. "Over there. Like a watcher."

Atencio and Dominga watched a raven glide across the open desert so far out he was just a black dot in the blue sky.

"He left, mama, before I could come home. I told him I'd come back and still he left before I could come home."

"Atencio, the cancer came so quickly. He did not know how it would be with the cancer."

Atencio turned and looked at his mother through blood shot, sober eyes. "*Ni yo,* mom. Neither did I."

Atencio slept on a blanket in the sand near the back door. Dominga came with juice and bread and sat with Atencio. But he hardly saw her. His body jerked and jittered and begged for alcohol all the night and then on through the next day. Even with the fear of the snakes looming like a mountain in his stomach, Atencio could not overcome the desire for a drink.

Before the end of the second morning, after Dominga left to teach her class in English as a second language, Atencio returned to the plaza bar and begged. The story of the snakes living in his house had rounded the village, and Atencio was given three beers and two of shots of vodka in the first hour. Everyone was thinking that Atencio was falling back into his old ways when he up and left his customary chair by the front window before dusk had completely fallen on the plaza. Atencio was numb with liquor but determined from fear, and he returned to his back step to wait for an answer, an idea, for a solution to find him.

Atencio sat on the back step in the silver dark beneath eight thousand stars and watched the horizon for the return of the moon. The waning moon rose after midnight and brought the stone step beneath Atencio to luminous life. Atencio watched the stone gleam like water under his black cotton pants, and he watched the answer surface from some old pool of memory. Atencio de Jesús was sitting on the answer: stone. Stone floors. He could lay hard stone over the mud floors.

Atencio lay awake on the blanket by the back door. Bits of knowledge flung far from his remembering fitted back together and made his idea whole. The road across the mesa country to a flagstone quarry unrolled before him— the old road, used twenty years ago by his father, Feodoro de Jesús, and his partner, Clay Koontz, and all the village men who helped them build the mercantile. Atencio was a boy when the men opened that road and drove their creaking trucks and trusted teams and ancient wagons across impossible terrain to lift rose-colored slabs the size of doors from the ground. Atencio's father had placed him on a ridge above the quarry with his lunch and a canteen. Day after day, Atencio watched them cut, wedge free, and then hoist from the ground stone that shone like the sky at sundown. It was a job so difficult Mi Ojo people talked about it years afterward like it was still happening.

When the mercantile floor was finished two months later, the road was closed and allowed to be reclaimed by the sand and the cactus and the tumbleweeds. There was a small hole, a scar, left in the desert, but Atencio's father said it was for a good reason: the making of a floor that could withstand a hundred years of people and weather and the changes brought by time. Something permanent, that stone floor, Feodoro de Jesús said, something beautiful.

Atencio did not need the road; he knew a shorter way, and he had a wheelbarrow. But Atencio de Jesús needed something permanent; Atencio de Jesús needed to find something beautiful.

Before the moon lifted to its zenith above the mesa country now shining like a sea of mercuric sand before him, Atencio's head flopped forwards onto the blanket wrapped loosely across his chest. His exhausted body slept like the dead, but in his dreams the ten glowing fingers of Atencio's hands were grasping the two strong arms of the wheelbarrow, and his feet were busy pushing something permanent, something beautiful, before him across the desert sand towards home.

Pastoral Airs

Dawn drifted over the eastern mesas in a slow tide of diffused sun, and a flock of piñon jays came to noisy life in the scruffy bushes near Whitney's truck. The light on the horizon was muted by soft clouds, but when the sun lifted above them, it was already hot, and Whitney's sleeping bag was immediately too heavy for comfort.

Whitney slid barefoot from the truck cab onto the red sand below. His legs remained numb with sleep and buckled under him, causing Whitney to sit down hard on the desert ground. The truck's bench seat was about twenty inches shorter than Whitney, and he remembered how he had attempted to straighten out during the night by hanging his legs out the side window.

Whitney rubbed his thighs and then stood with the aid of the truck door. He squinted into the sky and at the highway that aimed straight into the rising sun a few miles before dissolving into the red rock mesa country. Sixty miles to the east, the mountains of Santa Fe rose like a blue shadow off the earth. On the blacktop near the old station, three ravens pecked a breakfast from the furry corpse of a rabbit, perhaps one of the kamikazes Whitney had encountered last night. Behind him to the west, the two-laner was visible for half a mile, where it turned sharply into a bosque of cottonwood trees.

Whitney knew the trees followed a river. He had passed through this valley before, back when he drove around northern New Mexico looking for subjects to paint. The community of Mi Ojo was nestled in the valley made by the river. Water was the raison d'etre for small villages this far out in the high desert. Water and a deeply rooted, even stubborn, will to remain, were sometimes enough to forge communities that had outlasted hundreds of years of geographic isolation, extremes in weather, and finally the poverty introduced by modern, cash-carrying, cash-demanding America.

From far away east, Whitney heard the low drone of an approaching car. Whitney realized he was camped in a very public place and opened the truck and fetched his Stetson and sunglasses. He buckled the silver coiled snake that decorated the leather belt of his jeans and was just getting to his boots when the car roared passed him. Whitney lifted his arm to be friendly, but the passengers in the late model Lincoln kept their eyes on the road.

"Damned Texans," Whitney muttered as he pulled on his second boot and stood straight to stretch his back. "Don't they know it's illegal for them to leave the interstate?"

Whitney dug around the back of the truck for his water bottle and toothbrush and reclaimed his teeth while he walked the circumference of the adobe gas station. Even if the exposed bricks hadn't been so weathered and parched, the age of the place was evident in the upside-down-bottle shape of the gas pumps, and in the depth of the sand on the station floor. Behind the sinking building were enormous, barrel-trunked cottonwoods with arms that arched up and then over and back to the ground, where they embraced the back of the building like one of their own. Which it was, now, with few vestiges of human life, but plenty of the desert kind drifting in the front door and sifting through the glassless windows.

The vigaed roof covered only half the building. There was no door, and there was no floor other than the sand. Everything was speckled with glass from broken bottles and with the shiny, flattened remnants of crushed beer cans. From the front step of warped wood, the mesa country rolled southward, a shimmering red ocean melting into a sky so deeply blue it could not be focused upon.

Whitney leaned against the rusted, once red, gas pumps and decided the building was not worth reclaiming. For his desert studio he would have to look farther. He returned to the open back of the truck to find something to call breakfast.

To look farther, he was going to have to look better. Gringos carried enough unwanted baggage out in these villages without having the airs of the desperate or destitute. Whitney dug a clean but crumbled cowboy shirt out of his duffel bag. Before dressing, he vigorously washed his face with his bare hands and canteen water, and then spit-shined his scuffed and paint splattered boots. After munching half an apple, then popping a few aspirin for his tequila-spun head, Whitney was ready to enter the village of My Eye.

Back on the highway, Whitney drove the truck west into the bosque below the mesa upon which was built the village of Mi Ojo. The two-laner passed several hundred acres of irrigated fields that sprouted a thin, but hopeful, green. A few of the fields held small herds of cattle and sheep and mustang-like horses. Behind wood and tin animal sheds were small immaculate orchards of carefully pruned apple and pear trees. Immediately Whitney liked this little community that pushed up with determined life right on the edge of so much emptiness.

Whitney pulled off the highway into the parking lot of the Mi Ojo General Mercantile and Grocery. The mercantile was in full swing at barely eight in the morning. Whitney decided to stay seated in his truck where he could catch the local rhythms from a distance, at least until his head ceased pounding.

The Mi Ojo post office and its limp American flag were directly across the highway from the mercantile. Local residents parked at one and walked across to the other and back again. Some were dressed in city-type clothes, probably commuters to Santa Fe. After ten minutes, only pick-up trucks with ranchers and retirees remained parked around the mercantile and across at the post office. The eight o'clock ruckus of activity lasted only a few minutes; then Mi Ojo returned to what Whitney figured was probably its truer face: slow, rural northern New Mexico, where farmers drive out each morning to work and water their few irrigated acres; where part-time ranchers haul a couple of cows from one piece of open range to another; and young mothers with gaggles of children climbing over the car seat stop by the mercantile for milk and some chat with the neighbors. A community whose fragile pocket of green was forever enveloped in the spacious, hot world of the desert, whose acequias and planted fields, barbed wire fences and adobe walls supported a hamlet of humans under a painfully blue sky that might be speckled with lofty, white clouds by midafternoon.

Whitney looked across the highway and up toward the old village on the mesa. He could see the smooth, uneven backs of adobe dwellings built closely together like a fortress. Only the government-issue post office and a few trailer homes parked behind the roadside mercantile and the post office were down here on the highway. Thank God for high places, Whitney thought; for islands in the stream, or in the middle of the desert.

Whitney knew he was creating a small stir, sitting alone, watching from the truck. Each and every person who walked through the mercantile's open double doors shot a quick look at his truck. Some nodded, as if to tell him they knew he was there. Others seemed embarrassed to look at someone they did not know. Before Whitney aroused the suspicion worthy of an IRS agent, or a land-gobbling developer, he secured his Stetson over his unruly hair and left the truck.

Whitney walked the circumference of the mercantile's interior looking for orange juice. But he soon found it next to impossible to focus on food with his eyes so distracted by the floor. After stumbling around several aisles, and after finally stopping to bend over and touch the deep, rose colored flagstones, Whitney located the refrigerated foods section. Aware that he was being watched by the man at the counter, Whitney quickly chose a bottle of juice. He walked back to the front of the store and asked the clerk, a small sixtyish looking man in a khaki jump suit and cowboy boots, about the price of a bottle of orange juice, and how the store had come to get such an extraordinary stone floor?

"A thing of beauty, isn't it," the man told him. He was dark haired and tanned, but not Hispanic. His fluent Spanish to other customers, however, implied a long personal history with Mi Ojo. "A community venture, this floor. Laid in the 1960s. Hard times in this valley then. Men leaving to find work. The community was dying. It was just what Mi Ojo needed—a project to bring everyone together again."

"I have never seen a floor like this," Whitney said, squinting at the surface beneath him, "although it reminds me of stone floors found in the Mediterranean. Greek, Roman floors."

The man was studying Whitney, his mouth half opened as he chewed the end of a match stick.

"Mediterranean. Never been there, although my parents came from Eastern Europe. Orange juice is fifty-five cents. Need a bag?"

"Yes. No, I'll drink it now."

Whitney paid for the juice and then opened it, gulping half the contents in one tilt of the bottle.

"Not many use this highway anymore, not since the interstate was finished. You traveling northwest to Utah or southeast to Santa Fe?"

"I'm traveling from Santa Fe, but not to Utah. I might be looking for a place to live. Maybe near Mi Ojo. Ever hear of places for rent?"

"Hmm, well, could be, could be. Don't know. Just for yourself or do you have a family?"

"Just me, I'm alone," Whitney said, leaning into the linoleum counter.

"Can get plenty lonely out here in Mi Ojo, especially for a single man. What's your name and where are you from exactly? I'm Clay Koontz, owner."

"Glad to meet you, Clay," Whitney said, extending his hand. Clay stared at Whitney's long, slender fingers, at the skin and cuticles discolored by paint. "I'm Whitney Slope. I've been in Santa Fe eight years."

"Why leave such a nice little city? Good place, I'm told, although I don't care much for city living." Clay took the match stick from his mouth and stared at Whitney. "You're not a fugitive of some kind, are you?"

Whitney laughed, but Clay did not. "No! No! I'm just looking for a change of scenery. I paint."

Clay Koontz nodded and looked at Whitney's hands again.

"An artist. Been some here before. They like to paint the old church on the plaza up there." Clay pointed through the geranium covered windows at the dirt road winding up the mesa across the highway. "People around here are getting used to your kind."

"Beautiful church." Whitney was wondering about his kind, and if he was going to find a salon of escaped artists in residence up in that lovely village. Maybe he would go on to the outback of Utah after all.

Clay greeted two women as they walked past the counter. The young women gave Whitney a veiled once over before continuing their conversation in rapid Spanish.

"If you're really serious about finding a place to rent, I can ask around. We don't get many newcomers. And people don't leave here much, neither, so there's few empty houses."

Whitney nodded. He was relieved to know there weren't many newcomers.

"Except those that are real old, don't have plumbing or electricity. I suspect you'd like both? But there are a few places closed up that might be reopened. What can you pay?"

"Whatever's the fair price around here."

"What's fair to you."

Whitney pulled at each side of his mustache and smiled.

"A lot. A whole lot would be fair to me."

Clay smiled and nodded slowly.

"Come back tomorrow or the next day; I'll see what I can find." Clay leaned back on the windowsill behind him.

"Tomorrow would be great," Whitney said after swallowing the last of the juice. "I'm camping out of my truck. I'm ready to move in right away."

Whitney returned to his truck and sat with the door open. He had been thinking about moving, relocating, for the past year. But not actually beyond Santa Fe. Now he was looking for a house in the middle of nowhere, sixty miles from town, to call home. Connie would chuckle, but Alan would say this little flight without a charted course had set Whitney's progress towards maturity back a few decades.

Whitney looked at his watch. It was nine o'clock. Ten in Cleveland. Too early to call Caroline.

He sighed and turned on the engine. He would come back and use the phone later in the day. He turned the truck back onto the two-laner and headed east.

Magpies swooped from tree to tree along the highway. Crows or were they ravens? seemed to be everywhere apparent in the valley where the air temperature in the shade was probably already pushing eighty degrees. Whitney knew the hours ahead were going to pass very slowly. He knew there was going to be no absence of heat and boredom back at that gas station, or down in the shade of the bosque where gnats and flies had a firm hold on the biological balance. But Whitney was going to stay. It was west; it was under him, and he was going to attach himself to whatever came his way. Or did not come. House, no house; with or without plumbing, electricity; a roof, no roof. At least out here, Whitney knew exactly what was lacking.

Whitney passed the morning exploring the old gas station and the red hills surrounding it. After lunch, he slept against the enormous trunk of one of the cottonwood trees. By late afternoon, when the heat of the desert rose like a wall where the trees' shade ended, and the sand under the open sun burned the palm of a hand placed against it, Whitney was beginning to feel accustomed to the old place. He even stopped noticing the cars that passed him by without a friendly wave or even the smallest nod of recognition, like he was some untouchable, some nameless beggar living on the edge of the highway. Not even the state trooper who passed the old station several times that afternoon seemed particularly interested in Whitney's camp. Maybe the trooper had already asked Clay Koontz about him; maybe out here no one really cared what some citified Anglo was up to on the edge of the desert.

Before supper, Whitney returned to the mercantile to use the telephone mounted on its east wall. Whitney dialed the operator and waited. Behind the store, down a packed sand drive, a striking, swarthy woman with jet black hair that hung straight to her narrow waist, hung sheets on a wobbly clothesline. She glanced at Whitney in a friendly manner, but went into her trailer without speaking.

"Caroline?" Whitney said when his niece picked up the phone. "How'd it go, college girl?"

"Oh, God! It was fun! I wish you could have seen the backyard! I hung about a hundred lanterns and everyone danced, even dad, and Bobbie Burnett drank too much and got sick in the driveway!"

"Sounds like graduation, but I don't know what from. You know I'm sorry I couldn't have been there. Although I could have done without Bobbie's show."

Caroline laughed. "Yeah, I know. You would have been bored, Uncle Whitney. You go to all those fancy parties with famous people . . . how was your party?"

"I'm not exactly sure," Whitney said. Until just now, he had pushed The Show, and the skipped dinner party, to the far recesses of his brain. "I left a little early. I guess I didn't want to be like Bobbie Burnett. I'm old enough to know when I've had enough."

"Do you want to talk with dad? He's out back. One of his partners and his wife are here."

"No, tell him I called, Caroline. I just wanted to talk with you. I'll call later in the week. I'm out camping for a few days."

"Camping? Where?"

"Northern New Mexico."

"Painting and stuff?"

"And stuff," Whitney said.

"Are you okay?" Caroline added. She sounded so much like Connie. Whitney swallowed before answering.

"Of course I am. I feel better today than I have in, well, awhile."

"Take care of yourself, Uncle Whitney. And thanks for calling. I'm glad to know you're out there . . . I sure do love you."

"I love you, too, Caroline," Whitney half whispered. "I still can't believe you've grown up so much."

Whitney hung up the phone and stood beside the truck. The shadows were long from the trees, and the mesas were rich with the colors of late afternoon. Surrounded by such languid softness even the phone booth and the ugly trailer house took on pastoral airs.

Back at the abandoned station, Whitney prepared himself a cold supper of canned meat and tortillas bought from the mercantile. He uncorked a bottle of fine French wine brought from his Santa Fe kitchen and drank from the long, narrow bottle while evening sank into the mesa land around him. After the going-home commuter parade of local cars and pick-ups, the highway became as quiet and solemn as the desert. The cottonwood trees provided refuge for all sorts of birds who came for a chorus of collective song before final dark—meadowlarks, magpies, juncos, jays, ravens, of course. Even a silent, surveying hawk joined the plebeian lullaby and sat perched on a high branch, the visiting dignitary, distant, but still related.

After dark, the yips of coyotes and the murmurs of close but unseen crickets replaced the chorus of birds. Whitney watched the top edge of the mesas across the road become rimmed with blinking stars. He knew the moon was waiting to set sail just below the eastern horizon and that the total blackness was only temporary. Once he had slept out under the stars on the sand of beaches—it wasn't so long ago . . . before Caroline was born? Now she was a woman. More time had come and gone than Whitney wanted to remember. But surely he still possessed some of those survival skills?

Whitney's sense of isolation and exposure heightened with each new night sound, culminating with the arrival of a great hooting owl somewhere in the branches above him. It became a toss up as to which would be more uncomfortable—sleeping on the sand in the wild with the beasts seen and unseen, or on the front seat of the truck in a half-nelson around the steering wheel. Whitney considered unloading his belongings from the truck bed so that he could sleep in the camper shell, but there was no suitable place on the ground or in the station to pile his gear.

Whitney opted for a night on the floor of the gas station, come what may. What came was a face full of the half moon as it passed over the station just after midnight. The coyotes scampered and sang on the ridges across the highway, and the owl hooted voraciously from the upper branches of the cottonwood. But Whitney slept in deep, blessed oblivion, unaware of the clamor that surrounded him, and of the unearthly light that peered in at him through the open ceiling of the crumbling station.

Cañon de los Recuerdos

The next afternoon, when Whitney Slope drove into the mercantile parking lot, Clay Koontz stood leaning against the open door, enjoying a lull in activity. Whitney's hair was dirty; his clothes carried another day of Mi Ojo dust; and his face, although shaded by his Stetson, had become a darker brown under the blonde stubble around his mustache. Whitney sported the easy, unselfconscious smile of a person who has come to appreciate the social life of birds, katydids, and dry desert heat.

"Afternoon, Mr. Koontz," Whitney said over the gas pumps as he approached Clay.

"Mr. Slope," Clay said. "I've got a house for you, if you're still of a mind to live out here in the boonies?"

Whitney followed Clay inside the cool, almost dark store. Clay kept all of the overhead lights off during the heat of the afternoon. Without the glare of neon, the stone floors were a deep terra cotta rose.

Whitney removed his hat and ruffled his greasy hair away from his head. "I am; I'm still of a mind to live out here."

Clay stood near the counter and began unloading cigarettes from cartons into a pine display rack, vintage 1964. "Now, this particular house in Recuerdos Canyon is out a ways; you'll be having no neighbors to go to if you need something." Clay looked over the cigarettes at Whitney.

"That's fine," Whitney said, "who do I talk to?"

Clay walked past Whitney and motioned him to follow. They walked to the rear of the store and out the back door onto a small loading dock in the hot sun. Clay shaded his eyes with one hand and pointed with the other.

"That trailer there belongs to Dominga de Jesús. She's the caretaker of the house. I told her you might come and talk with her about it sometime today. Don't see her car just now, but it might be around back. A white Chevy wagon. Go on over and see. She's a good woman, a widow. Her husband, Feodoro de Jesús, was my partner here at the store.

Clay turned to Whitney, nodded, and left. Whitney straightened his hat, brushed off what dust was still loose from his jeans, and walked to the trailer's front porch. The door was open. He knocked on the screen, but no one was inside.

To the side of the trailer was the clothesline, emptied of sheets today. Beyond was an adobe shed with pieces of straw sticking out of the mud-plastered walls. As Whitney strolled past its open doors, he saw that it was inhabited by an old cream-and-white De Soto balanced on three wheels. Fifty feet farther, across a garden of prickly pear cactus, was an adobe house with no outward signs of life or use, save for two open, screenless windows.

Whitney walked down to the house and rapped his knuckles hard on the door frame. No one answered. Whitney could hear something like hammering from somewhere back of the old house. He left the door and wandered down around the side of the adobe. A shirtless boy, or man, was bent over a slab of stone, chipping with a hammer and chisel at one of its sides. The man, or boy, looked Asian, with black hair so long it touched his elastic-topped, black cotton pants. He was remarkably muscular and thin, like an animal in the wild who lives by wit and speed. The skin on the boy's back was smooth, like a child's, and was the color of aged cedar.

"Excuse me," Whitney said, touching the rim of his hat, "pardon my intrusion, but I'm looking for Dominga de Jesús."

The boy-man slowly turned his head over his shoulder and looked at Whitney. He then uncurled himself and stood with the hammer held against his side. Whitney saw that he was not Asian at all, but Hispanic, perhaps Indian, and that his eyes were an extraordinary green.

"I'm sorry to bother you like this, but I knocked up at the trailer house; no one was there. I thought maybe Mrs. de Jesús was down here?"

"She is not down here," the boy said simply. "I do not know where she is." He paused and looked up at the pitched tin roof of his house, and then back at Whitney. "She always comes back."

Whitney and the boy-man stood looking at each other in the hot glare of the afternoon sun. "I guess I'll wait for her up on her porch. I thank you for your help."

The boy, or man, bent down again and went on working. Whitney did not leave.

"Are you related to Dominga de Jesús?"

Cañon de los Recuerdos

"I am her son, Atencio."

"Nice to meet you. I'm Whitney Slope." Whitney thought about extending his hand; but there was the hammer, and somehow back here, facing the gigantic mesa country, social graces seemed ludicrous. "That's quite a piece of stone you have there. Quite a color. Same as the mercantile floor? I haven't ever seen that color in stone before. Not like that."

Atencio looked at the slab near his barefeet. "Yes."

"Are you making a walk, or step, adding to the patio out here?"

Atencio shook his head, and the hair down his back waved back and forth across his skin. "No. This is to keep the snakes out of the house." Atencio gestured with his head towards the door behind Whitney.

"Snakes?" Whitney asked, "In the house? This house?"

"Yes, snakes. But when I am finished they will go elsewhere." Atencio nodded at the mesa land and the foothills opening to his left. "They belong out there."

Nervously Whitney studied the sand and sage around his boots and then the base of the low adobe wall at the edge of the patio.

"You're putting in a stone floor? Isn't there a floor in the house already?"

"Yes. Packed mud. Now there will be stone."

Whitney brushed his mustache away from his upper lip and studied the stone again, squinting in the impossibly bright glare. "It must be quite a job with stone this size. Can you lift it alone?"

"Yes."

"Is someone helping you?"

"No. I have a wheelbarrow."

"You must be much stronger than you look," Whitney said. "I mean, I don't think I could do this job alone." Whitney heard a car's engine idling at the far side of the house.

"Dominga de Jesús," Atencio said.

"Thank you. I'll go up there now."

Atencio resumed kneeling over the stone, chipping off a sharp corner that was thinner than the rest of the slab.

"You know, stone masonry is a fine art, quite a skill," Whitney said. "I'd like to come back and see what you're doing inside your house." Whitney heard a car door slam.

"I'll see you again," Whitney said. Atencio kept his head lowered over the beautiful slab of stone.

Whitney walked hastily around the adobe house and up to the trailer. Dominga de Jesús was already inside when Whitney reached the door.

"Hello! Excuse me, is anyone home?" Whitney knocked on the screen door again.

A Hispanic woman dressed in a cotton dress, with gleaming black hair and light green eyes exactly the same hue as her son's, walked to the door. It was the woman Whitney had seen hanging out the sheets.

"You are the man looking for a house to rent?"

"Yes, I'm Whitney Slope. Are you Dominga de Jesús? Clay, over at the mercantile, told me to come talk with you."

Dominga opened the door for Whitney and then walked ahead of him to the kitchen. She lit the gas stove with a match and placed a lidless tea kettle on the burner.

"Please, sit down. I'm making myself some coffee. Would you drink some with me?"

"Thank you." Whitney took off his hat and settled into a chair at the metal dinette table near the window. He looked across the cactus-and-sand yard at Atencio's house. "I've been camping in my truck and haven't sat on a chair or at a table in two days."

Dominga smiled and sat down across the table from Whitney. She turned her head and gazed out the window towards Atencio's.

"Did Clay tell you about the house?"

"Just that it's up a canyon, isolated."

"*Cañon de los Recuerdos,* yes. It will need a little work. But it has electricity and indoor plumbing."

"It sounds perfect," Whitney said. "I don't need more."

Dominga smiled again and then looked at Whitney's hands on the table near hers.

"It's not perfect," she said. "But it was once a good home."

Whitney declined to stare at Dominga, although after staring at sand hills and sky, rusting pumps and crumbling adobe, a woman as beautiful as Dominga de Jesús was difficult to look away from. Dominga wore a sleeveless dress, and the skin on her arms and face was an even, warm brown. She was full breasted and full hipped, with a small waist and narrow wrists. Her straight, thick hair was bound in a knot at the base of her head. This woman did not resemble, even remotely, the widow Whitney had expected to find living in this green-brown trailer behind the Mi Ojo mercantile.

"I've been camping out of my truck, Mrs. de Jesús."

Dominga continued to smile. "I, too, love to camp, to sleep out under the stars. It is a very fine sky to sleep under." Dominga sighed and shook her head as if she had forgotten what she was going to say.

"Now, about the house," she began again.

"What is the rent, Mrs. de Jesús?"

"One hundred dollars a month. Clay said you were not worried about the amount of rent. Yes? Good. I'm not much of a landlord so I'll be learning how to, well, do this . . . as we go along."

The tea kettle's boiling water splashed onto the burner. Dominga left the table and removed it from the stove.

"The place belongs to my sister-in-law who lives up in Utah. I'm in charge because she's never here. I never thought about renting it before. People in Mi Ojo like to be close in to one another. Most of the community lives up on the hill over there, on the other side of the highway. Near the church, and the plaza."

Dominga threw several scoops of ground coffee directly into the tea kettle and then sat down again.

"Where is your home, Mr. Slope?"

"Whitney, please. I've been in Santa Fe for eight years. Before that, California, New York for school, then Greece, around."

"No family? Or do you not take them with you?"

"No, no family. Just me."

"Clay said you are an artist of some kind?"

"Yes. I paint."

"What do you paint?"

"Landscapes, mostly."

Dominga went to the sink and took a cup of cold water and poured it into the coffee pot.

"Cowboy coffee?" Whitney asked when she handed him a cup.

"Yes. I have the automatic maker over there on the counter. I use it whenever my sons are here. But for me, alone, I like to make it the way I make it in the mountains."

"You go into the mountains a lot?"

"No. But I think about the mountains a lot." Dominga sipped from her steaming cup and then set it on the table as she sat down again. "Tomorrow, my son, Tomas, can take you up the canyon. He will know about the electricity and plumbing."

"Okay. I'll be ready." Whitney looked out the window at Atencio's house. "That's quite a project your other son has going. Has he done stone work before?"

"No, Atencio has not worked with stone before." Dominga smiled apologetically. "Atencio has not worked with his hands, or with his head, or his heart, with anything of substance, excepting for a few months picking potatoes up north in Utah and holding highway signs near Tomita, in almost four years."

"I see. I'm sorry. I didn't mean to pry, to assume, well, I am sorry."

Dominga shook her head and looked back at the adobe house and its corrugated tin roof. "Everyone in Mi Ojo knows about Atencio. You should know, too." Dominga stood and went to the sink where she rinsed out a bowl and a single spoon.

"He is harmless enough. But he isn't always . . ." Dominga was looking out the window again, her spoon dripping in mid air, " . . . here. Atencio, isn't always here."

Whitney stood by the dinette with his hat in hand, preparing to leave.

"He was in Vietnam, Mr. Slope. And that is all I can tell you because that is all that I know."

Tomas de Jesús met Whitney Slope in front of Dominga's trailer the following noon. Tomas drove an orange truck with the state highway insignia on the door and three antennas and two red volunteer-fire-department beacons on the roof. Tomas was everything Atencio was not: overweight and thickly masculine, Tomas verged on hyperactive. He sported an army crew cut, pencil-thin black mustache, work jeans and construction boots. A Mi Ojo Merc baseball cap was pushed high on his forehead above narrow black brown eyes.

Tomas was in an obvious hurry when Whitney pulled up five minutes ahead of the scheduled time. He marched quickly to Whitney's truck and shook his hand through the window.

"Mr. Slope? Tomas de Jesús. Follow me. We'll go west up the highway two miles and then cut up a dirt road to the left."

Tomas used both hands to explain the route ahead. "Good you have a truck; it's not a county road, you know, not seasonally maintained."

Tomas returned to his idling truck and jumped into the cab with a dexterity his rounded torso did not suggest he possessed. He drove his truck onto the blacktop highway, spraying loose gravel onto Whitney's front grill. Whitney threw his own truck into gear and pursued, pedal to the floor. He followed Tomas across the bridge that spanned the Mi Ojo river, just a stream now in early summer, and then followed the dirt cloud left by Tomas's tires up the side road into the canyon.

Through the thick cloud of Tomas's trail of dust, Whitney could see heavy, old cottonwood trees and chamisa and tamarisk bushes that followed a small but lively stream along the side of the road. Twenty feet up the hills from the stream, the lush grass and trees gave way to piñon and juniper, cholla and sage. The little red hills beyond were nearly barren of vegetation, and seemed as hot to the eye as the stream seemed cool.

Whitney rounded a blind curve that cut suddenly to the left of a hill. After loudly scraping the back fender on a sharp dip in the road, he climbed a small mesa to the house. Tomas was out of his truck, the cab door left ajar behind him. He stood by the front gate. Whitney was chewing dust the way Tomas was chewing tobacco.

"Let's go on in and see what you're gonna need," Tomas said, after spitting black juice into the red sand. Whitney climbed from his truck, spit red saliva into the red sand, and followed Tomas through the half-hinged front gate.

Tomas opened the first door on the porch. It could hardly be called a front door, as there were four other similar doors opening onto the same covered porch down one side of the house's L and up the other. The house enclosed a patio where one tremendous, elegant catalpa tree grew. The patio was almost pure sand. Miraculously, irises and several large lilac bushes grew from the dry earth near the porch and along the outer adobe wall where the rain from the roof obviously collected during a desert shower. The patio wall was eroding to nothing in several places because the plaster on both the house and the wall was almost entirely gone, exposing the individual adobe bricks to the slow decay of the sun, wind, and rain.

Whitney quickly surveyed the exterior of the house before Tomas ushered him inside. The roof looked intact, and the wood of the porch was still solid. Whitney opened the screen door through which Tomas had disappeared. The door frame was too low for Whitney, and although he ducked in time to avoid concussion, his hat was knocked backwards onto the porch.

"Yeah, the place will need a little work," Tomas said, "but it looks good, it looks pretty good for a place this old—hundred, maybe hundred twenty-five. Belonged to my father's sister. She married twice, and lived here always. Never know today that she had five children here—and twenty-seven chickens; the back porch was a coop. All gone . . . yeah, she was widowed twice and then went to Utah for a new husband and money. Found both and never comes back except for weddings and funerals."

Whitney had never seen so much dirt collected in one place, except in nature, and maybe at the old gas station he had made his open-air home the past three days. At least this house still had a roof and finished wood floors, although the cracks between many of the floor boards were almost an inch in width, and the dirt below was pushing up into the house.

A few pieces of broken furniture lay at odd angles around the first room, which was long and wide with windows to the east, north, and south. Through every window was a view of the sand hills, the canyon, and a piece of the deep blue sky. If Whitney could get the dust out, repaint the foot deep window-sills, and clean the glass back to transparent, it would make a fine studio.

"Right here is the kitchen, Mr. Slope," Tomas was saying in the next room. "No fridge, but a good electric stove, and a sink made of porcelain. A little work, it should be just fine."

"No refrigerator? Where would I find a refrigerator?" The kitchen was in the same shape as the first room, only the floor had a lumpy surface of ripped and faded linoleum, with a stamped design redolent of a cheap 1940s parlor rug.

"Maybe up in Tomita; in Santa Fe maybe. But you have a truck. No problem, right? Now, the bathroom used to be down this way." Tomas rounded the corner and headed into the other arm of the L, walking down a step to the level of the next room. Unpainted dry board separated the bathroom from the hall and a small sitting room. Obviously the indoor plumbing had been added years after the house was built. The bathroom had a bathtub on legs, a sink on a pedestal, and a commode on its side.

"But the plumbing is all there, you see. Everything's in place. That's good, that's good," Tomas said, and left for the next room.

The last room was the bedroom, evidenced by an iron-framed, coiled-spring, double bed lacking a mattress. Tomas frowned at Whitney and pointed at the black frame.

"No problem, Tomas," Whitney said before Tomas opened his unhappy mouth, "I've got one in Santa Fe."

The floor in the bedroom was like the first room's, with old planks pulling away from one another and the earth below trying to restake its claim on the site. This was a large room and like the first room, the kitchen, and even the bathroom, had a door opening out to the patio. The catalpa tree's slender branches reached across the patio to the porch, and the lilacs made a tall fence over the south window. Beyond these, beyond the crumbling adobe wall and the trucks parked randomly near the wood gate, were visible the enormous red and yellow rock walls of what must be the end of the canyon, half a mile away.

After prying open the patio door, Tomas left the bedroom and walked outside to the catalpa tree to survey the roof.

"Is there a spring running out of that canyon?" Whitney called out the bedroom door.

"Yeah, sure is," Tomas called back. "I'll give this electrical box a look-see before I go."

Tomas disappeared around the side of the house near the trucks. Whitney remained in the bedroom. He wanted to see if the west window still opened. After tapping each side with his pocket knife, and then digging under the wood of the sill, Whitney managed to lift it two inches. Whitney returned to the view from the center of the room. He could almost see the heat from the mesas as it rushed in under the window to be absorbed somewhere behind him in the silence of the house.

Whitney held his hat in his hands and looked out to where Tomas had disappeared last. He wanted to call out to Tomas and tell him he did not really care if the electricity were turned on today. Or tomorrow, actually; next week; at the end of the month. Whenever. Whitney just wanted Tomas to leave. Whitney wanted to stand alone in the house in the canyon and begin to figure what he was going do to with so much silence and beauty and space.

☾

The silence and space did not wear off after the first twenty-four hours in the canyon house, but the beauty became lost temporarily in the tasks at hand: Whitney had to find a refrigerator, reinstall the toilet, replace both faucets in the kitchen sink, and devise a method by which to remove the half ton of sand drifted like dunes throughout the house's interior.

The initial cleaning of the house was so consuming that for the next two days Whitney thought of nothing else. Not of Santa Fe; not of The Show hanging at the gallery, the dinner party missed; not of work, of play; not of Anna, Connie, Caroline, or his new landlady. Life beyond the canyon house ceased to exist.

Tomas came to turn on the electricity the second afternoon and was positively jubilant about the flow of power through the house again. He could not enter a room without switching on the overhead light. Whitney waited for Tomas to leave so that he could return the house to natural lighting. He had purchased two dozen long-life, prayer candles from the mercantile's religious items department and placed them on window ledges and countertops throughout the house. He thought this sort of light suited the old house far better than the exposed bulbs in the center of each room's ceiling.

"You religious?" Tomas asked, picking up a tall, glass candleholder that had a full-color painting of some saint down one side.

"No, not in that way," Whitney said, taking the candle out of Tomas's hands and setting it back down on the kitchen counter. "I just like candles. They remind me of places I've been to in Spain and Portugal."

"World traveler," Tomas said, moving his chaw from one side of his mouth to the other and winking at Whitney.

The rejuvenation of the plumbing system was not the easy good deed the electricity had been. Tomas poked around the well house one evening after work, even though Whitney told him he would get to it himself, eventually. Tomas's ceaseless chat and chewing, and his darting back and forth from the house to his truck, left Whitney nervous and tired. After several hours in the well, and then at the base of the house where the pipes supposedly departed for the leach field, Tomas gave up.

☾

"We've got the pressure we need," Tomas said after successfully flooding the kitchen and bathroom floors with oxygen-bloated water that spit in unpredictable bursts from all faucets. "But I don't know why the drains are so slow. Maybe it's the line to the leach field. Might need a backhoe out here."

"No . . . ah, why don't I do some work on it tomorrow," Whitney said, finally able to turn off the charging water with a pipe wrench. "I've done this sort of thing before. I think I can figure it out without the aid of major machinery. Cheaper, too."

"I know a guy who could come up here and really ream the line out if you wanted it."

Whitney did not want some guy reaming out anything in the canyon.

"I'll call. Thanks; I'll call if I can't get it open myself. Clay has a snake at the mercantile. I'll start with that."

"Whatever you want, Mr. Slope, but a backhoe's got the muscle you need with these old pipe and sewer systems."

Whitney helped Tomas carry his tools back to his truck. At the door of the truck, for the first time since they had met, Tomas stood doing nothing. At least outwardly nothing: his eyes continued to scan the tin roof of the house.

"You're going to need some help with the roof on the north side there. It'll be flapping in the wind during the late summer rains." Tomas dropped his eyes to Whitney. "We do get rain here. Lots; fast. A nuisance."

"Yes, well, I suppose I will," Whitney answered reluctantly. "Any suggestions?" Whitney would not have asked if Tomas had not had a full-time job with the highway department.

"Maybe my older brother's boy in Gallina. He might come over on a Saturday. Or one of the boys in Mi Ojo. Jobs are hard to come by in these parts. You'd have your pick."

"Sure. I'd be happy to hire someone like that. What about your younger brother, Atencio?"

"He's not the best worker, you see."

Tomas gathered a particularly thick wad of tobacco juice in his mouth and then spit-fired it into the sand near his truck tire.

"Your mother told me a little bit. But, you know, maybe Atencio could use the work, the money?"

"He don't use money for anything but liquor. He could use the work, all right, but forget the cash." Tomas sighed loudly and adjusted his jeans, which had a tendency to slide down to his hips because they couldn't actually get a hold around his waist. "Atencio don't have a vehicle anyway. Except an old De Soto that was my dad's. Always has problems; sort of like Atencio, huh?! Atencio has a watch that doesn't work, too. My brothers and I, we told him years ago, 'Sell that ridiculous car and get something practical.' But he don't listen to anyone."

Tomas was eyeing the roof again. "Atencio used to fix up cars, had a touch, before he want over there. Before he went loco with war."

"Not a pleasant thing, that war." Whitney walked back to the front gate and studied the hinges. He was planning to buy new ones from the mercantile. "But if you think it would help him to have a job, a task, like work on this house, say for gas, or groceries, or something like that, I might be willing to work with him."

"Maybe, Mr. Slope. I'll ask my mother. Maybe. Like an exchange?"

"Exactly. Credit at the mercantile, or car parts. Whatever."

"Maybe. Maybe not. Atencio's not very predictable. Not very coherent. And besides, he drinks all the time."

"I saw him working on that stone, sober."

"What stone?"

"For the house. Floors. So snakes wouldn't come in."

"Oh jeez! Snakes, bears, owls, commies; it doesn't matter. Stone won't keep them out of his head."

"Well, he was sober when I met him."

"When?"

"In the afternoon behind his house."

Tomas stopped chewing a moment, then spit juice and shook his head. "No. Just a rest between bottles, maybe. You'll see."

Whitney finished his inspection of the rusted hinges and closed the gate between himself and Tomas. Still Tomas stood and chewed against his truck door while he studied the soon-to-be-flapping roof.

"Has Atencio been in Mi Ojo since he came back?"

"No, he was in the VA hospital in Santa Fe on and off for two years." Tomas looked at Whitney instead of the roof. "Two kinds of men out here: employed and not drinking or not employed and drinking. It don't change.

And we don't have any vet programs. But that didn't help Atencio, anyhow. He tried those in Santa Fe. Couldn't live there; he's a country boy. Freaked out even worse than just after Nam. Came home in bad shape. He's still walking around because of my mother—she won't let him go. And people still talk to him. He's one of theirs, I guess. Always."

Tomas looked back at the roof and sighed. "You know, he's damned near killing my mother."

"It sounds to me like he's damned near killing himself."

"You a parent Mr. Slope?"

"No."

"I am. Two kids. Girl and a boy. My wife already worries about them leaving, about the world getting them. I say hell, get them out of the house and on their own before they lose their nerve. Christ! My mother, she hovered just like my wife. Atencio, being the baby, never had an idea about the world beyond her skirts. The war hit him broadside is all, out where she couldn't help him none."

"Lots of men were affected, not just youngest sons."

"Yeah, but Atencio was sensitive. My mother said it just like that, *sensitive*. My father said, 'Hell, he can be sensitive in his spare time. There's a world of work to do before there's time to be sensitive.' Still, my dad babied Atencio, too, but pretended like he wasn't."

"All kinds of work in the world, the way I see it."

"Oh, yeah, you're an artist, aren't you? Easy life I'd imagine. Lots of women, right?"

"Lots," Whitney said sarcastically.

"You're probably sensitive, too, huh?"

"About certain things. And I like my solitude."

"Lots of solitude out here. Not many women, though . . . if that's what you like! Me, I like my solitude with a football game on TV, the beer cooler on the floor by my feet, the kids and wife at grandma's. That's solitude."

Whitney nodded and began to turn away from the gate, hoping Tomas would get into his truck.

"Now, Atencio has solitude with a bottle. He carries his solitude with him, along the highway, up to the plaza. You'll see him at the post office, too, standing by that sick tree. He's alone all the time. Him and his bag.

Up here, solitary." Tomas tapped his head. "Maybe Atencio's not even up there himself, you know?"

Tomas opened the truck door and put one leg up. He turned back before hoisting himself onto the seat.

"Like no one home, as they say." Tomas climbed into the truck and slammed the door.

"Maybe he needs some help getting home," Whitney said with more anger than he'd intended. But Tomas did not hear him over the roar of his four-by-four, four-on-the-floor departure.

Whitney sat on the porch floor, his back against a post, staring into the dusk sky. The canyon echoed as nighthawks cut the quiet air above it in eerie descending octaves, and an owl hooted intermittently from one of the cottonwood trees on the far side of the house. In between the sounds of the night creatures, the silence surrounding the house and canyon was like thick gauze against Whitney's ears.

Five days had passed since Whitney's departure from Santa Fe. Tomorrow he would send Caroline a note telling her where he was, how he was making this old adobe into a home. Whitney would sketch the little house nestled in the magnificent walls of Recuerdos Canyon on a post card. Alan would say it was decrepit, that Whitney couldn't be serious—a home? Whitney would say he had not felt more serious about home before in his life.

Whitney thought about calling someone—Jon and Sam, or the tortilla sisters. But he had so much resistance to the idea of explaining his actions, his departure; and the telephone was miles away, surrounded by trucks and cars and dogs during the day, mosquitos and a riveting silence at night. And then out in the engulfing isolation of Recuerdos Canyon, the actuality of the greater world evaporated into the dry air like a soap bubble.

Whitney unfolded his sleeping bag for another night on the porch. Eventually, inevitably, he would have to go into Santa Fe. There were things he needed from his apartment, and he needed to give the tortilla sisters a month's notice. He had asked the Mi Ojo post mistress for a mailbox. She said that was impossible, but he could use general delivery. Whitney would go by the Santa Fe post office and leave instructions for his mail to be forwarded.

Whitney lay naked on top of the sleeping bag he would need before midnight when the canyon turned cold. He watched the last sliver of the moon rise over the canyon and spill a soft light down the rock walls. Around his head the sand patio filled with the same smoky silver. Whitney turned onto his side and stared at the sand and thought about Atencio's beautiful stone.

Whitney had painted that rose color. He had mixed it, lightened it, darkened it, controlled and owned it on canvas. Whitney was famous for it. But he had never seen it. Never held it. Never really owned it, not the way Atencio de Jesús did. Atencio dug that rose spirit out of the desert womb, rubbed its dust beneath his palms, and felt the burn of its fire dig beneath the skin of his bare feet.

All this time, Whitney had thought the burning beneath his skin was from something trying to get out. But tonight, in the shivering shadows of the canyon, he understood that the burn was from something trying to get in.

Anna Farina

Except for the mysterious disappearance of its star attraction, the opening gala at the Mud Street Gallery was an enormous success. People important to Anna Farina had flown in from Dallas and Los Angeles. Buyers and collectors came from New York and Chicago and San Francisco. Business partners of Anna's husband, Jack, and old family friends had come late afternoon for preopening talk and cocktails at the house. The late night, postopening gathering of interesting, influential, and/or wealthy Santa Feans and out-of-town art collectors went as planned at the Farinas' four thousand square foot adobe and glass, Spanish mission-style home on Santa Fe's exclusive east side. Whitney Slope did not show, but the food, wine, music, and conversation were too perfect for anyone except Anna to be perturbed by the slight.

Anna had noticed Whitney's absence within moments of his departure, but did not equate it with anything more than a conversation on the balcony, or a visit to the men's room. At least not until an hour had passed, and no one had seen Whitney and his grey Stetson in or around the environs of the gallery or even on the plaza. At similar events, Anna had known Whitney to slip away for time alone at the High Noon bar. Whitney Slope was famous for ducking out of a social event or business meeting for a "rendezvous with a smooth Mexican and a few yarns with the tender," his way of saying he needed beer and time with Jon Gateworthy and their circle of confidants at the High Noon.

If the opening had not been going so well, Whitney's antisocial behavior would have spurred Anna into some sort of decisive, even punitive action. Like a talk in her office, or a messenger sent over to the cafe on the old plaza. But both Anna and Whitney were already considerably wealthier than before the show opened. Jack's Dallas friends, the Robertsons, had written a very fat check for the monolithic painting of Chaco Canyon hanging in the front foyer. The sale of that piece alone would pay Whitney's rent and Anna's overhead for the next six months. So since she did not seem to need him, anyhow, Anna simply chewed at her nails and allowed Whitney his little game of hard-to-get.

Jack Farina was not at the opening. He never attended Anna's gallery galas. He preferred to give her all the room she needed to do what he said she did best: look gorgeous, mingle, flirt, cajole, reassure, and, finally, sell art to her public. Anna had a fabulous business sense Jack himself had helped her develop. And she had also acquired a decent artistic one owing partly to her formal education in art history, and partly to her personal liason with Whitney Slope. Jack did not realize the scope of Whitney Slope's role in the development of Anna's artistic taste. He just chalked her perceptions and intuitions up to her sense of style, to that inherent, nebulous quality that enabled Anna to distinguish good art from not so good art. Jack could not see the difference most of the time, but he was glad Anna had found a way to sort it out. Her little hobby, as he called the gallery when she first bought it four years ago, had turned into a right profitable little venture.

Anna's little venture with Whitney, about which Jack was not privy, lasted three months. It was an off-again–on-again affair, nebulous and never one of the heart, although Anna Farina liked Whitney Slope. And Anna Farina did not remember ever liking a man, really liking him as a friend, before in her life.

Anna Farina was a busy person. When Jack was in town, she was the good wife. There was no sneaking around, no clandestine phone calls, or meeting in back alleys—ever. But Jack preferred the Dallas-Fort Worth metroplex to Santa Fe's unzoned, unstructured, third-world paradigm of life. Anna liked Santa Fe's dusty, slowed down society as long as she could climb on a plane for Dallas, or New York, or Los Angeles, whenever she needed to indulge herself in chauffered tours of designer shops, health salons, and penthouse grilles.

Of all her extramarital liasons, Whitney Slope had been the most rewarding. Whitney was congenial and good natured. He was the elegant loner, the handsome, intellectual cowboy, considered a coup among her friends in any part of the country. Whitney had continued to visit Anna's house and bed months longer than any of her previous lovers: sometimes because of his physical attractiveness, sometimes because of his easy conversation and advice, and sometimes because Whitney Slope made for an evening of good company, even without sexual exchange.

Whitney Slope's particular slant on life puzzled, attracted, and sometimes annoyed Anna Farina. Whitney seemed to have possession of something Anna wanted, but she would be damned if she knew what it was; or if she would ever admit to wanting.

There were aspects of each the other disliked: Whitney did not care for Anna's ostentatious house, her two special-order Mercedes stationwagons (one personal; one business), or for her husband's Texas-mafia connections. And Anna detested Whitney's 1983 four-by-four truck with custom shell; his three rented, usually disheveled, and hardly furnished rooms; and his penchant for daily drinks and down-home good times at the High Noon Cafe. Anna Farina did not drink. But even if she did, she would not sit over even one beer with the local people Whitney swapped stories with at the High Noon.

Whitney Slope knew a handful of details about Anna that no one else around Santa Fe knew. He knew all about her Texas childhood on the Becklesforth ranch that had its own twelve-seat ferris wheel, an eight-bedroom house designed to resemble a Rhineland castle, and a heated stable of twenty-eight arabian horses color matched and bred under strictest scrutiny. Anna told Whitney how her father was never home, but his demands and instructions were so thick upon the household as to be physically tangible even in his absence. The only time Anna saw her father smile was when she swallowed her fear and jumped her horse over a five-foot cement wall. Anna learned at the age of twelve to leave her mother alone when she remained in her room all morning, and to stay away from her father unless other people were in the house socializing.

Whitney knew that Anna's mother's death was blamed on drugs and booze, but that it was probably hastened by injuries she sustained when one of those overbred stallions attacked her in the stables one summer night. It took three men to pull Anna's mother out from under the crazed animal's hooves, at which time the horse reared, threw himself onto his back and broke his neck.

Whitney knew that Anna's personal life had been given second priority to her business life, even before she had a business life. The only environment Anna had ever trusted to be consistently cordial and predictable was found in her father's secretary's office on the top floor of his Dallas skyscraper, or in her husband's office complex directly across the Dallas Metroplex from her father's, or in her own beige-and-mauve office in the Mud Street Gallery in downtown Santa Fe.

"Some people never get any part of their lives under control," Anna told Whitney. "I've got my business well in hand."

"What about the, you know, private parts?" Whitney had asked her.

Anna remembered how she had snorted at him.

"I'm working on that. But for now, it doesn't seem to matter."

Most of the time it did not matter. Most of the time Jack Farina was in Dallas; Anna was alone in Santa Fe; and Whitney was available. Before Whitney Slope, others were available. Anna Farina was not missing anything. She kept telling herself that she was not missing anything or anyone. Not even Whitney.

Anna had to wait until Jack and his Texas buddies left Santa Fe for Dallas before she could begin her own investigation into Whitney's disappearance, or even acknowledge her escalating anxiety. Anxiety and anger. Anna was angry about Whitney's missing the dinner party, and about having to lie to Jack and his friends about Whitney's absence.

Anna Farina was very angry today.

Within twenty-four hours after the opening, all those in Santa Fe who cared about art and society, or art and money, or just art, even just Whitney, had scripted their own little dramas to explain what had happened to Whitney Slope. Everyone, Anna noticed, except Jack Farina, who did not care much for Santa Fe and so missed just about everything going on here.

When Jack left in his private jet the following afternoon, Anna returned to the gallery and began quizzing Candy about the local rumors.

"People seem to think it has to do with a woman," Candy told Anna. But the glint in Candy's eyes held more mischief than substance, and Anna dismissed her with a wave of her hand.

"Has Burt Rapp been around asking questions? Seems like the editor of the *Daily Duster* ought to be out sniffing for a good story in this one."

Anna sat at her glass and brass desk in the gallery office, looking through the mail and eyeing the phone.

"Burt hasn't been here." Candy leaned against the office door, twisting her long red hair around her fingers. "But I saw him at the High Noon; out front, anyway, at one of the tables after lunch today. Talking with Jon Gateworthy. But I can't say if they were discussing Whitney."

Anna paused and stared into the space between them.

"Hm . . . yes, they were," Anna said, opening her Rolodex and thumbing through the cards in rapid succession. "Leave me, I've got work."

Burt Rapp picked up his office phone after the first ring.

"Burt? Anna Farina. Now, don't get clever, just tell me what you know and don't say my name aloud in that circus you call a newspaper office."

Burt Rapp laughed into the phone and then cleared his throat.

"Can I say his name?"

"Hell, no. Let's just talk about the rodeo, okay?"

"Right."

Anna could picture Burt pulling at his salt and pepper beard, fumbling for a lighter.

"Well?" she asked impatiently.

"What a show it has been!" Burt said, "Now, let me think, what can I offer you about the horses? Not much. Just what the average Tom walking the streets has access to. Riders? Just about nothing. Today, anyway."

"What about Jon Gateworthy, does he know something?"

"Not that he's telling; not to me."

"But he might; is that what you think?"

"No, not really. He seems concerned, but not worried. I guess curious, even amused, might sum it up for Jon."

"Well, I am not amused. What did the reviewer write about the opening? Or is it too late to ask favors?"

"Not to worry. No favors needed. Great review, all the way round. It was, after all, a great show by a great painter—excuse me, rider. Isn't that what it's all about anyway?"

"Not necessarily. Burt, you'd tell me if you found out something wouldn't you?"

"I guess that depends on what I found out, doesn't it? He did say something about homesteading, or fly fishing . . ."

Anna hung up the phone and gave a disgusted groan towards the outer gallery. Candy reappeared.

"Nothing. Nothing at all. The biggest single show by a nationally acclaimed artist hangs on my walls, and I can't tell buyers exactly where Mr. Slope is. We could be handling the work of a famous dead painter, for all I know."

"Not Whitney Slope. He's out there. And the show is doing well; who cares where he is?"

Anna looked up at Candy and noticed her red leather mini skirt for the first time.

"Really, Candy, mini skirts are for college coeds, not professional art dealers. People are in the front room. Go tend to them."

Candy left. Anna remained at her desk, where she leafed through the mail, thought about miniskirts she had owned and worn sixteen years ago to the delight of her entire college community, and filed her nails, which had been chewed down to frayed stubs in the last fifteen hours. When Anna had reshaped them into respectable arcs over her fingers, she pulled out an emergency bottle of clear polish. With meticulous care, Anna glossed over the damage her nervous teeth had done, and thought how she did not miss Whitney; not exactly.

Anna had made up her mind about Whitney a month ago, and her mind was clear—end the affair, disconnect. But even disconnected, Anna had planned to talk with Whitney. Anna began to chew her barely dried nails. What if Whitney had left the country, gone back to Greece and his beloved studio over a butcher's shop? She wanted the affair to end because it was confusing issues; because Whitney was making issues. Anna had assumed Whitney would always be around. Anna put her hands under the desk where she could not nibble upon them. There was absolutely no one else she could talk to . . . if she wanted to talk, which she probably did not.

No, Anna did not want to talk. She just wanted to know where Whitney Slope had gone and why. And she wanted to know why his leaving made her so very angry at everything and everyone around her—enraged, actually. It felt like the sharp edge of some old knife was trying to cut its way through her Texas-tough hide.

Before Anna Farina went for her very first visit to the High Noon Cafe, she fleshed out five different scenarios to explain her appearance. Anna thought through each step she would take, each word, each question: Jon Gateworthy would be easier to talk with than Sam, although Samantha might have better information. Women were better at gathering personal information, but in Anna's experience, it was easier to obtain that information from men.

Even with a plan, the whole idea gave Anna an itchy feeling, like hives coming on after a chocolate binge. The High Noon Cafe. Looking for Whitney at the High Noon; questioning his intimates there: she would almost have preferred confronting a wife.

Twenty-four hours and ten phone calls later, Anna was prepared for a visit to the High Noon. She needed to see Jon and Sam's physical responses to her questions about Whitney. How else could she know whether to believe what they would tell her? Anna could tell a lot about people just by looking at them. At the same time, she prided herself in her ability to hide exactly what she was thinking, even from herself.

Anna's Italian leather sandals clicked rapidly over Santa Fe's portal-covered sidewalk between Mud Street and the plaza. Tourists and local store owners paused to watch Anna Farina walk by in her hand-printed, cotton batiste-flounced skirt and concha-belted silk blouse. Anna ignored her audience. This, she reminded herself as she crossed into the no-car zone of the old plaza, is a business visit. Business.

The High Noon lunch rush was over, but the outside tables were still crammed with coffee sippers and wine glass nursers. Anna did not miss a beat: she wove gracefully between the tables that, she noticed, were set too close together for any sort of privacy. Several bicycles had been left near the front door, and a shirtless guitarist strummed a forgettable tune from a seat just outside the cafe. It had been no error in her judgement, Anna thought, her avoidance of this scruffy watering hole all these years.

Once inside, Anna Farina was relieved to be lost in the dim, dusty interior of the famous High Noon. The ceiling fans created an unsettling wind that sent chills down Anna's neck, but at least she wouldn't begin perspiring. She attributed the profound lack of interior light to the need to hide the dingy, decaying atmosphere from the tourists suckered into lunch at the widely hailed historic cafe.

Jon Gateworthy was standing behind the bar. Anna walked over and took a seat directly in front of him. It was the first time in her thirty-eight years she had ever sat on a bar stool.

"Anna Farina, welcome," Jon said, walking over to Anna with a glass of ice water in his hand. "Lunch? Coffee? Margarita on the rocks?"

Anna's sense of mission, and discomfort, began to intensify. She had met Jon Gateworthy at gallery affairs, and once at Whitney's apartment, but never here, on Jon's turf. He was a tad too comfortable at his post behind the bar. In his starched white apron and rolled up chambray shirtsleeves, Jon Gateworthy had the wholesome demeanor of a prep-school soccer player. How he had managed to end up a bartender in an old saloon in northern New Mexico, Anna did not want to know. There were a thousand other refugees like him in Santa Fe, all wanting to bend an ear with their immigration story. Anna believed personal history was something to shoulder alone, not exchange like those embarrassing adolescent pictures traded by the dozens in grammar school.

The dusty dimness of the High Noon began to close in on Anna. Her hands began to perspire and she could feel her makeup moistening under her eyes. She should have called and asked Jon to come by the gallery. This visit into Whitney's other life was a terrible blunder.

"No, no lunch. Nothing."

People were beginning to watch her. Anna could see them staring at her back from the mirror across the bar.

"All right, coffee."

Jon smiled and poured her a cup from a pot under the bar. Jon was probably the same age as Anna, and although he and Sam seemed financially secure, they did not move in Anna's circle, here or anywhere. Except for Jon's past four years as the good-buddy bartender to Whitney, Anna would not be extending him any courtesy whatever.

"Thank you." Anna poured cream into her cup and stirred quickly. Jon stood directly before her, wiping the beer mugs soaking in the sink and surveying the High Noon clientele behind her.

Anna looked down the bar. Her nearest neighbors sat two stools down—a cowboy type and some woman he was leaning hard into. Anna had never seen them before. She decided they were not listening, and turned back to Jon.

"Jon," Anna drawled with her friendliest intonation, "we both know that Whitney has not been seen since the opening two nights ago. I need to know where he went."

Jon raised his eyebrows and set down the dry mug, picking up another wet one from the sink.

"I don't know where he went, Anna. Or if he went somewhere at all. I thought you might know?"

Samantha Gateworthy came out of the kitchen and walked quickly down the bar to Jon. She held a notebook, but she closed it when she saw Anna. Anna had never had a direct conversation with Samantha Gateworthy. Samantha always seemed to be in a hurry, about to break into a run. Today Sam looked Santa Fe casual and too thin in a summer shirt dress with epaulets, like for safari.

"I don't think I believe you," Anna said quietly, sipping her coffee between thoughts. "Samantha, do you know where Whitney went the other night? I know he thinks highly of you. He might have told you something. I need to know. Business."

Sam stared at Anna, and then looked at Jon, who was still smiling at Anna.

"He's telling you the truth, Anna. I wish he weren't. I guess if Whitney wanted it to be your business, or our business, anyone's business at all, he would have said something. Or sent a postcard."

Anna set the coffee cup down in its saucer and pushed it away from her.

"I'm really not amused by this." Anna's Texas accent tended to thicken when she was agitated. She noticed she had begun to double drawl her r's, like her father, but she was too annoyed to stop and correct herself. "I trust you will tell me if you hear something. I have a great deal of business with Whitney, responsibility, with the show in the gallery right now. I must find him. Please tell me if you hear something."

Sam sighed and shook her head as she walked quickly back to the kitchen. Anna opened her purse and pulled out her wallet.

"Keep it, Anna. On the house. First timer's treat," Jon said, placing both hands on the bar and then resting his torso into his long arms. Anna involuntarily glanced up into Jon's face, which was close to her own. Jon Gateworthy was not the sort of man Anna noticed, but he was attractive—blue eyes, brown hair, square chin, straightforward smile. For some reason, Anna felt very much like she'd been had.

"Come again and stay awhile," Jon said, nodding hello as someone walked behind Anna towards a table. "Our green chile is the best in the west, so I'm told."

"I don't eat chile." Anna stood and smoothed her skirt, then checked the positions of the sixteen silver concha disks decorating her belt.

"Yes, I'm told hot chile can cause quite a lot of disruption in the delicate system." Jon smiled and pointed to Anna's waist. "Quite a belt; Navajo?"

"Yes. One of a kind."

"I knew that," Jon said before he turned and asked the couple down the bar if they wanted coffee.

Anna snapped her bag closed and left the High Noon while Jon was not looking. The tables outside were almost deserted now, as was the plaza. The famous siesta hour. Her mother had used some similar excuse to shut herself in a dark room in the middle of the day. In Santa Fe, New Mexico, the whole population did it. And, Anna Farina thought, they had centuries of idleness and poverty to show for it.

Anna walked to the far side of the plaza and into a shoe shop in the old Santa Fe Hotel. She tried on four pairs of leather boots and two pairs of pumps, size seven narrow, in quick succession. Twenty minutes later, leaving a stack of disheveled shoe boxes in the center of the store behind her, Anna Farina departed, greatly refreshed and composed, ready to reenter the Mud Street Gallery and her world of business and businesslike people.

Apache Blood

The interior of the Capilla de Santo Tomas shimmered and wavered with the light from three dozen candles. Dominga sat in the last row and stared over the age-darkened oak pews she had just finished oiling. The good padre Leo told Dominga not to oil the pews this year, that one of the Hernandez twins would come in as soon as they were done with school. But Dominga had come anyway. She had been oiling the church pews since she was in high school.

Dominga put down her rag and set the can of wood oil beside it on the bench. The Hernandez girls were fraternal twins. They attended the same college in southern Colorado. They had no brothers. Their father, Floyd Hernandez, had saved his money from his job with the Forest Service to send his daughters to college. Floyd was very proud of the twins. The whole valley was proud of the twins.

How times had changed, Dominga thought: no one was about to give those girls away into marriage. There were still men who returned wounded in body and spirit from war and the crimes of man against man, but the women of the village were no longer expected to save them. Excepting, of course, the women who were mothers.

The *nichos* in the *capilla* walls held the santos carved years ago by Atencio. Dominga dusted them every week. No one else in Mi Ojo touched the santos. They knew the privilege belonged to Dominga. The privilege and the tragedy.

Dominga walked up the creaking wood plank floor to the altar at the front and turned to the bank of flickering votive candles in an assortment of jars and glasses on the left. Half of the fires flickering in this church had been lit by Dominga, all for Atencio.

Dominga picked up a match and lit another candle. She knelt and began her prayer for Atencio's salvation and return to sober life; for a good apple and alfalfa harvest in the valley; for the good padre Leo's health; for fat cattle and strong horses at the fall roundup. She prayed for fields full of lambs; for lusty sunsets and breathless dawns; for laughter, for clouds, for sheep. Not necessarily five, Dominga heard herself say aloud in the church, just *uno milagro* . . .

"*¡Dios mío!*" Dominga whispered.

Dominga lifted her gaze from the small white candle and stared up into the serene face of the Virgin who cast a sacred glance to Dominga's right.

"Forgive me," Dominga whispered, "it is a shameless time."

Dominga rose to her feet, then turned away from the Virgin and walked quickly to the rear of the church. She scooped up her rag and her bottle of furniture oil. After genuflecting, Dominga left the church and walked across the hot, sandy plaza to her car parked in the shade of the old cottonwood beside the bar. Dominga climbed in and turned the key in the ignition. The engine would not start.

Dominga took a tissue from the glove compartment and wiped the perspiration from her brow and her upper lip. She would wait a moment and then try again. It always started. The car always started, eventually. It was just God's way of reminding Dominga to stop and think over what she was doing. What she was asking for. Where she was going.

She had not even said good-bye to the good padre Leo. Dominga looked at her watch. Twelve noon. He would be having his soup, preparing for a nap. Padre Leo was becoming like a child. Old people did that, especially men. The women of the parish would look after him, bring him clean clothes and food, books and medicines. A woman's work was never done, the magazines said; a woman's work was never done because as children grew to adults, adults returned to children. There was always someone who needed tending: from out of the cradle or into the grave, the hands of mothers made the human passage smooth and easy.

Dominga tried the ignition again. The car started. She let it idle a moment. Where was she going? Back to the trailer?

Dominga's station wagon idled across the plaza and around the church. She headed down the steep road from the village to the highway. Atencio was not at the post office. Maybe he was still at the house, staring at the patio, remembering stone. Maybe prayers were answered. Maybe a mother's prayers just had to outlast the nightmares of her children.

Dominga looked up and down the two-lane highway and then across to her trailer. She had bread dough rising on the linoleum counter in the kitchen.

She had curtains for the padre waiting to be hemmed. She had nothing at all she wanted to do inside that metal box.

Dominga turned right and headed east down the highway. She knew Clay was watching her through the geraniums of the mercantile window. He would wonder if Dominga had a parish call to make out at one of the small ranches, or if she were going all the way to Santa Fe for supplies?

Dominga drove out of the river valley on the highway that lifted ever so slightly onto the desert plateau. Dominga drove slowly, and the desert beside the road passed like a dream, a mirage of silence beyond the car. When Dominga reached the old gas station, she steered the car gently off the road and around back of the old building. When the shade from the cottonwoods rested on the station wagon, Dominga turned off the engine.

It was fiercely hot. Dominga did not have a hat. Her skin would turn bronze out here, become the color of sand, the color of wild mahogany. Dominga would become like grandmother . . . the color of an Apache summer.

Dominga walked away from the car and the steaming station, out to the farthest trunk of the farthest tree and sat down. The atmosphere was so hot it pressed into her lips and sucked at her breath. She squinted into the sky. There were no clouds.

Whitney Slope had camped out at this station. People around Mi Ojo thought he was a tad loco, stopping here, the gringo who came out of nowhere into nowhere. But Dominga knew he was on to something. Or after something. Whitney knew it, too. Dominga saw it in his blue eyes: something big, something small, something he knew he could no longer live without.

The ravens flew into the cottonwood for refuge and sat quietly in the branches above Dominga. She looked at her new white sneakers; the left one was stained on the toe from a dollop of red chile sauce she had spilled yesterday. If Dominga washed the sneakers she would have to spend a day padding around in her bedroom slippers, or barefoot. The first would indicate that she was slipping into senility, into old age; the second, that she was losing her sense of decorum and modesty. Maybe she would wear her boots, her old ones, found in the shed where they had been chewed by mice, ruined by Dominga's neglect of what was important. Maybe in her old boots she could remember where it was she wanted to go and how, precisely, she was going to get there.

When Dominga was a girl, the soles of her feet were calloused like stiff jerky. She ran into the back field and out into the desert, around the prickly pear and over the spear grass, barefoot with the best of the boys. Maybe better. Dominga's mother used to say it was in Dominga's veins, the need to run barefoot, to escape the house in a shameless burst that made the piñon jays scatter and scold from the juniper trees. It was because of grandmother's Apache blood, mother used to say, all those generations roaming the plateau country; the sky the only ceiling, the sand the only floor.

Dominga closed her eyes. She wanted to see the spirits of her grandmothers sprinting across the plain, out of the reach of this time and this place. But all Dominga saw was the dough rising over the side of the plastic bread bowl on the linoleum counter in the trailer house kitchen, and the unbleached muslin of the good padre's curtains waiting in her sewing basket to be hemmed, ironed and rehung.

Dominga climbed back into the car and turned the key in the ignition. The car did not start. Dominga sighed. No, she would not waste a prayer begging God to start this old car. She waited, and then pumped the gas and turned the ignition. Nothing.

Dominga climbed out of the car. She would walk home. Atencio walked the highway all the time. Dominga took off her stained sneakers and flung them back into the car. She would walk as grandmother walked, as Atencio walked, at home under this sky.

Dominga was half a mile from the station when she heard a car approaching. She did not turn around. She did not want to explain why her station wagon was parked behind the old gas station, hidden from view; why she was walking shoeless over sand that burned tears into her eyes.

The car slowed and pulled onto the shoulder behind her.

"Dominga!" the driver called. "Dominga de Jesús, climb in!"

Dominga wiped her face with her hand and then turned around. It was her cousin, Miguel, in his shiny black state trooper's car. Dominga stared at the glaring front grill, undecided as to whether she would accept his help. After a moment, she walked to the passenger door and climbed in.

"What in blazes are you doing out here, Dominga?" Miguel pulled back onto the highway. His radio was calling someone back into the station. "Dominga? ¡Dios mío, mi prima! You don't even have shoes."

Miguel leaned towards Dominga and took off his sunglasses. Dominga held his gaze. The Hernandez sisters would have given anything—their college education, certainly the shirts off their backs—to be sitting, rescued, in handsome Miguel Gonzales' police car. Dominga chuckled.

"I was looking for something, back there, at the station," Dominga said. "My car wouldn't start."

"Your car's back at the station? I didn't see it."

Miguel swung the police car around and headed east.

Dominga chuckled again. "That's because I hid it around back."

"Why did you do that?" Miguel glanced at Dominga's feet. He was not amused, but he was curious. "And where are your shoes, Dominga de Jesús?"

"My shoes are in the car," Dominga said, inspecting the bruised skin of her feet. "I hid the car because I didn't want anyone to know I was out there." Miguel kept glancing at Dominga, frowning. "It's my Apache blood, Miguel."

"Apache blood?" Miguel's state trooper's frown disappeared and was replaced by his compadre smile. "I share that blood, Dominga. Does that mean I'll have days when I abandon my car and walk barefoot on scalding sand?"

"If you are very lucky." Dominga smiled at her young cousin.

Miguel shook his head and chuckled as he turned into the gas station. He drove around the old building and stopped behind the station wagon under the cottonwood trees.

"Well, Dominga de Jesús, you'd better find yourself a more reliable vehicle if you're going to be doing things you don't want people to know about. Come on, let's see if I can start it."

Miguel jumped from the car, leaving the door wide open behind him. His radio crackled and sputtered about someone's cow loose on the highway near Santa Fe, about cars veering to avoid it and at least one near-miss collision because of it.

Miguel started the Chevy's engine and then left the car idling and walked back to Dominga.

"Anything else I can do for you, Dominga?"

"No. *Gracias*, Miguel."

Dominga hobbled past her cousin to her car, and then climbed in behind the wheel.

Apache Blood

"*Hasta luego,* Dominga," Miguel called, and then he backed up and drove the police car quickly around the station and back onto the highway.

Dominga held the steering wheel and stared at her discarded, stained sneakers on the seat. Until just now, it had not occurred to her that she wanted to hide anything, or that she had anything to hide. But that was exactly what Dominga was doing. Hiding. Hiding something. Something she did not allow to surface even in her prayers.

The Weight of Open Space

Whitney entered the mercantile minutes after it opened. His truck needed gas, and he needed to make a few phone calls before heading into Santa Fe later in the morning. He also wanted to buy Juan one of the metal tackle boxes he had seen in the back of the store. Whitney did not know if Juan Lopez ever went fishing. The tackle box just seemed like a good birthday present. It was the thought that counted, after all. And the thought—standing beside a stream with nothing to do but stare into water and feel the sun on one's back—carried a good deal of positive weight for Whitney.

Instead of the usual random assortment of vehicles parked in no particular pattern around the mercantile, there was a cluster of trucks near the mercantile's west side. Whitney stopped to listen before entering the store. All he could decipher from the rapid Spanish laced with English was that more shovels were needed and that two lambs had died.

Inside, Whitney found Clay talking with three men in rubber boots and work jeans, all hovering over the farm supplies bin. Clay handed the men three new shovels, and they departed. From the front door, Clay watched all of the men and trucks head up the highway towards Tomita.

"Morning Mr. Slope," Clay called to Whitney, who was the only other male left in the store. Several women stood holding groceries bags, talking in the aisle. Something was up in sedate little Mi Ojo.

"What's up around here today?" Whitney asked. "People seem agitated."

"Yeah, well, they are," Clay said, returning to his perch on the window ledge behind the cash register. "Seems last night the dam twenty miles upstream had a little trouble maneuvering one of its gates." Clay chuckled. "Army Corps let out a wee tad more water than they wanted. It came washing down the Mi Ojo river like a tidal wave. The river could have held it and all, that's not the problem. Problem was no one warned the local ditch mayordomo; after all, it was the middle of the night."

Clay sighed, "Doubt those army engineers knew it themselves until sunup. The gates of the valley acequia were wide open, letting in the little trickle they're made to manage, and the water washed out the gates and then the sides of a quarter mile of the ditch nearest the river. Two fields got an unscheduled soaking."

Whitney nodded sympathetically.

"It makes for a damned nuisance in early summer with new crops under water, and then lambs washed downstream, and now a whole valley with no irrigation water to speak of," Clay continued. "Lots of animals are staring at an empty trough this morning. So the men are fixing it themselves."

Clay chuckled again. "Corps did offer to send some equipment down by tomorrow afternoon, at the latest of course."

"Sounds pretty bad," Whitney sighed. They were silent a moment, then Whitney remembered his truck out near the pumps and his gift for Juan.

"I need gas, too," Whitney said, "and one of those nice tackle boxes, the navy blue one that you have on the shelf against the back wall."

Whitney went outside and filled his truck's tank, staring up the highway and picturing the green fields of new corn devastated by mud and water.

"¡Hola, Mr. Slope!" Dominga called from her station wagon on the far side of the parking lot. "How is the house? You are sleeping well?"

"Yes, it's fine, wonderful, Mrs. de Jesús."

Whitney looked up the highway and then back to Dominga.

"Yes, the water, I know," Dominga called. She pointed at the back of her wagon. "My husband's best shovel. I am going there now."

Dominga waved and drove onto the highway before Whitney could replace the gas pump and walk her direction. He watched the rear end of the white wagon round the curve north of the village. Whitney walked quickly back into the mercantile.

"Clay, I owe you for the gas, the tackle box, and I'd like some of these rubber boots and a shovel from over here."

Clay watched Whitney from the counter.

"What are you going to do? Start farming up the canyon?"

Whitney pushed through the bin of boots until he found a pair almost his size. He walked to the next aisle and took the first shovel he found.

"You going up the road to help, Mr. Slope?"

"I am, just that, Clay." Whitney pulled out a fifty and paid for his gas, shovel, boots, and tackle box.

Clay followed Whitney outside to his truck.

"They might not need you, Mr. Slope," Clay said without opinion, "but they'll appreciate your trying."

Whitney drove up the highway where Dominga had disappeared seven minutes earlier. It occurred to him that not only had he not made any phone calls, he had also clearly swept aside any intention to visit Santa Fe today.

It was easy to find the drowned fields: trucks and old cars were parked along the side of the road and down the sandy shoulder. Dominga's station wagon was the last, and Whitney parked behind it. From the highway, the two fields, totaling about sixteen acres, glistened like Asian rice paddies. It was a haunting sight—one side of the highway wet to saturation; the other side as dry as the Dust Bowl, and almost as large, the sun blistering its brown hide from the pavement to the hazy horizon.

Because of the giant cottonwoods along the irrigation ditch, Whitney could hear but not see a tractor. All the other work was being done by hand—by the hands of Mi Ojo's farmers and ranchers and ranchers' fathers and uncles. There must have been thirty men along the ditch, or what had been a ditch until early this morning, all with shovels and wheelbarrows and broad hats.

The men closest to Whitney looked his way and nodded cordially but said nothing. It was early morning, but they were well on their individual ways to a soaking sweat. The task before them was enormous for men and shovels. Both sides of the ditch along the top of both fields were damaged. The acequia was emptied of water, and Whitney could see that in some sections up to half a foot of silt would have to be cleaned out before the ditch could be opened again.

Whitney spotted Dominga at the far end of the second field. She stood with the sheep in mud to her ankles. The sheep were filthy, their recently shorn torsos now sporting the same mud that lined the ditch bottom. They walked behind Dominga like she was Mother Nature herself come to save them from the follies of men.

"Mrs. de Jesús, hello," Whitney called when he was near enough to get her attention. His boots were stretching closer to his necessary size with each step, but Whitney still walked with a stilted bend of the toes. Even with the shovel, Whitney felt about as ill prepared to negotiate this flooded field as the sheep.

"Mr. Slope, what a surprise!"

Whitney reached the little island of mud Dominga and the sheep were standing upon. "I thought maybe I could help."

Dominga surveyed Whitney head to foot and then smiled.

"Of course you can. It is a big job. Come with me; I'm going to work at the very end." Dominga clucked to the sheep who for some reason continued to follow her. They all walked on a raised ridge up the field away from the river. Several lambs bounded between the adult sheep's legs as if nothing in the world had happened the night before.

"I heard some lambs were lost," Whitney called to Dominga. Dominga wore jeans and an old shirt, both obviously too large for her, probably out of her late husband's drawers. She was not tall, but she walked faster than anyone ought to try in heavy boots and thick mud, himself included.

"Yes, it is always the innocent that are harmed by such mishaps," she called back.

They reached the top of the second field, where two of the older men were beginning work on the ditch walls. Dominga opened a gate, and the sheep scurried obediently through, into the relatively dry field on the other side.

"Carlos, Jaime, this is the renter of the house in *Cañon de los Recuerdos,* Whitney Slope." Dominga picked up her shovel and walked a few paces down the ditch. "Mr. Slope would like to help us. He looks like he has a strong back, *¿verdad?*"

The men, who had to be in their sixties, looked over at Whitney and nodded. The man closest to him, Jaime, stopped his shoveling and extended a hand to Whitney. He did not say anything, but returned immediately to his work.

Dominga adjusted the bandana around her neck and the straw hat on her head and then began to dig in the bottom of the acequia. Whitney followed her lead and climbed down into the old waterway. It was lined with clay and was very slick; Whitney watched his rubberized feet take off under him, race forwards, and then rise above him. Both men and then Dominga, when she saw he was not hurt, laughed heartily. Jaime offered a hand, but Whitney declined, fearing he would pull Jaime in on top of him.

"These ditches are made for water and the things that glide in water," Carlos said, "I myself have avoided putting my bottom on the bottom for sixty-two years."

Carlos and Jaime laughed. Dominga watched Whitney. She looked a little worried so he raised a muddied hand and waved her back to work.

With the help of his shovel, Whitney stood up. His backside was coated with reddish clay. He did not try to clean the sludge off; it would just have to dry. Everyone in the field was bent over at work. Whitney wanted to be remembered for his strong back and his dexterity with a shovel, not for his visits to the ditch bottom.

The men began to talk about the past century's floods in English, then in English and Spanish, and eventually just Spanish. Dominga and Whitney worked along the north bank of the ditch, rebuilding its side with the earth that was washed halfway up the highway shoulder in this spot. They covered only a short distance in an hour's time. Carlos and Jaime did the same on their side, and everyone took turns climbing down the ditch and mucking out the bottom.

It was the same the whole length of the acequia across the tops of the two fields. The tractor continued to grumble from inside the cottonwood trees, where the gates to the valley acequia were being repaired and rebanked. Whitney thought how overwhelming a task this was with only one tractor. A second tractor was due to arrive after lunch, and then the Army Corps had promised their Caterpillar. But Carlos told Whitney everyone in the fields figured the Army Corps would arrive just about the time the job was done. If at all.

Late in the morning, the state trooper Whitney had seen from the old station stopped and spoke with the workers farther down the ditch. Without really looking his direction, Whitney knew the trooper had registered his presence. This cop missed nothing, and although he never took off his sunglasses, he seemed to hold no imposing aura over the workers. He stopped and talked with almost every man on the other field. Whitney thought he was about to pick up a shovel when the police radio began calling. After a short exchange with headquarters, the young trooper disappeared with lights on, but no siren, up the highway to Tomita.

Women appeared at noon with lunch. Dominga had brought her own basket and handed out sandwiches and tortillas and tin cups of iced tea from the back of her station wagon. Whitney found shade under a cottonwood near Dominga's car and watched. The women nodded at him, and the men said hello, but no one seemed interested in striking up a conversation.

Whitney was too tired to strike up one himself, so he sat against the tree's wide trunk and stared out across the highway at the desert and the mesas that were hot white under the noon sun.

It was the first time in more than a month that Whitney wished he had a pencil and a sketch pad. He studied his hands and noticed, with surprise and an almost embarrassing macho sort of pride, that they were red with blistered welts on the palms, and brown with sun on the backs.

Whitney looked over to Dominga. Out in the field, her hands had been covered by gloves; now they looked soft and feminine handing out tea and tortillas to the small crowd of men gathered around her car. Dominga never ceased smiling, and neither did anyone within ten feet of her.

Whitney meant to get up and serve himself lunch, but Dominga brought him two tortillas covered with butter and plum jam before he could get to his feet again.

"How is it I can hardly move, Mrs. de Jesús, and you are fluttering around like you just arrived and hadn't lifted a shovel all morning?"

Dominga sat down near Whitney and began to eat her own tortilla.

"Oh, it's a way of living, I suppose," she said, smiling and squinting at the open desert beyond the cars. "I've been outside most of my life, under this sun. I've always lived here. The body becomes accustomed to the feel of this heat. Before that, no amount of muscle, or determination, can really compensate for the, how would you say it, the feeling of . . . ?"

Whitney licked his fingers. "Being acclimatized?"

"*Sí.*"

"This jam is very good. Yours?"

"The valley's." Dominga smiled and stood up.

"You were good to come. It shows good intentions."

No one left after lunch except the women with children. Whitney had no desire to leave the field and, except for the blisters on his hands and the sunburn developing across the bridge of his nose, felt energetic about another couple of hours of ditch digging.

Jaime, Carlos, Dominga, and Whitney moved in concert along their section of the ditch all afternoon. Whitney learned more about Jaime and Carlos, who were brothers, born and raised in Mi Ojo. Carlos had been a rancher, but Jaime had left Mi Ojo after he returned from the second world war, to

---

work in a factory in California. All six of his children were raised there, and all but one remained in southern California.

"My house had walls like cardboard," he told Whitney late in the afternoon when the shadows from the cottonwoods finally reached their section of the ditch, "and the train tracks were so close to my kitchen cupboards my wife could not set out her china plates. We used plastic because they could fall against one another six times a day and not break."

Jaime and Dominga had heard the story many times, Whitney figured, but they laughed and sympathized with Carlos just the same.

"When I retired and returned home to Mi Ojo with my wife, Delia, the first thing she did, even before unwrapping her santos and crucifix, was to place those plates with the little rosebuds in the cabinet over the sink. Now we use them every day, just the two of us."

"*Sí*, Carlos, and even without the train through the kitchen, they have nicks," Jaime said, winking at Dominga.

"Oh, *sí*, and Delia loves them still!"

Whitney smiled and watched Jaime stand and straighten his back. Whitney was feeling stiff across his own spine. He couldn't imagine how old Jaime kept bending and lifting and bending again.

"*Cañon de los Recuerdos,*" Jaime said when he caught Whitney watching him. "*Mi* papa, Manuel, used to go up into the canyon and find his lost cattle, his stray sheep and disobedient goats. Everyone, *todos*, up in that canyon. Just like the name promises, *¿si?*"

"What does the name promise?" Whitney asked.

Jaime thought a moment, rolling his lips around his few teeth.

"It means, *en inglés*, something *como* the place of memories. The place of remembering . . . of *recuerdos, historias,* of some wisdom . . . a keepsake . . . something known long ago, something carried in the blood. The animals have the memory of water, the shade, safety. They return there to survive their own foolishness . . . *¡Dios mío!* . . . wandering out into the desert where they have freedom, but cannot survive. So they remember the canyon of water and that's where we find them. Unless the coyotes find them first."

"That's where Dominga's sheep were found," Carlos said after a pause. "But they were dead."

"Dominga's sheep?" Whitney asked, looking at Dominga.

"Oh, they weren't my sheep," Dominga said, scoffing at Carlos.

"Dominga saw them flying." Carlos held his old hands up and flapped them as if they were wings. *"Un milagro."*

Whitney looked at Dominga and waited for her to explain.

"Sí. I saw sheep carried by the wind when I was seven."

"But the canyon did not save them?" Whitney asked her.

"Who is to say death is not being saved, Mr. Slope?"

The sun reached far across the fields from the west and made shadows with the fence posts and the barbed wire between. Whitney leaned his chin into the handle of his shovel and watched the men inspecting the repaired acequia. Before water could be allowed in again every foot had to be closely inspected. Dominga told Whitney it was the same in the early spring when the valley irrigation system reopened. The old ditch was made of dirt with no cement except at the head gates, but the entire six miles of Mi Ojo's acequia ran like the best aluminum pipe when it was properly cleaned. And, Dominga told him, it was always properly cleaned.

"It is the valley's main artery," she told him, "and the river is the heart pumping life into it."

Whitney watched the colors of the mesas across the river deepen and settle into one another. Men shook hands, gathered shovels, and started trucks. Only the men with the tractor were going to remain. The water would be let in before sunset. Whitney thought about staying to watch, but then Dominga said she was leaving, and suddenly he felt like an outsider again.

Whitney pulled off his rubber boots and drove home barefoot. He was so tired he had to wrench his eyes from one side of their sockets to the other to follow the highway. After turning onto the road to Recuerdos Canyon, Whitney stopped the truck. He looked at his palms. The blisters were about to break open. They would hurt like hell when they did.

There was something Whitney wanted to remember, something he wanted to think about, and he was afraid if he waited any longer it would be lost to him in the exhausted collapse he knew he'd fall into when he reached the house. Whitney stared at the tamarisk and listened to the birds chirping somewhere inside the feathery canopy. It was a feeling worth chasing, a feeling he had glimpsed to one side all day.

At first Whitney had believed it was the urge to paint, to possess something beautiful with color and form, paint and canvas. But now he understood that it was more than the urge to paint: it was a feeling without boundary or color. It began with the sun resting on his back when he bent over to the earth; it was a sense of the space of the field opening behind him, the heat of the horizon everywhere around him, the weight of the sky out there.

The weight of space.

Whitney placed a blistered hand against his chest. What Whitney felt pressing against his heart and his head was the weight of open space.

The Weight of Open Space

Persimillion

When it was apparent there was nothing left to lose, nothing left to leave, Persimillion Ramirez agreed to cross the Great River into the north with her two younger brothers. Her brothers were almost grown men, although Alfredo was forever just a boy because he got caught, somehow, in birth. But they needed her; Persimillion could be a mother again. So she agreed to cross the border into the country where she would be no one.

Persimillion had love the size of the sun but no one to give it to after the babies died one night in their baskets on the porch. Something that happens now and then, here and there; maybe God knows why, the clinic nurse told her. Not Persimillion's fault, although there was no one else to care, no one who noticed, so this must be her doing, somehow.

Persimillion Ramirez had been fat before, years before, but when the babies died in the night for no reason she could fathom, she grew to a size that astounded even Pepé; even Alfredo the Foolish noticed. Maybe it was her body wanting the babies safe inside again, but Persimillion bloated and swelled like the cattle that dropped where they died in the Mexican sun. Persimillion began to drag under the weight of her unused giving. Even Persimillion wasn't large enough to hold so much unanchored love.

Crossing the river seemed the only way out after twenty-six years of life gone nowhere but to babies buried under infertile soil; of nothing going on, except to God, of nothing going out, except her breath and her hope. The Ramirez brothers chose a departure night just as the spring winds ended.

"We have suffered enough drought," Pepé told Persimillion. "We are going where there is enough water to wash cars shiny on Sunday afternoons."

Persimillion did not even lock up the old house. Her father's house; all her life, her only home. All these years alone without a husband to help, she had at least kept it clean. The shack was half cardboard, and had nothing inside to take, or leave or protect.

Persimillion left the empty baby baskets to wither on the porch. At twilight before their departure, she again touched the muslin linings she had sewn like they were to be the Virgin's gown. Now they were chewed and frayed by moths. Persimillion listened to the evening crickets that once came to sing to the babies who never grew past their first fat, never heard the song of summer, unless there was music on the road they took home to God. Persimillion, for one, had not heard any. Maybe she could have turned them back to the land of the living if some angel had opened its mouth and given her fair warning.

Half the village of Llosa had left and returned, and left again, for the big country, the rich country, the Americano country where babies grow into children plump and happy as pear cactus popping open with the late summer rain.

Persimillion and her two brothers walked all night to the river, to the spot they were told was crossable even through thick, pitch black. The last four months, Persimillion thought she was past caring for her own self. But after the thorns and barbs on the bushes ripped her blouse, then slashed the plump flesh of her arms and face, and after the gritty fall—pushed by one brother, pulling the other along behind—down into the cold black river, Persimillion remembered how it was with caring. It always came with pain.

Pepé knew Persimillion could not swim, but he promised her she would float, like a balloon. Persimillion did float, with her mouth full of the dirty Rio Grande, and her eyes sightless with sand. Pepé held tightly to Persimillion's arm, and Persimillion held Alfredo against her bosom. But their legs banged into the rocks under the river, and finally they were all separate in the strong, shallow current, bobbing about in the dark, afraid to call for help in a place where they were no one.

Pepé pulled Persimillion out of the water on the other side and dragged her up the bank into the cottonwood trees. Above her and to the east, Persimillion saw the first light of the rising moon. She could hear Alfredo sobbing somewhere near the river's edge, but she could not move to help him. Pepé went back for him, and dragged him to Persimillion's muddy side, where they all huddled together like dumped puppies in the thick trees.

They had heard about men roaming the border with shotguns and dogs, about friends who disappeared, others who were thrown back into the river like fish. So the brothers and Persimillion did not open their mouths to catch an extra breath or remove their clothes to dry, even stand to clear their heads of the river's confusion. If they had had a little money, they might have had someone meet them—others told them to find a *coyote*, not to cross alone. But before they actually crossed the river and felt the wet black fear, before they discovered that on the other side they were no one, the journey had seemed so simple, so honorable.

Persimillion lay on the ground only a few minutes. Then she pulled the mud from her eyes and hair, and dug the gritty sand from her ears and out of her broken sandals. Persimillion knew it would have to be her that gathered them up, figured out the next step towards safety. A good mother must do this, must care for her own before she cares for her self. She hoped dogs would not smell them, but they had to move. The bosque sand was not going to take her only remaining loved ones out from under her.

Persimillion lifted her mud-smeared and bloodied body from the ground and nudged her brothers with firm silence. It was time to go deeper into the big country where their best hope was to get lost.

God lived on the other side, and it was through his grace alone that Persimillion and the two brothers found a friendly driver with an empty pickup truck. He asked no questions and gave no answers. He drove them sixty miles into noon of the following day on a dirt road that crossed someone's ranch. The brothers slept like the dead, their faces full to the sun on a pile of straw. Persimillion sat erect and awake, methodically scanning the four horizons for whatever fear-giving forms might materialize in this new country.

It seemed to Persimillion Ramirez that no matter how many miles they put between their bodies and that border, something wanted was always about to be taken away. What could be of value here was beyond Persimillion's understanding, but when she thought of going back, she saw the tiny, soft faces on her lap, and the two cardboard boxes waiting to be filled with the remnants of her love. And then even the familiar soil of back home became unfriendly.

Persimillion Ramirez lifted her eyes from the past and returned her attention to the horizon ahead. The new country was too large to take in, and Persimillion prayed those same angels who guided her sleeping twins to higher ground were now singing a song for her.

Persimillion watched from dawn until dusk three days and into the fourth, for a stopping place. She was extraordinarily careful about each and every step she took because she had twisted her ankle crossing the great river. Although Pepé could not tell by looking, her ankle was swollen and painful. Persimillion was accustomed to the pain that no one could see and so they pushed ahead at a steady pace.

On the tenth day, they skirted the borders of a city and walked the desert and mesa land far from people but in sight of the northwest highway. Persimillion and her brothers slept on the open ground wrapped together in a piece of tarp left by the highway crew. The foolish brother carried the yellow canvas, rolled and tied in a thick jute rope, like it was a treasure. It was his first possession in the new country. Persimillion figured it was too dirty and old to be missed, so she let Alfredo cling to his prize.

There were thick, tall juniper trees shading the high desert country surrounding the city. This country would have made a good camp, Pepé told Persimillion. But Persimillion lay awake at night listening to the city sounds and thought how if she could hear them, maybe those city people could hear her; see her, and her brothers; eventually. And the one brother attracted so much attention with his perpetual grin and jerking walk. So on the morning of the eleventh day, even though the great river and all that was on its other side were now many more miles south than she could figure, Persimillion told her brothers they must walk further north.

While walking across a sage-scented piece of land, Persimillion and her brothers were picked up by a van full of Indian children. The Indians spoke their own language, a language not even Pepé could understand. Not English. Persimillion depended on Pepé to speak good English, like he told her he could. But in the van, no one spoke English or Spanish. So they drove in silence, the children staring at the three, dusty-faced strangers scrunched in the back row. They stared especially at the woman who needed half the van simply to turn around and set herself down.

But their curiosity was not hostile, or impolite. Everyone smiled. The children held out small, soft hands to share their pecans and fry bread, and little green apples. Persimillion wanted to watch the smiling, black-eyed children, but she fell, instead, into a light sleep, the hot wind blasting her face through the open window.

An hour later, the van stopped. Persimillion jerked to full consciousness. Even after remembering the soft palms held open with food, even surrounded by the friendly bodies of children, Persimillion felt her body slick with a heavy film of perspiration produced by fear. With her heart still pounding, and gasping for breath, Persimillion followed Alfredo and Pepé down the side steps and out of the van. She tried to convey her thanks to the driver and her love to the children, who she knew could not help but stare and whisper at the ragged threesome.

The van left them standing with their two solitary possessions—the now empty cotton bag that Pepé had carried from Llosa and the yellow canvas tarp—beside a two-lane highway of gray asphalt, the sun setting into the western mesas, night already engulfing the east where a solitary star glistened above the desert city fifty miles behind.

On the twelfth day, they risked walking along the highway, but always within sight of a large cactus or piñon, or an outcropping of rock they might make into a hiding place. Pepé had good eyes, and he watched for police cars, able to see more than a mile in either direction out here on the wide, flat land of New Mexico. Often this land looked like old Mexico, only these people, these cattle, had food to share and water to spare.

At high noon on the thirteenth day, the shrunken form of a crumbling gas station holding its own above the red desert sand appeared to Persimillion like the very doors to heaven. She knew in her heart they could stop here. It was something in the earth of the place. Persimillion did not know for how long, or where food and water might be found. But she knew they could stop here. Even if one or more of them died here, they had come upon some kind of home.

Persimillion settled her body down into the sand of the open doorway. Pepé and Alfredo walked around to the back of the adobe building to explore the cottonwood trees. They had not seen trees so large, so cool and shading, since the bosque of the great river nearly two weeks ago. Persimillion closed her eyes to the sun, and to the highway and the occasional car passing her by; she even closed her ears to the calls and shouts of her brothers as they explored the lush trees.

Persimillion knew she would be foolish to allow herself to feel safe; but she did allow herself to sink like a stone into the formless oblivion that oozed from every pore of the adobe wall melting back to dust around her. This moment of rest against the mud wall was a salve to her wounded body. Silence. It was a song that pressed like cool lemons against her parched lips. It was not the song of angels; no, Persimillion thought, this was just a little jangle, like a distant cowbell, ordinary, but vibrating with life, in the air above her inner ear.

The Good Padre Leo Brings Fruit

The good padre Leo knew that Mi Ojo, New Mexico, as a financial community, lived on or below the nationally defined poverty line. Its rural residents were therefore not really obliged to concern themselves in the rescuing of another country's poor. Yet padre Leo, himself a native of Mi Ojo, knew that even among the poor, there is a distinction between those who have and those who have not. Those facing daily life with some measure of peace of mind and a sense of place and stability are, come what may, partakers of the dream. The haves. So even though Mi Ojo as a community was not involved in any kind of sanctuary effort for the often constant flow of illegal workers and undocumented refugees heading north to Utah and Colorado, there were those in the valley who held out their hands with food and their hearts with friendship.

The good padre Leo was Dominga de Jesús' third cousin on her mother's side, and he was the only other living relative of the Mi Ojo state trooper, Miguel Gonzales. Miguel Gonzales's parents had both perished in a terrible fire that consumed two entire buildings on the old plaza of Mi Ojo fourteen winters ago. Miguel would have been legally orphaned had it not been for his *tío* Leo, the parish priest. Uncle Leo opened his arms and his two-room parish apartment to his only nephew, whom he raised as his own; or at least as much his own as was permissible for a priest of the faith.

Around Mi Ojo, and up the valley in Tomita, no one would ever insinuate the least bending of the law by Miguel Gonzales in regard to his only living relative's kindnesses towards the illegally squatting poor. But people of the valley knew that the law-abiding, law-enforcing Miguel extended, if you will, a certain tolerance to the padre and those he regarded as his children of God.

The three now living in the old gas station beneath the cottonwoods, where the great desert begins to suck the water from the roots of all but the hardiest desert flora and fauna, must have realized they were indeed children of God's when on the third day after their arrival, the local padre himself came to visit. He came in the 1968 Ford van that served as the Mi Ojo community center vehicle each Thursday when the senior citizens went shopping in Santa Fe; the Mi Ojo men's basketball team bus on Tuesday nights in winter; and the valley food bank on undocumented occasions such as this morning in early summer.

The good padre Leo—*el buen pastor* as his flock of Mi Ojo ranchers, farmers, mothers, fathers, widows, and other hard-working, church-going folks called him—pulled up slowly to the rusted gas pumps so as not to alarm the exceedingly large woman sitting on the sand near the door stoop watching him. He saw in her dark, lovely eyes the terror of someone who presumed no human rights, and maybe even less. He had seen the same look in the faces of cornered, half-frozen dogs scavenging the parish hall refuse dump in deep winter. Padre Leo knew those skinny, furless curs had no more chance than a baby chick once the sun went down, but he always found some leftovers to give them before sending them on to whatever might be their way.

Padre Leo smiled from the van before climbing out. He called a greeting in Spanish and then looked around for the boys he had seen with her yesterday.

But she was alone this morning. She looked a good deal larger up close than from a moving car on the highway. Padre Leo took a bandana from his dusty-black clerical jacket and wiped his dripping brow. He was nearly sixty, but padre Leo still had a head of black, glossy hair and thick eyebrows. Before he had taken his vows, there were many young women in the valley who brought him their sweet breads and mended his socks. Now he relived those days, not mourned but still remembered, in his nephew Miguel who was twice as handsome, but not nearly so shy.

The good padre had brought a basket of Dominga de Jesús' tortillas and a loaf of her heavy, hearty, whole wheat bread. He set the basket lovingly in the sand by the woman's huge ankles and, speaking softly in Spanish about the terrible heat of early summer, returned to the van to retrieve a cardboard box of apples and small pears. These he had brought from his own cellar, stocked last fall by the village children.

Mi Ojo and the other valley orchards had good crops last year. Padre Leo had been sharing the fruits of his full cupboards all year with various needy parishioners and shut-ins, with the three tired nuns up at the Tomita day school, and, including these three today, with exactly nine Mexican nationals waiting near Mi Ojo for a clue about their future.

Padre Leo sat down in the red sand near the large woman. Silently, she continued to eye the priest. She wore bright pink stretch pants and her white blouse, which was more like a tent billowing from her neck towards her thighs, was torn around her shoulders and back. Her face was scratched and recently scabbed.

"Where are your friends?" he asked her in Spanish, his own first language, although he spoke with the dialect familiar to northern New Mexico and laced, at times, with Spanish-Indian words passed on from his mother's Apache ancestors.

The woman nodded toward the road. She seemed almost relieved, padre Leo thought, that someone had finally acknowledged them.

"Out there?" Padre Leo pointed to the desert south of them. "It is hot to be out walking. They are walking?"

"*Sí.*" The woman stared off at the southern desert and the highway slicing it in two for a few miles until the heat waves from the sand consumed the asphalt.

"Why are they out there?"

"The younger one is foolish. He wants to find a ride home. With his thumb. The older brother went after him."

"I see." Padre Leo looked back at the woman and smiled. "I am padre Leo of the Mi Ojo parish." Padre Leo pointed northwest towards the mesas and the bosque. "I have food for you. I can help you if you want. Perhaps I could drive on down that way and look for your brothers? What is your name? I won't tell anyone. Just between us, if you like."

"Persimillion. My brothers are Pepé and Alfredo."

"Persimillion. I'll take the van and see if I can pick them up and bring them back, okay?"

Persimillion nodded. Padre Leo stood and brushed the red sand from his pants. He mopped his drenched brow again with his bandana as he walked back to the van.

Padre Leo caught up with Persimillion's brothers several miles down the highway. They were arguing on the edge of the blacktop. Alfredo stuck out his thumb when he saw the van approaching. Pepé yanked at his brother's extended arm, then turned and began to run out into the desert. But Pepé stopped before he crossed the barbed wire, and came back to stand next to his foolish, grinning brother.

When padre Leo stopped his van, Alfredo had the look of the saved, and Pepé the look of the captured—until he saw the collar around padre Leo's neck. Padre Leo, now in the final years of his parish career, had followed the cloth since he was nine, when he first held the bowl of holy water aloft for the priest. Yet he had waited a lifetime to experience the full radiance Spirit bestows on those who serve it without reservation. He felt it now when the two boys climbed into the van. The full tide of the long-awaited Holy Light struck his forehead, and padre Leo forgot how his face dripped with perspiration, and how his old polyester pants stuck to the van's vinyl seat beneath him. All padre Leo felt was the grace surrounding these filthy boys, and the gladness surrounding his heart to be serving them.

The good padre Leo wiped his face and his eyes with the damp bandana and placed his shaking hands back on the steering wheel.

"Your sister, Persimillion, asked me to bring you back to her," he said in Spanish after they were seated on the bench behind him. "She was afraid you were half way back to Mexico, or worse, by now."

In the rearview mirror, padre Leo watched the one brother shake his head in semidisgust at the younger brother, who smiled ear to foolish ear at the back of the good padre's head.

Padre Leo returned the boys to the care of their fat sister. He gave the three squatters drinking water, tin cups and plates, and clothes from the parish donation box. He told them he would return within a few days. He also told Pepé he could use some help later in the week rebuilding a bookcase in the parish library.

And then the good padre returned to his church on the dusty plaza of Mi Ojo, and life went on as usual. Only his third cousin, Dominga de Jesús, shared the details of padre Leo's visit to the old station. Dominga, like the good padre, reached out her hands and opened her heart to each and every person who crossed her path, or even came close to it, because, like the good padre, she felt the whole world of children to be her own.

Padre Leo knew there was a plan at work here: that maybe if Dominga could help them, help these three, or the three or four or nine to follow them, the day would come when she would know from deep within her heart how to help her lost son; her gifted, war-ravaged baby, Atencio. And he would find home, too. Not just home in Mi Ojo, in his grandmother's home behind the mercantile. But home inside.

It was a long journey, padre Leo told his parishioners Sunday after Sunday, finding home in such a world.

But padre Leo kept looking, kept the journey alive, because he knew there were women like Dominga de Jesús and men like Miguel—people of long faith and deep hope, who somehow sustained an abiding sense of forgiveness toward a world that inspired neither faith nor hope, and most certainly not love.

Heading for Santa Fe

As he drove east through Mi Ojo, Whitney gave a casual wave to the local men chewing and talking in front of the mercantile gas pumps. Two of the three men nodded back to him. Although most of the locals probably knew Whitney by name, they rarely initiated conversation with him. He figured in a rural place like Mi Ojo only longevity, and many seasons of ditch work, made a stranger into a neighbor.

It was two o'clock in the afternoon, and it was more than ninety-five degrees, but Whitney did not turn on the truck's air conditioning. He wanted the desert's scent to envelope him on his journey back to Santa Fe. On the seat beside him was Juan's tackle box and a list of errands. Whitney had consciously not washed the truck with the newly installed garden hose. The truck's silver sheen was now a dull, unremarkable grey under its fine coating of Recuerdos Canyon dust.

The hot wind blasted Whitney through the open window and kept the sweat from soaking into his shirt. With the tape player turned bearably loud, Whitney could enjoy Mozart over the engine noise. It was a beautiful drive, first through the bosque along the river, then out into the mesa country where the sand was populated with red rocks that stood in clusters like monuments to dead ancestors. He counted the corpses of five jackrabbits and one dog, its stiff legs aimed for the sky, along the road's side, and indulged for a moment in the humanitarian, yet ultimately foolish, impulse to feel sorry for desert animals.

Two boys, dark and poorly dressed, stood to one side of the old gas station, pitching bottle caps at a beer can set in the sand. Whitney raised his hand, figuring they were some of the boys from the village he had made small talk with at the mercantile or post office. The older one, who saw Whitney's gesture of greeting, stopped his bottle cap pitching and glanced over his shoulder at the trees. These were not Mi Ojo boys, Whitney thought as he sped on by: the boys around Mi Ojo didn't have that kind of tension in their posture.

The sixty mile view to the eastern horizon was interrupted only by the mountains of Santa Fe rising off the hazy plain. Santa Fe was a long ways across the mesa country, but the city's melody began to dominate Whitney's thinking with each highway mile that slipped beneath his tires. Unfortunately, the theme that came to play itself again and again in Whitney's mind was the one that resonated from the body and voice of Anna Farina.

That Anna would somehow orchestrate the ending to their friendly but nebulous affair was for three months an unspoken understanding between them. Even so, even as it happened last April, Whitney had missed it. It was only in retrospect, some thirty minutes later, that Whitney, sitting in his truck and looking at her enormous dark house, heard what Anna was saying. Or what Anna's housekeeper was saying Anna was saying. Anna did not involve herself directly in the affair's ending. She directed the finale from a discreet, antiseptic distance. Anna Farina liked clean hands. Whitney's, she used to say, were carelessly stained.

Whitney remembered their last night together. They were lying on Anna's daybed in what she called her dressing room—a closet larger than Whitney's apartment studio, decorated with Anna's formidable collection of clothes, shoes, hats, makeup, private business files, and her private phone—a whole universe of Anna Farina's existing separately from the bedroom she shared with Jack when he was in Santa Fe. Naked and tired, sexually spent and weary, Anna and Whitney were drifting back into their own bodies, slipping back into their own personal boundaries.

The soft lights from the terrace and the pool deck lit the lace curtains of the French doors. It was after midnight. Whitney was mentally preparing to leave. Although Anna often offered Whitney wine, cold leftovers, and a few minutes of quiet conversation before he dressed and drove back into Santa Fe, neither of them liked waking with someone else: Anna did not accept visitors or phone calls before ten in the morning. And Whitney liked to be in front of his canvas before the aroma of the tortilla sisters' dough rose up the staircase from their first floor ovens.

On this particular night in late April, Whitney and Anna fell into a conversation they'd had many times before. It was really an argument, frequently replayed between them, about art: could successful art avoid becoming just another business? Whitney knew his reminiscing about the good old days in Greece, about the years spent roaming Europe and the Mediterranean, painting, waiting tables, falling in love with white stretches of remote beach and the horizon line of dawn, would engage Anna in verbal battle. Still, on that last evening in the Farina mansion, Whitney could not help indulging himself in yet another energetic recounting of the old days. From forty-four, Whitney looked back at twenty-four and remembered with unrestrained fondness the simple poverty; the crowded, shared rooms with a view of someone's goat shed; days with a brush in his hand, nights at sidewalk cafes where the only permissible conversations were concerned somehow with art and freedom. Whitney remembered aloud to Anna the frequent career disappointments and occasional triumphs, the early years of his artistic pursuit defined by an absence of audience, income, or any tangible grounds for continuing.

"You're just wanting youth, like everyone," Anna said out of the dark beside him. "The specifics of your life aren't any different from a stockbroker's, or bank manager's: once you were young, now you're not so young."

"It's not being twenty-four I miss," Whitney said, "it's the not knowing from day-to-day, the possibilities unknown but sensed, sought, strived for in those days. It was a new land. A frontier of opportunities. Jesus! Anything could happen, anything at all! I loved it . . . loved it."

"You just want to be young, again, Whitney. Young and virile, your whole life ahead."

"Anna, I like my age. I like this time. I just miss the freedom to move sideways instead of forwards if that's what I want."

"Why? You, like me, have enough money to do what you like and want without having to ask anyone about it. That's freedom, Whitney, not living hand-to-mouth in some room without a sink off a smelly courtyard in Greece. It may sound colorful and precious now, especially in art columns, but I'm not fooled by your nostalgic embellishments of the past."

"I do not embellish. Except maybe on canvas, but not often. And you are not free, Anna. Freedom is not about money. Your money has been the very thing that's cost you your freedom. You're shackled by Jack's money, and expectations, just like your father's before. What is yours around here?"

Whitney waved his hand at the dark room.

"I have my own money from the gallery."

"Separate from Jack's?"

"Yes. But that is between you and me."

"Of course. But why?"

"Future insurance."

"Against what, Anna? Waking up and leaving?"

"I can leave anytime, Whitney. Anytime. Maybe tomorrow."

"Sure, Anna."

"Whitney, I don't have to leave Jack to prove anything to you or to anyone."

"Except yourself."

Anna sat up in the bed and moved her body away from Whitney's.

"You know, Whitney, it's not all that uncommon for people to have some soul-searching experience after someone close to them dies." Anna looked back at Whitney behind her on the bed pillows. "You're going through some guilt about Connie, and that's fine, but don't let it completely distort your sense of reality. You're at the center of the life you chose, an enormous success. Just because Connie told you you'd become everything she wanted to become and never would, you don't have to throw it all away in some misguided attempt at absolution."

Whitney folded his hands under his head and stared at the vigaed ceiling. "You know, in many ways success is very nearly antithetical to the creative. All these people with money looking over my shoulder makes for a very cluttered studio."

Anna sighed loudly. Whitney leaned forwards and found Anna's face. With his hand he gently pulled her towards him.

"Now your guilt, your absolution, that's another cluttered story, isn't it? But one only Anna Farina really knows."

Before Anna could drive, she received marriage proposals from rich widowers, soon-to-be-rich college boys, local oil men, and even a few close friends of her father. Anna thought they were flirtatious compliments, but her father believed her proposals were a very serious business, something to be dealt with very carefully, like all mergers.

Anna did not answer Whitney. Whitney let his hand fall from her face.

"You started your own business, just to get them all back."

"Them who?"

"Men who."

"No, I just realized where all the power was, and it wasn't at home, even in a rich one."

"And you sure as hell weren't going to be like your mother, were you?"

Anna looked across the dark at Whitney.

"Was your mother physically beautiful, Anna?

"I guess so. It was difficult to say the last few years. She was always in a nightgown. Or in the hospital."

"Why the hospital?"

"Depression."

"So all the pills?"

"I suppose. No one ever explained anything to me."

Anna sat up, pulling a sheet with her.

"Did he abuse her, your mother?"

"How would I know? She was an alcoholic."

"She wasn't born one. Maybe your father was why she was such a mess . . . "

"This isn't really any of your business, Slope. And she's dead."

"Why didn't she leave?"

"Sometimes you can't just walk out. Not in every situation."

"Who ever told you that?"

Anna was quietly picking at her fingernails.

"People will think you're unreliable. It makes for bad business."

"Jesus, Anna, we're not discussing business. We're discussing interpersonal relationships. Marriage."

"Like you know about that, Slope!" Anna laughed sarcastically.

Whitney sat up on his elbows and peered into the dim space between them.

"So whatever it was your mother had with your father, unbearable as it may have been, constitutes marriage? And likewise, what you have with Jack, a man with whom you share dinner parties and charge cards and whom you arrange to see as little as possible in a given year?"

Anna walked to the chair and retrieved her robe. She stood at the window, backlit by the pool's light.

"At least I try. You've never gotten that far. Don't ever pretend you know what constitutes marriage, Whitney Slope. And loving your sister and your niece with all your heart from fifteen hundred miles away does not pass for close family ties."

Whitney flinched with Anna's last remark. He thought maybe Anna was coming over to apologize, but she knelt down and dug around the floor by the bed looking for her slippers, instead.

"And my life is absolutely nothing like my mother's, maritally or otherwise," Anna grumbled over the side of the mattress.

"Except that you don't know how to leave, either," Whitney said.

Anna put on her slippers and moved away from the bed, to the door on the other side of the room.

"I have a headache," she said in a flat, distracted tone, like someone who has suddenly remembered a detail of extreme importance in another room. "I'm going to find some aspirin."

And then Anna was gone, pulling the door closed behind her. Whitney heard her slippers clicking down the tiles of the hall and then a door closing far away in the house. He was quite certain he remembered seeing an aspirin bottle in her vanity drawer.

Whitney lay on his back and closed his eyes, almost falling asleep, half listening for Anna's return. Several minutes passed and then a faraway door opened and footsteps clicked over the tile hall again.

The boudoir door opened. Whitney looked over and saw a body he did not recognize outlined by the light from the hall chandelier.

"Mrs. Farina has asked me to tell you that she has a bad headache. She wants you to leave."

It was Naomi, the Farina housekeeper. Naomi stood a moment more at the door and then said, "Did you hear me, Mr. Slope? Please let yourself out the back door. Soon."

The door closed again. Whitney lay another moment on the day bed, then rose and found his clothes in the dark. He had never used the back door. He wasn't even sure where it was, so he went out by the terrace and the shimmering blue Mexican tile pool, barefoot, carrying his boots under his arms. His shirt was unbuttoned and his belt buckle clanked ungracefully against his jean zipper.

Whitney reached his truck and climbed in. He sat with his hands on the steering wheel and stared at the house to which he had come for sex and a corrupted sort of companionship more than twenty times in the past three months. It occurred to Whitney as he shivered in the night air that the immense adobe house held no more personal familiarity to him than the moon. And its million dollar facade had none of the moon's beauty. Whitney started the truck's engine with a pronounced roar, giving the gas an extra throttle, and wondered why he had continued to return, week after week, to a place so devoid of sincerity and dignity as the Farina mansion?

Although they spoke almost daily the weeks before The Show, the midnight episode at the mansion had yet to emerge in any conversation. Between Whitney and Anna, anyway. Whitney had succumbed to telling Jon after the High Noon closed one night a week later. Samantha had already gone home. It was turning warm again in the evenings, and the windows to the plaza were wide open. The lights in the cafe were off except for the neon CERVEZA sign over the bar and the soft night light on Sam's desk near the kitchen. Even the cooks and kitchen helpers had left.

"I say be glad it's behind," Jon said passing a shared beer to Whitney who sat on a stool across the bar. "Leave it alone; get out while you can."

"We're still friends, Anna and me," Whitney said. "You're still worried about Jack Farina, aren't you Jon?"

"Always. The man's outside the law. And you know he's the jealous type. He's got that look in his eye. There are stories you don't want to hear about Jack's Dallas crowd. What he can't own, he cripples or destroys."

"He doesn't own Anna."

"But he doesn't know that."

"She's tough, Jon. She controls her world very exactly, and he knows that."

"No, Jack Farina knows that Anna controls her world within his world very exactly. There is a profound difference, my friend.

The tortilla sisters did not know about Anna. Not by name. They knew Whitney was spending nights with a woman who did not visit his apartment. A woman who hid her face.

"Any other woman would be staking her claim for the whole town to see," Aguelita explained when Whitney asked them why they assumed his mystery lady friend was married. "But not this one."

"God sees," Marguerite told Whitney, crossing herself and frowning. "You remember, Señor Slope, that God sees all."

God and Jack Farina. Jon said Jack Farina had his hands in everything around Santa Fe. Everything attached to money and power. Surely in Jack Farina's eyes, Anna qualified in both departments.

Traffic on the two-laner began to increase as the road neared Santa Fe and its surrounding foothill communities. As the truck climbed into the first mesas of Santa Fe's town limits, past the low-income trailer parks that hugged the high sides of arroyos, and then past the first foothill communities of expensive adobe haciendas, Whitney changed his afternoon agenda and decided he would visit the bank, the apartment, and then the High Noon, in that order. He glanced at the tackle box for Juan wrapped in last Sunday's comic pages. Whitney would call Mud Street after he shared a few conversations and asides with Jon and Juan, and the tortilla sisters; he would see Anna after he ate lunch and reconvinced himself that he had done nothing, and no one, wrong by leaving.

Back at the High Noon

Whitney's errands around Santa Fe were nearly completed. He had first visited the tortilla sisters, who thought Whitney had disappeared with either a hangover or a woman. When Whitney told Aguelita and Marguerite that it was neither, and that he was moving his studio home out to Mi Ojo, both sisters were more disappointed with Whitney's choice of neighborhoods than with his sudden vacating of the upstairs apartment.

"Nothing out there, Señor Slope," Marguerite said, frowning and shaking her head. "Just dust and flies. Oh, you should have let us show you some of the houses in the south end of town where we live. My son-in-law could have given you a very good deal."

"Why Mi Ojo?" Aguelita asked Whitney, holding his arm and making him look her in the eyes.

"I found a woman who makes better tortillas than you do, Aguelita," Whitney teased.

"No! *¿Es verdad?* You are lying to me!" Aguelita's eyes sparkled with excitement. "*¿La mujer?* Tell me all about her."

Aguelita placed Whitney in one of the chairs at the little table crowded against the wall under the street window. She gave him a *bizcochito* that was so warm he had to toss it from hand to hand.

"Actually, although I did meet someone who makes very good tortillas, I don't know her very well. And she's not the reason I'm moving."

"Oh, Whitney Slope!" Aguelita shook her finger before Whitney's face. "Don't you ever turn your back on good food or a good woman. *Sí*, isn't it true, Marguerite? Whitney will end up empty handed and alone, an old man with a shriveled heart and an empty belly!"

Whitney had packed the remainder of his possessions from his apartment into the truck. Even his full sized mattress was squeezed into the back on top of rugs, books, clothes, two chairs and a small drop-leaf table for his canyon kitchen. Whitney had then driven across town to the main branch of the Santa Fe post office and left a forwarding address—General Delivery, Mi Ojo, New Mexico.

"They have a post office out there?" the postal employee asked.

"Yes," Whitney answered. "Or something very much like one."

The High Noon Cafe was just beginning late afternoon happy hour when Whitney strode in carrying Juan's belated birthday present and his own belated appetite. It was the time of day when the regulars put up their booted toes and let the outside world of the plaza and the city slide from consciousness.

Whitney surveyed the lazy crowd, tipping his hat to a few acquaintances, and realizing just how much he enjoyed the old cafe's down-scale atmosphere. It was actually a modern-day miracle the way the High Noon Cafe had maintained its rustic, authentic, Old West ambiance when so many of its plaza neighbors had been renovated, gutted, razed, rebuilt, upscaled, or generally modernized. The High Noon Cafe was making money hand over first for the Gateworthys just by being today what it was yesterday, a sleepy little saloon always a half-step or more behind the outer world whirling around it. All who walked through the cafe's wide doors to sit at its unpolished pine tables or on the swiveling stools at its butter-smooth mahogany bar; all who sipped a salt-rimmed margarita and eyed the High Noon's sloping wood floor, cedar *latilla* ceiling, and two-foot-thick adobe walls that boasted not one right angle, could leave knowing they had partaken of something true to itself. Something that was not hoping for change, transformation, increase or decrease, in the foreseeable future.

Whitney had painted several canvasses of the cafe's interior, all of which were owned by the Gateworthys. In return for the canvasses, Whitney, and his immediate family, would eat and drink on the house for the next ninety-nine years. There was a rider in the agreement that stipulated the arrangement was null and void if Whitney suddenly took to conspicuous consumption, or radically increased the size of his immediate family. If anything, Whitney's family seemed to be decreasing, and with his move to Mi Ojo, his consumption of cafe food would certainly experience a decline.

If Jon Gateworthy was surprised to see Whitney walk into the High Noon, he did not show it. Jon just smiled his ivy league smile, pulled out a *Carta Blanca* from the cooler, and placed a heavy glass mug next to it on the mahogany bar in front of the stool back by the kitchen.

"Howdy, Jon," Whitney said as he strode across the creaking floor. "Have a Mexican for an old friend?"

Whitney and Jon clasped hands over the bar. Jon smiled and pointed to the beer waiting on the counter. Whitney winced and turned his sore palms towards Jon.

"Been digging ditches," Whitney said, looking closely at one palm and the scabbed blisters.

"Christ, Whitney, I thought you guarded your hands like a surgeon! Where the hell you been?"

"West," Whitney said, wrapping one hand around the cold bottle. "True west."

Whitney took a long slug from the bottle before pouring the beer into the cold mug. "Haven't tasted anything this good since I left."

"So you did leave? I'll call the *Duster* and tell Burt the mystery is over."

"Has it been that bad, a mystery?"

"Some people were looking for a body."

"No!"

"Really—you're a man with many fans, Slope. Prince Charles has nothing on you. Except maybe a Princess. And you've made compensations for that."

"Oh, shit howdy!" Whitney laughed good naturedly and placed his glass on the bar.

Jon took a margarita to a woman at the opposite end of the bar and returned with several magazines in his hand.

"Thought you might want to see these—you can have them. The reviews, the article about you in *National Art*—glowing. Good stuff."

"Thanks for the copies."

"So, you hadn't seen them yet?"

"No."

"You must have gone pretty far . . .someplace without a newsstand?"

"Yeah."

"And speaking of news headlines: Anna Farina came into this bar and sat at that bar stool down there, by the door, and drank coffee. Sipped coffee. Suffered through a cup of coffee. All she wanted was to know where you were. I said I couldn't be the one to tell her."

"Oh, God! Anna hates being the last to know."

"So she doesn't know yet? Have you seen her today? Wait, why don't you start at the beginning and fill me in, sorta chronologically."

Whitney recounted his week in lively detail to Jon: the gas station; the mercantile; Dominga and Tomas and Atencio de Jesús; the house in Recuerdos Canyon, and acequia digging.

"Why didn't you tell us you were planning this?"

"I didn't know I was planning it, Jon. Until it happened. Then I felt like I'd been waiting to do this for a very long time."

"So, are you painting? As I recall, you were down in the mouth the last few weeks with what you called a complete void of aesthetic imagery."

"Not painting just yet. But that's okay."

"It's okay to not paint?"

"Yeah."

"Are you in love? Or on some sort of native amphetamine?"

"Neither."

"What about Mud Street? Or do I get to tell Anna the details when she hears you've been seen and someone traces you here, and then she comes for me with both barrels?"

"I'm going to see her, next stop after here."

Jon made drinks for a couple of out-of-towners. Whitney ate a plate of tacos and finished his beer. When Jon returned, both he and Whitney looked at the empty mug and then at each other.

"No," Whitney said, covering the top of his glass with his hand. "I've got to see Anna. She dislikes friends who drink too much."

"So do bartenders," Jon said. "What's in the colorful package?" Jon motioned at Juan's present on the bar beside Whitney's plate.

"Juan's present."

Jon left to serve new arrivals at the bar. Whitney left his stool and walked back to the kitchen. Juan was standing before a vat of sizzling sopaipillas.

"I'm sorry I missed the fiesta the other night," Whitney told Juan as they shook hands.

"You had a big show."

"It wasn't just the show. But anyway, I want you to know Juan," Whitney said as he handed Juan the wrapped tackle box, "that this gift may mean more to me than it does to you. But I hope you'll take it with my best wishes."

Juan laughed and took the package. "Mmm, not a painting, no?" Juan unwrapped the gift and held up the metal box. "Tackle box. I didn't know you fished, Slope, or knew anything about it?"

"I don't, Juan. But it's never to late to learn."

"So, where did you go last weekend?" Juan opened the metal lid and pulled out the tray.

"Fishing."

Juan smiled conspiratorially. "When I was growing up, going fishing meant my mother was not to ask my father for details."

Whitney chuckled and shrugged.

"My brother-in-law takes his boat to a lake down south every weekend," Juan said. "He says I need to get away from the city, from the kids, more often. He just wants me to cook him lots of food! But now, I will take the worms and hooks. He can learn to cook, *¿sí?*" Juan laughed. *"Gracias,* Slope."

"De nada," Whitney answered, smiling. "And Juan, there really aren't any details, I mean, about my leaving."

"Not yet, *¡mi amigo!"*

Anna Farina's fresh and clean, impeccably powdered face showed not a single iota of emotion when Whitney Slope walked through the double wide doors of the Mud Street Gallery. Candy was just leaving. Whitney stopped before his painting of a white wall winding up to a hot plaza and open sky in Crete. He remembered that place well. He wanted very much to be there just now. Near the sea, alone on an island. Or in a canyon no one remembered except stray animals, storm-shorn sheep, and salvation seeking human refugees.

"Anna, you look wonderful. And the show is doing well, I hear."

Whitney took off his hat before Anna asked him to. For a Texan, she was tiresomely critical of cowboy hats.

"Hello, Whitney, I'm glad to see you're still among the living, although you look like you've been frying in the sun somewhere." Anna stood across the gallery from Whitney with her arms folded across her chest. She watched Candy walk up the street before speaking again. "I don't know what to say to you. I've been real angry with you, with everyone. But just now, all I feel is tired."

"I'm sorry."

"I'm sorry, too. I'm real sorry you didn't say something to me. Where the hell have you been, anyway?"

"I moved out to a village west of here," Whitney said. "I didn't tell you because I didn't know I was going to do it."

"Just like that, you decided to move out of Santa Fe? Why? I thought you were going to buy a place near town?"

"I felt the need for some distance. I've been having trouble getting my own attention."

"I can't imagine that!" Anna said sarcastically.

Anna turned around and looked out the windows at Mud Street. Late afternoon was sliding into early evening. This was usually a good hour for Whitney. The sun was razor bright, and the adobe walls of the old buildings gave off heat waves like ovens. But the mountains to the northeast had long, cool shadows down their sides. Anna turned around suddenly.

"You could have said something. Something. What would it have mattered, telling me you were leaving? You left me high and dry at that dinner party."

"I didn't feel up to being the main course—"

"Whitney, you're always telling me about the importance of friendship. And then you walk out on me, a friend, you say, without a word. For a whole week, nothing . . . "

Anna's sling back sandals clicked quickly across the gallery's tile floor. She stopped in front of Whitney with her arms still crossed tightly over her full breasts.

"You wouldn't have liked what I had to say," Whitney said, stepping back, "and I daresay you would have figured a way to stop me."

"Am I that much of a bully? No, don't answer."

Anna pushed at a blonde wave of hair that had escaped the silver and turquoise barrette above her left ear.

"Will you bring me new work by August? This show is selling fast."

"When I have some. I haven't painted in a while."

Anna stared at Whitney. "What?"

"I just haven't felt like painting."

Anna looked at Whitney as if she did not believe him.

"Since when?"

"Since I finished these." Whitney looked around the gallery at his work.

"Well, okay, take your vacation and then get back to work. I've got a lot banking on you, Slope. And don't forget we have that new calendar to finish by September, and two serigraphs for the San Francisco Christmas catalogue."

"Yeah, sure . . . "

"You're not going to go and change your style or something? Like painting cows in the field or something rural or pastoral like that?"

Whitney laughed.

"I don't know, Anna . . . I've been thinking a bit about sheep . . . " Whitney's hands imitated Carlos's impression of Dominga's flying sheep.

"I'm not feeling much like joking, Whitney. I don't trust you the way I did a week ago."

"Trust? You have a funny way of showing you trust me, Anna."

Anna sighed and walked to her office door.

"You're talking about Naomi."

"A wonderful, warm person your housekeeper."

"Jack's housekeeper. That was an error in judgment, I admit." Anna stopped and stared at her hands, lost for a moment in some thought Whitney was not sure he wanted to share. "So, you get the last laugh. You have one-upped me, Slope, walking out of Santa Fe, disappearing into thin air with an entire city watching."

"No one was watching but me. This was for me."

"Then you should have told me. Even if you thought I would get angry, you should have told me."

"Maybe I should have told you," Whitney said to Anna's back as she walked into her office.

Anna turned around and faced Whitney.

"You said it was important that we be open and honest, be friends, and then you do this."

Anna retrieved her keys from her desk drawer and turned off her reading lamp. Whitney followed her to the bottom of the stairs where she switched off the gallery lights, set the alarm, and then opened the front door. Whitney stepped into the bright sunshine of Mud Street. Anna pulled the gallery's heavy doors closed and locked them before putting on her sunglasses.

"Do you have a phone number you could share?"

"No. Just a post office box."

Whitney handed Anna a piece of paper with his new address.

"What if I have something important to tell you?"

"Write. It's overnight mail, I think."

"You think."

Whitney and Anna stood to one side while a small crowd of tourists sidled by, stopping briefly to look in the Mud Street Gallery windows.

"I thought you were different from other men," Anna drawled in a low voice so the tourists would not hear. "I really believed you were different."

Sharing Clouds

Dominga watched Whitney Slope's truck drive across the highway from the post office. It was midmorning. Nearly every morning, Whitney visited the post office and then the mercantile after a few hours of work in the canyon. Dominga continued to watch the silver truck as it pulled off the road onto the asphalt beside the gas pumps and then wound around and down the sand drive to the trailer.

Whitney turned off the truck and opened the door. Dominga scurried back to the box of clothes she was packing in the middle of the living room. Before Whitney reached the metal stairs to the trailer porch, Dominga had the box closed and lifted from the floor.

"Good morning, Mr. Slope," Dominga said cheerfully as she strode out the front door and past him to her car. "How is the canyon?"

"Here, let me help you with that," Whitney said, running ahead of her to the car door, "here, Dominga, maybe if I . . ."

But Dominga had a firm grip on the awkward box and smiled as she strode past him.

"Thank you, Mr. Slope," Dominga said, as she plopped the box down in the back of the station wagon beside several more boxes, and assorted piles of boots, shoes, overcoats, dishes, and blankets. "I'm actually a good deal stronger than I look."

Dominga straightened up and looked at Whitney. "And I look pretty strong."

"I guess you do," Whitney said, "but if you have more, I hope you'll let me carry something for you."

Whitney followed Dominga back into her trailer.

"There's coffee on the stove," Dominga told him. "Have some."

"Late spring cleaning, Mrs. de Jesús? " Whitney removed his hat but did not go for the coffee pot. "You look pretty busy around here today. I mean, you're always busy, but . . . "

"No, no," Dominga said as she walked down the narrow hall to the back bedroom. She took a discolored, water-spotted trunk by its old leather handle and dragged it behind her to the middle of her tiny living room. "This is not cleaning. This is uncluttering." Dominga sat down on the floor beside the trunk.

"You didn't come here to watch me throw out the de Jesús family clutter, Mr. Slope." Dominga looked over the trunk at Whitney, who was standing with his hat in his hands beside the dinette, looking down at Atencio's house. "Is anything wrong out at the canyon?"

"Oh, no. And Mrs. de Jesús, could we drop the mister and missus?"

Dominga lifted the trunk's lid and peered inside. Most of the clothes had belonged to the boys in high school: shirts and trousers long out of style but with plenty of use left in the fabric. Her old cowboy boots were on top. The leather down one side of the left boot was curled where it had been chewed. Dominga lifted the boot out of the trunk, examining it unhappily.

"I'm sorry, Whitney, I've been around *niños* and *viejos* for so long, I don't know how to talk with people in between."

Whitney poured himself a cup of coffee. Dominga watched Whitney's boots, worn but in their prime, as he walked past her to the chair by the door. She wondered if she still qualified as one of those people in between?

"I have a friend in Santa Fe who could fix that boot," Whitney said. "An old *viejo* I like to talk to."

"I wore these years ago. I used to ride with my brothers, up in the mountains." Dominga put the boot on the floor. "I can still ride. Still climb, too. But not in these boots."

"I have no doubt you can," Whitney leaned forwards and picked up the brown leather boot. "Let me take these to Alejandro. Really. He likes to restore good boots like these. It gives him a certain pleasure."

"All right. But I will pay for them."

"Maybe."

"And thank you for the calendar, Whitney," Dominga said. "I like your work very much."

Dominga pointed to the calendar hung over the telephone on the kitchen counter. "I especially like those clouds there, and the sunset above the mountains. Stratocumulus."

"Stratocumulus? Do you know clouds, Dominga?"

"Yes. I like clouds. I know clouds."

She looked at Whitney, who was still sitting in the chair by the door. She could not see his blue eyes, but she knew he was studying her. Dominga blushed and looked back down into the folded shirts.

"There was a time I never missed that weatherman in Albuquerque who explained about clouds. How they gather and disperse, why the rain falls on the eastern slope and not the western. He had those satellite pictures and you can watch the clouds form over the whole hemisphere! He explained why some rain never even reaches the ground. Virga, it's called. You'll see it—a veil hanging in the sky over the mesas in July. He retired. The new guy isn't a real meteorologist."

Whitney was still staring at Dominga over his coffee mug. It gave Dominga a giddy feeling that confused and embarrassed her.

"I used to imagine who could live in clouds. All that white. Appearing out of nothing over the planet. All that blue. Dissolving before your eyes."

"Angels," Whitney said.

"Yes." Dominga closed the trunk but did not lock it. "I guess if anyone lived in the clouds, they would be angels."

Dominga stood and looked out at the station wagon filled with her family's discarded possessions. "Maybe I'd better show these things to Tomas before I give them away. He's a saver, that one. If it still serves a useful function, Tomas says, it deserves a place in the closet."

"What if it doesn't serve a useful function?" Whitney asked.

"You should see his house. Tomas's wife's a big collector. It's one of their mutual hobbies—rescuing useful things. They get along well. You know, those kinds of shared habits can be the most important to a marriage."

"Really," Whitney said dryly.

Dominga chuckled and walked over to the old couch where she pulled the old crocheted afghan from the couch's soft shoulder and tossed it onto the trunk.

"Is he home?" Whitney left the chair and walked to the dinette and looked down at Atencio's house.

"No. I saw him leave early this morning, at dawn, with his wheelbarrow and his canteen." Dominga looked across the kitchen at Whitney. "Sometimes I am afraid this new floor will be too much for Atencio. It is so much work."

"But he wants to do it."

Dominga shook her head in agreement.

"It is a very precarious journey across that desert to the quarry. And there is no one to help, for miles. How would we find him? But I don't want him to stop. He is safer out there among the sage and the sand. At least the dangers of the desert are measurable, ¿sí?"

Dominga took Whitney's empty cup and placed it in the sink with her own. "Do you have children?"

"No. I have a niece, though, whom I care for a great deal."

"You must think I'm terribly boring, sitting in my trailer house watching my twenty-six year old son all day."

"On the contrary, Dominga," Whitney said, looking at her over the linoleum counter. "I think you are one of the most interesting women I've ever known."

"You must not have known many women, Mr. Slope."

"Not women who are grandmothers and who have the energy of schoolgirls riding horses in the mountains and studying the clouds, Mrs. de Jesús."

"I am very nearly forty-eight," Dominga told Whitney.

"I am very nearly forty-five," Whitney said, placing his long, tanned hands on the counter top.

"Well, then, fine. I guess we're old enough to have coffee and share . . . " Dominga fumbled for a word, but she did not know what she wanted to say.

"Clouds." Whitney said, smiling at her.

Dominga smiled and involuntarily touched the bandana on her head. Although Whitney had on his work clothes—a paint-spattered denim shirt and jeans—Dominga felt like an old widow woman in her jeans and another of Feodoro's plaid shirts. She looked at the trunk with the old afghan in the middle of the narrow living room. It occurred to her that most of her own clothes ought to be placed in that trunk.

"I think the junk in the trunk will stay in the trunk," Dominga said, "I won't tell Tomas about it, and he will never know."

Whitney helped Dominga load the trunk into the back of the station wagon.

"When does Atencio usually get back with his stone?"

Dominga shrugged her shoulders and stood where she had a better view of the adobe house under the cottonwoods.

"It depends on how much he tries to bring out. And that depends on the heat, which will be terrible today. So I can't say. Soon, maybe. Or not until noon, or later. He stays back there, sometimes, when it is too hot to push the wheelbarrow. But he left early. The rooster down the valley there was not yet crowing. Early. Whitney, did you want to see Atencio?"

"Yes. But I wanted to talk with you about it first. I have this idea, Dominga, about a stone patio, about hiring Atencio to come up to the canyon and put one in for me. If you agree, that is, that it would be a good thing for the house. I'd pay for it."

"Have Atencio work for you?"

"Yes. I believe he could do it."

"But he could fail, also. Atencio can be very unpredictable. Instead of a beautiful courtyard, you could be buying trouble for yourself . . . for the house . . . for Atencio."

Whitney leaned into the metal wall of Dominga's trailer where there was a needle's width of shade. Dominga shaded her eyes with her arm and looked at Whitney's face. His gringo skin was becoming a deep brown after three weeks in the canyon's glare. His eyes seemed a clearer blue and his unshaven beard caught the sun in its blonde stubble. Whitney Slope did not look like the men of her valley. And Whitney Slope did not look at Dominga like the men of the valley.

"I've already become involved in things I did not expect."

Dominga looked back at Atencio's house. "How would you pay him?"

"I'm told cash isn't the best stuff to place in Atencio's hands. How about grocery credit, or gas?"

"Yes, grocery credit. And enough gas to get his De Soto up to the canyon house. If he agrees, that is. Atencio still has an opinion about his life."

"He can use my truck—I mean, I'll drive it up to the quarry, if he'll take me. We can bring the stone out together."

Dominga turned and faced her loaded station wagon. Heat waves rose from the faded front hood.

"He won't be back for at least another hour. My cousin, the padre up at the church, is not a strong man. Perhaps you would drive up to the parish with me and help unload my car?"

"Of course."

Dominga drove across the highway and up the mesa into Mi Ojo. It was a hot, dusty, lazy noon in the pueblo.

"I suppose, except for trucks and cars, and the telephone wires and TV antennas, Mi Ojo looks pretty much like it looked a century ago," Whitney said.

"Yes, I guess it does." Dominga looked out across the roofs at the desert valley falling away below.

"You know, this plaza has all the elements of an island," Whitney said, leaning his head out his window. "High, aloof, the sky like the ocean between the walls of houses. See how the heat of the desert washes up the sides of the mesas like waves from the sea of sand below."

Dominga looked across the car at Whitney Slope. He spoke of the village the way she often thought of it. Maybe he would paint his words and then even as the village changed, as the good padre and Miguel Gonzales and everyone with any sense of northern New Mexico said it was going to, she would always have it in pictures. In paint. Maybe that's why Whitney Slope was here: to rescue the beauty of her village from the oblivion brought on by time and so-called progress.

Dominga waved at an elderly woman standing next to her garden. The old woman wore a broad-brimmed straw hat and had no teeth.

"Mrs. Archuleta," Dominga said after they passed. "She will be one hundred years old next month. Her irises are older than I am."

Whitney smiled and squinted back at the centenarian standing still as a fence post near her ancient flowers.

"Do you ever paint people?" Dominga asked.

"No. But then there was a time I did not paint clouds." Dominga looked at Whitney and frowned. "I just painted the blue," Whitney explained.

The inside of the Mi Ojo church was dark and cool, lit with the June sun filtered through four, narrow stained-glass windows, and a handful of flickering candles beneath the statue of the Virgin Mary. Whitney stood at the rear of the small church. Dominga genuflected and walked up one side.

"Atencio's saints," she said softly over her shoulder as she gestured at the *nichos* with the carved cedar santos. Whitney walked to the first mud ledge and looked at the wood saint.

"Atencio carved that when he was fourteen years old," Dominga said in half-whisper. "Saint Francis—always his favorite."

"Wonderful birds." Whitney said, touching a little winged creature on the saint's extended arm.

"Saint Francis had a way with animals—a language only they could understand."

Dominga sighed as she touched the face of the cedar statue and then walked quietly to a side door.

"They are nothing at all like the saints in my sister's church in Cleveland," Whitney said. "I like these; these saints are familiar looking chaps, huh? Local fellows with personable faces."

"Yes," Dominga said, opening the door to the good padre's office. "Some say the saints are simple folk who walk among us."

Dominga returned with the good padre Leo. The padre walked with his torso stooped forwards as he leaned into Dominga's arm. They had walked this way, arm in arm, for forty years. Only now it was Dominga who led and padre Leo who followed.

"My cousin, this is Whitney Slope, the renter I told you about," Dominga said to the padre.

"Hello Señor Slope. Welcome to our little church. You are welcome to come and share holy mass with us anytime."

The padre placed his hand in the air between himself and Whitney. Whitney grasped it. Dominga hoped Whitney would notice how the knuckles bulged with the debilitating gnarls of arthritis and not squeeze the old hand too hard.

"Glad to meet you, padre."

"And what has brought you to Mi Ojo, Mr. Slope?"

Whitney looked over at Dominga. "Oh, I don't know. Open space, sky; I don't really know just yet. Maybe clouds!"

"Mr. Slope is helping me move some things out of the trailer. Padre, I have a carful of discarded but still usable things. Some Feodoro's; some the boys'. Even some kitchen utensils, blankets; things you can find a use for, I know. Mr. Slope will unload them with me if you will tell us what you want and where to put it."

Dominga, Whitney and the padre walked out to the station wagon parked at the side of the church. The good padre Leo peered in through the glass at the boxes and piles of de Jesús family castoffs.

"Yes, Dominga, I think we can find good use for these things." Padre Leo straightened up and looked at his cousin and then at Whitney standing behind her. "You will not miss them? Feodoro's things?"

"No," Dominga said. "You have told me yourself, padre, that the dead have no need for the things of the living."

Whitney carried the trunk with Dominga, and then they returned for the boxes. The good padre carried small piles of clothes and shoes. It took ten minutes to move the items from the car into the parish hall. When they were done, Dominga sat down beside her cousin on a wood bench against the far wall. They both watched Whitney who stood by the open door, taking in the beautiful wall of the church garden framed by old cottonwoods and then the open blue sky over the desert.

"Some of this could be used right away, ¿sí?" Dominga asked her cousin.

Padre Leo smiled and rubbed his sore hands on his black polyester pants.

"Sí. I have some people in mind for clothes and blankets, and some of the other things," padre Leo said. He looked at Dominga with a serious eye. "But I can do that myself."

"No, mi padre, you cannot move all of that. Let me take the clothes to your friends myself. I do not mind. Whitney Slope could help me if we went right now."

The good padre Leo stared at his dusty black shoes and shook his head.

"No, Dominga, I think not. Even you might scare them."

"You mean the people in the old station, don't you?" Whitney said from the doorway.

Dominga and padre Leo looked at Whitney and then at one another.

"Yes, those people." Dominga walked over to Whitney and spoke softly.

"You see, these three are from Mexico, and the padre will help them while they are here. But, as you know, they are illegal visitors. Not in the eyes of God; no one is illegal in God's land."

Whitney looked down at Dominga.

"I've seen them, Dominga. Their secret is safe with me."

Dominga looked over at her old cousin whose hands were nervously, painfully, rubbing his knees. She had already told Whitney Slope about the clouds; and about that weatherman she still pined for. He knew about the sheep, and about the clothes she was hiding from Tomas in the trunk. What other secrets could be shared with this man?

"Sí, mi primo," Dominga said to the padre, "their secret is safe with Mr. Slope."

Desert Angel

Whitney had first passed the illegal squatters two days ago. There were three of them. One boy looked intelligent enough. But the younger boy had that unmistakable off-center quality exhibited by those with less than their full share of intellect. The boy waved at passing cars and trucks as if he were expecting company. And then there was a third, a woman, who Whitney had seen for the first time yesterday when he went out sketching on the southern plateau. The woman was remarkably large and was settled in the sand by the doorway. Only her head moved as her eyes followed the foolish one. Her body was that of a fattened beast, but her round brown face with its halo of black, frizzy hair belonged to the etheric realm of free-floating beings.

Whitney had meant to ask Dominga about them. Now, in Dominga's car, he was on his way to meet them.

Dominga was pensive as she drove the white Chevy east out of the bosque into the open mesa land.

"I will talk," Dominga said suddenly. "Or do you speak Spanish?"

"A little. You talk, Dominga. Somehow I think you're better at this."

"I've not met these three. But padre Leo says they are friendly. Frightened, of course, but friendly. The youngest brother is somewhat backward, the padre said. But the sister, Persimillion, and her other brother, Pepé, are fine, intelligent people."

"Her name is Persimillion?" Whitney looked across the seat at Dominga, who nodded, but kept her eyes on the two-laner.

"They have suffered, the good padre said. He does not know what, exactly. But they have suffered. There is something behind them they seek to forget."

Whitney turned his head back to the hot, richly colored mesa country opening wide and vacant to his right. South across the desert there was a barbed-wire fence. On the far side, as far as the eye could see, there were sand and prickly pear, yucca cactus, snake weed, sturdy sage, and small circles of grass. Occasionally there grew a cedar tree, its gnarled trunk fed by thick roots sunk deep into the dry earth. This country, Whitney thought, was not for the easily uprooted, the uncommitted.

"Yes, Persimillion, " Dominga nodded again as the gas station rose into view.

"Like a fruit," Whitney murmured, looking at the building he had once called home. "A plump, succulent, impossibly ripe cactus fruit."

Dominga slowed her old Chevy, and put on the turn signal, although there was not another vehicle for miles. Before she steered the car into the old station, Dominga turned her head and looked at Whitney.

"I suppose," Dominga said, "but a cactus is rooted."

Instead of the empty doorway that had greeted Whitney a month or so ago, the round, brown woman filled the door's open space side to side. At her feet in the red sand was the foolish boy, whose black-haired head was snuggled into her lap and shaded by her plump hands. The older boy was asleep with his back to the adobe wall, his head flopped onto one shoulder. Dominga pulled the Chevy in near the gas pumps, but Persimillion still did not move. As Whitney left the car, he was careful not to slam the door.

Dominga did all the talking. Whitney stood to one side, smiling when Persimillion looked up at him, trying not to be the aloof gringo. The brothers woke when Dominga began to explain who she was, and how the good padre Leo had sent her with this carload of clothes and supplies. Whitney could not understand all of what Dominga said, but he knew by her kind tone, by her smile and gentle gestures, that she was making the three refugees at ease. He knew because Dominga was doing the same for him.

"They'll help unload the car," Dominga said, walking back to Whitney. "The younger boy is Alfredo; the older is Pepé, who speaks some English."

The brothers helped Whitney unload the car while Dominga and Persimillion talked on the door stoop. Pepé moved quickly with the boxes, and was agile and strong. Alfredo the Foolish was more interested in Whitney's belt buckle than in the supplies. He kept pointing at the silver and grunting deep in his throat, like an animal. When the car was unloaded, Whitney sat on the back fender, removed his belt, and handed it to Alfredo.

Alfredo bobbed his head up and down while he studied the silver spiral snake with inlaid turquoise eyes. He then placed the buckle down in the sand near his bare feet and walked around it, tilting his head to one side and folding up his lips as if he were appraising it. Finally he put his hands on his slim hips and looked up at Whitney.

"I take it," he said in slurred English. "Good. I take it."

Dominga stood in the doorway, watching Whitney and Alfredo. Persimillion remained seated.

Persimillion said something to Dominga, who nodded and looked back at Whitney.

"Alfredo does not mean he will keep it, the belt," Dominga said across the gas pumps. "It is all the English he knows. He will ever know, Persimillion says. From the *mercado* in Juárez."

Alfredo lifted the belt and buckle out of the sand. He ran the smooth silver across his thin shirt, as if to shine it. When he was done, Alfredo looked down at the glossy silver in his palm. He moved it back and forth in the sun, which glanced off the silver and into Alfredo's deeply tanned face. The sun beam from the buckle shone like a dental lamp onto Alfredo's chin and mouth. Whitney saw the boy had no front teeth, and that his lips were cracked and sunburned. Alfredo handed Whitney his belt and watched with intense interest as Whitney threaded it back through the loops on his jeans.

"Here," Whitney said, digging around his front pocket, "you can have this. I have another at home."

Alfredo took the slim tube of lip balm from Whitney's extended hand. He seemed confused. Whitney bent over in front of Alfredo, and ran his fingers across his own lips.

"For your mouth, your lips, *por el sol,*" Whitney said, pointing to the sky.

Alfredo touched the tube to his lower lip and then burst into loud laughter. Before Whitney could show him how to remove the top, Alfredo slipped the tin tube into his own front pocket and ran around the side of the station where he disappeared into the silence.

Whitney looked across the gas pumps at Dominga and shrugged. He guessed it was too little, too late.

"Well, *bien, mi amigos,*" Dominga said, standing beside Persimillion and taking her hand. "I will come again. *Yo prometo.*"

"*Gracias,* Dominga de Jesús," Persimillion said. She stood up slowly, using the wall. "*Tu es un ángel,* Dominga de Jesús."

"Oh, no. No." Dominga shook her head. Whitney saw that she was blushing. "It was *padre Leo.*"

"*Un ángel,*" Persimillion repeated, holding Dominga's hand between her own.

Whitney and Dominga walked back to the Chevy. Whitney opened Dominga's door and waited until she climbed in.

"She called you an angel, didn't she?" he asked as he closed her door.

Dominga stared back at the three watching from the station doorway. Whitney walked around the car and climbed in.

"They believe you live in the clouds, Dominga."

"*Sí,* but . . . " Dominga started the Chevy and steered back onto the highway. "It is all really your point of view, isn't it? Who lives above, who lives below?"

Atencio's wheelbarrow was parked on its side near his house when Dominga stopped the station wagon beside her trailer.

"Atencio is home," she said, sliding out of her side of the car. "You can go see him now."

"Are you going to go down with me?"

"No," Dominga said. "It would be better for you to work this out alone with Atencio."

Whitney did not move immediately from the car. Dominga leaned back in the car window.

"Let me give you something to eat first. And then you can take Atencio some lunch."

Whitney took Dominga's lunch of blue corn tortillas, chile stew, and a hunk of cheddar cheese down to Atencio in a basket. Whitney was glad to have something to offer Atencio, even if it wasn't really his to offer. Although Whitney was asking Atencio to come work for him, he felt as though it was Atencio who was in the position of doing a favor.

Whitney knocked and called Atencio's name from the back door. Hearing Atencio's faint reply, Whitney entered the old house. Atencio was in the house, laying a triangular-shaped slab of the rose flagstone into the corner of his room. The room was about half done. The stones were exactly level. Whitney saw that Atencio did not bring back just any stone. These were individually remarkable in shape and color, varying a bit in shade and giving the floor a mixture of dark and then light hues of the same peachy rose.

"Hello, Atencio," Whitney said. "Your mother sent down a basket of food for lunch. Where would you like me to put it?"

Atencio straightened up and stood on the stone he had just finished setting. He was bare chested and wore the same thin cotton pants Whitney had seen him in before. But his hair was pulled tightly away from his face, giving his eyes and cheekbones a chiseled quality where before their exact shape had been shadowed.

"On the counter."

Whitney set the basket down on the wood planks that served for the kitchen counter top and then turned back to Atencio. Atencio was looking Whitney over.

"I was up at the church with your mother this morning. I came, though, to see you today."

Atencio continued to look across the room at Whitney. Whitney was struck by how truly motionless Atencio could be, like the stone itself. Not lifeless, exactly, but without detectable animation, like a tree under a windless sky. Whitney was going to have to carry this conversation himself.

"I have need of some help up at your aunt's old house in Recuerdos Canyon. Do you know the place?"

Atencio nodded that he did. Whether he was cognizant of the fact that Whitney was now living there, Whitney could not say.

"I would like to stabilize the outdoor patio, between the adobe wall, which needs some work, and the old porch, which has begun to rot from water running under it in the rains."

Whitney stepped into the room.

"What I'm thinking of having is a patio set with flagstones. These flagstones. Rose stone."

Whitney looked away from the floor and over to Atencio, who faced him now, his arms hanging limp to his sides, but with both green eyes alert and focused on Whitney's mouth.

"Would you be interested in setting a patio with the rose flagstones for some kind of exchange? Say, a grocery account at the mercantile, or gas and parts for your car in the shed out there?"

Atencio continued to stare at Whitney's mouth after he finished asking his questions. Whitney was ready to carry the conversation a little farther when Atencio stepped off the stone he had just set and began to survey the room around him. Whitney studied the floor, too, and was about to compliment Atencio on the careful fitting and placement he had done thus far, when Atencio looked up at him and spoke.

"The quarry is a long ways out. It would not be easy to bring out the stone for your patio."

"I have a truck we could use."

"You would pay me with groceries and gas?"

"Yes."

"You have spoken with my mother about this, haven't you?" Atencio was not angry. He was simply stating a fact they both knew to be true. "She does not believe I can hold cash without getting drunk."

Whitney began to object, but stopped himself. "Yes. I spoke with Dominga."

Atencio walked past Whitney to the kitchen and opened the basket. He pulled out the cheese and began to eat.

"I suppose it would be doing my mother a favor if I could buy my own food."

"Atencio, I hope you will accept this job because you want to do this job. Not as a favor to anyone else."

Atencio looked up at Whitney. They were only two feet apart. Atencio was bone and muscle, sinewy and spare, as indigenous to this country as the desert cedar.

"Jobs are usually a favor for someone else."

"When you can do work that allows your gifts to flourish and grow, it is not a job, Atencio. It is a pleasure."

Whitney watched Atencio study the basket of food.

"You could work half days, if you like. Or work a few days a week at the canyon house, a few days here. I'm very flexible, and I'm not in a hurry."

Atencio chewed cheese and looked at the floor of the kitchen.

"I still have a lot of work to do here," Atencio said after swallowing.

"We could get your stone at the same time we pulled out my stone. Then your house would go faster."

Atencio looked up at Whitney.

"I like going slowly."

"Would you like to think about this? I don't need to know today."

Atencio nodded and looked into the basket again. He pulled a tortilla in half and ate it quickly, brushing his hands on his black trousers.

"I'll come by in a few days, Atencio. We can talk some more then."

Whitney walked out into the sun. Atencio stood at the back door. Whitney realized how very tired his entire body was. His hands did not have blisters anymore, but his eyes felt like they might have developed a few out at the old station.

"*Adiós*, Atencio." Whitney walked towards the side of the house. He adjusted his hat and took his sunglasses out of his shirt pocket. It was discouraging, talking with Atencio. Especially after talking with Dominga. With Dominga everything seemed possible; with Atencio, the realm of the possible slipped hopelessly from human reach.

"Having the car would be a good thing," Atencio mumbled more to the open air than to Whitney. Whitney stopped and rested an arm against the side of Atencio's adobe house. "It is a good car. Tomas will tell you it is nothing but rotting metal, but I know: I've seen rotting metal, and the De Soto is not that."

"Are you saying you want the job, Atencio?"

Whitney did not mean to sound impatient, but it was nearly one hundred degrees now in the sun, and he could feel the first ruckles of perspiration gathering between his shoulder blades.

"I will think about it more," Atencio said. And then he vanished backwards into the adobe house like a shadow.

⁗

Upon returning to the canyon house, Whitney took a cold beer for a long soak in a lukewarm bath. After the bath, he stood naked in the studio.

Whitney wanted to paint. He wanted to put on a little Beethoven, open the bottles, get out the brushes, and put acrylic paint onto canvas. His head was crowded with color and form, with light and heat and the pulse of luscious, raw, poignant life. But Whitney was hesitant to disturb what he felt. When he put his hands onto this place he wanted to touch it with perfect equilibrium.

Whitney stood on the porch and listened to the canyon of midafternoon. Nothing moved. The sky carried nothing but blue heat from the horizon to the outer fringes of the atmosphere. The catalpa tree looked weary, its leaves limp. He would water at sundown when the plants could hold the moisture without a fight.

Cicadas droned and buzzed in the juniper and cedar trees up the sand hills above the house. The other life of the canyon—the birds and coyotes, the lizards and snakes and spiders, probably even the tiny insects that floated crucifixion-style on top of the stream, all of the even slightly sentient creatures of this place of remembering—lay comatose in the shade somewhere. Whitney realized only humans continued to scurry about in search of purposeful direction; only a human could be so faithless, so suspicious of the gifts that come from surrendering to what is, and to what will be.

The Blessed and the Damned

Atencio walked into the mercantile. He wanted to look around at the food and car parts and tools he might buy with the credit he was going to earn laying the patio at the canyon house. He knew there would not be much in Clay's store that would fit the De Soto. Atencio would need Tomas's help finding parts for the De Soto's engine, but it would not be hard getting the old car to work again: Atencio had taken very good care of his father's car all these years.

Atencio had not taken five steps into the store's interior before his eyes fixated on the floor. He knew, of course, about the stone floor in the mercantile: Atencio had watched the laying of the floor, stone by stone, as a boy twenty years ago. Even when Atencio was at school, or asleep, he watched the rose stones being set; fitted like a giant jigsaw puzzle one to another with fine, sifted stone dust, and sand from the arroyo near the quarry poured between the cracks. If Atencio had not been so young and small, too thin, his father said, to manage the stones, he would have worked between Clay and his father; he would have helped them choose the stones. Atencio would have sanded down their sides; he would have helped his father guide the precious rose stone into something beautiful, something permanent.

Atencio heard Clay Koontz talking to him from behind the counter, but it took another moment for him to let go of the floor and look up at the old face of his father's friend and partner.

"Still a remarkable floor, isn't it, Atencio?" Clay said. "I remember how you loved to watch."

Atencio walked a few steps closer to the counter and looked again at the stones. He was wearing shoes today, and he was unable to feel the smooth, cool surface against his soles. Atencio reached down and pulled off his canvas espadrilles.

Atencio heard Clay sigh.

"I see you still carry your father's watch, Atencio. Surely it doesn't work?"

"No, it has not worked in ten years," Atencio looked over at Clay. "My mother says things don't have to work to be valuable." Atencio paused and fingered the watch fob in his rear pocket. "I'm thinking of working, and I would get groceries or tools in exchange."

"I heard," Clay said, leaning onto the counter and rubbing his eyes with the backs of his liver-spotted hands. "Sounds like a good thing, Atencio. A good thing."

Atencio walked slowly up the aisle away from the front counter. Friends of his mother's came into the store, greeted him, and then turned to talk with Clay. Near the canned vegetables, Atencio knelt down onto his knees and felt the floor. His fingers followed the seams between the stones. This section was particularly tight. If Atencio studied the mercantile floor long enough, he could tell where one stone setter's work ended and another's began.

The friends of his mother began to whisper to Clay. Atencio knew his crawling about on the stone floor was causing a stir in the mercantile, so he crawled faster. He just needed a few more minutes to remember some things. Twenty years ago, Atencio knew this floor like the bones in his hands. But now, with all the shelves and cases and aisles, Atencio could not remember exactly where his father had worked.

"He's making a stone floor for his own house," Clay was telling the customers up front.

Clay wanted to be fatherly. But it was too late. There were things not even Feodoro could have made right. Clay knew. Atencio knew, too. Atencio's story had reached too far beyond Mi Ojo.

"And this one's the finest around," Clay said in a loud voice everyone in the store could hear, "like those found in the Mediterranean. You know, stone masonry is an art in many countries."

Atencio stood and brushed off his trouser knees. He carried his shoes in one hand and walked out of the mercantile, nodding his head when Clay called good-bye.

The blacktop of the parking lot had reached a temperature near red heat and was beginning to soften. Atencio put on his shoes. Across the highway at the post office, the single elm tree was thick green with summer. Spring had come and gone, summer was settling onto the valley, and Atencio had not noticed the change.

It was too hot to head into the desert for more stone. The stone he had brought out was already set. It was not lunch; it was not supper. The cool oblivion of evening was hours away.

"Atencio, my man!"

It was Burly, a high school buddy who was divorced and unemployed. Burly lived in his grandmother's house and cut firewood for city people in the winter months. During summer, Burly was an unanchored vessel of boredom and belligerency.

"¿Qué pasa?" Burly asked. He glided his grandmother's car, a maroon Fury, to a stop beside Atencio, blocking the gas pumps from further business for the duration of his visit.

Atencio leaned into the car. Burly had a six pack with three unopened bottles on the floor. There was also a brown paper bag of something more on the back seat.

"I'm okay, man. I'm working."

Burly raised his hands in mock wonder. *"¡Hijola!* That is news, my man! News. Atencio working. Why don't you climb in, and we'll beat this heat with a cruise down the valley to the river. The movement of the air, my man, will cool your head."

Atencio stood up and gazed across the empty highway at the elm tree. It was fuller in summer. Healthier looking. Like it wasn't so old and sickly, which everyone knew it was. He looked back at Burly, who chewed a matchstick and rolled his eyes with impatience. Atencio did not really want to spend the afternoon with Burly. But he did not want to stand under the elm tree waiting for cars, and time, to pass, either.

"Okay, a short cruise. To the river."

Burly and Atencio did not make it to the river. Not to the water. Burly stopped in the first cottonwood grove he could park grandmother's Fury, and then passed out. Or fell asleep. Atencio could not tell which.

Alone in the bosque, with Burly's three cold beers and an unopened bottle of red wine in the bag on the back seat, Atencio reckoned he had worked enough for one day. He did not set to drinking immediately. He settled onto the sandy ground where a little grass grew, and closed his eyes. In his mind he saw the quarry, a silent oven in the afternoon sun; he saw the stone he would bring out tomorrow, and the day after that.

Atencio opened his eyes to the sky and was satisfied he had not lost sight of his plan. Back in the Fury, its doors left open to flies and oxygen, Burly snored. Atencio picked up the first beer. He twisted the top off the bottle and placed it in his pocket because he had not one idea of what else to do out here in the bosque in the middle of a summer afternoon.

Hours passed and dusk infiltrated the bosque like grey smoke. Mosquitos came out in droves, and owls hooted from the trees along the river. Atencio lay flat on his back in the grass. Burly still snored in the car. Atencio tried to sit up, but his head was thick and groggy.

Atencio wanted to lie on his back, stare at the stars, and enjoy the numbness of the alcohol. But the mosquitos and then the river confused him: the buzzing and the sound of moving water pulled him out of his relaxed stupor. He knew Burly was someone familiar in the car. But the mosquitos and the moan of river water were not compatible with Burly asleep in the car. Old fear began to fester in Atencio's belly; he could feel his body tightening with the familiar poison.

Atencio had always had a good sense about direction, even drunk, or terrified. Using a tree for balance, Atencio pulled himself to his feet and leaned his ears into the bosque air, listening for clues. There was no sound other than the high whine of the mosquitos and the low moan of the moving river. Atencio left Burly and the car and moved deeper into the trees. Some old comfort found in brush lead him towards the river, away from the vulnerability of open spaces. He was almost within sight of the water when he caught the words of people. He crouched down in the bushes and waited.

Voices penetrated the alcohol jungle of Atencio's head. He sat in the brush, alert, but with his torso shaking and jerking with fear. Perspiration dripped from his forehead and slicked his palms. He might have spent the entire night hunched in half in the bosque scrub, but for sudden sobs. It was a child. Atencio sat up, his head exposed above the brush. A child cried and shouted for help. Atencio did not hesitate, did not evaluate his own safety, but sprang from his hiding place and ran towards the river.

He must have thought it a hundred times before, but tonight he responded: it did not matter, after all, if these children were of this side or the other.

Atencio saw the dark outline of a boy against the western sky. The boy was on the river bank, leaning out over the water towards a second boy struggling in the water. The second boy managed to wrap his arms around the first boy's legs. Atencio ran to the edge of the bank where the boy saw him and called loudly in Spanish.

"He is caught in the mud, the quicksand, and he will not let go of my legs. Help us!"

Atencio fell to his knees and grabbed the struggling boy's wrists, wrenching his hands off the other's ankles. The boy in the water was hysterical, like an animal frantic with the sense of approaching death. As soon as Atencio had freed him, the boy on the bank turned into the brush and began tearing at the limbs of the trees. Atencio fought the boy in the water, trying to hold him without being pulled into the river himself. The older boy returned with a long, narrow limb and yelled to Atencio to place the boy's hands on top of it. It was very difficult to get the boy in the water to understand that he was to hold onto the tree branch. But he did, finally, let go of Atencio and wrap his hands around the limb. Together, Atencio and the other boy pulled the frantic boy from the river. They dragged his wet, muddy body back into the grass where he fell sobbing onto Atencio. Atencio gasped loudly for air and space, but the boy would not let him go.

Ten minutes passed in the black bosque before the boy stopped crying and Atencio was able to sit up. The older boy sat on a fallen tree trunk. The night air was becoming cool, and each of them shivered. Atencio could not see the features of either of the boy's faces. He caught only the gleam in their black eyes when starlight crossed them.

Atencio followed the older boy out of the bosque and onto the desert. The younger boy clung to Atencio's waist. He now mumbled in a language that was part Spanish and part nonsense. The other boy said nothing. Atencio was too tired to answer; it was all he could do to keep walking with even the slight weight of the boy against him.

The older boy led the way. Atencio could see he was a good point man: he held his head high and surveyed the dark, starlit country around them with smooth, rhythmic turns of his head, first to the left, then to the right. Always watching; always alert.

They stopped when they reached trees again, near a decrepit building. Where they were, Atencio could not say exactly, but it felt safe, like they were home. Atencio waited at the door while the older boy went inside. The smaller boy still clung to Atencio. For the first time, Atencio could see the faces of the two boys found by the river. The older boy was dressed in a torn tee shirt and trousers of stiff, new denim. He stood just inside of the roofless building, speaking in Spanish to a woman sitting on the floor near a glowing kerosene lamp. The yellow flame cast a circle of light around her head. Atencio had never seen this woman before.

Pepé introduced his sister, Persimillion; his brother, Alfredo; and then himself to Atencio. Atencio looked down at the boy, Alfredo, whose arms were still wrapped around his waist. He was caked with mud and grass, and his lip was bleeding. Atencio took a corner of his own shirt and wiped the blood from the boy's chin. The boy smiled and began to dig in his front pocket. He pulled out a slender tube of lip balm and held it in the air near his face. After showing it to Atencio, the boy opened his nearly toothless mouth and guffawed. Atencio could not be certain because of the mud and the grass stains, but it seemed this boy was wearing one of Tomas's favorite old rodeo shirts.

Atencio's head whirled off center, and he sat down hard on the wooden doorway. The boy fell with him. He could hear the woman struggling to stand, and then he felt a cool hand against his head. She must have pried the boy's arms from his waist, because when Atencio woke several hours later, he was lying alone on the floor with a pillow under his aching skull.

Persimillion, her brother Pepé, and Atencio watched the sun rise like a gold marble off the horizon from the door stoop. The other boy, Alfredo, slept curled like a cat in the corner behind them. Atencio did not want to stare, but he was almost certain the blanket over Alfredo belonged to his mother, and the pillow he had found under his head was once his very own.

After coffee and bread, Persimillion made it very clear to Atencio that even though he had liquor on his breath, she had allowed him to sleep at their home because he had saved Alfredo's life at the river.

"This time will be an exception," she said without looking at Atencio. "But I do not allow men with liquor on their breath to share my food or my house."

Atencio nodded. "It will never happen again."

Walking home along the two-laner towards Mi Ojo, Atencio knew it would never happen again because he very much wanted to go back and share that woman's home and circle of light.

The Blessed and the Damned

Atencio looked back down the highway at the decrepit structure. He had forgotten all about that station until this morning when he sat on the door stoop and looked up at the old pumps. Then it came to him like yesterday—riding in the De Soto with his father, listening to the clanging of the gasoline meter as the gas was pumped into the car. Atencio remembered how it was raining one day, and his father kept telling him to close his window. But Atencio wanted to smell the gasoline and hear the bells of the pump, and he wanted to be close to his father who was laughing and talking to the station owner even though the rain was running in rivulets off his hat onto his shoulders. Feodoro de Jesús was not a man to let a little weather come between himself and a friendly conversation.

Atencio stuck out his thumb for a ride. No one stopped. Everyone just left him behind in their rearview mirrors. After the sixth car, Atencio kept his hands to himself and followed the edge of the blacktop with his eyes and his feet. His head hurt, but he was used to that. He was glad the shadows were long and cool under the yucca growing near the road: there was still time for him to get out to the quarry with his wheelbarrow before high noon.

Atencio walked up to his mother's trailer. He paused and thought about her coffee, which he could smell through the open door. He would ask her. Today he would ask for a cup before she offered one.

Atencio smoothed his crumpled, muddy shirt and walked up the steps to his mother's open door. Before he rapped on the screen door, Atencio reminded himself that it could all have been a dream. He would keep the events of the last twelve hours to himself just in case it was all a dream. Atencio had had dreams before in which he was both the blessed and the damned; the savior and the saved.

Cats in the Canyon

Whitney shelled peanuts and sipped beer on the porch, and thought about a cold supper of salad and homemade flour tortillas purchased from the mercantile earlier in the afternoon. He had gessoed five canvasses. They sat perfectly even, perfectly empty white space against the wall of his studio. Whitney had begun each of the last three days intending to paint, but on each of those days something had presented itself as more worthy of his time and attention: the back door frame needed new molding, and then there were wasp's nests under the roof near the end of the porch. Screens needed mending, and there was always work in the patio garden.

But really, the house was done. The renovation of the canyon home, excepting the patio, was completed. Although Whitney could find tasks to keep him busy, the house was now immaculate. The plumbing and the water system worked well enough to be forgotten. The second-, maybe even third-, hand refrigerator bought in Tomita from a self-proclaimed repairman was working its noisy heart out. Several times an hour the internal fans fluttered into action and resonated with the undertones of an idling tractor. But it kept the food cold, and with the doors into the kitchen closed, Whitney could ignore it.

It was paradise, Whitney thought, settling back into the porch post and the best time of day in the canyon. Dominga was right: it all depended on your point of view. On the east side of Santa Fe, this old adobe house would need fifty thousand dollars worth of renovations to qualify as marketable living quarters. But out in Mi Ojo, where people without names or papers called a roofless gas station home, the house in Recuerdos Canyon was a mansion; a palace.

Whitney had sent Caroline a post card with a pen and ink sketch of the Mi Ojo Mercantile on one side, and a scrawled message about how this was his new grocery store on the reverse side. He had drawn the telephone booth in vivid detail with an arrow indicating that he could be reached at this number. Whitney told Caroline he was making a home in this beautiful, remote corner of the world, but that it would not be a real home until his only niece visited.

From his porch seat, Whitney could see the towering red and yellow rock walls of the canyon. The very tops touched the open blue of outer space. Throughout the afternoon, small flecks of clouds unfurled and then vanished into the dry atmosphere in a pattern that eluded, yet somehow included, Whitney and his beer and solitude propped against the old porch post. Whitney could not see clouds now without thinking of Dominga, of asking her what they were called, why they had formed, where they would go.

Whitney wondered what the village residents, and especially the state trooper, thought about the squatters at the old gas station? Would the trooper move them on? Whitney had wondered if the trooper would stop and tell him to move on during his three day stopover at the same crumbling shelter. But Whitney had a late-model truck. Whitney's pockets carried dollars, and Whitney spoke English from lips that were surrounded by all-American, Anglo skin. Whitney was an alien here, but he was a legal one.

It occurred to Whitney that he was less alone in Mi Ojo than he had been in Santa Fe. It was not just because of Dominga and Atencio and his daily conversations with Clay and the postmistress. It was not just the people of Mi Ojo he felt a growing involvement with. It was the community of the canyon itself. Squadrons of jackrabbits flashed between the sage bushes when he walked into the foothills, and each morning several coyotes slinked home under cover of the brush that grew along the stream. There was a great horned owl's nest high in the rock ledges at the left side of the canyon. Swifts soared in and out of their cliff nests, beaks wide to inhale the swarms of insects in the air above the spring. Every day, several red-tailed hawks and scores of ravens took turns circling and hunting above the seeping sandstone walls, and then down along the stream's meandering, shaded path through cottonwoods and tamarisk. There was a sizable flock of iridescent blue-black piñon jays who flew noisily by the house each morning, sometimes stopping in the junipers on the mesa behind the house to squawk and scold before taking to the air again. Their laughing calls filled the canyon again in the evening when they returned to wherever it was they spent the night.

From the far side of the wall the hot silence was broken by what sounded like a cat. Whitney stood and listened, but all he could hear now were the jays who were making their noisy evening pilgrimage back down the canyon.

It was not until the flock had crested the mesa west of the house that Whitney was again able to discern the distinct voice of a cat.

Whitney left the porch and picked up the hose to spray the lilac bushes along the adobe wall. He leaned over and looked on the far side. It really was a cat. The cat was too rotund to jump up onto the wall, so it rubbed the base of the adobe and continued to yowl at Whitney when he saw that he had been noticed.

For a long moment Whitney considered spraying the cat with the hose and convincing him to move on. But it was nearly dusk and moving on meant a night up in the canyon somewhere. Whitney had not had a pet in thirty years, but he could not justify turning away the cat—especially when he remembered the size of the great horned owl about to begin his nightly rounds. Whitney walked to the patio gate and invited the cat in.

The cat was enormous. His black head was narrow and sleek, with a long nose. And his legs were long and slender. But his belly was swollen like a pumpkin gourd.

Whitney turned off the hose after filling a cup with water. The cat was not thirsty. There was the stream and, Whitney supposed, plenty of mice. The cat was just very, very tired.

Whitney sat on the porch. The cat settled down next to him with an audible sigh of relief. His rumbling purr continued to tell Whitney how appreciative he was until his eyes closed with exhaustion.

The cat turned onto its side, and Whitney saw it had protruding teats. This cat was no he: he was a she about to have kittens.

Whitney sighed and felt suckered. A house full of kittens. He stroked the now sleeping cat. She could have her litter, and then he would find them homes in the village. Cats and paints did not get along.

Whitney named the pregnant black cat Mousse. She slept on his laundry for four days, ate when he brought her a bowl of tuna or sardines, and gave birth to two white kittens in the early morning of the fifth day. Whitney heard Mousse's pushing and panting and slid off his bed to watch her in the soft light of a candle set on the floor. The waning moon in the western sky sent a silver beam through the window. Whitney lay in the beam of the moon on the old wood floor and waited for Mousse to finish. She washed the kittens and then fell asleep with them nuzzling her. Whitney returned to his own bed after the moon had set, and the candle had burned to a wax pool in its glass bowl.

In the bright light of morning, Whitney climbed out of bed and lay again on the floor. Mousse purred. The kittens were two, fluffy white balls beside her.

Whitney went to the kitchen and made coffee, then walked out to the porch to greet another canyon day. He was no longer alone. But he had never been alone here. A hummingbird fed from the yellow and white flowers of the old patio columbine whose fragrance Whitney had been breathing since dawn, and the jays squawked a clowns' greeting as they flew past the house. Whitney felt content in some tangled, almost paternal, sort of way.

"She had two—twins! A boy and a girl!" Whitney called hoarsely at the blue flock.

Whitney could not intellectualize, or easily direct, what washed over him as he stood in the sun on the porch. Not yet, anyway. Maybe tomorrow, *mañana*. Maybe so, he thought, squinting at the cloudless sky; maybe no.

Maybe it was watching the effort and beauty of Mousse's kittens' birth, or maybe it was simply the beginning of something that had only to do with him, but Whitney began to paint that morning. That morning became that afternoon, and then it was the next morning and afternoon, and the next. The days in the canyon studio glided by nearly indistinguishable one from the next. It was bliss. It was simplicity and self-centeredness known before only in childhood and the years just after college.

The pencil sketches of Mi Ojo and the desert hung about the studio walls with masking tape. Whitney was able to stretch ten small canvasses himself—only the large canvasses required professional assistance—and began working on three at a time. Whitney never used an easel, but leaned whatever he was painting against the wall on top of his large studio table.

Whitney began small, working on canvasses that were easy to move, easy to fill. The monolithic size he had become famous for in the last four years seemed presumptuous and out of place. He painted sky and sand, clouds and open space. He painted windowsills with dusk on the other side. He painted doorways to sand, doorways to heat, doorways to sky. Doorways to silence. Windows to vastness. Just the silence and vastness, sometimes, without walls or doors, or glassless window frames. He even filled one small canvas with only sky and another with only sand. Whitney hung these on his bedroom ceiling where he could view them flat on his back from his bed. The other canvasses were hung wherever Whitney placed a nail or found a ledge—the kitchen, the bathroom, the screened walls of the little back porch. From the catalpa tree in the patio, where the setting sun lifted the painted forms to life, Whitney hung a small painting of the gentle red-sand foothill across the road.

The fourth morning with the kittens, Whitney sat at his kitchen table and realized he had not gone into the post office, or the mercantile, had not left the canyon, in days. He did not know what day it might be, nor did he care. But he did care about finding Atencio and beginning work on the patio. And he wanted to tell Dominga about the cats. Maybe Dominga could explain to him the physiological need in forty-four-year-old men to become fathers.

The Stone Quarry

Whitney Slope woke just after dawn the morning scheduled for the first quarry expedition with Atencio de Jesús. He made a pot of strong coffee and took a cup to the porch. The kittens, hardly able to stand, but already determined to run and tumble, played on his lap and around his bare feet.

Whitney stared at the rocky, dusty, weed sprouting patio. This small plot of sand was the reason behind the coming morning's expedition. It was such a small patio. It could probably withstand another decade of rain and wind. It really wasn't imperative that it have a stone floor. Maybe he did feel sorry for Atencio; maybe Whitney's motivations were confused between saving the patio and saving someone who was not asking for his help. Whitney sighed and sipped the black brew. Maybe he was just hoping to score points with the gods of clouds, old houses, and condemned burro fields.

Whitney threw several pairs of leather work gloves into the back of the truck along with two shovels, a water bottle, and a loaf of bread, and headed down the canyon toward Mi Ojo.

Whitney considered seeing Dominga before he picked up Atencio—he was still twenty minutes early—but thought better of it when he saw Tomas's truck parked out front. Whitney did not need Tomas's commentary on the stone patio, or his choice of hired help. And Whitney was still holding on to the belief that Tomas really wasn't related to Dominga. Atencio might be half there, or here, sometimes, but he had an intuitive, gentle quality that linked him unmistakably to his mother.

Atencio was sitting on the back step drinking a cup of coffee when Whitney rounded the side of the adobe house.

"Good morning, Atencio," Whitney said unnecessarily loud. "Looks like a fine day for loading stone."

Atencio eyed Whitney over the rim of his tin cup, the kind most people would take camping.

"Every morning is a good morning for stone," Atencio said, setting his cup down on the ground.

"I like your attitude." Whitney leaned against the wall near the kitchen door and gazed out at the desert and mesa country to the north. "But pouring rain might be rough, even with four-wheel-drive."

"They moved the last six slabs of stone for the mercantile in pouring rain," Atencio said over his back to Whitney, "some people here in the valley believed it was the desert weeping for what had been taken away."

Whitney looked at the back of Atencio's head. His hair was tied back, ready for work. And his shirt was tucked into his black cotton trousers.

"That would be one way to interpret that sort of event, I suppose," Whitney said, putting his sunglasses over his squinting eyes. "Maybe the desert was happy, was washing her stones so they would shine their finest."

Atencio stood and turned into the kitchen.

"I have some water and some bread in case we get hungry out there," Whitney called after him.

"I will bring my canteen," Atencio said.

"Bring whatever you are accustomed to taking out there," Whitney said, "I'll get the wheelbarrow and meet you at the truck."

The ruts that had once been a road were even worse than Atencio had foretold. There were arroyos that crossed and paralleled the quarry road that looked easier to navigate, and Whitney wanted to leave the familiar path and try his luck up one of them. But Atencio was adamant.

"We will get lost or stuck. Stay on the old road."

"But there isn't an old road to stay on."

"In my head, I see it, and we won't get lost."

So Whitney dodged rocks that had slid fifty feet down the talus slopes, and circled trees and bushes that had sprouted in the last twenty or so years. Every few yards, Whitney stopped and surveyed the camouflaged track up close, climbing from the truck and bending down to study the clearance between his oil pan and a ledge of shale, or a sharply angled juniper tree root. It was very slow going. An hour later, they were within one ridge of the quarry.

"Just over that butte," Atencio said, pointing out his window at a narrow, red mesa that sported not a single tree or bush on its steep sides. "The quarry is beyond. You can see how the color begins here."

The desert around them was, indeed, shades of rose and peach. The mesas and arroyo were cut into wavering bands of pastel-colored rocks and sand bars. Gold and red sand flecked the peachy rose that swirled in the walls of the arroyo near the truck, and up the sandstone columns clustered like towers above the arroyo floor.

If there was a good rainstorm out here, this part of the imaginary road would become a bona fide river. Whitney mentally counted how many weeks there were between now, early July, and the desert equivalent of a monsoon that came in early August, or was it late July? In Santa Fe it had never really mattered. The rain just came. Instead of walking under portals for shade, everyone walked under portals to stay dry. It was never a life-and-death matter, or even a hindrance to work. At most, the rains were a nuisance to shop-keepers like Anna: Mud Street turned, or rather returned, into a mud arroyo, and everyone who entered her gallery tracked clay and silt "like plodding cattle" across her tile floor and oriental rugs.

Whitney used to say Anna could always move the gallery. It wasn't like she wasn't forewarned.

"It is, after all, called Mud Street."

Anna would say something about mud in his eye, and call in Candy to begin mopping.

Atencio jumped out of the truck, which Whitney continued to coax like a reluctant burro around a tight curve in the arroyo road. The road was headed straight up and over the sandy embankment next to the red butte, one side of which appeared to be sliding into the arroyo under Whitney's swerving tires.

"Where are you going?" Whitney yelled out the window.

Atencio did not hear him, or pretended not to. He ran ahead and disappeared over the bank of red sand. Whitney followed, inching up the last incline and scraping the back fender as the truck crested the angled ridge. For an instant, the truck's hood pointed to outer space and Whitney could see only sky through his windshield.

When the truck touched earth again, Whitney stopped and pulled the emergency brake. It was mostly for effect, for the terrain before him was flat and solid.

They were at the mouth of a canyon, a large canyon, much larger than the one Whitney lived in. This canyon was a half mile across and curved to the left, where castle-like rock formations rose a hundred feet above the west side, their color slurred in the heat rising from the desert floor.

Atencio sat in his customary Asian-crouch on a large, rose-colored boulder, looking down at what was obviously the quarry—a huge rose and peach hole in the ground.

"Quite a place," Whitney called to him. "How far back does that canyon go?"

Atencio looked up.

"Seven miles."

"How do you get in here from your house?"

Atencio turned and pointed southeast.

"I come through that little saddle there between the red mesas. It opens up on the other side. I follow some connecting arroyos. And then the plateau country north of my house."

"Why don't we drive the big arroyo in?"

"Because it has two dry waterfalls. Straight up. Or down."

Whitney nodded and walked to the edge of the quarry. It dropped twelve feet below him.

"How did they find this place?"

"Someone's cow wandered back here and died after getting her torso wedged between some boulders." Atencio stood up and adjusted his cotton pants. "She imagined greener grass, my father used to say, and forgot her own size."

Although Atencio's face did not seem amused, Whitney was amazed to hear something resembling a chuckle from Atencio's throat.

"When the rancher came back on horseback looking for her, the cow was stuck there, dead, between those two boulders. While he was wondering about what to do with his dead cow, the rancher got a glimpse of the stone."

"Did he leave the carcass between the boulders?"

Atencio jumped down into the quarry.

"She was eaten by coyotes and ravens, you see. There was just the skeleton. Bleached white, some on one side of the boulders, some on the other. My father and I came out to see the stone, and I took the bones home." Atencio took off his shoes and stood on the surface of one of the stones. "I used to believe bones were beautiful."

Whitney walked down the quarry's side, sliding in the shale and talus slope. When he reached the ledge with the large slabs, he knelt down and touched the exposed stones.

"How do you decide, Atencio, which ones to lift out."

"Like that, you touch them, feel their thickness, length, put the shovel under, start digging around them. You just know after awhile."

"I'll bring the wheelbarrow and tools down from the truck. You find a good place to begin, and we'll start." Whitney took off his hat and rubbed his hairline with his shirt sleeve. Atencio was putting his shoes back on. "It's not getting any cooler out here."

Within two hours, Whitney's truck was loaded at least to, if not beyond, its Detroit- makers' advertised limit. It took all four wheels in active service to pull the stone load away from the quarry. Exactly how he would navigate certain corners and dips in the upcoming nonroad Whitney could not say, but at least now he could follow his own tracks.

It took Whitney an hour and twenty minutes to reach the highway. The truck threatened to overheat, but then stopped short of the boiling point. Still, the sounds coming from down under the truck—from large stones trying to punch through the floor—gave Whitney serious second thoughts about continuing the project at all. When they reached the highway, Whitney was able to push the speed of the truck back up to twenty miles an hour. Finally they reached the Recuerdos Canyon road, and Whitney put the truck in low gear again for the last bumpy miles to his house. When he pulled up near the patio gate and looked at the load of rose stone in the bed behind him, the trouble and the wear and tear seemed worth it.

Atencio seemed to startle when Whitney turned off the engine. Whitney realized he had been asleep, or something akin to sleep.

"We're here," Whitney said, climbing out of the truck and walking to the rear to survey his tires. "Why don't we have some lunch inside before we try to unload this. You're hungry aren't you?"

Atencio nodded and opened his door. He walked to the patio gate, clutching his canteen against his side. Atencio did not open the gate, but stood back and waited for Whitney.

"Have you been up here before, back when your aunt lived here?"

"Yes," Atencio said. "But it was always noisy. She had children and lots of chickens."

"So I heard. Now there's just me here." Whitney looked at Atencio as he opened the gate. "Me and some cats who call this place home."

"Cats?" Atencio seemed to wake up again.

"Cats. A mother cat and her two kittens. Do you like cats?"

"I don't know. I never had one."

Whitney motioned to Atencio to follow him into the house.

"Cats are very smart. Smart and independent. They like us people because we have unusual foods and shirts to sleep on."

Whitney fixed a lunch of chicken sandwiches, pasta salad, and iced tea, pushing the beer to the back of the refrigerator. Mousse came into the kitchen and climbed onto the chair next to Atencio. Atencio was either mortified with fear, or overcome with reverence, as he did not move a finger, but sat like one of his wooden santos, watching her.

"She likes people. You can pet her. She won't bite or claw—she's the mother."

Atencio still did not move. Mousse began to wash, pausing every so often to look over at Atencio, to sniff the air between them.

The kittens appeared during lunch, jumping on their mother's back while she ate from her bowl, biting her tail and tackling each other under her belly. Atencio was so taken by their antics, he stopped eating and climbed down and sat on the floor to watch them.

"They're pretty amusing, aren't they?" Whitney said, eating his own sandwich and sipping iced tea. "You can watch them for hours, like a free show."

Whitney finished and cleared his dishes. Despite the satisfying meal, he was still feeling weary. Atencio looked tired, too. Still they had to unload the stone before he could drive Atencio back to Mi Ojo.

Atencio continued to stare at the cats. His face broke into a half-smile when Mousse was knocked over by the kittens as she attempted to walk across the kitchen.

"I'll be looking for homes for those kittens pretty soon. Maybe you'd like one of them?"

"I don't know how to care for a cat."

"Not much to it. Food, water, milk sometimes. And a lot of friendliness."

Mousse walked over and rubbed Atencio's ankles with her chin.

"I don't know if you've ever heard it, but cats are real good with snakes."

Atencio looked up at Whitney and then back at Mousse.

"It's true. Real good. Bobcats, domestic cats—I saw a film once, about how they play with them, how cats dance with snakes. They're fast. Snakes hate cats and avoid their territory."

Whitney retrieved his hat and headed for the patio door.

"Think about it, Atencio. Might be just the thing for you. A cat."

Atencio took his canteen to the sink and filled it with cold water, then splashed a handful onto his face. Whitney stood at the door and watched Mousse follow Atencio. She pushed her head into his leg again, then waited. The kittens had lost interest in ambushing their mother and were now lunging at Whitney's boot, their second favorite teething device. Atencio screwed the cap back on the canteen and then bent over to Mousse. With the gentlest movement of his fingers, Atencio touched Mousse's head. Mousse began to purr. Atencio touched her again. And then again.

"I'll be outside, Atencio. You can bring Mousse with you, if you want. She's a great watcher."

The Center of the Universe

After two expeditions to the quarry, Whitney and Atencio had brought enough rose stone to the canyon house to begin fitting and laying the patio floor. Although Whitney helped Atencio drag several of the larger pieces into place, the entire floor was designed by Atencio. Basically Atencio was on his own. Atencio wanted it that way. He did not say so in words, but Whitney could feel it in Atencio's gestures when they moved the first slabs into place near the adobe wall and the lilac bushes. Whitney felt he was somehow hurrying Atencio. Whitney spoiled Atencio's natural rhythm. Whitney knew exactly how Atencio felt, and left.

How Atencio avoided heat stroke was a wonder to Whitney. He did wear a broad-brimmed hat—a straw cowboy hat, not what Whitney would have pictured an in-country stylist like Atencio to favor. And after lunch, Atencio covered his bare torso with a shirt. But Atencio's body seemed unaffected by the inferno of the canyon. His feet were almost always free of shoes, even on the patio sand that Whitney knew would scald blisters into his own.

Whitney was working on a painting of a cedar tree from a sketch he had done on their last trip out to the quarry. Whitney kept leaving his work table, brush and paint in hand, to watch Atencio through the screen door. Atencio stood staring down at the rose stone laid randomly about his feet. After several minutes of complete absorption in the slabs, he would suddenly drag one into position next to another, and dig and chip, and dig some more, until the stones fit together, and then into the earth, as if they had been made that way in the quarry. It was very slow going, but Whitney knew the time would be worth the cost: Atencio was a perfectionist. From what Whitney had seen of his previous work, Atencio was very nearly a master of stone masonry.

During his second afternoon of work at the canyon house, Atencio came to the studio door. He needed a larger hammer. Whitney invited Atencio inside. With something like reluctance, Atencio opened the screen door and stepped into Whitney's studio.

"I'll buy a larger hammer," Whitney said, still dabbing his brush at a portion of the sky of his painting, "I'll get it from the mercantile tomorrow morning when I come pick you up."

Whitney put down his brush on the crowded work table and turned to face Atencio. Atencio was transfixed by the canvasses set against the walls and on the windowsills. He did not move towards them; he just fixed his eyes on one, and then another, until he had studied each canvass.

"This is my work, Atencio. Do you like it?"

Atencio did not answer.

"I'm trying something a little different for me. Less earth; more sky—space." Whitney watched Atencio's face, which remained expressionless. "Your mother has me thinking a lot more about clouds." Atencio continued to stare at the canvasses against the south wall.

"You don't have to like it. Some people don't care for this kind of painting—they like more detail, or more abstraction. As you can see, I don't like a lot of detail. I like a lot of light and shadow, and I try to get a feeling for a place, its color and form. I leave a lot to the imagination."

Whitney looked back at Atencio. His neck was sticking out like a goose to get a better look at the canvas on the southern windowsill.

"Why don't you go over and get a closer look, Atencio. I really don't mind your being in here, you know."

Atencio hesitated, then moved across the floor as if he were walking on glass. He stood before the painting of the patio wall, with the bare sand hill and a few fluttering clouds under a gigantic, hot-blue sky.

"I haven't worked this small in years. I'm enjoying the size, the simplicity. That one of the mesa across from the house there is one of my favorites." Whitney walked to a rectangular painting propped against the windowsill. "I might do another one, larger; different, but the same hill. Maybe with the house in part of the painting."

Atencio walked to the center of the studio. He looked out the door at the patio and the mesas beyond. The catalpa tree now shaded a small corner of the patio, but the cicadas of the canyon still buzzed with the joy they found in the high noon heat. Whitney studied Atencio's profile, which was classic Native American, with high cheek bones and a fine, straight nose. Atencio looked like his great grandmother's people, Dominga had told Whitney, Jicarilla Apaches from the northwestern plateau of New Mexico. Dominga's grandmother married a Spanish-speaking sheepherder's son. They met at an Anglo trader's house when they were teenagers. Grandmother loved her own people, Dominga had explained to Whitney, but grandmother loved grandfather more.

"I have seen this, too," Atencio said. He turned and faced Whitney. "I never knew it could be painted. How it feels. I thought paintings were just for how it looks."

Whitney noticed that Atencio's green eyes were rimmed with moisture. He held his hands, fingers locked together, over his stomach, as if holding an old wound.

"I've painted for a long time, Atencio." Whitney said picking up a favorite brush with a slender, pointed tip. "I rarely hear words that tell me someone has understood what I have painted. You have just paid me the highest compliment I could ever hope for. I thank you."

Atencio nodded that he understood. He looked again at the canvas on the windowsill, then moved noiselessly across the room and out the screen door to the patio.

Whitney stood before the half-done canvas that leaned against the wall behind his work table, brush in hand, not painting. He listened to the rhythmic chink of Atencio's hammer against the stone. Although the house remained fifteen degrees cooler than the canyon, even in the afternoon, the heat had settled into the studio, into Whitney's muscles and brain tissue, like a dense fog. Through the screened door, Atencio appeared to move in slow motion, cradling the stone, caressing the contours, the perspiration from his smooth, brown brow falling noiselessly onto the sand. Whitney had never known anyone to be so quiet.

Whitney walked to the door to tell Atencio to stop, to work when it was cooler. But then he saw Atencio's face as he turned to look behind at another stone: his was the face of pleasure, the face of joy—like a child's, full of itself with no apology, with no sense of time or exterior place.

Whitney stepped back from the door into the middle of the studio. He closed his eyes to the twenty-plus paintings of sky and sand, shadow and space, engulfing him in the hot room. Whitney thought how he stood in the center of the universe; how he had found what he longed for, even ignorant of the longing; how he had by luck or by miracle come to be in a place where art and reality fused into an inseparable matrix that had nothing and yet everything to do with paint and form, canvas and color.

Whitney set his brush down on the work table and returned to the studio door to ask Atencio if he wanted iced tea or water. Whitney caught his words midthroat: Mousse had jumped onto Atencio's shoulders and straddled his back and neck while Atencio worked to fit the stone in the sand before him. Mousse's claws clung to Atencio's back through his thin shirt, but Atencio smiled like a man in love. Mousse could not smile, but she purred so lustily she forgot to swallow. The drool formed sparkling balls on her furry lips before falling onto Atencio's shirt. Mousse's pleasure soaked the cotton on Atencio's shoulders to a shade just a tad darker than the perfect blue of her eyes, and just a tad lighter than the perfect blue of the summer sky.

Impromptu Infidelities

Atencio was working on his own floor today. Whitney did not go into Mi Ojo, but passed the day in the roar of the canyon's silence. He painted without pause until late in the afternoon. When the patio was completely shaded by the catalpa tree, Whitney took a beer out to the edge of the porch, where he sat and surveyed the rose stones Atencio had placed yesterday near the lilac bushes along the south wall.

The twin kittens, Clem and Clarita, heard him move out of the studio, where they were not allowed, on to the patio, and came bounding out from under his bed to yowl at the door. Whitney let them out of the bedroom and they began their hair-raising chase under the bushes. They were learning to jump. Soon they would be able to leave the patio, and Whitney would have to decide what to do with them.

Mousse sauntered out from the side of the house where she often slept during the heat of the day. Mousse settled against the branches of the lilacs on the rose flagstone near him and ignored her kittens. Self-preservation, Whitney thought, feline emotional insulation. She closed her sky blue eyes and drew within herself. Even drooling all over Atencio, Whitney thought Mousse was the most dignified animal he had ever known.

Whitney was adrift in a place inhabited by soundless forms of light and shadow when he heard a distant bark, and then a shrill yowl. The commotion stopped when Whitney came to waking consciousness. After shifting his back away from the sharp edge of an old floor board, he began to slide back into sleep, when the yowling, and then the barking and yipping, began again. Whitney opened his eyes and stared at the porch ceiling, straining to hear if the sounds were from this world or from a place he had been dreaming about.

Sharp barking came from the north side of the house. Whitney sat up and fumbled for his thongs and then ran out of the patio and around the back of the adobe, where he scanned the mesa behind. Halfway up the hill were three mongrel dogs circling and barking at a half-dead cedar tree. They were not playing. Their tails were down, and their teeth were bared.

From inside the protection of the tree, Mousse leapt, claws extended, at the eyes of one of the dogs. He ducked and backed away, and Mousse retreated back under the thick brush of the cedar branches.

Whitney broke into a clumsy run up the sand of the mesa which was stubbled with pear cactus. Mousse would not be so brave unless the kittens were up there, too.

"Yeah! Shit, git out of there!!" Whitney yelled at the dogs. But he was too far below them to give them pause. He scrambled upward again through the loose stones and sandy soil, but his rubber thongs were getting him nowhere at all. Too much time was passing. Mousse howled like a banshee from inside the brush, and occasionally attacked, lurching out with her small mouth wide open, her ears flat against her skull. Her claws flashed before the dogs' eyes and grazed their noses. But the dogs were getting hungrier. And braver.

Whitney watched Mousse and not the ground and one rubber thong caught on a jagged rock. He fell forwards and jammed his toe into a long prickly pear spine that pierced him clear to the bone.

"Argh!!!" The dogs heard him this time. They glanced back, but when they saw the man on his knees, they returned to their attack, circling the tree. The three were waiting now to catch Mousse with her back to at least one of them, just long enough to get a good bite. Whitney stood again and reached for a baseball-sized stone. He hurled it at the closest dog twenty yards above him. The stone hit the scruffy cur in the shoulder, and the dog retreated, yelping, up the mesa.

The retreat of the first dog broke the intensity of the attack. The other dogs soon followed him up the mesa where they all stopped to watch Whitney limp up the slide towards Mousse.

"Get out of here, you bastards!!" Whitney yelled, waving his arms in huge circles, and pretending to pick up another rock.

Whitney reached the cedar tree and called Mousse. She did not appear. Whitney scanned the mesa top again. The dogs could be lurking over the rim, waiting. Whitney bent down and pulled away the lower branches of the cedar tree. Inside the thin safety of the brush, Mousse still growled and hissed. Her fur was ruffled like a scrub brush straight out from her body. Whitney could see wet patches where either the dogs had mouthed her or her own perspiration had soaked her fur flat. Finally, Mousse blinked and stopped hissing, then began to pant. She seemed to half-recognize Whitney. Still, he decided he would not try to touch her.

Blood blackened the sand behind Mousse.

"Mousse, come here," Whitney said as calmly as he could despite too much adrenaline and his own heart pounding like a hammer into his ribs, "let me see what happened to you."

Mousse looked into the brush behind her and then back to Whitney. It was not Mousse who was bleeding. Whitney knew it was at least one of the kittens.

"Mousse, let me in there or bring them out. Come on, girl, let me help."

Mousse stood and turned around. Behind her, lying against the cedar trunk, tangled in the sage growing at its base, was one of the kittens. His, or her, rear end was caked with blood. The kitten did not move. Mousse began washing her baby's face.

"We've got to get her out of here," Whitney said. "I'm coming under, Mousse. I won't hurt the kitten. Where's the other one?"

Whitney crawled into the thick growth of branches and reached the kitten. From what little markings he could see on the belly, Whitney decided it was the girl, Clarita. When he was close enough to touch her, Whitney heard a timid cry near his ear. It was Clem, apparently unharmed, with his legs wrapped monkey style around a higher section of the tree's trunk.

"Come here, Clem," Whitney extended an arm, but had to pull Clem off the tree. He placed him on his shoulders where Clem sank his claws into Whitney's denim shirt. Whitney looked closely at Clarita. She was still breathing. He slid his hands under her white and grey body and gently lifted her, talking to both Mousse, who continued washing Clarita as he moved her, and to the unconscious kitten. When he rested Clarita against his stomach and began to crawl backwards out of the shelter of the tree, Whitney saw that the left rear leg had been bitten completely off and remained behind in the sand.

Swallowing rapidly and steadying himself, Whitney stood in the bright sun and looked far below at the old tin roof of his house.

"Mousse!" Whitney called, but she was already following. Whitney looked back up at the rim of the mesa, and wondered exactly how he could possibly protect the cats, or himself, from a second attack. But there were only the spiked swords of yucca leaves silhouetted on the mesa top.

The warm blood of Clarita oozed onto Whitney's hands and down his exposed stomach as he descended the hill. At the house he placed Clarita on clean rags he kept in a bucket in the studio. Clem clung to his shoulders all the way back to the bedroom where Whitney pried him claw by claw from his shoulders and back. Mousse remained in the studio, washing every inch of Clarita. After putting Clem under the bed, where he disappeared into the old wool shirt he was born upon, Whitney pulled his boots over his throbbing toe, found his truck keys, and returned to the studio.

"I'll be back with her, Mousse," Whitney said. Mousse continued washing her baby. She was doing an admirable job, considering the amount of dried and fresh blood that covered her kitten's body.

"You stay with Clem, Mousse, I'll be back."

Wrapped in rags and with a bandana tied tightly around the stump of her leg, Clarita lay motionless, except for the slightest movement of her lungs near her shoulders, on the front seat of the truck next to Whitney. It was an hour's drive to Santa Fe. In an emergency, Whitney had heard valley people say, it was possible to make it in forty minutes across the open desert.

Whitney would make it in forty minutes. By the time he reached Santa Fe, he would somehow remember where it was Anna took her pets to the vet.

The sun was beginning to set into the mesas west of Mi Ojo. When Whitney passed the mercantile, its adobe front was cast in a peach glow, reflecting the brightly lit clouds coloring the sky. Whitney felt unreasonably cold, and his torso trembled. He closed the truck's windows and forced himself to breath slowly. There were no other cars. Long shadows fell from the sides of the horses and cattle standing inert in the fields. The valley moved with the gentle ease of early dusk, except for Whitney's truck, which he pushed into high gear before rounding the last curve out of the bosque into the mesa land.

He had forgotten his hat, but had managed to remember his wallet. Fumbling around the glove compartment near Clarita's head, Whitney inadvertently saw how the rags were now completely red—scarlet red, not a red he would ever use, would ever wipe a brush clean of. Whitney shifted his eyes away from the bloody pile back to the road ahead, and wrapped his fingers tightly around the steering wheel.

Whitney was just getting the truck's speed up when the old gas station came into view. Whitney slowed, remembering the way the foolish boy often walked the highway thumbing for rides. The brothers were not outside the station, but Persimillion was. She stood alone, a frizzy-haired angel silhouetted in the doorway, gazing south across the highway into the sky over the desert where a faraway gathering of evening summer clouds were turning into heavenly mountains of purple and rose. Whitney loosened his grip and held up his left hand. He could not tell if Persimillion saw or recognized him, or if she even noticed a truck was passing by. Probably not, Whitney thought, lowering his hand and taking hold of the steering wheel again, and she would not have expected the driver to wave.

Whitney looked over Clarita and out the window to the desert. He had seen it, too: the rare, forgiving beauty of dusk's half-light on the earth that was so ruthless and hard a few hours before. Remarkable, really, this reprieve, this light on the world. A person did not have to paint it to know it. To hunger for it. Whitney could no longer see her—he was a half mile beyond—but Whitney held onto Persimillion's form, steady and reliable in the last light of the abandoned doorway, and the brutal images of the afternoon were pushed momentarily aside.

A red band marked the west, but night was completely upon Santa Fe when Whitney reached the city's limits. For the life of him, Whitney could not remember the name of Anna's vet, or where any vet might be found. When he crested the final hill into Santa Fe, he pulled the truck into a gas station and parked near a public phone booth. Whitney had to stand a moment staring at the booth's glass door before he could remember Anna's home phone number. Even as he dialed, he wasn't certain he had it right.

Naomi answered the Farina telephone.

"Naomi, this is Whitney Slope. Is Anna there? Is she home tonight?"

Whitney knew he sounded strange; his voice was tight, higher than usual. Naomi probably thought he was intoxicated.

"No, Mr. Slope. Mrs. Farina cannot come to the phone." Naomi spoke as if she had a very stiff collar around her neck. Whitney wanted to give that neck a firm, convincing squeeze.

"I did not ask if she could come to the phone," Whitney continued, taking a deep breath and trying to bring his voice down an octave. "This is an emergency. I must talk with Anna, now."

Naomi did not answer. Whitney was afraid she was placing the receiver down to cut him off. But then he heard Naomi clear her strangled throat.

"What sort of emergency? Mr. and Mrs. Farina have friends here from Dallas."

"Oh Christ, Naomi! Get Anna to the phone! My cat's dying!"

Naomi set the phone down hard on a table. Whitney heard her walk away into the house, hopefully to get Anna. Whitney rubbed his hand over his forehead and took another long breath to suppress the gagging sensation in his own throat. Why did people take so damn long to answer the phone?

"Hello," Anna said curtly. "What is it, Mr. Slope? I'm rather busy just now. Could this wait?"

"Anna, thank God! I need help. My cat was attacked by dogs. I need a vet, fast. Her leg was ripped off. Where should I go with her at this hour?"

"Oh,—your cat? When did you get a cat?" Anna paused.

"Where should I go? She's bleeding all over my truck seat? She's dying."

"Uh, let's see; take her to Dr. Morrow, at the north-side plaza. But he won't be there now. It's after hours. I'll call him. I'll have him meet you there. Do you know where it is?"

"No, no."

"By the flower market, and the cemetery—"

"I remember now. I'll be there. Call him. Fast."

Whitney started to hang up the receiver, but yanked the phone back to his mouth.

"Thanks, Anna."

But Anna had disconnected.

Dr. Morrow arrived at his office ten minutes behind Whitney. His assistant came a moment later, and together they examined Clarita on a table in the surgery room in the back of the building.

"You want me to try to save her?" Dr. Morrow asked, holding Clarita in his hands and calmly surveying the hole where her leg had been.

"Yes."

"It will be expensive. She's very young."

Whitney shook his head. "I know. But why don't you go ahead, just save her. If you can. Money is no problem."

Thirty minutes later, Whitney had not heard even the smallest sound from the surgery room. The outer office was dark and silent. Whitney leaned against the front window that looked out at the empty parking lot, and at the rows of identical war-memorial headstones in the cemetery across the road. One solitary street lamp lit the parking lot near his truck.

Anna's red Mercedes pulled in next to Whitney's truck. She walked quickly to the office door. Whitney unlocked it and let her in.

"I can't believe you're really over here," Anna said, peering into the dark waiting room and then back at Whitney. "My God, what I can see of you is really bad. What happened?"

Whitney lifted his shoulders helplessly, turned to a chair, and sat down. He fumbled with his unbuttoned shirt, but he could not work his fingers. His cactus impaled toe throbbed, and the skin of his shoulders burned from Clem's scratches. Everything and everyone seemed remote and unfamiliar. He realized he was glad, very, very glad, to see Anna.

"It has been an atrocious few hours."

Anna stood near him and looked down the hall, where light leaked out from under the surgery room door.

"Operating?"

"Yes. The leg was torn off."

Anna grimaced.

"Oh, that's bad. But he's very good, Dr. Morrow."

Anna and Whitney stared out the front window at the lamp post.

"When did you get a thing for cats, Whitney?"

"I didn't. They got a thing for me. The mother wandered up to my gate one day and stayed. Pregnant. With this one and another one."

"Why are you spending money for surgery if you don't want the kitten?"

Whitney shook his head and looked at Anna. She wore a very expensive and very fitted, black-sequined evening dress that glinted with the single light from the parking lot.

"I didn't say I didn't want her. I'm just saying I didn't go looking for a family of cats."

"Whitney, you're nobody's fool but your own." Anna walked to a chair near Whitney and sat down, crossing her long, silken legs as she touched Whitney's hands. Her hand was warm and light, but it made Whitney flinch.

"Nothing personal, Anna," he said, after she withdrew her hand, "I just feel like I'm about to jump clear out of my skin. It was a shock: the dogs, the blood; the dogs, more blood. Now here in a vet's office in the dark. And I don't remember eating dinner. Or even lunch, for that matter."

Anna fussed with her fingernails and then looked down the hall at the door to surgery.

"Dr. Morrow saved my cat, Scamp. She was bitten in the eye by a prairie rattler. They come in during droughts to drink water from the pool, right in town."

"I thought cats killed snakes, even rattlers?"

"Oh, they can. Usually. I interfered. I saw Scamp circling the snake as it slithered over the deck. I ran out with a broom and tried to knock Scamp away, or scare the snake back towards the fence he came in under. But they both ignored me. The snake struck right under the broom and got her in the eyeball. I was quite hysterical. But Dr. Morrow had the anti-venom waiting, and Scamp came out of it okay."

Whitney and Anna looked at one another across the dark. It seemed to Whitney he knew Anna better in half light. Anna was friendlier when the lights dimmed. It occurred to him that he had never seen Dominga in anything less than full light.

"The eye has no color or sight," Anna continued, "but at least he kept it."

Whitney sighed and rubbed his hands on his legs as if to stimulate circulation.

"I guess nothing's ever guaranteed," he said, "not even between snakes and cats."

"What?"

The door at the end of the hall opened and the waiting room was lit by the florescent lights from surgery. Dr. Morrow walked towards Anna and Whitney, drying his hands with a towel.

"Hello, Mrs. Farina. Mr. Slope, I can't say for sure yet; the kitten might make it. She's survived the loss of blood pretty well. Still, she's in shock; she'll have to stay here for a week or so. The wound has to heal very slowly. Then she could have a pretty normal life. On three legs, of course."

Whitney shook Dr. Morrow's hand.

"Thank you, Doc, for meeting me here and doing this for her. I really do appreciate it."

"I've known Anna Farina a long time," Dr. Morrow said, taking Anna's hand between his own. "She takes very good care of her animals. I'm accustomed to after-hours calls from people like her. Besides, I like to see them all make it."

ℰ

Outside in the parking lot, Whitney leaned his forehead against the cool metal of the truck's roof and stared through the glass at the seat and the pile of bloody rags. It was high-desert evening cool, and Whitney was beginning to shiver. He was thinking about the back door into the High Noon kitchen and some of Juan's enchiladas, when Anna's hands touched his shoulders and neck.

"You can't drive like this, Whitney. Let me make you something to eat first, and some coffee."

Whitney looked over his shoulder at Anna.

"Where? How? You have company. Anna, I didn't mean to impose on you like this. I just did not know anyone else to call for help."

"Thanks. I know that. I'm offering to feed you. Nothing more."

Anna smoothed Whitney's hair down against his neck. He rested his head into the truck again and felt Anna's long, manicured nails against his scalp.

Nothing more had been so much more. Oh so much more. Whitney was not sure he wanted much more. Or if Anna did. But God! He needed some food and time to recoup.

Whitney turned around and straightened his back. He smoothed his bloody shirt and did his best to smile at Anna.

"You're right. I simply cannot drive home like this."

"All right, follow me back to the gallery, and I'll dig up something from my office fridge. Might only be cheese and some frozen fish balls leftover from your opening. They've only been in there a month—I can heat them back to life."

Whitney leaned away from the truck door, but Anna did not move. Instead, she pressed her sequined body against his blood-and paint-smeared shirt, her hips into his sand scuffed jeans, and her perfumed head into his chest. Before Whitney could decide whether or not to put his arms around her, she pulled away.

"Follow me."

If Whitney had not been so fogged by shock, starvation, and the general disorientation of being in Santa Fe, he might have given more credence to the large knot of worry congealing like thick pudding in his stomach. But worry and judgment seemed superfluous now.

Anna parked in the alley behind the gallery. Whitney pulled his truck in behind. He knew, climbing out of the truck, that he was violating his own *numero uno* rule about never parking behind Anna's car anywhere, especially in a Santa Fe alley. But Anna did not say anything or seem disconcerted about the proximity of their vehicles, so Whitney decided things really had changed. There was no reason to feel, or act, like furtive paramours. For some reason, the knot in his stomach loosened. Whitney took in a long draught of the evening air and gazed skyward, just to get his bearings, before entering the Mud Street Gallery.

Alone in the dark of the gallery balcony, Whitney waited while Anna prepared him supper. He was struck by how brief a time had actually passed between this moment now and that moment at the opening when he had first glimpsed some other side of life, a side defined by the very horizon line he now beheld. Whitney had crossed that line; he had made the other side his own. Maybe only a very little bit his own, but his own, nonetheless. Whitney looked down at the top of his truck. He needed to eat. But soon he wanted to be on the road home again. The road to Recuerdos Canyon.

Anna served Whitney a platter of fine cheeses and fish balls and some kind of black bread. On two chairs brought up from the gallery, they sat near the balcony wall, eating in silence, watching the sky for shooting stars, a common enough phenomenon, even over Santa Fe, to make it a reasonable pastime on a summer night. Due west the twinkling lights of Santa Fe ended where the desert opened into a dark galaxy beyond.

"It is very dark where I live," Whitney said, lifting his wine glass and pointing west. "At night. No lights save the stars anywhere. Anywhere at all. Only over the ocean have I ever seen such total black."

Whitney stretched out his long legs and dug his boot heels into the tile before him. He thought about removing his boots to free his aching toe, but it seemed too intimate a gesture.

"Do you like the isolation? I mean, really like it?"

Whitney opened his mouth to answer, but Anna went on talking.

"Doesn't anything make you afraid, or a little nervous, Whitney?"

"I've been nervous for months, Anna. No, really, I have. Since Connie died, I've been anxious about things."

"So you moved? And you're not anxious anymore?"

Whitney thought a moment.

"Most of the time, out in the canyon, I am not anxious. I am happy; I am sad. But I am not anxious."

"It's the people, isn't it, that made you unhappy here," Anna said.

"No, actually, it was the lack of people . . . of people who saw me as just a person sharing life on the planet . . . trying to find my way along."

Anna stared into her seltzer water, her long fingernails tapping the glass.

"I don't want to leave here—my house, my business," Anna said after a long pause. "But things are going to have to change. And change makes me very nervous. Because change can make for disruption and chaos. I don't like my routines disrupted. And I do not like any sort of chaos."

"No one does."

Anna sipped her seltzer and twisted a curl of her hair.

"What are you up to, Anna Farina?"

"It doesn't involve you. It's better if you don't know."

"Did you ask Jack about Burro Alley?"

"Oh. Yes. He didn't say much; just that he and Robertson put together a group of investors who were buying Santa Fe real estate."

Whitney closed his eyes and sighed loudly, sinking into the chair and tilting his head back. When he opened his eyes, he saw the black, star-speckled city sky and felt Anna's warm hands on his thighs. He looked down at her kneeling between his knees.

"Anna, you are, as always, a most gorgeous woman in a black dress on a dark balcony. And, ignoring my own appearance, which must be akin to a prehistoric hunter after a bungled kill, if you are not looking to get us further entangled, then just what are you doing?"

Anna rubbed Whitney's thighs with firm, slow movements. When she pressed her pink glossed nails into his jeans, dust showered the air near her hands.

"I see your desert escapade hasn't cured you of extrapolating and expounding at unnecessary length about intimate matters. I'm not trying to do anything. I'm here. You're here. Some things never change. Like the way you squint at me, half in interest, half in challenge."

Whitney set his glass on the floor and took Anna's silver bound wrists in his hands.

"We don't have to go farther. I didn't mean to challenge you. I did not come here expecting that."

Anna pulled her wrists out of Whitney's grip and placed her hands on the hem of his bloody shirt.

"I know that, Whitney. Neither did I. But maybe I need more impromptu activities . . . you told me once I needed to loosen up."

Anna lifted the open shirt away from Whitney and lightly touched the skin exposed above his belt. Whitney shook his head.

"Anna, no, let's not . . ."

"Is there someone else, Whitney?"

"No."

"Then you should take off this remarkably disgusting shirt. People will begin to talk."

In one smooth movement, Anna pulled the shirt off his shoulders and down his arms, dropping it in a heap on the balcony floor. She stood and looked at Whitney's shoulders where tiny puncture wounds marked Clem's clutch for dear life four hours earlier. Whitney's skin prickled with goose bumps, but before he could improvise another way to get warm, Anna pulled him from the chair and down onto the oriental rug on the balcony floor. She turned him over and lay on top, pinning him with her hips and thighs. Anna's sleek, perfumed body was hot and fragrant, and Whitney forgot how cold he was when Anna pushed his hair back from his forehead and kissed his lips. Whitney realized his last chance for a protest had vanished and reached for the black zipper on her back.

The long-stemmed candle Anna had placed on the balcony wall was nearly burned to its brass base when Whitney was once again able to focus on something beyond Anna's, or his own, body. Looking at the sky beyond the flame of the candle, Whitney saw that the pattern of stars above the balcony had changed.

"The earth has moved," Whitney said in a half whisper, wondering just how much noise had echoed into the rafters and drifted over the balcony wall and down the alley during the past half hour?

Anna laughed into Whitney's neck, and pulled a cotton shawl from the chair over her back.

"What I mean, exactly, Ms. Farina, is that the stars I use to navigate have shifted a bit to the west."

"Time to go home, right Slope?"

"No, that's not my point." Whitney lifted Anna's face from his chest and kissed her on the lips.

"My point is that time flies when you're . . . occupied."

Anna kissed him again and sat up. Whitney had seen Anna a hundred times in candlelight, but never outside, not here. She was remarkably lithe and muscular. He knew she worked at it. But it was her carriage, too. Anna liked her body, and anyone who looked at her knew it.

"I have to go. You can spend the whole night here if you want, Whitney, but I have to go home. Jack's in town."

"I know. Naomi made a point of telling me that. Oh, Lord, what have we done?" Whitney sat up on his elbows and gazed skyward again. "We said never when Jack is in town."

Anna began dressing, staying low so that anyone below in the alley would not see her over the top of the wall.

"It doesn't matter. It's different now. Between you and me; between me and Jack. Different. You know that, don't you?"

Whitney looked at Anna and then reached for his jeans on the tile floor under one of the chairs.

"I do know, about us. But not about Jack. And it still matters. To me. About Jack finding out."

Anna sat on the chair and pulled on a black sling-backed sandal.

"Why do you care if he finds out?"

"Because it's sleazy sleeping with another man's wife. Even with Jack Farina's wife. And I'd like to live another forty years or so."

"I should probably be insulted," Anna said quietly, "and the fact that I'm not, well, what does that say?"

Whitney watched Anna finish with her sandal and then glance at her watch.

"How's it different with Jack, Anna?"

Anna looked at Whitney, but did not seem to hear him.

"Is it hard to be alone all the time? What do you think of when there's no one around and nothing to do? When no one cares what you do . . . or if you even get out of bed in the morning?"

"You think a lot about yourself," Whitney said. "Or your cats. Sometimes about your past, people you've loved—lost. I guess it's hard if you're not used to it."

"How do you get used to it?"

"By doing it, even when it's lousy."

Whitney studied Anna as she picked up the tray of food and blew out the candle, leaving him in the black of the balcony. Whitney draped his shirt over his shoulders after deciding he was not about to put the blood stiff cloth against his body again.

When they reached the alley, Whitney took Anna's keys and opened her door, and then took her hand and helped her into the car.

"You saved me tonight, Anna Farina," he said, kissing her hand.

Anna closed her door, took the keys from Whitney and put them in the ignition.

"You saved me a little bit, too, Whitney. You turned this into a very nice evening. Good night."

Whitney watched the lights of the Mercedes disappear down the alley and into the street before he started the truck. It was after midnight, and the streets of Santa Fe were deserted. Whitney passed only one other car before reaching the edge of town. Once out on the open highway, speeding head-long into the merciful black of the desert country, Whitney thought back over the evening on the balcony. It wasn't that he had been unfaithful to someone else when he told Anna there was no one. No, it was worse. Whitney had been unfaithful to himself and to everything he had worked to secure in the canyon.

Company

Persimillion had never known a man who stayed. She had known men who stayed overnight; back in Mexico, men stayed for beer afterwards, or for a cup of coffee sipped in haste on the front stoop of her *casita* the next morning. But Persimillion had never known a man who stayed.

Atencio de Jesús stayed. Not for entire days, not often overnight. Atencio's staying was the kind that involved Persimillion's heart. Persimillion might have asked Atencio to stay, but she knew he had a house and a mother three miles up the highway in the village of Mi Ojo. Persimillion did not expect Atencio to give those up for nothing.

Atencio always came to the old station on foot, but he said he had a job and a car in the village. Pepé's eyes followed Atencio around like he was a millionaire or a king, or the favored son of one, after Atencio mentioned the car. Or maybe it was because Atencio had a job. In Mexico, any car, any sort of job, meant opportunity. Atencio de Jesús had all the opportunity Pepé had ever dreamed of.

"I do not have money," Atencio told Persimillion one evening, "but I can buy groceries or parts for my car. Soon, I will drive my car here, and we will all go for a ride into the mountains."

Persimillion Ramirez had never been in mountains. Not up in mountains, the world somewhere far below and the sky and then heaven above, only closer. Persimillion had walked around mountains, had seen them far away like clouds, and then close before her like an endlessly rising wall. She nodded in agreement to Atencio's idea about driving up into mountains, but Persimillion did not imagine such a journey to be anything more than words: Atencio might be gone by then; Atencio might forget about the mountains, about her, after his car was fixed. Or his car might never be fixed. Back home in Mexico, most cars were never fixed. Maybe cars were fixed for an afternoon, only to leave the owner stranded even farther from home with worse problems than he had the morning before.

Atencio might remember about the mountains and about offering to drive her up into the mountains, but Persimillion could be gone by then, sent back to Mexico on a bus, or pushed on ahead, somewhere up the narrow highway, when that policeman who pretended not to see them moved them on. Good things often came too late. So Persimillion enjoyed good things, like Atencio's car taking them into the mountains, in her head, just in case they never came to be.

It was a nice thought, Persimillion told Atencio. "It doesn't need to happen to be nice."

Atencio de Jesús spoke Persimillion's language, and he understood even more. Even so, Atencio did not say much. He arrived at the station door just about supper time, barefoot, sometimes, but always standing straight and clean. And Atencio never came empty handed. He brought his mother's tortillas and chile stew; he brought apples and water, beef jerky and coffee, in a pack he carried over his shoulder.

One late afternoon, when Persimillion believed the heat should have kept him home in the shade of his house, Atencio brought an old watch for Alfredo. Just like Persimillion knew he would, Alfredo threw it in the sand and then circled around it.

"My father's old watch," Atencio said as he watched Alfredo's inspection of the watch under the cottonwood trees. "It doesn't work, you see." Atencio looked across the sand of the station at Persimillion and Pepé. "Things don't have to work to be valuable."

"It works for Alfredo," Pepé said.

The first evening Atencio returned to Persimillion and the old station—the first visit after the incident with her brothers at the river—Persimillion was wary. She did not stand for him, but remained settled on the door stoop. Persimillion felt the old apprehension, the worry, all the familiar predecessors for pain, press in around her head. But by dusk, when the mourning doves began their song in the cottonwoods, she knew Atencio did not come looking to share her blanket, or touch her breasts.

Atencio de Jesús touched Persimillion with his green eyes and his soft voice. It was a pleasure, like being full, being pregnant, having Atencio beside her sharing her door stoop and her view of the southern sky. After two visits, Persimillion knew Atencio came to share supper and a few words, silence, too, and evening calm. Atencio wanted to share calm; like Persimillion, Atencio wanted to find the calm that would stay.

Even Alfredo the Foolish got so he remembered a few moments of calm each day. Alfredo seemed to have a frenzy building in his head, and it was difficult for him to fall asleep. But each afternoon, Alfredo waited by the gas pumps for a sign of Atencio the Calm walking towards him on the highway.

"He won't come every day," Persimillion would say to Alfredo. But she got so she watched Alfredo while he watched for Atencio. Persimillion wanted to know the moment Atencio came into view, a thin stick following the highway's side, as he moved out of the protective shade of the green bosque into the riveting glare of the open desert.

When Atencio came into view, Persimillion raised her huge body from the ground of the doorway. With laborious joy, she folded all the blankets, smoothed her hair, and adjusted her pants evenly around her waist. She set sticks for a fire out back of the station, and rubbed the tin plates and cups shiny clean with the hem of her blouse.

"Pepé!" Persimillion called out back into the cottonwoods, "bring your matches. Start the fire. Tonight we will cook! Tonight we have company!"

Atencio told Persimillion about his stone floor, about the quarry across the desert where the stone shone like sundown, a place where his father used to take him. Persimillion knew Atencio's father was strong and alive in that quarry, and that it gave Atencio courage, walking way out there and talking to the stone. When Atencio spoke about his dead father both of the Ramirez brothers listened: Persimillion knew they were listening to Atencio and thinking about his father like he was their father, too. Everyone needed a father like Feodoro de Jesús. No wonder Atencio still wept for him.

Like a father, Atencio took the boys fishing. Atencio had found a way to keep Alfredo away from the water by giving him an empty can and telling him to fill it with worms. Pepé and Atencio caught fish in the evening while Alfredo dug in the dirt for worms. Alfredo always found worms, but the can was hardly ever full because Alfredo ate them before they could become bait.

There was a consistency to Atencio's visits that calmed the Ramirez family. But Persimillion knew that Atencio was not always calm, that he made an effort to be calm and peaceful so that Alfredo and Pepé would feel calm and peaceful.

After a late supper, more times than not, Atencio left the station before midnight and walked into the dark, a sliver of the summer moon guiding him home. Persimillion watched Atencio until he was just more of the black, and then she watched longer in case he turned back.

Sometimes Atencio was too tired to walk the three miles back home in the descending cool of the desert night. On these nights, he curled up alongside the brothers with his head on Persimillion's lap. Atencio fell asleep like one of her own. On those nights, Persimillion made an extra effort to remain awake. Instead of lying down on her own blanket, she sat happily exhausted, her family safe in the nest of her thighs, her back against the cooling adobe of the station wall.

Persimillion knew Atencio de Jesús liked to watch the last of the firelight flickering in her black eyes. His eyes rested in her eyes until he slipped down inside himself and fell into a restful sleep. And then Persimillion's eyes became Atencio's eyes. Persimillion could see perfectly what Atencio saw. Persimillion could see the fears following Atencio. And she could see what Atencio was looking for up ahead, tomorrow, or farther, in heaven, maybe, because Persimillion was looking for it, too: a place where the fears couldn't keep calling after them. A place where the past couldn't keep claiming them as its own.

Full Hands

The good padre Leo believed he had his hands full even before his nephew, Miguel Gonzales, walked into the parish library in full uniform and greeted Pepé in fine, flawless, formal Spanish.

"*Buenos días,* Pepé," Miguel said, removing his hat and then his sunglasses, which he placed in his uniform pocket. "And you, *tío* Leo, *mi padre,* how are your hands today? Are you cutting that board yourself, or are you letting your hired hand do that for you?"

Padre Leo was, indeed, holding a freshly sawed board he himself had cut; and his hands were, indeed, aching like they had been pounded by something worse. But it was not padre Leo's hands that made him ache. It was his handsome nephew, holster and handcuffs gleaming against his black clothes, walking into the parish library where he knew full well the boy Pepé was this morning making book shelves.

"*Sí, sí,* I am letting him help. He is doing far too much as it is." Padre Leo put the new shelf down onto the floor and marked its future position on the wall with a pencil he kept behind his ear.

The good padre knew without looking directly at him that Pepé was frozen in midhoist over the library desk. Padre Leo knew from the way Pepé was looking at Miguel that Pepé was finding it hard to breathe.

"This is my nephew, Pepé, my only nephew, Miguel," padre Leo said in Spanish to Pepé.

The good padre watched Pepé climb down from the ladder and timidly set the tape measure and hand saw on the table between himself and the six-foot-one–inch state trooper. Padre Leo wanted to tell Miguel he had bought these tools for Pepé, but his tongue seemed stuck to his teeth. Instead, padre Leo thought how Miguel must have recently shined his boots, for they reflected the sunlight of the open parish window like pools of black water. The good padre swallowed loudly and found his tongue:

"Please, my good friend, go on working while we talk in the next room."

Padre Leo placed a throbbing hand on Pepé's thin shoulder before turning to speak to Miguel.

"It is so nice to have you stop by today, Miguel. If you had called, first, I would not have been so busy."

Pepé remained paralyzed near the library table as padre Leo and his nephew left the room.

"You have given him quite a scare, you know," padre Leo said to Miguel in a hushed voice when they reached the inner office. "Why did you come today? Why did you not call first?"

Miguel smiled and then shrugged. "I cannot change the laws, my good uncle. We understand one another, you and I, but this time you are pretending not to notice the passage of time. I cannot feign so much ignorance."

"I know it has been a month."

"More, *tío.*"

"But there are complications with these."

"There are complications with all of them. They are illegal immigrants. They are called aliens by my superiors, may God forgive them. And I emphasize *illegal* and *my superiors.*"

The good padre shook his head and rested his lumpy hand on Miguel's shoulder, which was nearly a foot above his own.

"I have asked too much of you. God knows I would not ever want to jeopardize your job and hard-earned respect for anyone. But what can I do for them? They are hardly able to move on, anywhere. The woman is so . . . large. The other boy is so, so . . . incompetent."

"He should be in an institution. He will hurt himself you know. It is himself he will harm." Miguel bent down and looked into his uncle's eyes, waiting for agreement.

"Possibly. But the woman, she has lost so much, her children; I do not even know how. The grief has strangled her memory; the words are lost in her throat where they choke her. It is difficult to walk, to move at all, Miguel, with so much grief to carry. How would they move on, to where, to what?"

"They got this far, *mi padre.* Give them credit for getting this far."

"It was luck, Miguel, that they have survived here this long. Luck and the grace of God."

"And which are you providing, uncle? Are you the luck, or are you the grace?"

Padre Leo smiled at his nephew. He always admired Miguel's gift for words, even when they cornered him.

"I think I am a little of both. But I am hoping to find more of the grace before I leave this earth."

"You would just give it away, *tío*. And then wait for a little more, and give that away, and then a little more, on and on. You would never stop and save yourself some."

"God's grace cannot be taken away, Miguel. Or owned and saved. It can only be shared."

Miguel sighed and put his black hat on his head. Before putting on his sunglasses, he glanced at the closed door to the library.

"Share a little more, padre, but only a little more. I am living too much with my eyes looking the other direction."

"God bless you, Miguel. Only a little longer."

Miguel left by the back door to the garden. Padre Leo took out his bandana and wiped his damp forehead and the skin of his thin neck, which stuck to his clerical collar. Before he reentered the library, he held his hands up before his eyes. The pain curved them into bony balls. He really did need help. Pepé's being here was a good thing because the good padre Leo could no longer pull the tape measure from its casing, and he could hardly cut a straight edge across a board, even with the old, familiar handsaw his own father had given him half a century ago. Padre Leo was not fooling himself; he could not do his work alone.

When the good padre Leo opened the door to tell Pepé what a good helper he was, a Godsend—how padre Leo could not continue his work without him—padre Leo found an empty room. The high noon heat slowed padre Leo's sense of sadness, but he still felt an ache, not from his hands, but from his heart, when he saw Pepé's half-sawed board left against the wall. Padre Leo shuffled slowly to the table and touched the smooth wood handle of his father's antique handsaw. Set carefully beside the old saw was the new tape measure padre Leo had bought just this morning, down at the mercantile. The good padre had carried it home in his pocket, up the slow climb of the hill to the church on the plaza. While he walked, he thought about how it would be Pepé's first gift in New Mexico, his first job. It brought a sense of his own boyhood back to padre Leo, and the joy of building with one's father.

Padre Leo had held the tape measure against his hip, kept it cupped in his curved palm, until Pepé came in for work.

"This is not just for your work with me, Pepé," padre Leo told him when he brought out the measure from his pocket and put it into Pepé's hand. "It is for all the work ahead."

"What if there is no work for me here?"

"God has work for all of us on his earth. Take this measure in good faith. The work will come."

Padre Leo had tried to explain: this was for Pepé. Padre Leo picked up the measure and held it between his two hands. Padre Leo could not use it. He set it back down on the table. He would save this measure for Pepé.

Comprende

Whitney Slope was stretching the last corner of a three-by-five-foot canvas onto its pine wood frame when Tomas's truck roared up the side of the house and stopped. Whitney squinted into the sun of the patio and wished the orange vehicle were a mirage.

"*¿Qué pasa,* Slope?" Tomas slammed the door behind him and leaned against the truck. He gazed, once again, at the tin roof Whitney had yet to nail down before the monsoons. "Looks like I caught you in the act of working. How 'bout that?"

"You can catch me most any day, Tomas," Whitney said, shooting the last staples into the wood to secure the canvas. "Why aren't you at work today?"

"Oh, just a day off. They say I work too much. The state ends up owing me money. But, you know, it's funny: I'm more at home with my highway crew most of the time than with the wife and kids. Must be the man in me."

Whitney straightened up and squinted again at Tomas. He lifted the stretched canvas and took it into the studio, not bothering to invite Tomas to follow. Tomas would follow.

"So, you painting some expensive ones, Slope?" Tomas had brought a beer in with him, and he popped its top while he surveyed the paintings around the studio. Whitney needed to move some of them into storage until he decided whether to show them or keep them.

"I just paint. The rest of the world decides if I'm painting something expensive or not. Frankly," Whitney paused and sat down on his stool in front of his table of paints and brushes, eyeing the ungessoed canvas leaning against the wall in front of him, "I don't give a blessed damn if these are worth a dime. These are for me."

Tomas sucked at his beer and raised his eyebrows at Whitney. Whitney picked up a brush and then set it down, picking up the larger one next to it.

"What are you doing out here today, Tomas? Something for the house? Or are you socializing? I really need to use the rest of the afternoon getting started on this canvas."

Whitney swiveled the stool and faced Tomas.

"A bit of both. I wanted to look over what Atencio's been doing to the patio. Told my mother I'd check it out and make sure he's not going to drain the water from the roof back into the house or something. You never know with Atencio. Never know."

"You walked past it." Whitney pointed the brush at the studio door and the patio beyond. "He's about three fourths done. And I can't see a thing wrong with it. Your brother is a very fine stone mason. Very fine."

"Gifted, huh?"

"Yeah, he is. Gifted. But it's not a curse, you know?"

Tomas walked to the door.

"Yeah, it is—out here," Tomas said. He viewed the patio from the studio, sipping his beer.

"But what does he do next, Slope? You got any more suggestions?" Tomas turned around and spoke to Whitney, who remained, brush in hand, watching Tomas. "That's what worries me, and my mother, I imagine. Now what? Sure, he's done okay while he's had this work here. But there isn't a big need around Mi Ojo or Tomita for new patios. We live with the sand, or the mud. The artist of the stone floors isn't in big demand out here in *el valle de los mexicanos-americanos. ¿Comprende?*"

Whitney swiveled back to his canvas and twirled the brush between his fingers.

"*Comprendo*, Tomas. But there are people in Santa Fe who would hire Atencio. If Atencio wanted it, he could have a lot of work. He's that good."

"In the gringo world? Atencio would be gobbled up, spit out. *Un muerto.* And he's that unreliable. You know, just like I do, that Atencio is a walking emotional time bomb. *¡El fatal!*"

"I don't think so, Tomas. I've been with him a lot over the last three weeks. He's changing. He's trying. He wants this to work."

Tomas tilted his beer can skyward and finished it.

"Well, so, how are you liking life in Mi Ojo? The loneliness getting to you yet?"

"Not hardly."

"You've caused quite a stir among the young ladies in the valley. *El Huero Misterioso.*"

"I'm just an ordinary kind of guy, Tomas."

"My mother thinks you're nice enough."

Whitney did not respond, although Tomas was obviously waiting for him to say something profound. Whitney was side-tracked thinking about Dominga's talking to Tomas about him.

"She's been dressing different, my mother." Tomas waved his hand around his shoulders. "Skirts, barefoot doing the laundry. She's been leaving her hair down, like a girl. Like Atencio." Tomas had to stop and think about this last observation. "Next thing you know, she'll be walking the highway in those foreign pants." Tomas sighed, the weight of the world on his chest. "I found an envelope from the registrar of the Capital City Community College. Imagine, college at her age."

"She's not that old," Whitney said. "And even if she were, she could still go to school. This is the late twentieth century, Tomas."

"My wife thinks Dominga just needs more children," Tomas continued, chuckling. "Adopt a few more. There are plenty in the valley who could use her loving care."

Whitney turned Tomas's direction.

"Adopt more?" Whitney asked.

"Yeah. She adopted me, and Dennis and Robert. Our mother died when I was a baby."

"Of course she did," Whitney said. He nodded at the canvas while he took in this latest and very important fragment about the life of Dominga de Jesús.

"Clouds," Tomas said suddenly, pointing at Whitney's painting on the windowsill closest to the patio door. "She wants to study clouds. Now, what would a woman her age do with clouds?"

"I don't know, Tomas." Whitney stood up and with his hands on his hips, brush still in hand, faced Tomas across the studio. "But I know that if you don't let her do something of her own while she still has the inclination, you're going to lose her. One way or another, you're going to lose her."

"What the hell does that mean, Slope?"

"It means that there's more to Dominga than adopting children and taking care of her house. Or her trailer. She's trying to remember what those things are. You might try, too."

Tomas whistled through his teeth and shook his head. "Women's liberation! That's in Santa Fe, Slope. In Mi Ojo, we don't have the luxury. No revolution out here. We just survive."

"Is there anything I can help you with before you go, Tomas? I have a lot of work to do on this canvas."

"I'll just look at the patio." Tomas was still chuckling to himself as he left the studio. Outside, he walked around the flagstones. Tomas stopped and stood on each of the rose stones, kicking their sides and looking for one to shift. Whitney watched. He knew not a one of them would budge. They were set for life in that sand, and fitted so tightly, water would have a hard time seeping between.

Tomas looked over at the studio door and saw Whitney watching him.

"Not bad for a skinny kid. Not bad. Maybe he's building some muscle after all."

"He can lift more weight than I can," Whitney said, opening the screen door and standing on the porch. "Atencio has many talents no one can see."

"Now, that cow he's dating seems to know about his unseen talents," Tomas said, chuckling and shaking his head. "Have you ever seen anyone so large? Only Atencio would try to put his arms around a bull mama like her. God! I guess when you're desperate, you take what comes your way. Sweet Jeesus!"

"I can't imagine it's any of our business," Whitney said. "And looks aren't everything."

Tomas guffawed and waved his arm skyward in protest.

"¡Hijola! Slope, I'd bet my truck you've never made it with a woman who was less than semigorgeous. I mean, I've seen Juárez whores with more physical attraction than that fat sister at the old station. People like her should be herded back to Mexico. And will be, soon, if they don't move on."

Whitney looked at the rose stones, at their gentle fluctuations in color and size. Mousse had come to sit by the kitchen door where she washed her back and paws. Clem and Clarita, who had returned from the vet last week, were asleep in his bedroom. Whitney hoped they would not come to the door: he had a feeling Tomas would have something ignorant and insulting to say about Clarita's three legs.

"The difference being, Tomas, the Juárez whore doesn't give a damn about you, or herself, although she might pretend to with her favors and moans and all; and that woman, Persimillion, probably cares a whole lot—about herself, about Atencio, about the whole damned world that doesn't even deserve it, or her."

Whitney knelt and put his hand on Mousse's head. Mousse started to purr and pushed her ear into Whitney's open hand. "Give me a choice, Tomas? I'd take the fat sister any day."

Tomas snuffled his doubt into his hand and walked to the porch.

"Well . . . " Whitney stood. "I've got work. You tell Dominga the patio's coming alone just fine."

Tomas walked the length of the porch to the patio gate and then turned around.

"I'm on to you, Slope, ¿sabe? People like you like to think you can rescue people because you have money, huh?" Tomas looked across the hot air of the patio between them, his eyes direct but not hostile. "And you know what, Slope? We'll probably end up having to rescue you."

Tomas chuckled and looked down at his boot that dug into the edge of one of the stones. He managed to loosen a little sand, but not enough to unseal the stone.

"You know, he's got to find some real work. He's got to face the real world one of these days. Get his head out of the clouds. People like Atencio can't live like you, Slope. He needs a job. He needs a schedule."

"I have a job," Whitney said to Tomas's back as he opened the truck door. Tomas waved a skeptical hand and laughed back over his shoulder.

"Imbecile," Whitney muttered under his breath as he walked back into the studio with Mousse on his arm.

Tomas started his truck and left. Whitney held Mousse against his shoulder and listened to her throaty purr.

"Comprendo," Whitney told Mousse. *"Comprendo."*

Tomas was the one who did not understand. Because, in fact, there was a revolution going on in Mi Ojo. That was exactly what was going on out here. Individual uprisings: individuals rising up into the face of their individual captors.

The Blush of Midsummer

Dominga carried an armful of oranges that had arrived at the mercantile this morning on an old migrant worker's truck. She planned to make orange juice and take it to Atencio and the padre Leo. Dominga balanced the large oranges against her chest and waited at the counter for Clay to give her a sack. Someone walked up beside her. Dominga turned and faced Whitney Slope.

"Good morning, Dominga," Whitney said, taking off his hat and pushing his hair back from his forehead. "You like oranges, I guess."

Dominga laughed and looked down at the plump fruit balanced on her arms and breasts. She was blushing, an infuriating habit she seemed to have developed around Whitney Slope.

"Yes, well, the good padre Leo loves orange juice. And Tomas gave me an electric squeezer a few birthdays back. I'll make a pitcher of fresh juice from these."

Clay was watching: actually, Dominga noticed, he was looking at her full, red- and purple-flowered skirt.

"Clay, a bag, please," Dominga said. "What brings you to town this morning, Mr. Slope?"

"Well, Mrs. de Jesús, I needed some groceries and my mail." Whitney leaned onto the counter beside her. Clay placed the twelve oranges in a paper bag. "And I wanted to talk to you about the patio."

"The patio?" Clay asked.

"Yes, the patio Atencio is putting in for me in the canyon," Whitney answered, still looking at Dominga. Dominga picked up the bag of oranges.

"*Muchas gracias,* Clay."

Dominga started walking to the door. Whitney followed.

"Is there a problem with the patio, Mr. Slope?" Dominga asked. Clay had left the counter and gone to the other side of the mercantile where he was unpacking a box of canned goods. But Dominga knew Clay was still listening.

"Oh no, there's no problem—Dominga, is there some social law or something around Mi Ojo that says you have to call me Mr. Slope in public?"

Dominga laughed and glanced over the aisles at Clay. In truth, she had not even noticed that she was calling Whitney Mr. Slope.

"No."

"Then why do you do that?" Whitney followed Dominga out into the sunshine and then across the asphalt towards his truck.

"I don't know." Dominga saw that Whitney was not going to his truck, but was walking her home to the trailer. She was afraid to look around the mercantile or across the highway at the post office to see who was watching them. But what did it matter, anyway? She was a grandmother. Dominga shifted the bag onto her hip and headed down the side of the store towards her house.

"I really hoped to have some coffee with you, Dominga," Whitney said. "Do you have a few moments?"

"Yes." Dominga climbed the trailer steps and opened the door before Whitney could reach it. When they were both inside and she had set the oranges down on the kitchen counter, Dominga turned and faced the tall Anglo with blue-stained cuticles and eyes to match.

"Tomas said you were painting a lot of clouds."

"I am. And Tomas told me you were thinking about going back to school to study them."

Dominga put the water pot on the stove and lit the burner.

"Yes, I am. Sounds foolish, I know."

"Hardly. Dominga, why should it sound foolish?"

"Because of my age. Because of my, well, I haven't done anything outside of Mi Ojo since I was a teenager at the Archdiocese's summer camp near Santa Fe."

Whitney sat down on the overstuffed sofa. Dominga was glad the old afghan was gone; she wished she could rid the room of the old couch as easily.

"Don't discount your needs, Dominga."

"Tomas thinks I am abandoning Atencio, and the grandchildren, thinking about going to college in Santa Fe. I'd still come home every night."

"Of course. Lots of women your age go back to school."

"My car doesn't work very well. Tomas says I could get stranded in the city."

"You could. But you could find help. From what I've seen, you're a very resourceful woman."

Dominga stared out the window at the adobe house. Atencio was standing by the De Soto. What if her decision to go to school caused Atencio to lapse into drinking again?

"It's not necessary, though, for me to go to school. Maybe it's just a passing fancy. I have so much to do for the church, for the English class I teach, for my family."

Whitney sat forward on the old sofa, his hat in his hands.

"My sister died before she gave herself the chance to find out which passing fancies in her life were necessary."

Dominga heard the water boiling, went to the stove, and took the pot off the burner. She was flushed, again, her shoulders pink with heat. Not because she was embarrassed, but because she had never seen Whitney forceful or insistent. He was almost angry with her.

"I'm sorry," Dominga said, as she measured some ground coffee into the boiling water. "I'm sorry she died. You cared for her very much."

"Very much." Whitney gazed at Dominga across the trailer. "I miss her, although I saw Connie only twice a year or so. She was a very talented artist. She could draw animals that a biologist would admire. Only she never had a chance to show herself or the world— even her daughter—what she could do."

Dominga sat down at the dinette. "I see."

"The last things she drew were like maps to the insides of her body . . . the territories of the cancer. Her daughter, Caroline, found them. Connie had titled the sketchbook "The Approach of My Death." I haven't seen it yet."

Dominga looked at the house across the sand from the trailer, and up at the blue sky over the thick green cottonwoods. No clouds today. But soon it would be late July, and the rains would begin. The approach of the rainy season would signal the death of midsummer. Everything would change with the rain.

"That's why you wanted Atencio to work at the canyon," Dominga said.

"I don't understand."

"It was never about a job, or money, for Atencio. You wanted him to have a chance to show himself what he could do."

"I never thought of it that way," Whitney said.

Dominga returned to the kitchen counter and after adding cold water to the pot to settle the grounds, poured them each a cup of coffee. She handed Whitney his mug and then sat down at the dinette.

"Tomas says I am filling Atencio with ideas he can never use," Whitney continued. "What do you think, Dominga?"

"I do not believe he drinks at all anymore," Dominga said. "That could be the result of the work at his house, or your house. He's been tinkering with the De Soto's engine in the early evenings. Or maybe it's Persimillion. You know, Atencio has taken those boys under his wing. Seems silly, his wings being so fragile—but he gets some kind of security from them. Or maybe from himself, seeing himself the father."

"Tomas told me Atencio is with Persimillion a lot."

"Yes," Dominga said, smiling. "Atencio loves Persimillion's heart, which he says is the size of the sun and twice as bright."

"It is not surprising," Whitney said. "She is a woman of enormous proportions."

Dominga chuckled good naturedly.

"I make extra food for Atencio. I know he shares everything he has with Persimillion and the boys. People around the village are always giving me various accounts and opinions about Atencio's visits to the gas station."

"Does it bother you, Dominga?"

"No. Their opinions are uninformed. They see him walking home at midnight, or dawn, along the highway. They assume certain things. I tell them he's a grown man; his life is his own."

"Just like you," Whitney interrupted.

"I don't walk the highway at night," Dominga said. Although she had thought a good deal about it—at dawn, at midnight, lying awake on her bed, the trailer window wide open to the stars. Dominga had thought about walking barefoot out onto the desert, of crossing the acequia and dropping her nightgown into the cool waters.

"No, Dominga, I mean that you're a grown woman. Your life is your own."

Dominga looked at Whitney. He had not touched his coffee. Maybe he did not come for coffee. Or to talk about the new patio in the canyon.

"Mr. Rodriguez told me he often sees Atencio in the late afternoon fishing with the brothers at the river," Dominga said. "Two days ago, the boys were downstream from Atencio. Something happened, and the young boy, Alfredo, began to scream. Mr. Rodriguez watched Atencio carry him through the thick sage and grass along the edge of the bosque. Mr. Rodriguez asked me if I knew what had happened.

"I asked Atencio about that," Dominga continued, "he told me Alfredo was stung by a bee and that the boy just collapsed. Atencio carried the boy up to the church where the good padre Leo pulled out the stinger and put ointment on the wound—and prayed. Alfredo wanted the padre to pray for him. He said, 'Pray me go home.' So padre Leo prayed that God would guide Alfredo home."

"Atencio is very strong," Whitney said to Dominga after a long silence. "I am continually amazed by his strength."

"They say the boy is foolish, completely ignorant of the ways of the world," Dominga said, gazing into the space between her and Whitney, "but I told the good padre Leo, 'That may be, but that boy is not ignorant of the ways of God.' Like a newborn, wet and wrinkled from the womb, Alfredo has one foot in heaven."

Dominga looked out the window at Atencio's house.

"Alfredo is with Atencio today. He pretends to fix the car . . . he imitates Atencio's every move."

Dominga watched Atencio come out of his house with a tool box. Alfredo followed at his heels. Atencio opened the De Soto's door and bent down under the dash. Alfredo did the same.

Whitney extricated himself from the deep sofa cushions and walked to the window that looked out at the De Soto.

"My God, that old car is standing evenly on four tires."

The glass on the front windshield was clean and shiny, as was the chrome around the fenders and headlights. The De Soto gleamed with dignity and purpose in the cactus-infested sand between the trailer and the old adobe house, like a landlocked ship waiting for its return to the open sea.

Atencio opened the hood of the De Soto, then walked around and climbed into the car and turned on the engine. Alfredo sat beside him, his furrowed brow imitating Atencio's as he listened to the engine. Atencio revved it for a few minutes, then turned the evenly idling engine off. When he closed the car door behind him, he carefully wiped the chrome of the handle with a rag he had in his pants pocket. Alfredo did the same with a similar rag Atencio must have given him.

"When did he get the new jeans?" Whitney asked.

"I ordered them from Clay's catalogue," Dominga said. "Atencio was reluctant to wear them. He says they are hot and stiff. But for work on the car, he agreed they are better protection."

"Will he drive it soon?"

"When he passes the driver's test again," Dominga said. "His license expired six years ago."

"He has done a wonderful job on that old car," Whitney said before sitting down at the table across from Dominga. She saw that his coffee remained on the end table near the sofa.

"We used to say God spoke through Atencio's hands," Dominga said, "But I don't know anymore."

"Why not?" Whitney asked.

"Could God have wanted Atencio's hands used for war, and death? How does a mother reconcile such things? What can God be saying? I do not know, Whitney. I cannot justify these things to my own heart. Perhaps the heart of God feels differently. Perhaps God is more forgiving of the ways of men than mothers are."

"Perhaps," Whitney said after a painful silence.

Dominga felt Whitney's eyes on her. She looked at him over her coffee mug.

"How old was your sister?" she asked.

"Forty-eight."

"And you wonder what God is saying when he takes someone away who has so much yet to do, ¿sí?"

"Sí."

Whitney stared out the window at Atencio, and Alfredo beside him. Dominga studied Whitney's face and eyes.

"How are your cats, Whitney? The kitten is all right?"

"Clarita is fine. I call her Three-Legs now." Whitney was still lost somewhere in another thought. Dominga waited for him to return. After a moment, he sighed and looked across the table at her. "Three-legs follows me around all day and sleeps under the bed sheet with me at night. Her twin brother, Clem, still goes walking with me. He always has one eye on the horizon, but he's a good sprinter and climber. You know, even Three-Legs can scale a tree in the flash of an eye."

"You sound like a father talking about his children."

"I guess I do." Whitney looked back at Atencio and Alfredo near the De Soto. "When Atencio works in the patio, Mousse is his shadow. She sits within reach of him, or perches on his shoulders and back. Atencio has a way with the cats. I have even seen Mousse ride Atencio's shoulders when he walks about the patio examining his work, and then back and forth to the truck, or into the kitchen for water. Has he told you about her?"

"Not the cat," Dominga laughed. "Only about Persimillion."

"They belong together," Whitney said.

"Persimillion and Atencio?"

"No. Well, maybe. I mean Mousse and Atencio." Whitney drummed his long fingers on the table and stared at the adobe house.

"Did you not like my coffee this morning?" Dominga finally asked.

Whitney was not listening to her. "I'll ask Atencio if he wants Mousse to live with him. I'll give him a large supply of cat food and an old shirt." Whitney looked at Dominga. "The rest will be up to Mousse."

Dominga cleared Whitney's coffee mug and walked to the sink. Whitney watched her.

"I have to make this orange juice," she said. "I want to take it up to the padre."

Dominga pulled the squeezer out of the cabinet under the sink and rinsed it under the tap.

"Will you come and see the house, Dominga?"

"Your house?"

"Yes . . . your sister-in-law's house."

"Well, of course, sometime." Dominga fumbled with a hair pin that was becoming loose near the nap of her neck.

"How about this week? For lunch? I want you to tell me what kinds of clouds I'm painting."

"Lunch? This week? I'll see."

"Tomas wouldn't approve, would he?" Whitney asked.

"You don't like Tomas, do you?" Dominga took the hair pins from her hair. "Tomas is difficult, I know. He's opinionated and brash, but he makes up for his rudeness by having a very steady head. Tomas will never surprise you. Tomas isn't unpredictable."

"Like Atencio, as Tomas is always reminding me." Whitney's eyes, like Dominga's, followed Atencio and his foolish, hobbling apprentice as they walked away from the De Soto and around the side of the adobe house.

Dominga's braid unraveled in her hands. She began to braid it again when Whitney stood and walked around the counter and took her hair in his hands.

"I used to braid my sister's hair," he said quietly. "And then Caroline's. But she cut it last summer."

Dominga closed her eyes as Whitney's experienced hands pulled and laced her hair down her back. She felt his arm as he reached over her shoulder and took the rubber band from the counter and snapped it around the bottom of the braid.

"Thank you," Dominga said. She turned around and faced Whitney. Dominga's head reached the middle of his chest. Her cheeks were flushed and she looked away, but Whitney's hand took her chin and guided her face back toward his.

"De nada, Dominga de Jesús."

But Dominga could see in Whitney's eyes how he was lying.

Mousse Loves Atencio

Atencio was ready to believe the snakes were gone. He had not seen a sign of them in more than a month. But the stone floors were not yet completely finished in the house, and until they were, Atencio would sleep outside—on the rope hammock Whitney Slope had given him.

Or so Atencio intended until the cat with the deep blue eyes came to live with him in his grandmother's house. Mousse walked into the old house one evening like it was the friendliest place she had ever set paw. She jumped up onto the kitchen table and began to wash her black fur, pausing to sniff the night air that was fragrant with the flowering tamarisks that bloomed along the acequia's banks. Mousse purred in the dark kitchen just like she had purred in the high noon light of the canyon patio.

Atencio almost stopped his trips to the quarry after Mousse moved in with him. But then he reconsidered: he was so close, now, to completion. And he had not completed more than short sentences in so many years; the stone floor was a goal he was beginning to believe he would actually reach.

The snakes of the past were buried beneath the people and places of Atencio's present. There was the De Soto, close now to mobility. And there was Persimillion and her brothers, who had no mobility whatsoever, but who would need it—and therefore Atencio and the De Soto—one day soon. Atencio had known people like them before, over there, in Nam, people at home nowhere and everywhere. But the people over there, in the past, had not spoken his language; they had not welcomed Atencio and his attempts to help into their lives; they had not looked at him like a man whose hands and heart they trusted.

And there was the cat, Mousse. Whitney had her spayed in Santa Fe and then told Atencio she was his cat now. Three days ago, Mousse had come back from the canyon with Atencio. She had worried and fretted in Whitney's truck, had first clawed Atencio and then hidden beneath his feet until they stopped at his house fifteen minutes later. Atencio was so nervous about Mousse's coming to his house, he had stayed up the entire first night with her, sitting on the back stoop watching her fall asleep on his lap. But the last two nights, she had slept on top of his chest on the hammock. Atencio felt her ears lifting and moving to sounds in the night he did not hear, felt her body expand as she sniffed a wild scent. Even so, Mousse stayed. It was good having the cat with him: Mousse knew instinctively what should be feared, and what should be ignored.

The first morning with Mousse, Atencio gathered up his knapsack of tortillas and cheese, filled his water bottle from the kitchen tap, secured his work hat on his head, and stood by the wheelbarrow. Mousse watched from the stone wall of the old garden as Atencio lifted the wheelbarrow's arms.

"I will be back by noon," Atencio told Mousse. Mousse blinked her eyes and sniffed the air. It was not quite seven o'clock, but the hands of the July sun were already hot and invasive; the cool air had fled the garden. Mousse would move into the shade soon.

Atencio pushed the creaking cart before him down the slope between the yard of the house and the beginning of the back field, across the acequia following the path his previous twenty-four trips to the quarry had pressed into the sand. He wanted to look back at Mousse, to cluck and call to her, but he kept his eyes on the wheelbarrow and the ground passing under it. The open desert was no place for a fur-laden cat.

From Atencio's left side came a dark streak and a long jump. Mousse landed with a soft thump in the center of the wheelbarrow's bed. Atencio stopped in surprise. Mousse circled once and then sat down on her rear haunches, face forward into the open country ahead. Atencio resumed his pushing, more carefully now, avoiding the larger rocks and deep jolts he had grown accustomed to on previous journeys. He was always careful—moved slowly, smoothly, over the sand—coming out with the barrow laden with the rose stone. But now the journey in would be as precious.

While Atencio removed the stone slabs, Mousse watched from the shade of a cedar tree that grew on the side of the quarry. Atencio gave her water whenever he stopped and took some for himself. Mousse left the shade to rub his legs every hour or so and once during the morning roused herself from her stretched-out snooze to chase a lizard foolish enough to believe the cat was too hot to pursue. Atencio knew Mousse would catch the lizard—she always caught any reptile she surprised, but she never ate one. Her prowess proven once again, Mousse just pinned the luckless fellow alongside her with one paw clamped over its head. Atencio caught site of the lizard fifteen minutes later, running for its life across the rocks of the quarry, unaware that Mousse followed its every move down the cliff.

Mousse kept an eye on the sky, too, on the hawks that circled the rose quarry, and the ravens that squawked and flapped noisily past. She pulled her whiskers forwards when a piñon jay flew too close to her cedar tree, and clucked with anticipation if one landed. But the birds left her quickly for the open sky, and Mousse's wide blue eyes settled back to small slits as she turned inward again.

Atencio saw he had been wrong: the open desert was as much a part of Mousse's world as the canyon, or the patio, or the kitchen table; and she partook of each with the same enthusiasm and skill.

Persimillion Loves Alfredo

For weeks, Persimillion had been watching Alfredo for signs of an idea taking hold of his foolish head. It was inevitable, like the sun's passing across the sky. Sooner or later, Alfredo would get a foolish idea that would cause them all trouble.

Persimillion was grateful for the distractions the good padre Leo brought—old tools, torn children's picture books, colorful clothes for Alfredo to change into and out of again. Atencio had given Alfredo a watch that did not tick, but it gleamed like real gold in the sand. Alfredo was content to live within the world of the beautiful watch face for almost a month. But both Pepé and Persimillion had been watching for the dawn, or the afternoon, or the middle of the night, when Alfredo would turn inward, or inside out; when Alfredo would be suddenly filled with an inner longing they would not be able to shake from him with words or promises they all knew they could not keep.

Persimillion heard the padre, and then Atencio, talk about the coming rain, a rain that would make the desert sink into a gloom of mud and thunder. And then it would bloom, they said, soon after, into a fresh glory of sun and green growth. It was not a long rain, not like a tropical, ocean rain; this was a desert rain, which meant too much water where there had been too much sun. Water that would inundate the desert and make it impossible for the dry earth to hold itself, causing it to slide and sink, to drown in itself. The sun would return, everyone said, just when the earth of the mesa country could endure no more. Life would return to normal—to the dry heat of fall, to the cool tepid warmth of winter—and the swollen cactus flowers would shrivel to handfuls of colored dust on the desert floor.

But even with the roofless house, the coming rain did not worry Persimillion the way Alfredo did. Persimillion knew that Alfredo would get an idea. She wondered what form the idea would take out here in a new country? She watched the horizon for the shadow of approaching rain, and she watched Alfredo's foolish face for the shadow of approaching trouble.

The trouble came in the late afternoon, the hour when Alfredo usually watched the highway for a sign of Atencio's coming. Alfredo began to speak in jumbled syllables about the police. About walking along the highway and seeing police. Persimillion and Pepé explained again and again about the police: about the danger. Alfredo understood about the danger. But he misunderstood the words about danger and going home.

Persimillion heard Alfredo talking to his watch out near the gas pumps. He was telling the watch about the danger, but then he was telling his watch how the dangerous car would take him home. And somewhere in his tangled mind, Persimillion knew Alfredo was seeing home; and wanting home; and understanding, in terms only Alfredo could comprehend, that only a police car could take him home again. The idea sprouted right there in the watch face in the sand near the gas pumps, with the first clouds of Mexican moisture forming in the sky like an ominous visitor from the south. Persimillion struggled to her feet in the doorway.

"Pepé!" she called to the back of the station. "Pepé! Come quickly!" Pepé came running. "He has an idea about going home, Pepé. Alfredo has an idea about the police car driving him home."

Persimillion and Pepé watched Alfredo all morning. Neither of them slept in the afternoon, but sat over Alfredo, watching, waiting. Alfredo's ideas were not to be ignored. His past ideas had led him to sit naked on glowing coals, to be kicked by an outraged cow upon whom he had tried to suckle, and to perform minor surgery on the birthmark under his left eye after he heard the nurse at the village clinic reprimanding Persimillion about his lack of cleanliness.

"He only wants to make life easier," Persimillion was always telling Pepé after an incident with Alfredo and his ideas. "His ideas are his way of making things right."

"His ideas are not ideas, they are death wishes," Pepé said when they discussed Alfredo in the shade near the north wall of the old station. "We keep his wishes from coming true. And most of the time, Persimillion, I don't know why."

"Because, Pepé, you and I are his guardians, his family. We understand about life, about death, and Alfredo doesn't."

But even when Persimillion said these things, she wondered in her heart if she really believed them? Thus far, the best of her life had gone down death's road and had left behind the living, hollow and empty handed. Maybe it was Alfredo who understood.

Pepé and Persimillion woke one morning to find that Alfredo had disappeared. Usually Pepé or Persimillion woke before Alfredo, or heard him stirring and opened one watchful eye, but on this particular morning, Alfredo had slipped noiselessly away.

Pepé searched the desert north of the station. When he found Alfredo's unmistakable footprints—the left foot digging a shallow trench in the sand beside the imprint of the right—Pepé went for Atencio. Persimillion stayed at the station in case Alfredo returned home on his own, which was doubtful.

Pepé and Atencio followed Alfredo's footprints into the desert country with Mousse the cat, who seemed to understand that this was a search-and-rescue mission and so ignored all lizards, birds, insects, and other desert life she would normally have paused to pursue. Pepé told Persimillion later how Atencio and Mousse the cat seemed to move in unison across the plateau country, how they glanced at one another, exchanged information in some language of the body and eyes that only they understood.

They found Alfredo in a boulder pile. Alfredo's leg was wedged into the stone. He had lain there, caught, for several hours. His skin and hair were the same color as the rock, and his lips, which he'd smeared hourly with Whitney Slope's tube of balm, were caked with red sand. Alfredo smiled and laughed loudly when they found him. Neither Pepé nor Atencio smiled or laughed, although they were relieved Alfredo was not seriously hurt.

"We were lucky to find him so quickly," Atencio told Persimillion back at the station. "We could have carried home a skeleton."

Pepé had snorted. "There is not much difference between Alfredo the Foolish and a bag of old bones."

Persimillion was very angry: not at Pepé, who always likened Alfredo to something dead, but at herself for not seeing how far away Alfredo's mind had wandered.

"He was looking for Atencio's stone quarry," Pepé explained. "Alfredo wants to be like Atencio, big and strong." Pepé chuckled. "He wanted to make a home out there in the stone. What he found was a grave."

Persimillion looked at Pepé and Atencio, and then at Alfredo. His left ankle was swollen but not broken. It would mend. Even bones could mend.

But what about Alfredo's head? He was living on instinct, now, raw, animal instinct that was leading him farther into the clouds of confusion.

Pepé suggested the rope. Persimillion did not want to tie their younger brother like a dog. But less than twenty-four hours after his journey alone into the desert, Alfredo ran at a passing black and white vehicle—not the state trooper, but a frightened old man who nearly lost control of his car trying to avoid Alfredo. Reluctantly, Persimillion agreed; Alfredo had to be contained. There were no doors or windows in the station. There was nothing between Alfredo and his delusions except the gas pumps, and Pepé, Persimillion, and Atencio. Persimillion decided it was more humane to tie Alfredo to her body than to one of the cottonwoods or the rusted pumps. So Pepé secured one end of a rope around Alfredo's waist, and the other around Persimillion's.

Persimillion had to change her sitting patterns for Alfredo. Alfredo liked to move, to run and circle the station, to roll in the morning sand. When Pepé was not working for the padre, Alfredo was tied to Pepé instead of Persimillion, and together they went to the bosque or walked into the mesa country like before.

Persimillion knew Alfredo's predicament distressed Atencio. She saw his uneasiness, how Alfredo's captivity dampened Atencio's green eyes. She knew it did not sit well with him. Even so, Atencio shook off his own feelings and agreed there was little else to be done.

Atencio took Alfredo for walks in the evening while Pepé and Persimillion rested from their round-the-clock watch. Atencio held Alfredo's hand when they sat in the evening watching stars fall across the black sky, or contemplated the July moon. Alfredo curled his body into Atencio's while Persimillion made a supper. Sometimes Atencio fed him, placing tiny morsels of food at Alfredo's mouth like he was a wild, wounded bird tied to the ground by the frayed rope. Persimillion watched Atencio holding Alfredo. Atencio understood how a bad idea could take hold on someone and make him miserable.

No one mentioned it, but they all three knew: something would have to change. Otherwise they would all go mad, tied to Alfredo in the crumbling gas station, with the only promise headed their way the fearsome desert rains.

Unholy Alliance

It was the last week of July, and the thunderheads above the southern rim of Recuerdos Canyon's walls were climbing thirty, forty, fifty thousand feet above the desert floor into the great outer blue of space. Whitney was stretching small and medium-sized canvasses with Atencio, who was very adept at getting the corners tight. Atencio and Whitney both stopped their work on the porch to watch the billowing of the accumulating clouds.

"Cumulus congestus that will build to cumulonimbus," Whitney said, chuckling. "Dominga explained it to me."

Atencio smiled. "I grew up with the clouds. Winter or summer, my mother loved to stop the car and point. 'Nimbostratus that will bring rain for a long duration if the winds are northeast to south; cirrus fibratus, ice clouds . . . good weather if winds are from the west.' My older brothers would groan. But my father would hold up his hand and say, 'Boys, your mother is a wise woman. She will never be surprised by the weather.'"

"Monolithic," Whitney said looking again at the kingdom of white over the canyon.

"I would like to touch them," Atencio said, his left hand held open to the air.

It was on this morning in late July that Whitney knew it was time: time to begin painting what he felt most about this place—space. Expansion. Monolithic forms and gigantic stretches of color had begun to press in on Whitney when he ate, when he dozed, when he held a brush. So one morning with Atencio's help, Whitney built the frame and stretched a canvas that measured five feet by ten feet. When he drove down to the mercantile that afternoon, he stood at the pay phone and over the noise of idling, unmuffled engines and barking, yapping dogs, ordered five more oversized canvasses, stretched and gessoed, from the Santa Fe Art Supply.

And so Whitney had committed himself to something big: The Window to the Desert. At least the one he saw opening between his hand and his interior eye.

The rains that began that week were a thing of rare and religious beauty in the canyon: the saturated sage filled the house with a bittersweet fragrance that was invigorating and heady. The pale gold and red hills near the house lost their muted colors and turned to rich, tropical beaches with water running down their sides. The rain collected on the mesas above the canyon and gathered in a spraying waterfall off the top of the cliffs, carving another season's grooves into the ancient sandstone. The stream that followed the canyon road was now a rushing, bubbling river that threatened on some afternoons to overtake the roadbed. Although the road to the house became deep, sticky clay, the sun returned each and every morning and remained until noon, drying the mud enough to make Whitney's road passable.

Where earlier in the summer there had been cracked clay fields with thorny bushes and a few straggly scrubs, there were now new varieties of weeds and grasses. The limbs of the cholla sprouted crimson-purple flowers between the cactus spines, and the once flat prickly pear were bloated and bulbous with water, their fruit fattening each day. And just like Tomas had repeatedly foretold, the tin roof flapped like a flag in the wind that whipped through the canyon with the afternoon thunderstorms. But there were no leaks in the old roof, and Whitney got so he hardly heard the flapping tin.

Atencio's flagstones channeled the water down the patio and away from the house, half of it into the bushes and flowers growing along the side yard, the rest spilling down the small hill to the canyon road. There was substantial erosion where the water crossed the road, but the whole canyon was slowly becoming an arroyo, anyway, and the rut by the patio wall was no greater than the other thirty between Whitney's house and the highway.

People around Mi Ojo swore the rains never lasted more than two weeks, three in a wet year. Whitney figured the road had been here a century already; it wasn't about to slide off the surface of the earth now with just his truck passing over it. Even so, Whitney kept rubber boots and a rain slicker, his tool box and acequia shovel, in the truck so he could dig out of the mud, or dig the mud off, or slog through the mud on foot, if nature ever overwhelmed the four wheels of power drive he could now honestly call necessary for his daily transportation.

Atencio's work on a new flagstone walk out back of the kitchen porch was halted temporarily by the monsoons because Whitney and Atencio could not get to the quarry. During the last week, Atencio had worked at his own home, finishing up the stone floor in his now snake-free house. Maybe it was Mousse living with him, but Atencio had lost his fear of the snakes. He had returned Whitney's rope hammock, and had moved back inside the old adobe dwelling. Mousse's moving in with Atencio coincided with a lot of changes: Dominga said Atencio was now making his own meals when he was not out at the old gas station. Atencio had recently taken to wearing, at least outdoors, a pair of canvas sneakers Whitney had bought him when they began work in the quarry: at first, Atencio refused to try them at all, and went barefoot, or in his jute-soled slippers, even over the scorching surface of the quarry. He told Whitney he did not like tying shoe laces. Atencio still did not tie the laces—he had taken them out—but he did wear the shoes on his sockless feet.

When Whitney asked about his new living arrangement with Mousse, Atencio told Whitney good things followed Mousse the way bad things used to follow Atencio. As long as Mousse was beside him, or just ahead of him, Atencio said without humor, good things were within Atencio's reach.

"God sees how Mousse loves me," Atencio said. "He sees how I am ready, now, for other good things."

Although everyone in the valley knew the De Soto was not among those Mi Ojo vehicles registered within the last decade, Atencio had begun driving himself up the canyon in the old car. It was a comical sort of vehicle, a giant beetle rolling on four wheels. But Atencio was oblivious to the De Soto's size and outdated features. Atencio kept the car immaculate outside and in. The two-tone tan fabric interior had no visible wear, and everything—the plastic ivory fittings on the door handles and window fixtures, the wood grain moldings, the ashtray and instrument panel lights, the rearview mirror— everything was original and in working order. Whitney thought the car even smelled like it must have when it left the production line in 1941. Atencio drove the custom four-door De Soto with a slow reverence that gave the beige and white sedan an aura of importance and purpose. Whitney never once heard the old gears grind under Atencio's guidance, an amazing feat considering the size, age, and temperament of the De Soto's clutch and transmission.

After a morning of work in the studio on the window painting, Whitney drove into Santa Fe to pick up the canvasses and other paint supplies he had ordered. After loading up the truck with rolls of canvas; several large, prestretched frames; and bottles and tubes of paints at the art supply, Whitney headed for the plaza. The afternoon deluge began just as Whitney climbed from his truck and began walking towards the tortilla sisters' shop. He ran the last block, which was covered by an old portal. The A & M Tortilla Factory was bustling with customers, most of whom were old-timer Hispanos sitting out the rain in the always warm to hot shop.

"Whitney Slope! *Cómo está,* my friend with the blue fingers?" Aguelita took Whitney's hand and looked at his cuticles. Marguerite was serving fresh *bizcochitos* from the oven to an elderly Hispanic couple who ate them standing where they were in the middle of the shop. After letting go Whitney's hand with a sigh, Aguelita walked around to the warming oven and pulled out a tortilla, which she slapped onto a napkin. She slid it across the counter to Whitney.

"¡Dios mío! You look like an *hispano,* Whitney, brown and healthy! Who is cooking for you?"

"I am, Marguerite," Whitney said, biting the edge of the soft tortilla. "Business is good?"

"God bless the rain," Marguerite said. "What are you doing in town to-day?"

"Shopping. Can I have a half dozen of these to go?"

Aguelita stopped in the center of the shop and looked at Whitney. "Are the tortillas not so good in Mi Ojo, anymore?" Aguelita asked, lifting a conspiratorial eye.

"Oh, no, the tortillas are just fine, Aguelita. But I cannot come into town without wanting a few of yours."

Aguelita chuckled and shook her head. "Some men can never make up their minds. Here or there; this one or that. But one day, you're going to have to make a commitment. *¡Sí,* even you, Whitney Slope, will prefer the cooking of just one woman!"

Whitney's shoulders and boots were soaked after the short walk up to the plaza and the High Noon. He stood in the doorway trying to shed himself of some of the mud and water, and then went to his favorite stool at the end of the bar. Through the cafe's open doors he watched the rain running down the gutters of the covered portal to the street and the storm drain. The city drain had already reached maximum capacity so most of the High Noon's water joined the bustling current headed for Mud Street and a reunion with the water funneling off the upper plaza and the north side of town. Whitney would have enjoyed nothing better than to sit alone here at the mahogany bar with a beer and the newspaper had he not been thinking about the canyon and the same storm passing through, and about how he was missing it.

Not any of the old regulars were hanging around the High Noon this afternoon. It was the sort of afternoon that would provoke Anna into a rage about the weather, the incompetence of Santa Fe's founding fathers, and the thoughtlessness of people with muddy boots. Now that he lived in Mi Ojo, Whitney guessed his boots were always muddy.

Whitney decided not to visit Anna. Whitney reminded himself during a long, penetrating stare into the mirror over the wall behind the bar, that the last time he had visited Anna, he had come out with more mud on his feet than he'd traipsed in. Murky waters, Jon would say. Fooling around.

"Whitney, howdy!" Sam said, striding out the kitchen, purse and straw hat in hand. "Why didn't you tell us you were coming in? Can you stay for dinner later? Jon's at the dentist. He'd love to see you."

"I didn't think about calling, Sam," Whitney said, giving her a hug when she reached his bar stool. "When you don't have a telephone you stop thinking about using one."

Sam held Whitney by the shoulders and looked him up and down.

"I daresay, you look different, Whitney. What can I get you?"

"Just a beer. I'm running errands and then going home. I'm working."

Sam pulled Whitney's Mexican beer-of-choice from the refrigerator and placed it and a mug on the bar before him.

"Now that's good news." Sam leaned her elbows on the counter and stared out the open doors at the rain. "My God! I always forget how much rain comes when it comes. What's your new house like? Wet?"

"No, it's dry. But the road is a bog, and you wouldn't want to drive it after dark 'cause you can't see the tsunami of mud coming. But it's just wonderful out there. You and Jon should come visit."

"We'll do that." Sam was staring at Whitney now, frowning, chewing her bottom lip.

"You didn't see Burt's editorial in the *Duster* two days back, did you?"

"No, why? Should I?"

"That's a matter of opinion."

Sam walked back to her desk near the kitchen. Whitney watched her. He saw Juan in the back and waved. Juan lifted his head in greeting.

"Señor Slope! I went fishing last weekend. I caught nothing but some sunburn. But my brother-in-law liked my tackle box. Filled it with all sorts of worms and bugs and feathery things. He said, 'Now, *mi hermano*, now at least you look like you know what you're doing!'" Juan laughed loudly and turned back to his chile pot. "Nothing! Not even tadpoles! Nothing at all!"

Whitney laughed. "Fishing's not about food, Juan. Remember that!"

Whitney heard Juan laughing in the kitchen as Sam returned with a copy of the *Duster*, which she slid across the bar to Whitney.

"What's it about?" Whitney asked, thumbing through the paper for Burt's column.

"Burro Alley." Sam and Whitney exchanged looks. "Whitney, I've got to go to the bank before it closes. I'll be back in about thirty minutes. Will you be here?"

"Maybe," Whitney said. He read the first lines of Burt's editorial: "For those of you who don't know, who aren't in the know, or for reasons personal and emotional would rather not know, let me be the first to tell you: that dusty, unimproved nine-foot-wide path between Cristo Rey and Cathedral Avenues called Burro Alley—where historical record claims both burros and people have coexisted for more than two centuries—has been sold to a Texas-based real estate developer."

Whitney sighed.

"Did you know?" Sam asked. Whitney nodded and went on reading.

"Yes, it's true, my friends," Burt wrote. "Not even the most dilapidated, fly-and-pie-ridden corner of indigenous beauty in our town is safe from the slick, speculative hands of outside investors."

Whitney stopped reading again and looked up at Sam, who was frowning and chewing her lip.

"It's not as bad as it seems. It's not your fault, Whitney. It's all of our faults: the whole damned world wants a piece of Santa Fe."

Sam put on her hat, which would do little against the pouring rain, and walked out of the cafe and across the street towards the bank.

Whitney continued reading. Halfway down the column, Burt named Jack Farina as one of the investors hoping to make Burro Alley into an upscale hotel complex with shops, galleries, and croissant-serving cafes:

Jack Farina is the husband of Anna Farina, who is the owner and general director of the Mud Street Gallery. The Mud Street Gallery has recently enjoyed national recognition for its exhibits of work by outstanding Southwestern artists. While I applaud Ms. Farina's taste in art, and wholeheartedly agree with national reviewers that several of these artists are indeed among the best in the western world, I cannot help but wonder how much of the profits reaped from the sale of their work has served to underwrite the seizure of two blocks of Santa Fe's oldest terra firma? What this suggests to me is an unholy alliance, albeit an unknown and inadvertent one, between those people who truly love and respect Santa Fe's native cultural attributes, and those who view our little community through self-serving, profit-hunting eyes.

Whitney stopped reading when Juan placed a plate of blue corn enchiladas before him. Juan said nothing, but Whitney knew he had read the editorial.
"*Gracias,* Juan," Whitney mumbled.
"*De nada.*"
Whitney continued reading:

We can no more regulate art than we can regulate morality. An artist paints what he loves; a landowner may sell if he chooses. If Mr. Albert Romero chooses to sell Burro Alley to a Texas conglomerate, it is his right. His family has owned the alley for five decades.

And it is my right, or rather my hope, to wish never to see the day when the burros born and raised between the adobe walls and *jacal* fences of Burro Alley are asked to move on, along with their neighbors—those low profile shopkeepers who fix vacuum cleaners and boots, who sell fresh chile from the valley in the fall, *farolitos* at Christmas, and hand-carved *retablos* before Lent. For if their leaving comes to pass, how much longer can it be before this scruffy old-timer and his old family station wagon are no longer welcome at the plaza? Before only Mercedes, BMWs, and immaculate, mud-free Range Rovers line its upscaled parking meters?

At the end of the column, the header **IRONY** preceded Burt's closing thoughts:

My little paperback dictionary says, among other things, that irony is an incongruity between what might be expected to happen and what actually occurs. Now, one could say it is ironic that the finest and most talented painters of our time, such as my good friend Whitney Slope, would have, literally, a hand in the demise of Santa Fe's oldest neighborhoods through gorgeous and even otherwordly depiction of their physical and etheric facades. But then again, haven't we ordinary taco-and-sunset-loving folks come to realize that what is happening to our little city is not what we hoped for, but is certainly what we have come to expect?

"Oh, Jesus!" Whitney mumbled under his breath. He picked at his enchilada, but his appetite was gone.

Whitney folded up the paper and looked behind him at the bar. It was empty. He looked at his watch. Sam would be back in about twenty minutes. He still needed to pick up Dominga's boots at Alejandro's. If Alejandro was still speaking to him.

Whitney drank the remainder of his beer and studied the long, uneven mud-plastered wall across the cafe. Whitney had always wondered why that wall did not have a window. Sam said they did not put in many windows in the old days for defensive purposes. And it faced west, true west, so it would be hot in the summer. Still, Whitney thought, there must have been a truly beautiful view from this place some two hundred years ago: the mountains, the desert, the sky. And clouds: clouds coming and going, moving in and then back out. Clouds, the clothes of the angels.

Whitney took a napkin and scribbled Sam an apology about his leaving before she returned. Juan came to the kitchen door.

"Juan, will you make sure Sam gets this? I have to go."

"Of course," Juan said. "Was there something wrong with my enchilada today?"

"Oh, no, Juan!" Whitney said, putting on his hat. "I just don't feel up to eating today."

"The burros?"

"Yes."

"I didn't know you were so fond of animals, Whitney Slope."

"You'd be surprised, *mi amigo,* what I have come to be fond of."

Death's Partners

Whitney found Alejandro across the alley from his shop in the shed beside the burro field. Whitney skirted the narrow walkway between the adobe wall and the back of the shed where he was showered by the tall, drenched feathers of the old tamarisk. Wonder, the white coated baby, shook her pink ears in greeting to Whitney. The fragrance of the wet tamarisk mingled with the smell of wet manure and damp burro fur: it was a primitive place, Burro Alley, right here in the middle of the urban world. Whitney loved this place. He placed a hand between Wonder's impossibly large ears and felt his heart clutch, knowing that all of this was about to be buried in history.

"*Buenas tardes,* Alejandro," Whitney called into the low roofed shed.

"Oh, Whitney, *¡buenas tardes!*" Alejandro emerged from the unlit shed. Built of rough hewn lumber some eighty years ago, the little edifice was never given electricity. Someone tried to paint it in the fifties, Alejandro remembered, but the porous wood sucked up so much paint that the do-gooder just gave up. One side of the shed still sported a hint of leather brown latex.

"I'm just cleaning out some of the stuff in this old shed," Alejandro stared back into the dark interior. The doorway was very low. Whitney could not see anything through the dim opening. "I have to be out in two weeks. If Eliza doesn't come over here and decide what she wants to keep, I'm going to throw it away. *¡Dios mío!* How did we get to have so much stuff!"

"Where will the burros go, Alejandro?" Whitney followed Alejandro back along the adobe wall to which all of the burros had now come to stand.

"My cousin, Raphael, lives on a little *rancho* east of the mountains. He's a *viejo* with less eye sight than a bat, but he says he can take the burros." Alejandro paused before reaching the alley and looked back at the five burros, still watching the men. "They're not really mine, you know. They belong to the alley . . . their granddaddies were here. No one remembers who first brought them in. Everyone used them to haul wood, or wool, or their children. I heard old Mr. Salazar used to bring in Christmas trees from the mountains above Santa Fe on the backs of the burros. We all take care of them. They've never been owned, exactly."

Alejandro looked up at Whitney "Sort of like all of us *nativos*, huh, *mi hermano?*"

Whitney nodded.

"You've come for the lady's boots, *¿sí?*"

"Yes, if they're ready."

Alejandro motioned to Whitney to come across the alley and into the shop. Inside, Whitney surveyed the circumference of the room. It was different. There was less clutter. There were vacant, clean shelves, and Alejandro's bottle collection had been removed from the ledge above the back door.

"Oh, they're ready. Good boots, too. She was wise to have them repaired." Alejandro handed Whitney Dominga's brown leather boots. They were freshly polished. The supple leather looked elegant in an experienced, trail-worthy sort of way.

"She is one wise woman," Whitney said. He could not say exactly where the leather had been chewed. Dominga would be pleased. Dominga would be able to wear these boots for many years to come. "I suppose you saw Burt's editorial about Burro Alley?"

"*Sí.*" Alejandro sat on the tall stool beside his work bench and turned on the little light. He had a leather sandal on his lap that needed a new ankle strap. It looked like something Samantha would wear. "I saw the editorial. Nothing new, heh?"

"No. Just more of the same bad news. Especially about Mud Street. About me. You had it right all along, Alejandro."

Alejandro shook his head in disagreement. "I don't know, Whitney. Your motives do not leave a bitter taste in the mouth. Now my old *vecino*, Albert Romero, I cannot spit far enough to get the bad taste he has given me off my lips."

Alejandro cut a long strip of brown leather with his knife and then held it up next to the sandal.

"It is not only the *rico* gringos . . . it is *la gente*, my own people. Albert knew. And still he sold to people without eyes; without heart." Alejandro tapped his chest with his knife.

"It makes me sick to see you leave here," Whitney said, walking to the open doors. Thunder rumbled to the south somewhere. It would rain again.

"It makes me sick and tired of everything men do when I think about these old buildings coming down. Of the burros being herded out."

"*Sí.* It is an ache that will never stop." Alejandro carried the sandal to the doorway and peered skyward. "It will rain all night. I think it will be a very dark night."

"What do I owe you, Alejandro?"

"What does she mean to you, Whitney?" Alejandro's eyes sparkled. "How special is this *mujer?*

"She is . . . " Whitney looked down at Alejandro holding Sam's sandal, chewing a toothpick, smiling. "She saw sheep flying in the wind when she was a child. And she still watches the sky, the clouds, for their return."

"Oh, *sí*, Whitney, *es una mujer especial.*" Alejandro laughed and pressed his hand into Whitney's arm. "These boots are my gift to you and your new life. You think of me when you see this woman in her boots. You remember me and the burros, and the time we watched pass by this door."

The highway across the desert between Santa Fe and Mi Ojo was fifty miles of the straight and narrow. On this particular evening, Whitney was glad for the road's monotonous design, as he was having a bit of difficulty focusing through the sheets of rain on anything much beyond the hood of his truck.

The truck's tape deck pressed Chopin's simple chords of beauty and angst into the warm cab, but it was Burt Rapp's words that played the loudest refrain in Whitney's head. Over and over, *unholy alliance* scurried past Whitney's ears and eyes, until it was no longer Anna with whom Whitney had slept, but was Jack Farina.

As Whitney neared the mesa country east of the old gas station, or what he believed was the country east of the station, he remembered how half the mud building's roof was missing. Whitney imagined the floor in that little adobe cell would be just about swimmable by now. Maybe Atencio was there tonight? Looking for a landmark, Whitney squinted into the rain flashing like shards of broken glass past the beams of his headlights. Without the stars defining the tops of the mesas, he could not tell if he was ten miles out from the station, or some three beyond it.

The rain stopped. The abrupt silence was somehow louder than his engine, and Whitney slammed into it like a wall, temporarily losing mental contact with his hands. He did not hit a tree, which for one horrifying moment seemed inevitable, but managed to veer the truck back to the middle of the highway. Whitney was concentrating so much on the mechanics of steering that he forgot to slow the truck before the final curve into Mi Ojo. As the truck regained its balance on the right side of the highway, and Whitney felt the heat of relief and the ensuing surge of adrenaline shoot down his legs and arms, a shadow leapt at him from the right side of the road. It catapulted high into the air out of the bushes and weeds Tomas's highway department crew never trimmed, straight into Whitney's front headlight. A muffled thump followed. The shadow dropped back into the bushes like a kicked ball. Whitney would have driven the remaining five miles home without a backwards glance—he had hit jackrabbits and prairie dogs before—but for the turquoise blue illuminated by his headlights in the eyes of the animal he had felled.

Whitney slowed the truck at the far side of the mercantile and pulled onto the road's shoulder. He opened his window and hung his head out the side, partly to listen for he did not know what, and partly to give himself some air. There was not a bone in his body that wanted to go back to find that animal. But Whitney turned the truck around and drove slowly down the highway in search of it.

On the far side of the road, partially hidden in the bushes, was what he hoped he would not find. Whitney pulled over and turned off the truck. Before opening the door, he took a long breath to oxygenate his heaving heart. It began to rain again, a slowly building drizzle that soaked Whitney to the skin by the time he reached Mousse. He bent down and watched her for movement, but she was quite still.

Whitney looked over his shoulder and up the road at the dark post office. He had forgotten his hat, and the rain plastered his hair against his skull like a cap. Whitney wiped his eyes with the back of his wet shirt sleeve and looked up into the dark bosque trees. Not even Dominga's solitary porch lantern was visible through the black branches.

Everyone was asleep. There were no witnesses. There was just the rain and the somber, soaked bosque, and a narrow road around a sharp curve that claimed animal lives like so many miles under the speeding tires of cars and trucks every week of the year.

The rain ran off Whitney's face and onto Mousse's already soggy fur. Whitney carefully scooped her off the pavement and rested her body against his chest. He stood by the edge of the highway stroking her wet coat, listening for cars or other sounds of life. But Whitney heard only the rain smacking the highway pavement and splashing through the branches of the giant cottonwoods behind him. No thunder, no lightning, just ceaseless black rain.

Whitney placed Mousse's limp body on the truck seat beside Dominga's boots and the brown paper bag filled with tortillas and started the engine. He pulled on the headlights and made a U-turn back towards Mi Ojo. As the truck idled past the mercantile, Whitney's hands began to shake, and his teeth chattered. He could wake Dominga. But then what? Ask for comfort? For forgiveness?

There comes a time when there is too much even for someone as devout as Dominga to forgive. When explanations are simply a smoke screen between men and the devil. Still, if someone stopped Whitney now, if someone stuck out a thumb or flagged him down for help, Whitney would try to explain. Whitney would try to explain what had happened, show them what he had done. Here was the beloved body, the truck's headlight, the rain, the dark—all beyond his control. And here were the murderer's hands. Who did they belong to? First they had annihilated Alejandro's and the burros' innocent corner of the world. And now they had killed a cat, a beautiful, miraculous cat who had helped lead a war-weary boy home.

Where was Miguel? Or the good padre? Where were the police and the priests when someone really wanted to confess?

After a considerable battle between the truck's tires and the bog of mud that engulfed his road, Whitney reached the canyon house. Whitney's first concern was to keep Clem and Three-Legs from seeing, or smelling, or sensing the way cats do, the dead body of their mother. He did not turn on any lights, and he closed the cats in his bedroom where they had been sleeping.

Whitney found an empty wine crate on the kitchen porch. He wrapped Mousse in a clean towel and placed her in the narrow box. Whitney then vigorously washed his hands in the dark bathroom, and, although his hair and clothes were still dripping wet, he splashed cold water from the tap onto his face.

There was no blood. There were no deep cuts, and there was no gruesome tangle of limbs and bones. Still, tiptoing in his muddy boots around the house and yard, the loose tin on the roof flapping like an alarm when he retrieved the shovel from the rear of the truck, Whitney Slope felt like the earth's newest embodiment of murder and mayhem.

The extent of Atencio de Jesús' mastery of stone masonry was brought to Whitney's attention when he began to unearth one of the rose stones of the patio. It took Whitney more than two hours to remove one of the smaller flagstones near the patio wall, dig a deep grave for the wine box, and then fill and reset the stone again. The first two parts of the task were the easiest. But resetting the stone with even half of Atencio's expertise was impossible. Four times Whitney raked, smoothed, and leveled and then reset the oblong slab, before it was even remotely similar to those set around it.

Whitney was not conscious of his intention to hide the grave until the third time he pulled the stone and began again to rearrange the heavy, wet sand with his hands. And then the exact motivation behind his actions struck him like a hammer. His hands moved about far below him like artificial appendages; these were not the graceful hands that joined color and form into universal, transcendent beauty—these were frantic, deformed hands; these hands were death's partners.

Whitney knelt on the wet stones, his shoulders now covered with a slicker against the persistant rain that came and went in nonsensical patterns. It was not only from Atencio and Dominga that Whitney wanted to hide the grave. He wanted to hide it from the gods of the canyon, too, and from the nameless, good sheep who came here for some remembered shelter, and who became the hosts of a miracle, instead.

Whitney bent down until his forehead touched the slick surface of the reset stone. He would tell Atencio. Tomorrow he would find the strength of body, the courage in his heart, to tell Atencio.

Whitney stood and shuffled to the porch. His hand touched the door to his room, but he did not open it. Instead, he slid to the porch floor and sat with his back against the old wood of the door. The canyon around him shuddered with the tide of rain that blew in ahead of the predawn light. Before the sun began to send crimson fingers to warm the eastern horizon, the storm subsided. With the first light, Whitney Slope finally shed his tear-and rain-soaked clothes on the floor of the porch, and then crawled naked into his bed beside the warm, forgiving bodies of Clem and Three-legs.

t·h·i·r·t·y

The Arms of the Fathers

Atencio came to Dominga's trailer before six in the morning. He rapped hard on the aluminum screen door and then walked in. Dominga heard him and hurried down the hallway in her pajamas.

"Mom, have you seen Mousse?" he asked her. He was barefoot and disheveled, his long, black hair loose around his back, uncombed and matted. Like the old days.

"No, *mi hijito,* I haven't seen Mousse. I am only just now getting up."

Atencio walked back to the door and out onto the trailer porch. After a night of rain, the new sun struck the mesas, the village roofs and the dark green leaves on the cottonwood branches like they were glass. It was such a relief to see the sun. Dominga looked at the sky: no clouds. But there was too much moisture rising off the desert; there would be thunderheads—the air would become saturated with the rising vapor and the water would condense into clouds. First cumulus humilis, bright white clouds of clean, fluffy lamb's wool; then after hours of steady vertical buildup, the sky would choke with the mountains called cumulus congestus, bringing dark, angry rain.

"Atencio, wait, have some breakfast." Atencio did not turn to Dominga, but tapped his hand on his thigh, staring at the mercantile.

"Perhaps Mousse was closed in by Clay last night," he said.

Atencio hopped down the trailer porch, skipping the steps entirely. He ran swiftly over the sand and around cactus to the rear door of the mercantile. It was locked. Dominga knew Clay would not come for another hour.

"I have a key, Atencio!" she called, standing on the porch in her cotton nightgown.

Atencio ran back and waited while Dominga retrieved the mercantile key from the wall above the telephone. She glanced at Whitney Slope's calendar painting of a wooden shed with the blue, blue sky seen through the window of it's empty interior. It was good not to see clouds in this painting: Dominga had told Whitney there should be clouds in the August painting, but on this

---

morning when Atencio seemed like he was struggling once more against the current of his own salvation, she was glad the sky of the calendar was clear.

"Here," she said. Atencio took the keys and ran back to the mercantile. Dominga went into the kitchen and put on the coffee. She did not watch Atencio enter the mercantile, but she could feel her son's growing desperation like a hardening sap ball in her belly as he searched but did not find the cat. When he returned, Atencio said nothing. He handed her the key and turned on his bare heel and left the trailer. Dominga watched him sprint across the highway and up past the post office. He paused beside the bushes, and then jogged up the hill to the village.

"Dear God, let him find the cat," Dominga whispered. She lit two candles on the kitchen counter and said a rosary before the water boiled. It was not like praying for sheep. Or was it? Dominga measured and poured the ground coffee into the water, but did not wait for the brew to darken. She went to her bedroom and dressed in her jeans and her flannel shirt, socks and sneakers. Dominga knew that she could only prepare superficially for what this day was going to bring her.

When Atencio returned an hour later, Dominga was sitting on the front steps. She had managed to eat a token breakfast of buttered toast. She held her untouched coffee between her hands.

"Atencio, have some breakfast!" Dominga said as he strode past. He seemed oblivious to her, but then stopped before he was past her parked car.

"Have you seen her?"

"No."

"Maybe she is at home now." Atencio began to run again, down across the sand to his adobe house without a sideways glance at the sparkling De Soto.

Clay was sweeping the back stoop of the mercantile, watching Dominga and Atencio.

"*Hola,*" he called across the humid sage. "*¿Cómo está,* Dominga?"

"Clay, have you seen Mousse? Atencio's cat?"

"No. Atencio already asked me. Twice." Clay leaned against his broom. Even from such a distance Dominga could hear him sigh. "I told him cats are mighty independent creatures."

"*Sí, es verdad,*" Dominga said. "But you keep your eye out for her, Clay."

"Of course."

The Arms of the Fathers

An hour later, Atencio came past Dominga's trailer again. He had run halfway to the quarry, but had turned back when he did not see Mousse's prints. Dominga pretended to be darning one of the good padre Leo's socks, but her fingers were useless and unmanageable.

"Atencio, Mousse will come back when she's ready. Why don't you work on the floor, or go up the canyon and see Whitney. He said you have work yet on the stone walk. It is sunny this morning. You could work, *¿sí?*"

Atencio was not listening. He was watching something inside his head, something that was leading him farther and farther back into the catacombs of his brain, where Dominga could not follow.

"Please, Atencio, *mi hijito,* calm down."

Atencio looked across the trailer at his mother, his green eyes locked for one gracious moment into her own.

"I must find her. Maybe Persimillion and Pepé have seen her."

And then Atencio turned away, and Dominga knew he was gone.

By 9:30, Dominga decided to go look for the cat herself. Sitting in the trailer only heightened her sense of approaching doom. She snatched up her purse and keys and went to the car. It would not start. Dominga drummed her fingers on the steering wheel.

The Hernandez twins drove up beside the mercantile gas pumps in their little Honda civic and waved at Dominga as they climbed from their new car. Dominga waved and forced a smile. She would wait a few minutes, and the Chevy would start. It had to start. There was no one to call. Dominga pumped the gas and then tried the ignition again. Nothing. Clay would loan her his truck, but then he would know how worried she was. Miguel would probably drive her up and down the valley, lights on, but such a display might make Atencio more agitated than he already was. No, this was something Dominga had to do on her own, like her descent down that canyon wall at dawn. If she waited for external confirmation, she would end up doing nothing at all.

Dominga tried the car once more. Nothing stirred under the old hood. The Hernandez twins finished pumping their gas and went into the mercantile. Dominga left her station wagon and stood staring at the little blue car by the pumps. No doubt the keys were in the ignition. No doubt no one in Mi Ojo would blame Dominga when they knew all the facts—that Atencio was falling apart again, that Atencio's cat was gone and he was slipping away.

No one would blame the widow de Jesús for stealing the Hernandez twins' car to rescue her baby son.

Dominga closed her eyes. Shameless. A sob strangled her throat. She turned and walked quickly across the sand and back inside her trailer. Dominga dropped her purse and her keys on the carpeted floor and then sat down at the dinette and wept.

Someone was knocking on the screen door. Dominga wiped her face and looked up. It was Whitney Slope.

"Dominga?"

Dominga fumbled for a tissue on the counter behind her.

"Yes, Whitney." She blew her nose and motioned for him to come inside. He stood in the middle of her trailer beside her purse and car keys. Each of his hands held one of her old riding boots.

"Dominga, I have something to tell you." Dominga stared at the boots: beloved leather that had known three decades of sun and wind, horsehair and saddle soap, mountain pine and desert bone. Whole again. Her boots were home, and they were in one piece.

"I've been trying to get out of the canyon all morning," Whitney said. "I had to wait for the sun to dry some of the mud."

Whitney seemed to remember what he was holding and handed Dominga the boots. She held them against her chest. They were warm from the sun. They had probably been on Whitney's truck seat all morning.

"It's about last night," he continued.

Dominga looked at Whitney to thank him. He bent over and retrieved her purse and keys from the floor. When he stood, she saw how his face was contorted with compassion, like those cedar saints flickering in the candlelight of the *capilla*. Was he holding a great love in his eyes, or was it some profound grief?

"Dominga, have you been crying? What's wrong?"

Dominga shook her head. "Yes, well, . . . "

"Is it Atencio?"

"Yes. He is not acting well this morning. He can't find Mousse."

Whitney took off his hat.

"Oh, God, Dominga . . . it was me. Last night, in the rain, I hit Mousse on the highway." Whitney pointed out the door at the road. "Out there. She jumped at my truck. I couldn't stop . . . I couldn't stop!"

The Arms of the Fathers

"¡Dios mío!" Dominga breathed. She stood up with the boots pressed against her chest. *"¡Dios mío!* Dead?"

"Yes."

Dominga walked over to Whitney and looked up into his face. She saw, now, how red his own eyes were.

"We must go and find Atencio."

Whitney nodded.

Dominga sat down on the overstuffed chair and untied her sneakers. She kicked the canvas shoes across the room and then pulled on her old boots. When she stood up, she pressed her heels down against the familiar soles. *"Gracias,* Whitney. The boots . . . "

Whitney nodded.

"I'm ready," Dominga said. "But my car won't start."

"We can take mine."

"I'll drive," Dominga was surprised to hear herself say as they left the trailer and walked to the mud-encrusted truck. "I'm not sure yet where we are going—Persimillion's first."

Whitney said nothing, but handed her the keys. Dominga climbed up into the cab. Whitney climbed in beside her.

"I used to drive Tomas's truck," Dominga said as she moved the seat closer to the steering wheel.

"Of course," Whitney said.

Dominga gave the engine a good throttle and put the truck in gear. She adjusted the rearview mirror and glanced at Whitney. He was almost smiling, only neither one of them could smile just now. Beyond, up at the mercantile, Dominga noticed with embarrassment and relief that the Hernandez sisters' car was gone. For a moment, she pictured herself having to explain things to Miguel Gonzales, how she had only followed his advice and found herself a more reliable vehicle.

It was a story that quickly circulated the village and environs of Mi Ojo: within four hours, everyone knew Atencio was missing because of his cat. Clay asked everyone who came into the mercantile whether anyone had seen Atencio. Dominga knew the gossip that followed her—how she was driving that new gringo's truck, looking for her Atencio who everyone with any sense of the predictable knew was curled around a bottle somewhere.

By early afternoon, Dominga and Whitney had visited the old gas station, where Pepé told them Atencio had come earlier. Pepé had not seen Mousse, and Persimillion and Alfredo were gone to Tomita with the padre to see about Alfredo's still bruised ankle, so Atencio left. Dominga had driven Whitney's truck to the village plaza and the cemetery above the pueblo three or four times each. They looked in the trailer and the house around back every time they passed the mercantile.

The afternoon rain began as a light shower, but the clouds had black rims along their bottoms and thunder in their sides. Dominga knew as well as the weatherman that it would pour before the afternoon was through.

"We should go to the quarry," Dominga said as she headed the truck west toward Tomita.

"We could be stranded, Dominga," Whitney said. Dominga pulled off the highway where the quarry road led off across the mesa country and stopped. "We can't help Atencio if we're stuck out there."

"What if he's there?"

"If he's there, at least he's not at the bar."

"That's true," Dominga said. "He would be safe out there."

Whitney laid his hand on Dominga's shoulder. It was warm. Dominga took his long fingers and laced them between her own as the rain pattered with increasing vigor on the top of the truck. Dominga looked at Whitney, at his arm stretched across the seat, at his shoulder, at this man she hardly knew. If Atencio were safe, if Mousse were at home, if the pain of the world would cease for just a few hours, would she allow herself to curl up into this man and remember the pleasures of hand and heart that men and women shared?

By late afternoon, the torrential downpour had soaked the valley of Mi Ojo to the bone. Dominga and Whitney stood in the trailer, eating tortillas and cheese and looking out at the adobe house. Clay had seen Atencio last: Atencio had come in to ask about the cat, again. And then he had slipped out of the mercantile and like a *brujo*, Clay said, vanished into the rain.

"What will we do now?" Whitney asked. Like Dominga, his shirt and jeans were damp.

"I don't know. I don't know what to do."

But she did know that she had a few dry shirts in the back.

"Just a moment."

Dominga walked back to her bedroom and pulled two of Feodoro's remaining flannel shirts from her drawer.

"Here, it's getting cold," she said, handing the red and white plaid to Whitney. "Put this on." Whitney pulled off his denim shirt and slipped on Feodoro's cotton flannel. It was too short in the arms, but Whitney was slender through the torso and could button the front. It embarrassed Dominga, the way she noticed Whitney's chest and bare shoulders; the way she thought about this man's body, flesh and blood, when her own son might be slipping out of his.

Dominga went back to her room to change her own shirt. Even her bra was damp. She took it off, but did not look for a dry one.

They stood in the kitchen drinking the morning's reheated coffee. Dominga could not think anymore. The fear had begun to swell in her heart, making her feel lopsided and sick. Perhaps this was the senility other mothers chose when what cannot be changed begins to consume them from within.

"Whitney," Dominga said suddenly.

"What?"

"Will you still care for Atencio, even if he drinks again?"

"Dominga, what kind of question is that? Of course I'll still care for him."

Dominga set down her cup and buried her head in her hands. She began to sob. A moment later, Whitney's arms were around her, and she was pressed into the familiar cotton flannel of Feodoro's shirt. Nothing had changed. Only now Dominga was a woman in pain, instead of a woman who let everyone else's pain obscure her own.

"Dominga de Jesús! Hello!" Dominga and Whitney pulled apart and looked over at the door. It was Mr. Lopez. Dominga could hear his miniature dogs yapping in the truck cab behind him, even through the noise of the rain on the trailer roof.

"*Hola,* Ramon," Dominga opened the door. "Come in."

"No, no. I just wanted to tell you, I was out fishing after lunch, just before the clouds came, and as I was leaving I saw Atencio and Burly drive into the bosque."

"¡O, gracias! ¡Gracias, Ramon!" Dominga turned to Whitney. "We must go to the river."

Whitney drove the truck off the highway and onto a path made by car tracks through the grass into the dense trees. The rain was less insistent in the bosque. Dominga peered ahead, looking for Burly's maroon car. It was there, parked close to the river, one door swung open.

"There they are," she said, pointing. "Oh, God, let him be all right."

Dominga left the truck before it was stopped. Whitney jumped out behind her. When they reached the car, they both looked inside. Burly was asleep behind the steering wheel, his empty beer cans scattered over the front seat and on the floor.

"Burly?! Where's Atencio?" Through the open door Whitney took Burly by the shoulders. Burly opened one eye and laughed.

"Gringo man! ¿Cómo está?" Burly looked at Dominga standing beside Whitney, holding on to his arm. "Oh, sí, you've taken the pretty Señorita de Jesús for a drive in the bosque! Sí, you like our little pueblo!"

"Where's Atencio?" Whitney took Burly's face and aimed it back at his own. "¿Dónde está Atencio?"

"The river, man. He was loco, in a fever. He ran to the river."

"¡Dios mío!" Dominga gasped under her breath as she ran towards the cottonwoods that lined the river's banks.

"Atencio!" Dominga stopped and pulled at the dark green brush at the base of the trees. The rain spattered down through the blackened branches. "Atencio!"

Whitney was calling farther down the bank. The river before Dominga was swollen and seemed to be rising into the grasses along the edge of the channel. Dominga's boots stumbled through the thick underbrush near the water where she searched for any sign of her son.

"Atencio!" Dominga called again and again. Her voice seemed to be drowning in the rain. "Atencio!"

"Here!" Whitney's voice cut through the rain. "Dominga! Over here!"

Dominga ran with her arms before her face, her lips and eyes whipped by wet leaves and stems. She pressed through a stand of young cottonwoods and found Whitney bent over Atencio who lay prostrate on the ground.

"Oh, God! Is he okay?" Dominga fell on her knees beside them and lifted Atencio's head from the wet ground. His hair was tangled in the grass and

The Arms of the Fathers

weeds. "Atencio, it's me, mama." Whitney took Atencio's shoulders and folded him into a sitting position. Behind him in the grass was an empty vodka bottle slowly refilling with water and mud.

"Atencio, we've got to get you out of this rain," Whitney said gently into his ear. Atencio drowsily opened one eye. "Can you stand?"

Atencio lifted one arm with great difficulty and grasped Feodoro's flannel shirt with one hand.

"Papa! I can't stand, papa!"

"All right, I'll carry you," Whitney said, glancing at Dominga.

Atencio pulled his face into Whitney and began to cry into his chest. "Papa! You came back! *¡Mi papa!*"

"Atencio, it's me, Whitney. And your mother."

"Mama! Did you tell papa?" Atencio let go of Feodoro's shirt and rolled back onto the ground. Whitney picked Atencio up by the shoulders again and wiped the hair and mud from his cheek.

"*Sí*, Atencio, I told him everything." Dominga took Atencio's face in her hands. "*Sí*, papa knows everything. Papa loves you, Atencio."

"Do you still love me, papa?" Atencio was staring into Whitney's face. Whitney looked at Dominga. She nodded.

"Of course, Atencio, of course I still love you."

"Oh, God! It hurts!" Atencio closed his eyes and held his belly. He began to rock back and forth. Whitney and Dominga struggled to keep him from reeling over onto the ground again. "It hurts, papa. It still hurts."

"What hurts, Atencio?" Whitney asked, finally securing both arms about Atencio's thin torso.

"I wanted to tell her how I was sorry. So sorry, *mi hijita*. So sorry to kill your papa."

"You didn't kill papa," Dominga said, grabbing Atencio's face again and making him look into her own. "He was sick. He had cancer in his stomach."

"*Sí*, but I killed that little girl's papa." Atencio's shoulders folded inwards with sobs. Whitney moved around behind Atencio and tried to lift him from under his shoulders, but he would not move. "God knows. God saw. And so he took my papa!"

"No! *No es verdad,* Atencio. God did not take Feodoro to punish you. No!"

Atencio sobs wracked his body.

"I'm going to pick him up, Dominga," Whitney said. "Can you help me?"

"Yes."

Whitney placed one arm under Atencio's back and another arm under his knees. Dominga steadied his head and shoulders while Whitney struggled to stand.

"Okay, I've got him. Let's go."

"It hurts, papa!" Atencio cried. "It hurts!"

Dominga led the way back to the truck, pushing aside branches and bushes, and throwing a thousand Hail Marys ahead into the rain as they fought their way out of the drenched trees. Dominga kept looking back at Whitney carrying Atencio. Unlike Atencio, Dominga did not mistake Whitney for Feodoro. But she understood how very much like a father's the arms around her son had come to be.

t·h·i·r·t·y - o·n·e

Down Around Santa Fe

Anna Farina sat in the kitchen eating a sandwich. From Anna's hilltop perch, Santa Fe and the desert to the south and west of the city opened like a brown palm. It was hot today. It was muggy, humid, like Texas in late summer.

Jack Farina was packing and preparing to leave on his private jet. Anna tried to appear nonchalant, but she was counting the minutes until he was out of the house. The last twenty-four hours between them had been unusually strained. Maybe it was her imagination, but it seemed they couldn't exchange a sincere sentence. Only sarcasm and underhanded insults passed between them when they were in the same room. Maybe, Anna thought, that was how it had always been, only she had chosen not to notice. Maybe the unholy alliance in her life was not the adulterous one after all.

Naomi came into the kitchen and poured a glass of iced tea for Jack.

"Mr. Farina wants you down the hall," Naomi said, her eyes flicking across the mess of bread and cheeses Anna had left on the counter. "His cab will be here in ten minutes."

"He knows where I am, Naomi," Anna said, still staring out at the pool and the city below. "You can remind him, if you want, where the kitchen is."

Candy was leaving the gallery at noon for her sister's wedding shower. Anna would have to handle the gallery alone all afternoon. It was still heavy *turista* season. It would be busy. A lot of questions and probably very few sales. Anna thought about closing up shop, staying home, putting her feet up with a magazine, maybe going for a swim before the rain began. If only Jack would leave and let her get on with her day. Her life.

"My dear, you're eating in the kitchen like a maid," Jack said. Jack held his iced tea in one hand and his briefcase in the other. He traveled lightly, as he had two sets of whatever he needed, one in Dallas, one in Santa Fe. And maybe, Anna often thought, another set in a house she didn't know they owned somewhere she had never been. And never wanted to go.

"You asked me last week about Burro Alley?" Jack said after a long draught on his iced tea. Jack drank iced tea instead of water. No matter where he was, he had a glass of iced tea in his hand or beside it. "We're thinking of a hotel with shops. A restaurant on the third floor with a large balcony. Perhaps the gallery on the first floor, off the courtyard and fountain."

"This is with the Eric Robertsons?"

"Yes."

"I like Mud Street. It's weathered a lot of storms."

Jack shrugged and sipped his tea. "But you're paying someone else rent money. We could up the profits substantially."

"My profits are fine. By the way, how are the Robertsons enjoying the Chaco painting in their new office? It's the best major piece Whitney has done this year. I thought about keeping that one, buying it for the house, you know. Was their foyer large enough, or did they have to buy another office building?"

Jack placed his half empty glass near the sink and shifted his briefcase. He smiled at Anna as if she were a child asking adult questions.

"I thought I told you, Anna. They decided to sell the painting to a friend, a new partner, who simply had to have that particular view of that particular mud ruin." Jack laughed. "You know Eric; he turned quite a profit in the space of about two days."

Anna picked crumbs off her plate with a wet finger. She looked out the window again; this view was getting all too familiar to her. It was time for a change of scenery.

"I let that painting go early for you. I gave them a dealer's discount because they were friends of yours. You knew all along, didn't you, Jack?" Anna looked across the kitchen at her husband who stood near the door ready to exit for Texas. "I asked you quite specifically not to ever do this again with artists in my gallery. Or me. No turn-around art sales. It makes me the middleman in a deal that compromises the artist."

Jack shrugged and looked at his watch.

"Oh, Anna, you've done it for years. It's the world of business, my dear. You play; so play along."

With a deft and muscular snap, Anna threw her china plate onto the tile floor near Jack's Italian leather shoes. Pieces of mauve and blue china sprayed the hallway behind him.

"How much did you pocket, Jack? How much did you make off with after scuttling the little wife, you shit?!"

"Don't be crude, Anna." Jack lifted one leg and looked at the mustard clinging to the cuff of his white linen pants. "Maybe this business is getting to be too much for you. Or maybe it's the company you keep around this sorry town?"

Anna left the kitchen and bumped into Naomi in the hall.

"There's a mess in the kitchen," Anna said loudly.

"I'll split the profit with you, Anna," Jack called after her. "I was planning on telling you; you'll get your share."

Anna stood in the middle of the enormous bedroom, three sides of which were walls of glass. Anna knew she had come here for a reason, but the reason had yet to crystallize.

"What about Whitney Slope's share, Jack?"

"Mmm, Mr. Slope." Jack stood at the door, pointing at his watch. "I have a meeting tonight in Dallas. I have to hit the road. Seems a little late in life to have an attack of conscience, doesn't it? Slope doesn't have to know, honey. He's well enough off, I'm told."

"Slope will know because I will tell him. I'll split my share. It's the least I can do."

"You can—and do—a great deal more for the man, my dear. Don't be so modest. But he keeps Mud Street floating on the art high seas so I guess he pays you pretty well, huh?"

Jack winked and then turned and walked down the hall. Anna chewed three nails at once and looked at the empty doorway. She could hear Naomi telling Jack the cab had arrived, and to have a pleasant trip.

Anna pulled suits and sport coats off the closet rack and ran down the hall and out the double front doors where she heaped them onto the gravel in front of the cab's fender. Jack was closing the trunk, and Naomi was standing beside him holding his half-full iced tea glass. Anna ran past them and back into the house. She returned to the bedroom and pulled the drawers of Jack's bureau onto the floor. They were too heavy to be carried, so she scooped up an armful of his underwear, the undershirts and boxer shorts, the initialed linen handkerchiefs, and socks, and ran back down the hall and outside to the drive. Naomi was already picking up the dumped suits, still on hangers, but Jack watched calmly through black sunglasses. Anna took the second pile out to the fountain that bubbled in the grass courtyard. She pushed everything into the dribbling water that was spit twenty-four hours a day from an expensive stone imitation of a Mexican sun god.

Anna walked past the cab and stopped so close to Jack she could feel the heat pulsing off his brow.

"You can move out Jack; you can take what's yours, which does not include me, or this house, or my gallery, and fly on back to Dallas where scum like you aren't so noticeable."

"This won't be easy, Anna. I own Mud Street, and the house. You can have your clothes. Have you thought about seeing a doctor, my dear? Hysteria runs in your family as I recall. I have many . . . "

"Don't waste your breath threatening me, Jack. I have many, too. I have so much on your business dealings it could fill a book. I don't particularly want to waste clean paper with the filth I know about you, so leave me alone. Leave me what I want, and we'll call it even."

Jack gazed over the cab roof at his clothes in the fountain. The soaked pile was causing the carefully measured trickle to overflow into the grass beneath it.

"Anna, I have never liked *even*. Naomi, after you clean up the mess my deranged and spoiled wife has made, feel free to leave here. I know you've been unhappy. I'll accommodate you at my home in Dallas."

Jack climbed into the back seat and waved at the driver to leave. The driver forgot about the clothes piled in front of his tires, and the cab thumped over the suits Naomi had not yet removed from the driveway.

"Leave the damned stuff, Naomi!" Anna yelled. "Just get your personal things out before I get back this afternoon."

Anna stormed back into the house, slamming the door behind her. She walked quickly through the living room and kitchen, and out to the pool.

Clouds obscured the entire southern view. There was still sun beating heat into the city, but within the hour, the rain would hammer Santa Fe.

Anna reached down and pulled her white lizard pumps off her swollen feet and threw them into the water. She watched them sink gracefully to the bottom, where they rested like placid fish. Anna dipped one hot foot and then the other into the deep end of the Mexican tile pool. And then she plunged into the water head first, kicking and flailing until she touched the smooth blue bottom.

t·h·i·r·t·y - t·w·o

Another Miracle

The tires of the De Soto could not turn in the mud. Atencio left the car where it was near the right side of the road and began to walk the remaining mile up the canyon to Whitney's house. The rain had stopped over an hour ago, but the mud was deep and slick with clay. Atencio would have to walk quickly through the thick quagmire to reach Whitney's house before complete dark claimed the canyon.

Usually the De Soto could slither and sputter its way up the canyon road, even after an afternoon of rain.

"It's so damned heavy," Whitney had said the first time Atencio drove up to the house after a cloud burst, "it's like a tank, or a turtle, drudging up that road. Who would have guessed it could make it?"

"I would have," Atencio had replied. They had stood together in the warm drizzling rain staring at the De Soto's whitewalls that were no longer white. "My father used to drive this car all over the county, even up into the mountains, in bad weather—rain, snow in the winter. This car never stranded him, never stranded nobody."

Until tonight. Today, the rain had burst angrily from huge black clouds that had rolled low and fast over Mi Ojo. Much of the canyon road had been overrun by the stream that was now a swift river where rocks were bounced and smashed under the current like bowling balls. Even the prehistoric weight of the De Soto could not push the car through the muck to the house. But Atencio was determined to reach Whitney's house. It had been nearly a week since he had worked at the canyon.

Four mornings ago, Atencio had awakened in his mother's trailer, in her bed; Whitney Slope was sitting in a chair beside him. Dominga had brought Atencio coffee and then had sat down on the edge of the bed while Whitney told him about Mousse's death. Together, they had wept. And then Atencio had left his mother's bed and walked alone out onto the front porch of the trailer.

It was a sparkling, clear morning. Atencio knew that the rain would return by midafternoon. The dark storms were not over. His sorrow was not over, either, but Atencio looked into the brilliant blue sky and knew it was good to be alive. It was good to remember hope.

After Atencio, Whitney, and Dominga had eaten breakfast, Pepé appeared at the trailer door. Even though Dominga had gone to Persimillion after they found Atencio in the bosque, Pepé seemed relieved to see for himself that Atencio really was okay. Alfredo, he told them, was not eating at all. Persimillion thought maybe Alfredo was going to starve himself in some attempt to get home to Mexico.

Atencio had planned to return to the canyon with Whitney and resume his work on the back walk. But it was suddenly very evident that unless Atencio could convince Alfredo to eat, Persimillion and Pepé would have more problems than they could handle. So Atencio had spent three days at the gas station. This morning, when Whitney came by to see how they all were, Atencio had told him he would begin working evenings, when Alfredo seemed content to sleep.

Atencio walked slowly along the road. He glanced back at the mud-stalled De Soto backlit by the golden sky above the canyon. Dusk.

Alfredo had a fixation on the De Soto. Atencio could not drive Persimillion and Pepé and Alfredo anywhere—he explained how they could not go up into the mountains until Atencio had a license—but that did not matter to Alfredo: since the afternoon when the De Soto was parked alongside the gas pumps like it was getting a fill-up at the old station, Alfredo had fixed it in his head that Atencio was going to drive them all home. Atencio and the De Soto were going to answer Alfredo's prayers—the journey back home to Mexico was about to happen.

Despite the makeshift wooden roof Atencio and Pepé had fashioned over part of the station to keep them all dry at night, worries were pressing in on the Ramirez family. Persimillion worried about how they would move on, and where. And Pepé, who was working with padre Leo at the church, was very nervous about the policeman he met there. Atencio had explained to Pepé that the policeman was a friend; for now, anyway. He would not sneak up and take Pepé away. Still, Pepé had dreams about that policeman, about his black glasses, about his heavy black boots that made the parish library floor shudder when he walked across the creaking boards.

Pepé did not walk along the highway, anymore; he cut through the bosque when he went to work for padre Leo, even though it meant an hour more of walking each day, and dozens more mosquito bites added to the itchy welts already covering Pepé's face and arms.

This evening, it was Atencio who did not want to be walking along the road. In the swiftly lowering light, the muddy canyon road frightened Atencio. It was not like walking the highway to the old station, with familiar cars passing, with the white line along the edge of the blacktop to follow. The canyon road had no lines, and tonight it seemed to have no boundaries. Atencio knew Whitney would be along soon. Even if Atencio became stuck on foot, had to climb onto the boulders at the base of one of the small mesas and wait, Whitney would be along soon. Whitney always came when he said he would come.

But the walk still frightened Atencio: the black mud, the disappearing light, the dripping sounds from the trees and cactus, the stream alongside the road gushing like a frothy river. Night hawks had begun their evening hunt and cut the air above the road with rapid, shrill whistles as their bodies sliced the atmosphere like tiny missiles. Atencio liked the great horned owl that lived at the end of the canyon, but tonight his hooting song haunted him. This road was not a place Atencio wanted to be.

Atencio kept his eyes on the road immediately before him, and turned his mind to thoughts that did not agitate and entangle him: he remembered how Whitney had told him he had friends, the Gateworthys, in Santa Fe who were rebuilding a house. Whitney had asked these Gateworthys if they wanted a stone floor and they had said yes. They would hire Atencio. They would even provide the stone ("Not your stone," Whitney said, "stone from another part of New Mexico"), and they would pay Atencio cash. Good money. All Atencio had to do was get his car registered and renew his driver's license. And stay off the beer and vodka.

Tonight, slopping alone up the muddy canyon road, waiting for Whitney to drive up and take him home, he still thought the job in Santa Fe seemed too big, too much. Whitney had told Atencio not to worry about it in advance, to take it a step at a time. Get the car registered. Get his license. Finish the canyon house.

The sky to the west suddenly lightened. The sun was freed as the clouds slid north and for a few minutes yellow light touched the top edges of the mesas surrounding the back canyon. The rocks that had been dirty brown were bright peach and orange, and the sky behind was navy blue with swirls of purple. Atencio wanted to run towards the blazing rocks of the back canyon, away from the dusk already behind him, on the road. But he could only pick a slow path through the mud, and the sun on the mesas disappeared within another moment.

Atencio walked barefoot, carrying his sneakers in his hands. Glancing back over his shoulder, he could still see the De Soto's bottom deep in the mud at the last curve. He would retrieve it in the morning. Whitney would have to drive him back home tonight. He hoped Persimillion would understand, but Atencio would not be able to visit her at the station until tomorrow afternoon. Persimillion would be exhausted by then, exhausted by Alfredo at the end of his rope.

Alfredo's insistence about returning home, about crossing the river and going back to the old village, was making life for everyone around him misery. There was no rest from Alfredo's demand, from his need to be walking the highway. Alfredo stuck his thumb out for rides even when he was inside the station and could see no cars pass. Tied by the rope to Persimillion, or Pepé, Alfredo slept with one arm stretched out on the dirt floor, his hand folded into a fist, his thumb pointed south. Persimillion said Alfredo was dreaming foolish dreams of the happy life he never had in Mexico.

Atencio wanted to be like a father to Alfredo. Atencio remembered how his own father walked into the house in the evenings before supper, and, just by sitting at the kitchen table, brought calm and order to the de Jesús home. Atencio remembered how Feodoro stood out by the back garden and looked over the mesa country at the freshness of morning. Feodoro rested his hands on his slender hips, and with his hat cocked lower over one eye, puffed on his pipe. His mouth was stern with the coming day's work, but Feodoro's eyes smiled, always, and he whistled as he walked up the sandy road for another day at the mercantile.

Feodoro de Jesús never balked at hard work, unhappy situations, or difficult decisions. He did not complain when the roof of the mercantile caved in during the August rains, nor did he hesitate with his gun the evening his favorite cow pony broke her leg during the fall roundup in the upper pastures above Mi Ojo.

"These sad things in life are just reminders," Feodoro told his sons, "what's here is here. No use looking the other direction, looking behind. That's when you stumble. A horse who can't keep her eyes on the trail below her will fall right off the side into the tangling thick of it."

Atencio slogged along in the deepening dark and listened to the low idle of Whitney Slope's truck far away behind him on the canyon road. Here was the mud and the wet night Atencio did not care to be walking through, but here it was. Here it was, a canyon in New Mexico, not a rice paddy, not a foreign place; here was Whitney's silver truck making its way up the road, not a tank aimed on his, or anyone else's, death. There was no war here.

Atencio plucked each foot out of the mud behind him and plopped it back into the mud in front of him. He sucked in the moist evening air of late August. Here was home if he wanted it. He could make his way through the dark bog by himself, even with a fist of old fear punching at his belly. Feodoro de Jesús could look down from the pale, evening clouds and see how his youngest son had his two bare feet and his two green eyes on the trail before him.

Before the headlights of the approaching truck rounded the curve near the parked De Soto, Atencio heard an unfamiliar vibration in the engine. Realizing it might not be Whitney, he stepped off the road and slipped behind a large chamisa bush where he could watch the truck approach and not be seen. The western sky was now as dark as the road bed, but enough clouds had cleared away for the first stars to twinkle above the mesas. Atencio looked at the pattern of the stars. The rains were nearing their natural end; there is a season, Feodoro de Jesús would remind him, a time for everything to come and to go under heaven.

Headlights flashed like searchlights up the sides of the mesas ahead of Atencio as the approaching truck swerved hard before regaining traction. Atencio peered through the chamisa branches. These were not the headlights of Whitney Slope's silver truck. These headlights were rectangular, and there were red lights across the top of the vehicle. Tomas had red lights like that on top of his truck, but his headlights were round, like Whitney's. Atencio crouched down onto his ankles and huddled over his knees, making his body a small shadow at the foot of the old bush. He buried his eyes in his shirt sleeves so that the headlights would not reflect them and betray his hiding place. The truck roared past Atencio, spraying the bush, the rock slope behind, and Atencio's head and shoulders with greasy, pebble-shot mud that stung his scalp and arms.

It was too dark for Atencio to see the color of the vehicle, but he knew he did not recognize the lights or the outline of the hood. It was not a truck from Mi Ojo. Atencio knew all the trucks of the valley, even at night.

Atencio stood and walked onto the road. He watched the truck disappear around the next mesa into the canyon. As Atencio walked, he listened to the engine until it reached Whitney's house three quarters of a mile ahead, where it was turned off.

The last section of the canyon road was not as muddy because it was on a slope, and the water ran down and off to one side instead of into deep grooves in the middle. Atencio hastened his pace, partly because it felt good to walk quickly again, and partly because of his nervous curiosity about the truck up ahead at Whitney's house.

Atencio cut across the mesa and up the back hill that offered a shortcut between the road and the west side of the house. There were no lights at Whitney's house. Atencio crouched down and listened. The legs of crickets and the echoing hoot from the old owl broke the canyon silence. He continued to walk, but bent nearly in half now, through the chamisa and the tall cholla cactus.

Atencio knew this place behind the house: he had hauled fill for the patio from this sandbed with Three-Legs and Clem watching from the safety of the cottonwood near the back porch. But Atencio was very careful: the stars were hardly sufficient light to discern and avoid the clusters of yucca spines aimed for the sky, or the long, sprawling prickly pear patches that covered half of the mesa.

Atencio moved smoothly across the wet sand. His bare feet eased into contours between small pebbles, oblivious to the thorny stabs from goatheads, his breathing fast but absolutely silent. The beam of a flashlight moved around the inside of Whitney's kitchen and struck out the west window onto the sand flats surrounding Atencio. He froze near the ground, his sneakers folded in his hands beneath his belly, his eyes averted. When Atencio looked up at the house again, the kitchen was dark.

Atencio crept like a shadow along the north wall of the house until he reached the back porch. The rose flagstones he was about to lay were set in low piles near the porch door. He could hear voices, now, and low laughter, and then a sharp, searing sound of something ripping. Atencio stopped mid-step near the back door, his hand on the screen. It was an ugly laughter: it was ugly and it came from a dark house. Whitney Slope was not inside.

Atencio's throat clamped down; he felt his air supply shut off from his lungs. A loud guffaw jolted Atencio out of himself, and he began to breathe again. He crept past the back porch towards the north window of the studio where he slid down the adobe wall of the house and sat on the ground.

"God damned! Ain't this fine art, Billyboy!"

The beam from the flashlight cut jagged yellow knives of light into the cottonwood behind the house. Atencio's head and arms began to shake, and he clenched his jaw so his teeth would not chatter or bite down on his tongue.

"Give it a good slice, like that!" Atencio heard ripping and tearing again. "Don't take much, does it, to put this stuff in its place? Museum quality, wouldn't you say, Joe?"

Wood splintered and boards cracked apart in the studio above Atencio's head. But he did not move. He held his legs against his chest and pinned his mouth closed with his knees.

"My wife would like this one! Too bad! Shit, I should just take it to her. She likes those little pointy hills with clouds, like a sand box, she says, when we drive down south into the Big Bend country."

"I been there, Billyboy. But I myself don't care much for the clouds or for little pointy hills. Let her rip, sucker!"

The splintering of frames and the cutting of canvas continued without comment for several minutes. The light from a flashlight occasionally whipped past the cottonwood across the sand from Atencio.

"How much longer we got? Let's get the hell out of here; leave those."

"No, if Slope comes Jack don't care if we mess with him a little. We got the time. I'm hoping he comes. We could take him down. Faggot artist."

"Like to be here when he sees his precious mess; probably weep like a baby over these spilled bottles."

Glass shattered inside the studio, and then more glass and more glass. Atencio covered his ears with his hands and bit his lips to stop the scream gathering just below his Adam's apple. And then it was silent. A door slammed on the other side of the house and the truck with the rectangular headlights started up and roared down the drive to the road.

Atencio did not leave his hiding place beneath the studio window until he could hear nothing but the crickets in the junipers and the rushing gurgle of the stream; until he heard again the hooting of the old owl from his lookout high in the cliffs at the end of the canyon, and saw the half moon, a golden eye of familiar calm, lift gently above the sand hills. The sky was almost clear with only thin strands of clouds passing across the moon.

Atencio stood and leaned his back against the adobe house. He could see the bushes and the boulders, the rabbit brush and sage far up the mesa, in the bleached silver light. Atencio listened to the whishing thud of his blood passing through his head. When the thud subsided to only a soft thump against his temples, Atencio walked around to the front of Whitney's house.

The rose glow in the patio and the soft wind passing through the long branches of the catalpa tree gave no hint of the massacre that had just transpired inside.

Atencio sat down on the porch with his bare feet on the flagstone patio. Atencio knew Whitney's house was not locked, but still he did not go inside, not even into the kitchen when he let the cats out. Atencio could not go inside alone. But he could watch over the patio and the cats. Atencio sat with his back against one of the porch posts and waited for Whitney Slope to return.

The cats played in the bushes along the patio wall and then, finally tired, came to sit on the porch near Atencio. Their fur was white, with black around the ears and face, and on their small paws. Not like Mousse's black coat. But they had their mother's blue blue eyes. Even in the moonlight, Atencio could see the opaque black iris floating in a sea of blue that was Mousse, that was Three-Legs and Clem.

Atencio fought back a surge of sadness swelling up in his belly. He reached over and brought Three-Legs tenderly to his lap where she curled up and purred. Clem came to join them. Atencio stroked them both and felt their warm heat rise up into his hands. Life was here. Death was here, too, but Atencio was reaching for the life.

Whitney's truck lurched up the slippery drive and parked near the house. Atencio stood up as Whitney opened the gate.

"I saw the De Soto," Whitney said as he strode noisily up the porch. "I can give you a lift home now, or we can wait until morning. The road is not getting drier; we won't get the De Soto out 'till tomorrow."

Another Miracle

Atencio nodded, but looked away from Whitney.

"I'll have to put up with my refrigerator for at least another week," Whitney said walking up to the door. "What is it, Atencio? You look like you've seen a ghost."

"Something happened here. Men came. They were . . . "

Atencio pointed at the studio door.

"Men came here? What did they want?"

"I did not talk to them. They never saw me."

"Good lord . . . "

Whitney opened the studio door and groped for the light switch. Atencio remained on the porch, his eyes on his feet that again wore sneakers.

"Oh Christ . . . oh Jesus Christ! Oh my God, look what they've done!"

Atencio followed Whitney into the studio with his eyes still on his sneakers.

"Did you see them, Atencio? Who were they?"

Atencio slowly raised his eyes. The floor was splattered with blue and brown and white paint spilled from the gallon tubs Whitney kept near the work table. Stuck to the puddles of paint were pieces of canvas, shards of glass, and splintered scraps of wood frames. Atencio lifted his eyes to the walls and the windowsills, but there was not a painting left intact anywhere.

"Did you see them?"

Atencio thought before answering. He had a mental picture of the men, but he had never actually looked at them.

"No."

"Were they in a car? No, of course not, no car could get up here tonight. A truck? A jeep? Could you see?"

Atencio nodded. "Two men in a jeep."

"Had to be Jack's men."

Atencio's head jerked to look at Whitney.

"Did you hear that name, Atencio? Jack?"

"Yes."

"Jack Farina, the bastard! The bloody Texas bastard."

Whitney stepped around the piles of destroyed canvasses, picking up the remnants of an especially large one near the north wall.

"They got 'em all; sweet Jesus, they got 'em all."

Whitney left the studio and walked through the kitchen back to his bedroom. Atencio sat down on the floor near the door. He wanted very much to throw up, but he pinned his lips together and concentrated on his sneakers.

He had done nothing to stop them, and they had desecrated and defiled everything. He had not stopped them. He had crouched in fear and protected himself—been little more than an accomplice. He had seen such evil men before. And just like in Nam, he had not moved; he had remained mute, had closed his eyes and waited for the evil to end.

Whitney stood at the studio door holding the remains of more paintings.

"They got the paintings in the kitchen and bathroom . . . they even found the ones on the ceiling. Jesus Christ! They even got the one I had packed to send to my niece! Christ!"

Atencio could not look up at Whitney, nor could he get his feet under him to stand. Atencio's chest began to heave like a balloon. Then he began to moan, and soon he was sobbing like a child.

"Oh, Atencio, no." Whitney exclaimed. "It's not your fault! Atencio, this has nothing to do with you."

Whitney pushed aside a piece of a painting still connected to one corner of its frame and dumped what he had in his arms onto the floor, before kneeling down beside Atencio. Atencio buried his face into his knees and tried to conceal his sobs. Whitney slid an arm around his shoulders.

"Oh, God, I wish you hadn't seen this," Whitney said. "This is all mine, mine, Atencio; this war is all mine."

"I didn't stop them," Atencio choked his words through deep sobs. "I watched; I could have stopped . . . they never saw me . . . I hid."

"If you . . . if they had seen you, they might have hurt you. These were bad men, Atencio. God, I should have known!"

Whitney slumped down against the wall beside Atencio. Atencio cried until he was empty. When his belly stopped filling with pain, Atencio looked over at Whitney. Whitney's knees were pulled up under his chin, like Atencio's. His eyes were small slits, and his fingers held his head on either side of his skull.

"Shit," Whitney mumbled, "Goddammitall. I should have seen it coming."

Whitney looked at Atencio.

"It was all so perfectly expected. Sometimes the obvious is so obvious we simply don't see it coming at us."

Another Miracle

Whitney sighed loudly and then stood and walked around the studio. "Really, this is no surprise."

Atencio saw Whitney's beautiful, talented hands trembling.

"You will begin again." Atencio stood and touched Whitney's elbow from behind. "What you see, here in your head, is yours. If they do not get your spirit, then you can begin again."

"My paintings seem to bring nothing but trouble," Whitney said. "Not just to me, but to all the people I care about . . . Alejandro, my sister, now you."

"Your paintings gave me back my memory," Atencio said simply. "They helped me to remember what is beautiful . . . what is permanent . . . "

Whitney reached out a hand and touched Atencio's shoulder, trying to smile.

"Actually, Atencio, you did the same for me," Whitney said.

Atencio shook his head. He did not understand.

"You, Atencio, and this canyon, and Mousse, Dominga . . . I had forgotten how much I needed life that was not made with paint."

Atencio looked across the floor strewn with torn canvas and wood. "I had forgotten how much I missed life that was not diluted with alcohol."

Atencio walked out onto the patio and across the flagstones to the rose slab that was not level with the others. Mousse's grave. Atencio removed his sneakers and placed his bare feet upon the wet, cool stone and closed his eyes: instead of remorse and sadness, Atencio felt a warm surge as if Mousse's spirit were rising up through his legs and wrapping itself around his heart.

Whitney came and stood on the porch behind him.

"I did not do a very good job," Whitney said softly. "You can reset the stone, if you want."

"No . . ." Atencio's toes curled over the lifted edge of the grave. "This is how it should be. It is a stone, a story, worth remembering."

Atencio turned and looked up at the sky over the tin roof.

"Whitney, where is the big one?"

Whitney looked up at the stars, puzzled. "What big one?"

"Is it still out back?" Atencio asked.

Whitney stared uncertainly at Atencio. Atencio left the patio and jogged around the side of the house to the back porch. Whitney followed.

"It's here! Christ, it's here!" Whitney cried. They each held an end of the huge frame. "They never saw it. Oh, God, they never saw it!"

Atencio pressed his fingers into the hard wood that was safe and strong beneath the plastic he had so carefully enshrouded the canvas in two days ago.

"*La Ventana de Dios,*" Atencio said.

Whitney looked at Atencio from the far end of the ten foot painting. They stared at one another, two ghost forms in the haze of the back porch, their ghost hands rubbing the top of the frame between them.

"*God's Window?* That's what you call it?"

Atencio nodded. He could feel Whitney trembling through the frame.

"*Sí.* But now I think it is *La Ventana de los Milagros.*"

"Miracles?" Whitney sighed. "Are all the miracles in this place related somehow to tragedy?"

"*Sí, mas o menos,*" Atencio said. "But you can see, now, how Mousse returned to this place, to watch over the canyon. Like the sheep, a death that leaves the living with a sense of hope."

Whitney rubbed his forehead with the back of his hand, which still trembled in the moonlight.

"*Es verdad,* Atencio."

◎

Atencio sat at Whitney's kitchen table. A kerosene lamp made sputtering sounds every few minutes when the moths that fluttered through holes in the door screen reached the flame. From up the canyon, they could hear the owl, and coyotes were yipping noisily on the open desert.

"I don't think I can drive just now," Whitney said. "Would you mind sleeping here? You can have my bed, or you can sleep on the porch on the hammock, in my bag. Your choice. Please stay, Atencio."

Atencio walked to the screen door and looked out at the gleaming patio. Clem and Three-Legs were waiting by the door. Behind them the moon was halfway to its zenith in the cloudless sky.

"I'll sleep on the patio."

Whitney brought Atencio his sleeping bag and a pillow from the bedroom.

"I'm sure Clem would stay and sleep with you. Three-Legs is afraid. She can't shake the memory of those dogs."

"Okay."

Atencio turned.

"You know, Atencio," Whitney was looking at him across the kitchen. "I understand some of the pain." Whitney touched his belly. "I have that pain, too. My only sister died of cancer last fall. There was so much I wanted to say. There was so much left to be done. And I don't know who to blame. Except myself."

Atencio looked at Whitney's belly and then back at his face.

"Persimillion believes God took her babies," Atencio added. "I do not know what to tell her. My mother says we must be like the sheep sacrificed in the wind; accepting the fate that takes us; the death that chooses us; and, in-between, the miracles that sustain us."

Atencio opened the door and left the kitchen. He picked up Clem while Three-Legs scurried into the house with Whitney.

"Thanks for staying, Atencio," Whitney said from the far side of the screen. "I'm so damned thankful they didn't see you."

"It's because I am so quiet," Atencio said. "Stealthy. They said Indians are sneaky by nature."

"Who said?" Whitney opened the screen door and leaned out towards Atencio and Clem.

"Over there."

Whitney frowned.

"But you're not really even Indian. You speak Spanish. You're Hispanic."

"I look Indian. And my great grandmother was Apache. Over there, I was always, always, point. Point man. And if a man got killed, even if he was a hundred yards away from me, I felt like I had failed him."

"It was a jungle. You were outnumbered, Atencio. No one could see them all."

"I wanted to," Atencio said to Clem, "I even believed, for a while, that I was that good. That if I were good, really good, no one would die."

"But they would . . . they did . . . and you are that good." Whitney stepped out through the door. "You are that good. I would follow you, Atencio, through any jungle."

It was too warm a night for a sleeping bag, so Atencio lay exposed to the canyon air. Atencio was very tired, but he was not sleepy. One arm rested on the stone above the grave, and his other arm held Clem warmly against his ribs. Atencio watched the moon drop in the west, and the stars and their brilliant universe of infinity roll towards him. When a gentle wave of sleep finally lapped against Atencio's body, he slipped into somnolent waters that carried him under the stone and into his heart: Mousse was here.

t·h·i·r·t·y- t·h·r·e·e

A Window in the High Noon

It was forecast by the local weather people to be a clear day in northern New Mexico. Whitney listened on the kitchen radio to their promises of blue skies and fluffy, waterless clouds. Dominga had explained how the rains would end when the jet stream no longer scooped water out of the Gulf of Mexico or California and carried it northeast into New Mexico. The rains might return for an afternoon or two, later in the week, but the monsoons carried by the anvil-shaped cumulonimbus clouds were about spent. Just like everyone who lived below them, on the land, Whitney figured. Spent: emptied, hollowed, rinsed—cleansed.

In a month or so, everyone around Santa Fe, around Mi Ojo, would complain about the dry heat of fall. But for today, anyway, the population of northern New Mexico were united behind the weather caster's gleeful declaration that the rains of August were past.

Whitney and Atencio had spent the morning mopping up the studio floor after hauling the ravaged paintings to a pile behind the house. Whitney chose a sandy spot far from the cottonwood's old branches for his bonfire. But when all the frames and canvasses were out of the studio, he did not immediately take a match to the paintings.

"I'll wait until dark, when I can really see the fire," Whitney told Atencio. But Whitney knew, and he figured Atencio knew, too, that he could not let the paintings go yet.

Before Atencio left in the De Soto, freed easily once the morning sun laid its hot arms on the road that clung to the De Soto's tires, Whitney asked him to help move the sole surviving painting into the rear of his truck. It did not fit, of course, but stuck out a few feet into the space over the bumper. But the painting was wrapped and tied securely with rope. The *Window of Miracles* was safe for travel.

"Where will you take it?" Atencio asked. Whitney thought Atencio was looking a little forlorn about the window leaving the canyon.

"Some place safe; some place where it will be appreciated, maybe. Where people can look at it, or through it. You'll see it again, Atencio, I promise you."

"Will you sell it?"

"Not exactly. I'm thinking that I'll auction it off for charity. Give the money to the Children's Hospital. Or the V.A. Hospital, in Santa Fe."

Atencio continued to look at the wrapped canvas as if it were his best friend departing for another part of the world.

"I'll paint you another one, Atencio," Whitney said. "A smaller one you can put in your house. Okay?"

It was mid afternoon when Whitney pulled the truck into the alley and parked at the rear entrance to the High Noon. Juan opened the back door for Whitney and ushered him in with an inquiring nod at his mud-caked truck parked where delivery vehicles usually stopped.

"You getting especially old, Whitney, needing a closer parking place?"

Whitney removed his hat and sunglasses and rubbed his eyes.

"I've aged, Juan, but I'm really just making a delivery. How's the fishing going?

"I left the tackle box on my brother-in-law's boat," Juan said, apologetically. "He uses it like his own all the time. I use it when I go out with him, but I still take all the food."

Whitney chuckled.

"Is one of the Gateworthy's around?"

"*Sí*, Jon and Samantha both."

Whitney strode into the outer cafe and surveyed the room for its owners. A tourist family, easily identified by their oversized canvas bags, and the sunburn that shone on their cheeks, noses, and tops of shoulders, were finishing a late lunch at a table in the very middle of the cafe. The Gateworthy's were sitting side by side at the bar drinking through straws stuck into a single pop bottle.

"Good Lord almighty, Samantha, it's that vagabond and ne'er-do-well painter, Whitney Slope." Jon raised a hand and gestured for Whitney to join them. Whitney took the seat next to Sam and placed his arm around her waist.

"Looks like the good life lives here, sipping soda with your sweetheart on a summer afternoon."

"Let me get you one, Whitney." Sam stood up and went around the bar before Whitney could stop her. "Would you rather have a beer?"

"No, soda is fine."

Sam put the soda down on the bar with a tall glass of ice.

"What are you in town for?" Jon asked. "Were your ears ringing, or did Anna send someone out with the news?"

"What news would that be, Jon?"

"Anna, well, she seems to have thrown Jack out," Jon said. "Literally—boots, hats, saddles, pistols, and all into the front fountain. I guess you wouldn't know, not having a phone."

Whitney shook his head.

"No, I wouldn't know," Whitney said. "But someone did come out with the news, in a manner of speaking."

"Who, Whitney?" Sam asked.

Whitney looked over his shoulder. The tourists were busy trying to cool their salsa-burned lips with ice water.

"Jack sent some men up my canyon last night. They were in my studio. They carved up my paintings . . . tore up the studio. Everything."

"Oh my God, I can't believe it!" Sam said.

"I can," Jon said. "I'm sorry to say that I can believe it."

Whitney fidgeted with his glass and looked at Jon down the bar.

"Everything?" Jon asked after a moment.

"Yeah, all of it."

"Good stuff?" Sam asked.

Whitney did not answer. The bad feeling he had had earlier this morning, before he and Atencio had cleaned up the studio, came back to nest in his stomach.

"Of course it was good stuff," Jon said quietly. "Why would Jack Farina destroy anything less?"

Whitney drank his soda. Jon went to the ice machine and filled another pitcher with water for the sunburned family. Sam bit her lip and watched Whitney.

"It's not been an easy pill to swallow," Whitney said when Jon returned and stood across the bar from him, "but at least no one was hurt, and most of my heart is still beating this morning."

"Will you press charges?" Jon asked.

"No. That would just escalate it all, involve innocent bystanders."

Jon nodded and looked down the bar and out the door to the plaza.

"I wish I could think of something to say, Whitney."

"*I told you so* would not be out of line," Whitney said. Everyone at the bar sighed. "Actually, there was a little gift from the spirits of the canyon: one painting survived the massacre." Whitney gestured to the kitchen and the back door to the alley. "If you two will have it, I have a business proposal for you'all."

"Anything. What do you have in mind?" Jon asked.

"I have the spared canvas out back in the truck. I want to hang it here and put it up for auction—you know, take silent bids for a few weeks. I don't want to show this in the gallery."

Whitney looked across at Sam and then over at Jon.

"Not to be spiteful or anything; just because. The profit from this one isn't for me. Or Anna. It's for . . . intangible debts. Call it a penance of sorts. I need a place big enough to hang it, and you've got the perfect wall. What do you say?"

"Can we see it first?" Jon asked. "I'm assuming I'll like it, but maybe your style's changed out there, what with all these spirits and what-have-you."

Whitney chuckled. "Let's go."

Burt Rapp was sitting with a newspaper spread open before him at the corner table when Whitney and Jon and Sam carried the wrapped painting into the cafe from the kitchen. The tourist family had left.

"Good lord, he has been working this summer," Burt said to the room in general. "What's this one, Slope? I can see, of course, that it's very large."

After leaning it against the mud wall, where it reached across half the length of the room, Jon, Sam and Whitney carefully untaped the green plastic wrap and uncovered the painting.

"Oh, God, it's wonderful, Whitney," Sam spoke first. "This is . . . fine."

The resonating blue of the sky seen through the long, narrow, white-trimmed window glowed even in the dim and dusty, hardly lit High Noon Cafe. The mud of the painting's wall and the High Noon's blended together like intimate neighbors, and the low horizon of faraway red hills brought the heat and space of the summer desert into the small cafe.

"Yeah, this is good, this is, well, just real good." Jon looked up at Whitney and then back to the painting. "Like it should be, isn't it? A window there to all that sky. The clouds, like they are alive. Of course we'll do the auction."

"Auction? You're going to auction this one? Why?" Burt Rapp left his table and approached the painting. "Why not Mud Street?"

"He's donating the proceeds from this one to charity," Sam said.

"Tax problems?" Burt asked.

"No, Burt, no tax problems," Whitney said. "Just because I want to. It's the thing to do with this one."

"Anna Farina's not going to be real keen on missing out on this sale. You know, *mucho dinero* slipping past her fingers. And *dinero* is something she may be needing this fall."

Whitney shot Burt an inquisitive glance, but did not ask what he knew.

"How can we hang it, Jon? It's terribly heavy," Sam said, walking away from the painting and viewing it from another part of the cafe. "It's wonderful, what a window. What's it called, Whitney? *Perfect View of the Perfect Desert?*"

"*The Window of Miracles,*" Whitney answered.

"You've gotten religious?" Burt asked. "Those little villages are living relics of Old World Catholicism. But who would have guessed Whitney Slope would be born again in one?"

"Actually, it was someone else's name for the painting; it just seemed to fit."

"Oh, get me my pencil, I feel a story coming on. Now Slope, don't go shaking your head like that. I could build it around the auction, charity and all. You know it will bring in more with publicity, Whitney."

Whitney surveyed Burt, who was chewing on a stub of a pencil because he could not smoke in the cafe. If there was such a thing, Burt was a discreet editor.

"Okay, you're on. But let me help them hang this first."

Burt Rapp and Whitney sat at the bar, each sipping soda from a tall glass and munching tortilla chips still warm from the kitchen. Burt's notebook lay open between them on the bar.

"This is all you have from a summer of work out there in, what's it called, Mi Ojo?" Burt waited for Whitney to answer before he began scribbling notes again.

"Mi Ojo, yes. But drop the name. No names."

Whitney looked at Burt. "You know, Burt, I'm as sick about Burro Alley as anyone."

"I know that, Whitney. It was nothing personal, the editorial."

"Well, it is personal. You're right, for the most part, but it's still personal."

"Mi Ojo, the place you're living now? You know you can keep that sort of paradise a secret for only so long." Burt set his pencil down on the bar and began fidgeting with but not pulling out a cigarette.

Whitney looked Burt squarely in the eye. "It's not paradise, Burt. It's poor. It's dry. The people have nothing but their land and one another and this old faith in the seasons and the heavens."

"It's beautiful, isn't it?"

"The people are beautiful," Whitney answered.

"So you're painting people now?"

"No." Whitney said. "Just clouds and sky . . . territory that even the developers haven't been able to lay their hands on yet."

Burt raised his eyebrows. "You and I know there are those who will try. So, why is this the only painting from the summer?"

Whitney held a chip in the air and studied its salty surface.

"Don't print this, but vandals got the rest. That big one is all that's left."

"What?" Burt stared at the large painting. He whistled and then leaned into Whitney. "Farina's people got the rest, didn't they?"

"I didn't say I knew who wrecked them, just that they're gone."

"Oh, well, I know," Burt said.

"What do you know, Burt?"

Whitney cracked chips between his teeth and squinted at Burt in the mirror across the bar. Burt waited a moment and then answered:

"I know that Anna threw Jack Farina out of the house several days ago—piled his clothes and personal affects into the front fountain there where her nosy neighbors had a view of the whole altercation—and that she is divorcing him. Jack Farina is going to lose some big investments here, including Mud Street. Anna's got herself a very good lawyer. She has, I am told, very thorough proof of his illegal doings, even stuff from his books, hard ball, and that leaves him pretty much with his hands tied in the settlement. Jack Farina doesn't like having his hands tied, especially by his adulterous wife. I would think Farina could be very imaginative in cutting his losses and slapping Anna, and her lover, all in one fell swoop."

Burt rubbed his eyes under his glasses. "Are you pressing charges?"

"No. No, I'm not. What would it change? What good would come of it?"

"What will you do?"

"I'll just start over again."

Burt whistled again through his teeth. "What I can't print will kill me for sure." He turned around to face Whitney. "I'm looking to understand you, Whitney. Maybe there's less to figure out about you than I used to believe. Once in a while, folks like me like to think folks like you struggle a little bit. Today I'm thinking you do."

"I struggle just like you, Burt. Maybe even more."

"Can I quote you some day on that?"

"Yeah, you can."

Whitney swiveled his stool around and faced the painting with both elbows propped on the mahogany bar behind him. There was not a stroke he would change on that canvas. Not a color he would add or subtract, not a cloud or a hill he would raise or lower. Whitney had studied that window, that horizon, in his head and on the canvas for two entire weeks of mornings. The deep red of the sand, the hot white on the window ledge, the blue deepening into more blue, the drifting clouds floating into infinity had lived in his arms and swirled in his belly like a smooth liquor for fourteen days and nights. A painting like that was an addictive drug that did not dissolve from the blood.

Connie would have loved that painting: not because it was beautiful, nor because it was large and well done, well drawn, as she used to say; but because of the breathing, palpable life that orbited Whitney while he worked on the canvas. Connie knew that art had to, eventually, finally, wed reality. Art could never be separate, could never be held at some antiseptic distance.

Whitney looked at that window and heard Atencio's hammer chinking at the rose stone, heard the cats' wrestling bodies thumping happily on the old linoleum of the kitchen, and the cicadas on the mesa junipers buzzing zealously in the escalating heat. He was sorry Dominga had not seen the painting out in the canyon. He would bring her here, to the High Noon, for lunch one day soon.

"A good struggle, Burt," Whitney said as he swiveled back to face the bar. "Make sure and say it was, it is, a good struggle."

Burt smiled and stood up as he closed his notebook.

"Slope, I'll do a story another time, when you know what the story is about. For now, I'll just mention the auction and the *Window*, the V. A. Hospital. Art news, you know; nothing more."

"Fine."

ℚ

Whitney stepped out of the High Noon kitchen into the sun of the back alley and found Anna Farina standing in the shade of his truck's cab, staring at her shoes. She had not heard him open the screen door, nor the sound of his boots on the pavement of the alley. Whitney had never seen Anna so oblivious to her surroundings, especially when her surroundings consisted of the alley near the detested High Noon Cafe.

"Anna Farina," Whitney said as he put on his hat and sunglasses. "Anna Farina."

Anna straightened up and moved away from the truck, obviously startled.

"Whitney," she said, shading her eyes. Anna usually wore sunglasses, but Whitney noticed she carried neither her glasses nor her purse. Anna was uncharacteristically empty handed. "I was waiting for you. I saw the truck."

"Saw the truck? Were you out strolling Santa Fe's lovely alleys, or did you just happened to look waaaay down here?"

"No, actually . . . Burt called me. Don't be angry with him. I asked him to, if he saw you in town."

Whitney kicked some dried mud off the left front wheel well of his truck.

"I'm not angry. You've been standing out here all this time?"

"Half an hour or so." Anna paused and sucked in a small breath. "I'm divorcing Jack."

Whitney shook his head and bit his lower lip.

"So I heard, Anna."

"I would have called you, but I couldn't," Anna said. "I wanted you to hear from me, not through the grapevine. I'm sorry about that . . . the gossip."

"Oh, I don't care about that, Anna." Whitney surveyed Anna's face: she wore almost no makeup, and her eyes were swollen and small. She was putting up a remarkable front considering the condition she was in. So, Whitney realized, was he.

"You've made the right decision, Anna. That's what really matters, not the gossip. How have you been? It can't be easy right now."

"I'm okay, thankful really. Forty-eight hours have passed; Jack's still gone, and my house is still standing. Mud Street, too. He can't take them from me. I expected something. But I was very careful. He's not going to win this time."

Whitney stared at his boots a moment. He felt like the grim reaper the way he passed out bad news today.

"There's something you must know . . . it's about Jack. And you and me. Actually it's about my paintings. It's that Jack sent his men up to my house last night. They destroyed all of my work."

Anna let out a strangled cry. Whitney took her shoulder and bent over near her face.

"Anna, no one was hurt. That's the thing."

"No, the thing is, the thing of it is, Jack always wins."

Anna pulled from Whitney and faced the alley away from him.

"You see, Whitney? It's that good people don't win. It's the bad that have the power. Always. And if you don't play by their rules, play dirty and mean, you lose. You do."

Whitney turned Anna around by her shoulders. She was crying.

"No, that's not true. You are going to win this time, Anna. You've won. You're out. You've got yourself and your business; you can take care of yourself. Don't let him win . . . let it go."

"All your work."

"I'll do more work."

Anna studied Whitney's face. Whitney wiped her cheeks with his hand.

"How can you be so forgiving?"

Whitney smiled and let go of Anna's shoulders.

"Because I've been forgiven all my damned life, that's why."

Anna sighed.

"I guess I should feel better. I mean at least I don't have to lie awake wondering what Jack's going to do to me. He's done it. And Jack is a one shot killer. Once he hits, he doesn't strike again. That wouldn't be sporting."

Whitney leaned against the truck's hood. He was developing a headache from the heat and the glare of the sun in the alley. Anna looked just as withered.

"I suppose you'll want to change galleries," Anna said. "I wouldn't blame you, Whitney. No one would."

"No, I don't want to change galleries, Anna."

"Really?"

"Honest to God," Whitney said, holding up his Boy Scout fingers.

"What do I sell this fall?"

"You have a gallery full of fine artists. Promote them. Back them, Anna. They need that, too. Their time is coming—or here. Remember six, seven years ago nobody bought my work. Not even you."

Anna chewed her thumbnail, which was chipped of it's high gloss finish.

"I really am on my own, aren't I?" Anna said, holding her hand away from her body and frowning at her nails.

"You've waited thirty-eight years for this, Anna. Embrace it—it could be the time of your life."

Anna dropped her hands and lifted her eyes to Whitney.

"This is the moving sideways, isn't it?"

"What?"

"Or is it forwards?"

Whitney understood and nodded.

"No, this is forwards," Whitney said forcefully, but smiling. "It is, all of it, forwards."

Anna left the side of the truck and walked quickly to Whitney. She wrapped her slender arms around his waist and pushed her face hard into his chest. Whitney stroked Anna's hair.

"You dumped his clothes out in the driveway? Did you really do that? What did the neighbors say?"

Anna chuckled through congested nasal passages.

"I did. I did that. Every last boot, every bolo tie, every turquoise watchband; even his shaving stuff. I only wish I could have burned it without getting arrested."

"I have some burning to do myself. I'll think of you when I light the match."

Anna eyed Whitney.

"I'll think good things, Anna. Only good."

Whitney pointed to the truck.

"Can I drive you back to the gallery, or your car, or the house?"

"No, I really want to walk. I even wore flats, see, just for this occasion."

"Okay. You walk carefully, Anna B."

"Like you drive, Whitney?"

Whitney opened the truck door and climbed in.

"Like I'm learning to drive; yes, like that."

t.h.i.r.t.y - f.o.u.r

Another Death on the Highway

Persimillion was familiar with the habits of mice and rats, but when Alfredo began to gnaw on the rope between them, she did not respond with her usual alacrity. Some part of her slumbering self knew she was in New Mexico. Persimillion had never seen a mouse or a rat anywhere near the old station. Too many large wild birds, Pepé said.

Persimillion went on dreaming. Her dream was not about the station; nor about Alfredo, ropes, or rats. Persimillion was high in the mountains and although she was alone in a country she did not know, she knew in her dream heart that Atencio would find her here. The higher the mountain beneath her dream feet, the clearer the air became. In such clear air, Persimillion knew Atencio's green eyes would easily find her.

She was almost out of reach of everything that followed her, was taking the last steps to the summit that touched the bottoms of the clouds, when a cry from far below stabbed her and jolted Persimillion to consciousness. She noticed the frayed rope beside her on the mud floor. And then she noticed how large the station seemed with just herself lying on the floor. She noticed the full, nearly round moon, too, directly overhead, exactly where the station's half-roof ended. And before she sat up, she remembered how Pepé and Atencio were not here because they were together at Atencio's house working on Atencio's car.

The cry came again: it was a call, first, then a scream and a thumping sound, and then silence. Persimillion struggled to rock her body off her buttocks and stand, but it took several attempts before she could find her balance. There were people out there on the highway calling to her, talking loudly. But Persimillion stood unable to move, staring at the frayed, short rope dangling from her waist.

She wanted to hurry, to run, because she knew that Alfredo was on the road, silent. And she feared his silences more than his seizures, more than his angers or hungers. She walked to the station door and on across the stones and sand of the gas station's old parking lot. She knew the moon cast more than enough light on the highway to give her a full understanding of the commotion awaiting her, but Persimillion chose to walk with her head down, her eyes on the stones and the sand and the cactus that had become home.

When she reached the blacktop and the people talking in nonsensical, loud English, she knelt down—almost falling—and placed her head on Alfredo's chest. She knew there was no pulse—there was far too much blood on his shirt and in his hair and splattered about between his feet and the car's fender—to hope for a pulse. But Persimillion had said death's good-bye before and she knew it was important that she do so properly now.

The Americans cried and bent down beside her. Persimillion said nothing. Other cars came and stopped, and soon there were people all around her, many even speaking Spanish and asking her what they could do? Persimillion wanted to say there was nothing to do, but she could not part her lips to speak. She settled herself down onto the blacktop and pulled Alfredo's head and shoulders onto her lap and began to sing to him. While she sang, she wiped the blood from his face with her blouse and took each of his hands and placed them across his thin chest. The rope was still tied about him; laying on the highway was the chewed end, like a cut umbilical cord. Someone above Persimillion placed a white, silk handkerchief in her hand. Persimillion knew it was for her face, her tears, but she used it instead to clean Alfredo.

The police came before the ambulance. Persimillion wondered for the first time since waking exactly where Pepé was and if he were safe with Atencio. She prayed that he was faraway and ignorant as the officers gently, but firmly, lifted her away from Alfredo. The ambulance men brought a stretcher and a white sheet, and began to wrap Alfredo's body. When they lifted him onto the canvas stretcher between them, Persimillion reached down once more and touched Alfredo's cool cheek with one warm hand.

"He was foolish, you see," she told the officer beside her. The policeman nodded and looked down at Alfredo.

Two policemen lead Persimillion past the people watching along the side of the road, past the ambulance parked uselessly in front of the gas station, to one of the police cars. Before they helped her into the back seat, someone stepped up to Persimillion and held out Atencio's father's watch.

"This was in the road," the officer translated for Persimillion. "Was it the boy's?"

"*Sí,*" Persimillion said, taking the watch and staring into its shattered face. "But the insides were always broken."

Miguel Gonzales Takes Pepé Ramirez Home

The good padre Leo was not a sound sleeper. Padre Leo needed a nightly respite from the goings-on in the valley and in the village around him, but more times than not, he lay awake listening to the coyotes yipping and barking up at the village dump, to the cries of colicky babies across the plaza somewhere, and to the occasional siren of an ambulance driving down the valley from one of the northern communities en route to the Santa Fe Children's Hospital.

Padre Leo lay awake pondering the dry stillness that descended on Mi Ojo after the rains of August. On this particular night, padre Leo was aware, too, of the air of agitation rising off the valley floor. Maybe it was because of his swollen bones pressing against one another in his brittle joints, but the good padre was unusually sensitive to the subtle changes in the air over Mi Ojo: not just changes in climate, but in the soil and the valley's flora and fauna, too. Padre Leo's skin prickled the dawn the cholla cactus birthed their first blossoms into fiery bloom, and he was itchy the evening the tarantulas returned to roam the valley fields, their black, furry bodies boldly, foolishly, crossing the highway en route to remembered migration grounds.

When the night air lifted the muslin window curtains Dominga de Jesús had mended, padre Leo could sense the changes that came to the people of Mi Ojo: the heavy breath of grief when death swept away someone's elderly parent a few houses up the road, or the snarling wind of anger that would whorl in the padre's belly even before an audible ruckus from two or more frustrated souls could reach his ears, prompting him to sit up and pray for human understanding and divine forgiveness.

The night was not a time of rest for the good padre Leo. Padre Leo was thankful for the moon's company on those nights it drifted brilliantly aloof above the earth of Mi Ojo, a celestial keeper of the light during the good padre's long nights of lonely vigil.

Padre Leo felt the commotion below on the highway east of Mi Ojo and sat up on the edge of his bed to view the moon. The moon would be full and perfectly round tomorrow night. Padre Leo closed his eyes and listened. Even those lunatic coyotes up the canyon above the village dump had been silenced by something, something bigger than their ancestral love for the moon. Padre Leo stared into the moon and listened. Tonight there had been an accident of some kind down the valley, below in the mesa country east of the village. Padre Leo began to pray, his ears alert for the first distant call of a siren.

The siren came from the east, from Santa Fe. The yowling of the Mi Ojo dogs joined the song of the siren. Padre Leo wondered if the coyotes joined, too, or was this only the song of man and his misery? If he were able to walk quickly, padre Leo would have left his apartment and headed down the hill to the highway. But he could hardly move his legs from the bed, so the good padre dressed slowly and then hobbled across the parish courtyard to the church.

Padre Leo knelt at the foot of his beloved Virgin in the flickering light of sixty-four candles in the *santuario* and waited. He did not mean to be waiting, and was shamed by his inability to place his whole mind, his whole heart, on the words of the Lord he whispered over his rosary. Maybe it was a father's reflex, always worrying that it might be Miguel in trouble? Padre Leo's whole body ached for news it did not yet possess in pictures, but felt in meaning. When the side door to the church creaked open thirty minutes later, it was with both relief and anxiety that padre Leo rose to greet his nephew.

Miguel Gonzales was not in uniform, but was dressed in faded jeans and a sleeveless T-shirt, wearing the sneakers he played power forward in for the Mi Ojo community basketball team. It was very dim in the church, especially in the corner near the side door. Padre Leo could not make out the face of the slender young man standing behind Miguel, gripping his nephew's long arm like a rooted tree found during a violent storm.

"My son, come in." padre Leo stood clumsily and stumbled forwards, catching himself on the pew beside him. "Ah, I am so stiff in the middle of the night, *como un viejo.*"

"Padre, there has been a terrible accident." Miguel drew the hidden person into the half-light of the candles. "I have brought Pepé. He needs refuge, padre, and I cannot do anything more. Do you understand?"

"*¡Díos mío!* Come here, Pepé, what has happened?"

Pepé released his grip on Miguel's arm and shuffled across the wood floor to padre Leo's open arms. Pepé bent his head over and with his chin touching his chest, began to sob. Padre Leo lifted his crooked arms around Pepé's torso and held him gently, looking at Miguel who remained near the door.

"Tell me, Miguel, what has happened? Where is the sister, and the other brother?"

Miguel put his hands in the front pockets of his jeans and shook his head.

"I did not get there first, *tío,* I was not home, or near the car radio. Or I might have gotten there first."

"Gotten to where?"

"The old gas station. I was up in Tomita, with Lila, and I drove as fast as I could, but the sheriff was already at the scene."

"The scene? Tell me, Miguel, was someone hurt?"

"The other brother, Alfredo. He was hit by a car. He was killed, padre, on the highway east of the gas station."

Pepé began to moan loudly, and his legs folded under him. He allowed the padre and Miguel to place him on the pew.

"Oh, *¡Dios mío,* no! Oh, Pepé, I am so sorry." Padre Leo crossed himself and then pressed his eyes closed with his free hand.

"He—he wanted a ride home," Pepé hiccuped in Spanish into his dirty shirt sleeve, "Alfredo broke the rope when Persimillion was sleeping. I was . . . gone."

Pepé's sobs came from deep in his throat, like an animal's. Padre Leo held Pepé's thin body down against his lap and let him rock and moan. Miguel stood in the shadows of the doorway, one hand pressed around his forehead.

"When I drove up, the sheriff's department had Persimillion," Miguel said in English. "They were about to take her in. She sat in the middle of the highway, padre, with Alfredo's . . . with his face resting on her lap. She tried to clean his face with her blouse . . . " Miquel's hand reached helplessly into the air before him. "When they asked her what happened, she told them—before I could stop her—that her brother wanted to go home to Mexico. It took three men to move her, to lift her away from Alfredo and take her to the sheriff's car. They took her to Santa Fe, to the state detention center for illegal immigrants."

Padre Leo looked down at the boy cradled in his arms. Pepé was still now, as if he were asleep. Padre Leo responded in English.

Miguel Gonzales Takes
Pepé Ramirez Home

"Miguel, you have risked so much to bring Pepé."

"Pepé and Atencio were working on the De Soto behind Dominga's trailer. Apparently Pepé walked home because Atencio was not done with the car and it was getting late . . . that's when Pepé saw the ambulance. The accident. I found him under the cottonwoods behind the station."

Miguel paused and took a long breath.

"I thought he was unconscious, the way he lay in the tangled brush, curled in a small ball. He did not move when I spoke his name. I had to carry him away from the station and leave him further in the bosque. He did as I told him and waited for me to return. After the sheriff left, I went back and brought him here."

Padre Leo stroked Pepé's straight, black hair. "He will stay with me for now. In the morning, perhaps, I will think of something to do. Miguel, I am so thankful for you."

Miguel Gonzales walked to the center of the church and genuflected. He then walked over to the table of flickering candles and stood a moment staring into the waxy glow at the Virgin's feet.

" I have broken a law I swore to uphold, *tío*. Of what good is my word? What sort of man am I?"

"Tonight, you upheld God's laws, Miguel," padre Leo said from the pew behind. "You are a man whose word is better than most, my nephew, because yours is a word spoken for everyone."

Miguel turned around and faced the empty church. His eyes were bloodshot. Padre Leo longed to stand and hold his only nephew—his first child, always, may God forgive him, his only son—but his hands were full with Pepé. And padre Leo could see that even wrestling with confusion and despair, Miguel Gonzales had his feet firmly beneath him.

"I must go and tell Atencio and Dominga what has happened. I must go now, *tío,* and move my car away from the church. The longer I am here, the more trouble it could cause everyone."

"*Sí, por favor,* go quickly, Miguel, you must avoid trouble."

Pepé lifted his face as Miguel walked past the pew towards the side door. "Thank you, Officer Gonzales," he said in English halted by sobs.

"You must do what the good padre tells you now, Pepé. And please, *hermano, yo me llamo Miguel.*"

⟲

Miguel Gonzales Takes
Pepé Ramirez Home

After the heavy carved door was pulled closed, and after padre Leo heard Miguel start his car and idle away from the church, he closed his eyes and sat back against the pew.

"Dominga de Jesús always said Alfredo had one foot in heaven." Padre Leo spoke in soft Spanish to the top of Pepé's head. "Tonight, I believe he has placed both feet in heaven."

Pepé remained huddled low in the good padre's lap, sniffling, quietly soaking the padre's black polyester pants with what felt to the good padre like a lifetime of tears.

t·h·i·r·t·y-s·i·x

Los Milagros de la Gente

Whitney sat with his coffee and toast and two cats on the edge of the porch, his bare feet on the cool flagstones, his face lifted to the sun just risen over the canyon. Behind him in the studio were three new canvasses, stretched and gessoed the evening before, after his bonfire. A gallon bucket of Perfect Sky Blue—Whitney's own formula—and quart bottles of Desert Terra Cotta, Deep Mesa Red, Light Cloud Blue, Deep Twilight Blue, Sand Gold, Sand Brown, Sand Yellow and Sand Rose, were freshly mixed and waiting on his table in the middle of the room.

Caroline had a reservation on a plane bound for Denver, and then Santa Fe, on the fifteenth of September. Whitney planned to paint the next two weeks, then put the brush aside and explore northern New Mexico with his niece for a week.

Whitney sighed: Alan had not been particularly pleased with Caroline's independent decision to use her summer earnings on a plane ticket to the outback of the Southwest. But during Whitney's and Alan's forty-five minute phone call last night, even Alan seemed to remember how very much Connie had wanted to make this same trip; how Whitney was now and would always be Caroline's only living relative on her mother's side. How, after all the differences in lifestyle and politics and location were said and done, Whitney was family.

Whitney stood and stretched his bare arms high to the sky. The bean pods of the patio catalpa were almost a foot in length. Whitney wondered how much longer the tree would be able to bear the weight of its own fertility?

From faraway down the canyon, Whitney heard an approaching car. It was not yet seven in the morning. It seemed impossible to Whitney that a car was actually coming up his road. Whitney walked out to the patio gate and listened. The piñon jays had already passed his door en route to the box canyon and the water at its base. The drone of the car was momentarily muffled by the mesa and the ensuing quiet was so total Whitney heard his own blood thudding rhythmically past his temples. Thinking perhaps the car had turned around, Whitney turned back himself. But by the time he reached the house, the engine's hum had resurfaced. Whitney grabbed a shirt he'd left on a kitchen chair and returned to the porch.

Clem and Three-Legs sat on the patio wall, washing and readying themselves for company. Whitney pulled the shirt across his chest and buttoned it as the De Soto rounded the mesa, then headed up the driveway to the gate.

Whitney was relieved to see Atencio, although he was surprised Pepé Ramirez sat beside him on the front seat. Pepé had never come up the canyon with Atencio. Only Atencio climbed out of the car. He walked with an urgency Whitney had never seen in Atencio. His stride was reminiscent of Tomas's head-first march when he'd arrive intent on imposing or performing some task on Whitney or the house.

"Atencio, good morning."

"Whitney, we, I, very much need your help," Atencio said as he reached the gate. "This morning I must go to Santa Fe. You must drive me to Santa Fe, now."

"Atencio, it's seven a.m. What's the rush?"

Pepé was leaning across the front seat so he could see Atencio and Whitney through the driver's window.

"Persimillion was taken last night, and we have to go and get her out."

"Out of where?"

"Immigration. They will send her back to Mexico if I don't get her."

"Wait, wait Atencio, how can you get her out?" Whitney squinted into the De Soto at Pepé. "Where's Alfredo?"

Atencio's green eyes flickered to the ground for just an instant.

"Alfredo was hit by a car last night," Atencio said softly. "He was killed on the highway."

"Oh Jesus! Oh, God, no!"

Whitney turned away from Atencio and leaned against the blue gate, shaking his head.

"Miguel Gonzales came and told me and my mother last night," Atencio continued. "My mother and I sat up all night with the good padre and Pepé at the church."

Atencio's words were spoken with a determination and forcefulness Whitney had never heard in his voice.

"Miguel cannot help with this. It is up to me. Miguel said if I go imme-diately to Santa Fe I might be able to get Persimillion out. Maybe. My mother said you, Whitney Slope, would know how to handle this situation. You have lots of friends in Santa Fe. But we must go now."

"Atencio, even if we find her, how are we going to get them to let her go? She's a Mexican national; she doesn't have any papers."

"She's my family," Atencio said matter-of-factly. "My family needs me, Whitney. I'm going to marry her."

"Marry her?" Whitney asked. "You know, you don't have to marry her, I mean, just to . . ."

"I have to marry her," Atencio said. "I love Persimillion and I have to marry her."

Whitney turned around. Atencio was leaning over the gate towards him, his hands gripping the top of the blue painted wood. For the first time, Whitney noticed how meticulously Atencio was dressed—in a clean, almost new shirt tucked into his new jeans, his usually bare feet in sneakers, and socks. Whitney had never seen Atencio de Jesús in socks. Even so, Atencio would stand out in a crowd. Atencio, even dressed in his citified best, seemed to belong to another realm. Persimillion belonged there, too. A realm of free-floating beings, where money and power meant nothing, and love and compassion were the primary sources of sustenance. Of course Atencio would marry Persimillion.

"I understand, Atencio," Whitney said softly.

"I could drive myself illegally, but I am afraid that when I get there, I will not know what to do. You will know, Whitney, what to say to save her."

"Oh, I don't know, Atencio, I've never done this before."

Atencio frowned and looked over his shoulder at Pepé in the car.

"Of course, I'll go with you, Atencio." Whitney touched Atencio's shoul-der over the gate. "Let me get my boots and my hat. We'll take my truck."

Whitney opened the gate and motioned for Atencio to follow him back to the kitchen door.

"You have to drive the De Soto," Whitney heard Atencio say from the porch.

"What?" Whitney stopped in the kitchen and walked back to the porch door where Atencio stood. "Why?"

"Because we won't all fit in the truck," Atencio said, shrugging his shoulders. "You see, there is Persimillion, and then Pepé and me, and you . . ."

Whitney squinted at the truck and at the De Soto beside it. The De Soto was the larger.

"I see. But it's not registered. It's not insured. We don't want extra trouble on this little journey."

"Tomas registered the De Soto and paid the first insurance bill last week," Atencio said.

"Tomas? I'll be damned!" Whitney walked down the hall to his bedroom and sat down on his bed to pull on his socks and boots. Atencio walked down the porch and peered at Whitney through the screen of the bedroom door. Dominga was wrong, Whitney thought: Tomas could surprise him.

"Will you go with me?" Atencio pressed his face into the screen and watched Whitney pound his heel down into his boot.

"I will go with you. May God and all the saints your mother prays to help us."

Whitney grabbed his hat from the windowsill and then checked his jeans for his wallet.

"I sure as hell better have my papers," Whitney muttered to himself. "I'm going to have a hard enough time convincing myself I know what we're doing, let alone any state authority types."

Atencio opened the door for Whitney.

"I would drive if I had my license. I have this."

Atencio pulled out a folded piece of paper and opened it and handed it to Whitney. It was his birth certificate. Whitney studied it and saw that Atencio de Jesús was born at home in Mi Ojo, New Mexico to Dominga de Jesús exactly twenty-eight years ago this week. Dominga would have been about twenty. At that same time, Whitney was in high school in Ohio. Connie was at the University of Pennsylvania, impressing her art professors. Whitney carefully refolded the thin paper and handed it back to Atencio.

"I don't mind. Really, Atencio. What are friends for? Just don't you mind how I drive the De Soto, okay?"

Whitney put his arm around Atencio's shoulders as they walked down the porch. Pepé was standing next to the car, his neck stretched so he could see over the roof of the De Soto's humped back. After Whitney closed the gate, Pepé opened the back door and climbed into the rear seat of the car.

"*Buenos días,* Pepé," Whitney said opening the door and sliding onto the immense couch that served as the front seat. Whitney studied the grain of the wood dashboard as Atencio put the key into the ignition. The car could have moved off the production line yesterday for all the wear it showed.

"I am so very, very sorry to hear about Alfredo," Whitney looked at Pepé in the rearview mirror. The mirror seemed to be the same size as the one over his bathroom sink. "I liked Alfredo; he was a special sort of person. I will never forget him."

Pepé nodded. Whitney looked across the seat at Atencio.

"Does he understand me?"

Atencio nodded that he had. "Pepé's English is very good. He doesn't miss much."

"We'll find Persimillion, Pepé," Whitney said into the mirror, "and we'll bring her home."

"Give her a little gas first," Atencio said when Whitney placed his hand on the ignition. "She's warmed up already, it won't be hard."

"She?" Whitney said, looking across what seemed to be a barn to where Atencio sat on the other side of the car. "Have you thought of moving in here, Atencio? *She's* got the room."

Atencio chuckled and then pointed again at the ignition.

The De Soto started effortlessly. Whitney was beginning to feel confident in his ability to drive the old car safely, and without embarrassing incident, to Santa Fe, until he tried to disengage the clutch. Whitney let the clutch out smoothly, but too quickly, and the pedal jumped up from the floor like it had been punched. Whitney's knee rammed into his stomach, and the De Soto lurched forwards six feet and stalled.

Whitney looked into the mirror at Pepé, who's eyes were the size of small dinner plates, and then across the seat at Atencio, who was buckling his seat belt.

"Good idea," Whitney said, searching around the side of the seat for his own belt. "Who put these in? Your mother?"

"My father," Atencio said.

Atencio looked out the front window as Whitney again started the De Soto. This time Whitney put the car in gear slowly, with one hand holding his knee down near the seat. The De Soto began to move forwards, and Whitney steered it with two hands around the front of the truck, across the sand and back to the driveway to the road. Clem and Three-Legs watched like two black and white owls on top of the adobe wall, blinking only when absolutely necessary, their eyes and ears riveted to the immense vehicle idling by them. Whitney wanted to wave, but he was afraid to remove even one hand from the gigantic wheel.

When he had the De Soto safely in the center of the canyon road, Whitney fumbled for the column shift and jerked the car into second gear.

"I'll get it, Atencio, don't worry," Whitney said after the gears stopped grinding, "at least I won't have to shift much once we reach the highway."

Atencio was concentrating on the road ahead. Whitney wished he would talk—say anything—about the car, about the weather, about his mother. The De Soto rounded the mesa and crossed the lower part of the canyon road. Whitney adjusted himself in the seat and moved the rearview mirror to a better position for his height. The cottonwoods along the stream passed by in slow motion. Whitney felt like the navigator of a great dirigible whose destination was land, but whose exact route would be hit or miss at best.

As the De Soto crossed the desert highway comfortably at forty-five miles per hour, Atencio told Whitney the details of the accident the night before: how Alfredo chewed free, how Pepé was at his house helping him work on the De Soto, about the sheriff's car, how Pepé returned to the gas station just as the ambulance arrived, and how he hid in the bosque until Miguel Gonzales came and took him to the good padre Leo.

As they passed the old station, Whitney saw how all of their separate paths had crossed on the decrepit doorstep. Crossed and intertwined. Whitney thought about how he would bring Caroline here: how he would stop the truck and they would stand in the middle of the dissolving room while he told his niece the story of the lost painter, and of the burros and the ravens who led him west into a part of himself nearly forgotten; he would tell her of the family from Mexico, and of the solace and sadness that lived in the walls of this house of sky and sand. And most of all he would tell Caroline how very much he loved her; and how very much he loved Connie.

The detention facility of the state immigration office was on the south side of Santa Fe. Before driving across town, Whitney called Burt Rapp from a pay phone and asked him for directions, and for a brief summary of immigration laws and other details concerning illegal aliens and American citizens and marriage. When Whitney was somewhat confident he understood his mission—nothing more than convincing the authorities that Atencio de Jesús' intentions were on the up and up; that Persimillion was in her right mind; and that releasing Persimillion was not in blatant defiance of federal immigration laws, which, Burt assured him, it was—Whitney returned to the De Soto sporting his best false smile and headed south across town.

Whitney explained to Atencio what Burt Rapp had told him on the phone. Atencio remained silent, as did Pepé. When the De Soto reached the parking lot of the immigration offices and detention center, Whitney looked at Atencio. Atencio was perspiring profusely. Water dripped from his face and ran down his arms and chest, and moisture rose up through his shirt. Atencio looked back at Whitney and tried to smile.

"I'm sorry, Whitney."

"There's really nothing to be worried about, Atencio. This is all legal. What's the matter?"

Atencio rubbed his damp hair away from his forehead.

"This is like the hospital," Atencio said, pointing across the parking lot at the drab, uninspiring stucco building. "When I came home . . . the VA Hospital. I wasn't sure I would ever leave."

Whitney reached over and held Atencio's damp shoulder.

"You're going to leave here today, Atencio. With Persimillion, if she's in there. I'm leaving here; you're leaving here; Pepé; we're all going to leave. We're going to drive back together to Mi Ojo, back home, today. I won't leave you here. Okay?"

Atencio nodded. "Okay."

Whitney checked his pockets, but he had forgotten to bring a bandana or handkerchief.

"Do you have something in the car to dry off with?"

Atencio opened the glove compartment. Inside were neatly folded papers and maps, and a box of tissue, the kind Dominga used in her trailer house. Atencio blotted his neck and face, and then his arms, with several tissues.

"Okay," Whitney said. His own hands were perspiring from the past fifteen minutes and the amount of shifting and directional navigation he'd had to perform pulling into and out of Santa Fe traffic. Whitney did not look down at his own torso, but he was very certain his underarms were soaked and that the back of his shirt would have to be peeled like cellophane from the seat when he climbed out of the De Soto.

Whitney and Atencio left Pepé in the car in the parking lot. After speaking with various immigration personnel, they were escorted to the office of someone at the top of the department.

The someone at the top turned out to be High Noon head cook Juan Lopez's boat-owning, fish-loving, tackle box-claiming brother-in-law, Randy Gallegos, a sometimes regular at the mahogany bar of the High Noon Cafe. Randy Gallegos looked as surprised to see Whitney Slope as Whitney was to see him.

"Whitney Slope? Well, what can immigration do for a man like you?"

Randy Gallegos leaned around and looked at Atencio standing motionless in the doorway behind Whitney.

"We need some advice as to how to extricate this man's fiance from your detention facility."

Randy Gallegos motioned towards two metal chairs side by side against the office wall. He returned to his own chair behind a big, black metal desk and lit a cigarette.

"Why don't you tell me the particulars, Slope?"

Atencio fidgeted with a nub in the nap of his jeans in between glances at Whitney and Randy Gallegos.

"Mr. de Jesús, born and raised in Mi Ojo, New Mexico, is engaged to marry a certain Persimillion Ramirez who has been detained here since the death of her brother on Highway 54 last night. She was in a state of shock and forgot to tell the officers in charge about Atencio, who was at his home in Mi Ojo."

"She is an illegal alien, am I correct?"

"Yes. But when she marries an American citizen . . . "

"Yes, but this is all highly irregular, as you can see. They should have a marriage license and blood tests; there are legal procedures, you know, for marriage between a Mexican national and an American citizen. Why wasn't this taken care of before this morning?"

Randy Gallegos sucked on his cigarette and frowned at Atencio. Whitney looked over at Atencio, but Atencio did not look up at Whitney.

"When you live way out on the desert," Whitney continued, "the proper legal procedures seem abstract at best; they are not always applicable to daily living which is rooted in subsistence agriculture and community tradition and church law . . . "

"For heaven's sake, Slope, I know all about it! Jesus, you don't have to lecture me. I was raised north of here, in a little village, Gallina."

Atencio's head jerked out of its catatonic position.

"I have a brother in Gallina—Robert de Jesús. He married Flora Jaramillo. Her father is the postmaster."

Randy Gallegos stubbed out the cigarette and fingered the pack on the desk. "Yes, I know Flora's family. I even know your brother, Robert. He owns a welding shop."

Randy Gallegos sat back in his chair and stared at the ceiling.

"So, Atencio, is your mother the girl who saw sheep fly? As a child, the Garcia girl from Mi Ojo?"

Randy Gallegos's eyes dropped from the ceiling to Atencio's face. He was smiling.

"*Sí, es mi mama,*" Atencio said.

"My mother told me that story when I was a boy. My mother's last years, when she could not remember her name or my name or who she had been married to—*¿comprende?* Well, she remembered the Garcia girl's sheep. She sat by the back door and peered through the screen waiting to see those sheep. It sounds a bit loco, *sí*, but she was happy when she died. She was going to fly in the wind with God's sheep!"

Randy Gallegos looked over at Whitney and laughed. Whitney smiled.

"A miracle," Whitney said.

Randy nodded and leaned back in his chair again. "Yeah, *milagro* . . ., but we are talking about federal law here. Not many miracles in the federal building!"

Randy lit another cigarette and then looked through the smoke at Whitney. "What is it you want me to do?"

"Let us take her out of here with us," Whitney said quickly. Atencio was watching Randy Gallegos, acting more at ease now that their familial and spiritual ties had been firmly established. "I'll take them to the court house, get the blood tests done, whatever; we'll do all the paper work right now, today. It will all be legal."

"No, it won't, Slope. It will all be illegal enough to cost me my job."

Randy Gallegos stood and looked out the small, aluminum window behind his desk. Whitney wondered if he were eyeing the De Soto, and if Pepé was doing anything out of the ordinary in or around the flamboyant car?

Randy Gallegos walked across the office and closed his door.

"We're all *hermanos, sí* Slope? *La gente.* So, today, and just between us, I'm going to treat you like family."

Atencio and Whitney were both leaning forwards on their metal chairs while Randy Gallegos stubbed out his second cigarette in an ashtray on the windowsill.

"He will need to sign papers of intent to marry, and you must send copies of the marriage license and blood tests to me personally. And Miss Ramirez? She will have to go back down to Juárez and recross the border into this country legally. I need some proof of your residency here in New Mexico, Atencio."

Atencio was already holding his birth certificate. He unfolded the thin paper and gave it to Randy Gallegos. Whitney hoped the certificate was not too damp to read.

"The state of New Mexico frowns upon marriages that serve to allow illegal aliens to migrate into the United States for purposes other than serious and sacred union. You must sign papers swearing this is not a marriage of convenience with the intent to defraud our country. Have you any other identification Mr. de Jesús?"

Whitney saw Atencio's eyes doubling in size and cleared his own throat to answer. But Atencio spoke calmly.

"I am a United States veteran and could bring you discharge papers and other veteran identification."

"Okay. Not today. I just want you to sign these papers now, right here. While you do this, I'll send someone down for your fiance, Mr. de Jesús. Persimillion? I remember her. It was a very tragic accident out there. The sheriff told me about the boy. Very tragic."

Whitney looked at Atencio and nodded towards the parking lot. Atencio did not understand.

"There's one more matter connected to this . . . family matter. Persimillion has a second brother. If he wanted to be a legal, you know, worker, how would he do that?"

"I suppose he's not sitting on the south side of the Rio Grande waiting for an answer, is he?" Randy Gallegos chuckled into his cigarette pack. "Well, he needs to have papers saying he has employment here. Then, being that his sister will be a naturalized citizen, it shouldn't be too hard for him. Get confirmation in writing about a job first. To me."

"Okay," Whitney said to Atencio. "That should about do it for today."

Atencio took the papers from Randy, who left the room. Whitney watched Atencio sign each document; he was still perspiring like a sweatshop worker, but his face and body were relaxed now.

Persimillion was standing by a uniformed officer in the front reception area when Whitney and Atencio finally left Randy Gallegos's office. Atencio ran down the hall to her. Persimillion cried out and opened her short, plump arms to greet Atencio. People sitting in the plastic chairs of the waiting room gawked and mumbled about the skinny man and the rotund woman crying and hugging, but Atencio and Persimillion were completely oblivious to their audience.

"Come on, let's get out of here," Whitney said, walking up to the embracing couple. "Pepé's probably roasted by now in the car."

"Pepé? ¿Aquí?" Persimillion wiped her face with the back of her hand and looked at Atencio.

"¡Sí, en mi carro, aquí!" Atencio wiped Persimillion's cheeks with his hand and then led Persimillion out the front doors.

After what seemed to Whitney to be an afternoon of greetings and sobs and hugs in the parking lot beside the De Soto, Whitney coerced everyone into the car. Pepé moved up front with Whitney; Persimillion and Atencio sat holding hands in the back seat. As the De Soto made its way back into Santa Fe, Persimillion's body was alternately shaken by laughter and sobs. She spoke Alfredo's name again and again. Whitney listened as Atencio told her in Spanish about padre Leo and the Mi Ojo *capilla*, about mass and *muerte*.

Whitney eased the De Soto into two diagonal parking spaces in front of the brick and tile Santa Fe County court house. Atencio took Persimillion into the medical center next door. Forty-five minutes later, he escorted her into the court house itself.

Whitney remained with Pepé. He was at a loss about what to say to Pepé about Alfredo, about Mi Ojo, about a life where hope and new beginnings were constantly at war with poverty and loss. So they lay on the grass before the courthouse in silence, staring up through the old elm trees at the deep blue September sky. As Whitney felt himself beginning to doze, he wondered whether Pepé, ever poised to run, could manage a catnap of his own.

Atencio and Persimillion reappeared an hour later, both ragged and weary, but smiling. At Whitney's insistence, they went to the High Noon Cafe for a late lunch. It seemed like the thing to do. Everyone was starved; it was hot as the blazes, and Whitney could not face the lumbering drive back across the desert to Mi Ojo on an empty stomach.

"Everybody's practically legal, and I'm paying, so no arguments," Whitney said after they reloaded into the De Soto. But no one seemed interested in objecting. Normally, Whitney would have left the car parked where it was and walked the few blocks to the plaza. But it had taken Persimillion two minutes just to climb up the court house steps and across its veranda; Whitney knew that what was a casual walk for the rest of them would be an overland journey for Atencio's bride-to-be.

Whitney parked the De Soto in the alley behind the High Noon, already figuring the cost of a parking ticket into their lunch bill. He went ahead into the kitchen where Juan and Jon stood watching, actually gaping, through the back door.

"My God, where did you get that car, Whitney?" Jon pushed the kitchen door wide open to get a better look at the De Soto. "What a colossus! The tires look a little bald. But what a gem. Where, Whitney, did you pick that up?"

"Not mine, Jon, it belongs to Atencio de Jesús, the young man who is going to lay your stone? He's here."

Whitney walked past Jon and Juan and through the kitchen. He looked into the High Noon's dining room to size up the crowd, which was small. Whitney returned to the kitchen door where Juan and Jon remained staring at the car and at Pepé and Atencio escorting Persimillion towards them.

"Come on in, this way," Whitney said. "Excuse our forbidden entry, Jon, but we've had some kind of day, and, well, I really had to park back here."

Jon's eyes moved slowly from the three entering the kitchen to Whitney.

"Well Whitney, last time you parked out back, you brought me a master-piece to auction," Jon mused. "What exactly have you brought me today?

Los Milagros de la Gente

"Jon Gateworthy, I'd like you to meet my friends from Mi Ojo." Whitney pointed to Atencio first. "Atencio de Jesús, the artist of the stone floors, among other things; his fiance, Persimillion Ramirez; and her brother, Pepé. The Ramirezes are recent immigrants to Nuevo Mejico. But then, we're all mostly immigrants here, aren't we?"

"We certainly are," Jon said as he shook hands with Atencio and then with Pepé. He smiled at Persimillion, then took her hand.

"Juan," Jon said over his shoulder, "please go and ask Sam to set our guests a table, would you?"

Juan slipped out to speak to Sam and returned to lead Pepé, Atencio, and Persimillion into the cafe. Whitney walked to the sink and rinsed his face and neck with cold water, then removed his hat so he could splash his hair, too. Jon watched the parade through the kitchen door into the cafe and then turned to Whitney. Whitney let the water drip off his chin and down his shirt.

"Where would you like me to begin?" Whitney asked. "It began like any morning. But then there was a death in the family, Persimillion's family, and she was taken to immigration detention, and Atencio proposed marriage, but he doesn't have a license, for driving or marriage . . . "

Sam walked into the kitchen with Juan.

"You are here! Where's this car?" Sam touched Whitney lightly on the arm and then leaned out the back door. "That's quite a vehicle, Whitney. Does it steer?"

"Great car, Samantha. Room enough for the whole family, which is exactly what I brought in today. Did you meet Atencio, the guy I told you lays stone floors?"

"Yes. I hear they're celebrating their engagement," Sam said, standing close to Whitney, "but that someone's brother died last night? Seems a strange time to, well, celebrate?"

"The way I see it, Samantha," Whitney said, "it's all relative: they've had loss and more loss. When the opportunity for something other than loss finally appears, there is a sense of thankfulness. Of hope. *¿Comprende?*"

Sam stared at the door into the cafe.

"Comprendo, Whitney. *Comprendo."*

"Could you make us some enchiladas?" Whitney turned to Juan. "And bring some of that fresh salsa and chips, and a few baskets of sopaipillas. Make a lot of food for these people. A lot of food."

"*Sí,* I already figured that," Juan said, winking at Whitney.

"By the way, Juan," Whitney said as he followed Juan to the main stove on one side of the kitchen, "I saw Randy, your brother-in-law, today . . . you know, at immigration?"

Juan smiled at Whitney.

"I understand."

"Nice man, your brother-in-law."

"Fishing makes for all sorts of *compadres,*" Juan said.

"Yes. Fish and sheep."

Juan cocked his head. "Sheep?"

"Next time you're out on the water," Whitney added, "ask Randy about the sheep."

"Please, join us?" Whitney asked Jon and Sam before he left the kitchen. "I really would appreciate your company."

Sam brought freshly squeezed lemonade, and they all sat at the long pine table under the painting. Atencio could not stop talking about Whitney's painting, in English, in Spanish, and sometimes in both; how Whitney had worked on it day after day, how it was first the outline of a window into nothing, and then there was just a line of red sand, and then a blue sky, and then the fluffy clouds emerged, and then the wall, and then light and shadow, heat, and space, and then it was done.

Atencio, Persimillion and Pepé spoke together in Spanish and soon were absorbed in a conversation that did not include Whitney and the Gateworthys.

"Have you heard about the auction?" Jon said after a silence at their end of the table. "I sent you a note about it two days ago. With the Pony Express mail service around here, you probably haven't received it yet."

"No, tell me. Someone has bought it?"

"Well, it's actually going to be a trade, not a sale," Sam said.

"Trade with whom, for what?" Whitney asked, frowning.

"With Anna Becklesforth Farina," Sam said, leaning towards Whitney to get a better view of his face. Jon stood and walked back to Sam's desk. He returned with a legal-sized envelope, which he handed to Whitney.

"We haven't figured out the exact legalities of this yet," Jon said, sitting down again. "But we're working on it with your lawyer. I sent you the details in the letter."

"What's this, cold cash?" Whitney opened the envelope and peered inside.

"No, Whitney, it's an agreement, a letter of intent to quitclaim all rights to a certain piece of real estate," Jon said.

Whitney extracted the papers.

"To Burro Alley!" Sam cried, before Whitney could read it.

"Oh, God!" Whitney said. "Oh my God!"

Whitney looked at the painting on the wall behind the table, and then at Jon and Sam. Atencio was watching him.

"This is very good news," Whitney said to Atencio. Atencio looked relieved. "Very good . . . this is well, this . . . does Alejandro know?"

"Yes," Sam said. "Jon called Alejandro last night, at home. And Burt Rapp knows, too."

"That's not all of it," Jon said. "Anna turned around and donated the painting itself to the High Noon. To that wall. You must have said something to her once, huh? Way back when, about the wall without a window . . . a view? She told me the cafe looked like a different place—a place 'with a classy, rustic ambiance'—her words—with that window hanging there. So it stays."

Whitney shook his head in disbelief.

"I didn't tell her. I really can't believe Anna gave it to you; don't that just about beat all?"

"Anna said to tell her who to quitclaim the deed to—the Historic Preservation Trust, the Santa Fe Museum board, whatever—and she will have it drawn up by her attorney."

◎

The High Noon was quiet except for the overhead swish of the ceiling fans, one of which had developed a moaning creak somewhere in its rotation. Whitney, Atencio, Persimillion, and Pepé finished their lunch of blue corn enchiladas just as the supper crowd began sidling into the High Noon. The September crowd was three-quarters locals; the remainder were old-time tourists, people who returned to Santa Fe year after year, always in the early fall after the summer rush, to enjoy the slow, almost vacant cafes, the cool evenings, the lengthening shadows on the plaza, and the golden sheen of the aspens that would soon wash over the mountains. It was a relaxed crowd, an easy, accepting gathering of cowboys and local business people who gave

Whitney and his friends at the long table against the far wall mildly curious glances and then forgot them.

Whitney studied his painting above Persimillion's head: the window and its desert view were so large even Persimillion looked small beneath them. There was enough space even for Persimillion's dreams in that desert. Whitney gathered up his hat and pulled out his wallet, preparing to leave. That window reminded him exactly where it was he wanted to be.

"No, this is on me, Slope," Jon said at the bar.

"I think there's a clause about family size," Whitney said, taking several bills from his wallet.

"Well, we'll have to rewrite our contract. Remember, we got the *Window of Miracles.*"

Whitney and Jon smiled at one another across the cafe. Atencio walked to the bar and stood before Jon.

"You have been kind to us," Atencio said, putting out his hand to Jon. "I look forward to laying your floor. It is an honor to have been asked to do such a job."

"We're honored to have you, Atencio," Jon said, shaking Atencio's hand. "We'll start in about three weeks, if that's okay with you?"

"Yes. I will have my driver's license by then."

Jon walked Whitney out to the De Soto and inspected the insides of the car while everyone else loaded.

"Right out of another time, Whit," Jon said as he ran his hand across the chrome of the door.

"It's right out of another place, too . . . a place you read about in books, but don't really expect to find."

Jon closed Whitney's door and stepped back. Whitney started the De Soto and carefully put it in gear.

"If this alley were any narrower," Whitney breathed, as the car began to glide over the cracked pavement away from the High Noon. In the rearview mirror, Whitney waved goodbye to Jon, Sam, and Juan, who stood transfixed in the alley like three school children who have just seen the circus for the very first time.

t·h·i·r·t·y - s·e·v·e·n

Homecoming

Only the gentle hum of the De Soto's engine interrupted their drive home across the desert. Before they were ten miles out of Santa Fe, Pepé fell asleep against the far door, his feet curled under him on the wide seat like a small child. Persimillion and Atencio sat shoulder to shoulder in the back seat, holding hands and sharing through Atencio's window a view of pink clouds draped like ribbons of shredded silk over the far southern sand. Whitney had a slight cramp in his right buttock from holding his boot just so on the gas pedal; otherwise, all things considered, it was an easy enough, pleasant enough, journey home.

Word of their pilgrimage to save Persimillion from deportation had swept through the village, and people close to Atencio and Dominga were waiting at the trailer behind the mercantile when Whitney pulled the De Soto into its usual parking spot near Atencio's house. Padre Leo, Miguel Gonzales, Tomas, and Clay Koontz joined Dominga on the trailer porch. There was much hugging and a few tears when Atencio and Persimillion and Pepé left the car. Dominga had prepared enough food for the entire parish, and Whitney had no choice but to stay and join the repast, which was part mourning supper for Alfredo, whose body lay in a wooden casket up at the church, and part engagement feast for Atencio and his fiance, Persimillion Ramirez.

When Whitney climbed out of the De Soto, Dominga took him by the arm and led him up to her trailer where Miguel Gonzales stood holding a can of soda. It was a strange gathering, Whitney thought, everyone but him blood- or marriage-bonded family to these three people, all trying to accommodate the extremes of loss and rebirth in one supper. Everyone was hungry except for Whitney and Pepé: Whitney had eaten one too many enchiladas at the High Noon; Pepé had yet to exhibit much of an appetite, but seemed genuinely thankful to Dominga for trying to feed him.

"What a day you must have had," Dominga said, holding Whitney by both shoulders so that he would face her. Dominga wore a full, gathered skirt and a loose cotton blouse. Her hair was untied, and she was wearing her riding boots. She smiled when she saw Whitney studying her feet. "What a time it has been!"

Whitney looked at Miguel and nodded a greeting, then extended his hand.

"Miguel Gonzales," Whitney said, shaking the trooper's large, muscular hand. "You're a man of many talents, I am told."

"It is best, around these parts, not to believe everything you are told," Miguel said as he shifted his gaze to Dominga.

"I believe nothing and everything around Mi Ojo," Whitney said, also looking at Dominga who remained wedged between them.

Dominga guided Whitney and Miguel through the trailer door. They were followed by the good padre and Tomas, Clay, Atencio, Persimillion, and Pepé. Dominga put platters of warm tortillas, meat and cheese, salad, and corn and a huge ceramic bowl of *posole* on her dinette table and began urging people to serve themselves. Whitney took a token portion and then stood against the kitchen counter with Tomas and Miguel. Several devotional candles burned near his elbows, below the *retablos* and carved cedar crosses Dominga had gathered into this one corner of her kitchen.

"Just goes to show you," Tomas said to Whitney and Miguel, "that you have to be careful who you go letting wear your old shirts."

Tomas pointed to Pepé, who was sitting with padre Leo on the sofa.

"See that one there—the checkered cowboy shirt, red pearl buttons, an old favorite—looks like it's wrapped itself around my brother's future brother-in-law." Tomas lifted both hands in exaggerated disbelief. "I'd be watching your clothes, your possessions, Slope; you, too, Miguel, for the ever-sharing hands of my mother. She has this talent, you know: she'll get you to see things her way—believe 'em, even—to do things. It don't matter what you say."

Miguel chuckled between bites into a tortilla filled with meat and cheese.

Whitney watched the changing light on the desert through the small window beside the dinette table. Atencio sat near the window, the glaze of sundown catching his cheek bone like an angle of stone. Atencio felt Whitney's eyes upon him and looked back at him across the counter.

"Mr. Slope, you look a bit tuckered out this evening," Clay Koontz said from his seat at the dinette table. "I never would have taken you to be the community rescue sort when I first laid eyes on you."

Whitney squinted at Clay. He was almost too tired now to make social conversation. But he kept trying.

"Clay, I'll take that as a compliment . . . "

Whitney's eyes left Clay's face to follow Dominga as she helped Persimillion settle herself and her plate of food into a chair.

"I hear you're thinking of staying the fall, into the winter, out here?"

"I'm thinking of staying, just staying."

"Maybe you would teach a little art class," padre Leo said over the plate balanced on his lap. "How wonderful it would be for the children, after school, in the parish hall. There is not much to do when winter comes."

"Yes, the children have never had a drawing class," Dominga interjected energetically. "Think of what you could show them, Mr. Slope."

Whitney studied Dominga's face, which was radiant with sun and relief.

"Mr. Slope?" Whitney asked her.

"Whitney." Dominga looked at the room of people watching them. She smiled and took Whitney's arm. "Yes, just think, Whitney, of what you could show them."

"I'll do just that, Dominga." Whitney smiled down at her. "I'll give it some thought."

"So, Slope, I'm headed up to Tomita," Tomas said, setting his empty plate in the sink and rinsing off his hands. "Your road is on my way. Want a ride?"

"Yes."

Whitney began his good-byes to everyone in the crowded trailer. Atencio came and stood beside him. Whitney could see that Atencio, like he, was too tired to speak, to say words that came close to expressing what existed between them.

"Come up to the canyon whenever you want," Whitney said, resting a hand on Atencio's shoulder. Atencio nodded. "Bring Persimillion to see the patio . . . and the cats."

Dominga walked Whitney outside onto the porch. Tomas was already in his orange truck, listening to his radio.

"I would like to come up to the canyon, too," Dominga said, holding Whitney by the hand. Whitney gave her hand a gentle squeeze. "I have registered for school. I have the catalogue of classes. I am thinking about the stars."

"The stars? Not clouds?"

"Oh, I'm still thinking about clouds," Dominga said. "But I've started thinking about what's above them."

Whitney smiled. "How about Thursday?"

"Thursday. At noon?"

"No, how about at six, for supper? Afterwards we could take a walk and watch the stars come out. And then the moon."

Dominga stared at Whitney and then smiled. *"Bueno."*

Tomas and Whitney sat in silence as they drove up the canyon road. When the truck rounded the curve that had stalled the De Soto in the August rains, Whitney looked out his window and down at the packed clay where an impossible quagmire had so recently held Atencio captive: only ruts, now, the rains of August fading into yesterday.

When the roof of the house came into view, Tomas began to talk:

"Looks like I'll be getting the trailer in the next year or so."

"What trailer?" Whitney asked, glancing at Tomas and then back at the beautiful evening.

"Dominga's. Seems that Atencio plans to build a little *casita* for himself and the missus, and the boy, out there near the acequia. Out of adobes, like grandfather."

"Is that so? Makes sense. Atencio's mighty good with his hands." Whitney thought about Atencio making adobes, barefoot in the mud. Maybe Whitney would help; shed his shirt and shoes for a season and build walls, ceilings, floors. Homes.

"Dominga will move back into her mother's house," Tomas continued. "She said I can have the trailer, if I want it. Of course I want it! I might even be able to sell it for something!"

"You're quite the rescuer, I'm told."

Tomas chuckled.

"You know, Slope, you got to rescue the living. Ol' brother Tomas here got to retrieve the dead. Yeah, I went into Santa Fe for the body. And the casket."

Tomas chewed at his tobacco and leaned onto his arm resting on the open window. He looked to be thinking so hard Whitney kept silent and thought about Alfredo's body riding in the back of Tomas' pickup a few hours back, and about how much Alfredo had wanted to ride somewhere, anywhere.

"You and me both, Slope—my mother and Clay and padre Leo, too— know Atencio and his bride are going to have a mountain of problems to overcome, even out here in Mi Ojo where everyone will try to take care of them. There's just so much help people in need themselves can offer. This valley ain't no river of affluence and prosperity. Love don't pay any bills."

"I know that, Tomas," Whitney said after pulling his head back into the truck. "But don't you figure they have about as much chance as anyone? I mean, look around. Trouble doesn't seem to have an exclusive grip on the poor."

Tomas sighed and said nothing.

"Speaking of helping," Whitney said after a pause, "ol' Pepé has to secure a job around here before he can think about getting a green card. Maybe you could use your influence?"

Tomas looked across at Whitney, his eyes a bit wider than a moment before.

"Maybe," he said, "I'll think about it."

September was stealing the evening light a little each day, but there was still sun on the catalpa tree when they reached the canyon house. Before climbing out of the truck, Whitney leaned across the cab and gently punched Tomas on the shoulder. Tomas lifted one hand in farewell, spit some juice into the sand by the patio wall, then reversed the truck and left Whitney standing alone at the blue patio gate.

Thirty minutes later, the upper rock walls gave up the light, and the lower canyon fell into first dusk. Whitney sat before the gessoed canvas he had left in the studio thirteen hours ago. He really wanted to paint. He wanted to paint the line of Atencio's cheekbone. Not a portrait, exactly. But a portrait, somehow, of someone he knew, someone he loved. Not tonight. Tomorrow, first light, would be soon enough.

Whitney left his perch on the stool in the studio. Clem and Three-Legs were washing one another on the patio. Whitney stood near them, his bare feet warmed by the heat still held in the rose slabs. Whitney stepped from stone to stone, pressing his soles into the hollows and over the hills of each.

When he reached the edge of the patio, he knelt and placed his palms onto the grave.

Whitney looked over at Clem and Three-Legs: they sat down on their haunches, readying for sleep, blue eyes closed but black ears still alert and moving to catch the first sounds of the wild night beginning in the canyon. Whitney closed his eyes and listened, too.

Whitney could not hear what the cats heard, but he could see past them, backwards, and a few moments forwards; he could see beneath the rose stones, under the earth; he could see and almost understand all the sundowns and sunups, midnights and high noons, that had brought them all in this perfectly timed dance to this twilight now, to this sliver of shared life that would slip away like the waning moon, behind them not even the faintest trace of a shadow left to explain how it was when they were all here.

Only the saints of sheep and of cats would remain. Would remember.

Whitney left the patio and returned to the dusky studio. He knew the canyon house like the back of his hand and needed no light to find his best brush and a small jar of Perfect Blue. Whitney carried them back outside and under the now awake and curious eyes of Three-Legs and Clem, painted MOUSSE in brilliant blue on the grave stone's smooth surface, just as the canyon mourning doves joined their voices for an evening lament, and the first twilight stars emerged gold over the mesa tops.